HUNTING LICENSE

Earl was leaning forward, holding onto the back of the folding chair in front of him. "I've already cleaned up one of your mistakes. You wouldn't be coming to us unless you want somebody else to bleed on your behalf."

"You've got me all wrong." Stricken clucked disapprovingly. "This isn't one of mine, but it was one of the task force's teams that responded to investigate. Intel said this should've been a cakewalk, turned out it wasn't. That team has gone missing."

"Surprised you care."

"There're always more things looking for a PUFF exemption to replace them." He shrugged. "But I do hate losing valuable assets, especially pretty redheads."

The metal in Earl's hands snapped in two.

"See you around, Earl. Enjoy your conference."

"No!" Earl stood, flinging one hand outward and sending four chairs clattering across the room. "Son of a bitch!"

A picture appeared on the TV screen. Three figures were walking down the lowered back ramp of a gray C-130 cargo plane. They were dressed in multicam and combat gear, carrying rifles. There were two men in front and an attractive woman in back. Her red hair was rather striking in a shot so filled with bland, dusty colors.

"Heather..." Earl whispered. After a few seconds, the picture disappeared and the TV changed to silent static. "Damn it!" Earl smashed his fist into the TV.

"Earl?" Cody asked. "You okay?"

"Team leads, collect your men. We're going hunting."

Baen Books by Larry Correia

Monster Hunter International
Monster Hunter Vendetta
Monster Hunter Alpha
The Monster Hunters (omnibus)
Monster Hunter Legion

THE GRIMNOIR CHRONICLES
Hard Magic
Spellbound
Warbound

WITH MIKE KUPARI
Dead Six
Swords of Exodus (forthcoming)

To purchase these and all Baen Book titles
in e-book format, please go to www.baen.com.

MONSTER HUNTER LEGION

Larry Correia

MONSTER HUNTER LEGION

This is a work of fiction. All the characters and events portrayed in this book are fictional, and any resemblance to real people or incidents is purely coincidental.

A Baen Books Original

Baen Publishing Enterprises
P.O. Box 1403
Riverdale, NY 10471
www.baen.com

ISBN: 978-1-4516-3906-3

Cover art by Alan Pollack

First Baen paperback printing, July 2013

Library of Congress Control Number: 2012016683

Distributed by Simon & Schuster
1230 Avenue of the Americas
New York, NY 10020

Pages by Joy Freeman (www.pagesbyjoy.com)
Printed in the United States of America

MONSTER HUNTER
LEGION

CHAPTER 1

Most of the things Las Vegas has to offer to its hordes of tourists don't hold much appeal for me. Having been an accountant, I am way too good at math to enjoy gambling. As a former bouncer, I'm not big on the party scene. Strip clubs? Happily married to a total babe who could kill me from a mile away with her sniper rifle, so no thanks. Sure, there were plenty of other things to do in Vegas, like overpriced shows, taking your picture with Elvis, and that sort of thing, but as a professional Monster Hunter, I'm pretty jaded when it comes to what constitutes *excitement*.

However, there is one thing in Las Vegas' extensive, sparkling arsenal of tourist-from-their-dollars-separating weapons that I'm absolutely powerless to resist, and that is a kick ass buffet.

The flight in had taken forever and I was starving. So first thing upon arrival at our hotel, I had called up every other hungry member of Monster Hunter International that I could find and we'd set out to conquer the unsuspecting hotel buffet.

This was a business trip. Normally, *business* for us meant that there was some horrible supernatural thing in dire need of a good killing, but not this time. Las Vegas was the site of the first annual *International Conference of Monster Hunting Professionals.*

The conference was a big deal. Sponsored by a wealthy organizer, the ultra-secret ICMHP 1 had been billed as an opportunity to network with other informed individuals, check out the latest gear and equipment, and listen to experts. There had never been an event like this before. Every member of MHI who could get away from work had come, and though we were the biggest company in the business, we were still outnumbered five to one by representatives of every other rival monster hunting company in the world. In addition, there were representatives from all of the legitimate supernaturally attuned organization and government agencies, all come together here to learn from each other. Despite just oozing with all of that professionalism, we had all taken to calling it *Ick-mip* for short.

The conference started tomorrow morning, which for most of the Hunters meant a chance to party or gamble the night away, but for me, it was buffet time. As a very large, high-intensity-lifestyle kind of guy, I burn a lot of calories. I may lose at the gambling table, but I never lose at the dinner table. Plus the food at the upscale establishments tended to be above average, and since Hunters made good money, my days of eating at the dumpy places were over. Besides, all of the ICMHP guests were staying at the new, ultra-swanky, not even totally open to the public yet, Last Dragon hotel. The Last Dragon's buffet had actual master chefs from around the world, and was supposed to be one of the best new places to eat in town. The internet had said so, and who was I to argue with the Zagat survey?

My team had just gotten back from a grueling mission and most had simply wanted to crash. I'd only been able to coerce Trip Jones and Holly Newcastle into coming, though Holly had complained about watching her figure and said that she was going to *take it easy*. When it came to food I had no concept of easy. Despite his aversion to being around humans, Edward had been tempted by my wild tales of hundreds of yards of glorious meats, none of which needed to be chased down and stabbed to death first. However, his older brother and chieftain, Skippy, had forbidden it. Turns out that it is really difficult to eat in public with a face mask on. It is tough being an orc.

There had been an incoming flight due shortly with a couple of Newbies onboard, and Milo Anderson had volunteered to stay and be their ride to the hotel. Earl Harbinger had said these particular recruits were especially talented, so they'd earned the field trip. Lucky them. My Newbie field trip had been storming the *Antoine-Henri* and fighting wights.

Last but not least for my team, my lovely wife Julie had said she was tired, encouraged me not to hurt myself at dinner—she knows how I can sometimes be over-enthusiastic for things that come in serving sizes larger than my head—and then went to bed early. She had been feeling a little under the weather during the trip.

After ditching our luggage, which mostly consisted of armor and guns, we'd snagged a few of the other

Hunters staying on our floor. Most of the floors of the Last Dragon hotel were still in the finishing stages of construction, so the place hadn't even had its grand opening yet. Officially, the hotel wasn't ready yet, but since ICMHP was supposed to be secret anyway, it was a perfect place for several hundred Hunters to stay, and the ICMHP organizers had even gotten us a killer discount. ICMHP would be the first ever event for its conference center, but luckily, the casino, shops, and—most important—restaurants were already open to the public.

"Wow..." Trip whistled as he looked down the endless food trays of the top-rated all-you-can-eat place on Earth. "That's one impressive spread." It really was. Lots of everything, cuisine from a few dozen cultures, all of it beautiful, and the smells... They were absolutely mouthwatering, and that wasn't just because I'd spent most of the day squeezed into a helicopter smelling avgas fumes and gun smoke, this place was awesome. "This is how Vikings eat in Viking heaven."

"Valhalla," Holly pointed out. "Viking heaven is called Valhalla."

"I know that," Trip answered. "Surprised you do, though." It was a lame attempt at teasing her, since everyone present knew that Holly just worked the dumb blonde angle to manipulate people who didn't know her well enough to know that she was an encyclopedia of crafty monster eradication.

"Sure I do. I had this really sexy valkyrie costume one Halloween," Holly answered, completely deadpan. "The chain-mail bikini was *so* hot... Though it did chafe." And then she started to describe it in graphic detail. Watching the always gentlemanly and borderline prudish Trip get too embarrassed to respond coherently was always fun for the whole team, but luckily for him, the hostess called for Owen Pitt and party of ten, and seated us before it got too bad.

I'd managed to gather several other Hunters who hadn't been too distracted by the pretty flashing lights and promises of loose slots to forget dinner. The Haight brothers were from Team Haven out of Colorado, and though Sam was dead and Priest had been promoted to be their leader, they would always be called Team Haven. Cooper and my brother-in-law, Nate Shackleford, were from Paxton's team out of Seattle. Gregorius was from Atlanta, and since the last time I'd seen him he'd decided to ditch his old military grooming standards, and I had to compliment him on the quality of his lumberjack beard. My old buddy Albert Lee was stationed at headquarters in Alabama and he was always fun to hang out with. VanZant was a team lead out of California and Green was one of his guys. I'd worked with all of them at one point or another, either from Newbie training, battling Lord Machado's minions at DeSoya caverns, or fighting under the alien insect branches of the Arbmunep.

The Last Dragon's buffet was in a large, circular glass enclosure inside the casino's shopping mall. The whole place slowly rotated so that the view out the windows was constantly changing murals, gardens, and fountains. The diners got to watch as one story below us, hundreds of consumers blew all their money on overpriced merchandise. It was kind of neat if you liked people-watching as much as I did. Inside the restaurant there were even ice sculptures and five different kinds of chocolate fountains.

After heaping food on our plates, we took our seats. It had been a while since I'd seen most of these particular coworkers, and in short order my arm had been twisted into talking about the case we had wrapped up just that morning. In fact, my team hadn't even thought we'd be able to attend ICMHP at all, because we'd spent two fruitless weeks trolling the crappiest parts of Jackson, Mississippi looking for our monster. It was January, and we'd gotten rained on the whole time. Bagging that aswang at the last minute had been a stroke of luck, giving us an excuse to pack right up and hightail it to Las Vegas where we could be much warmer and dry for a bit. I like telling stories, but whenever I started exaggerating to make the monster even more disgusting, Trip would correct me. He always was good at keeping me honest. Besides, since the damned thing had been an imported mutant Filipino vampire with a *proboscis*, you didn't need much hyperbole to make it gross. This was not the sort of dinner conversation that you would have with polite company.

MHI tended to be a noisy, boisterous, fun-loving bunch, and as you filled them with good food and drinks they just got louder. Soon, everyone else was cracking jokes and telling stories too, interrupted only by the constant trips back for more food. Green was skinny, and VanZant's nickname was "the hobbit" because he was maybe a stocky five foot four, but even our small Hunters had appetites, not to mention that Gregorius was about my size, so we were putting a hurting on the place. However, as Nate pointed out, at seventy bucks a head, we were darn well going to get our money's worth. Luckily, they had seated us far enough to the side that we weren't bugging the other, more normal patrons.

They had stuck together a few tables into a long rectangle for us. I was sitting at one end across from Green and next to VanZant. Green was bald, hyperactive, and had been a San Diego police officer before MHI had recruited him. I'd accidentally broken his collarbone back in Newbie training, but he'd never seemed to hold a grudge about it. Green was a scrapper, one of those men that wasn't scared of anything, so getting severely injured in training was no biggie. I'd lost count of how many beers he had drunk, and apparently he'd already hit the minibar in his room before coming down. The waitress just kept the refills coming, because since we had to walk past slot machines to get out of this place, the management probably wanted their guests as incapable of making good decisions as possible. His boss, VanZant, just frowned as Green got into a noisy argument with bomb expert Cooper over the proper use of hand grenades.

VanZant was a courteous man, so he waited until there were several different conversations going on before leaning in to ask me quietly, "So how's Julie doing?"

The question was understandable. VanZant had been with Julie when she'd been injured during Hood's attack on our compound. He was one of the few who knew something about how she had survived, her lacerations sealed by the lingering magic of the Guardian, leaving only black lines where there had once been mortal wounds. "Pretty good. Mostly we don't think about it." Which wasn't true at all. The thought that she had been physically changed by magic from the Old Ones was always there, gnawing away at our peace of mind, but there wasn't much we could do about it.

VanZant's concern was evident. "Has there been any... change?"

He meant to the supernatural marks on my wife's neck and abdomen, reminders of things that should have killed her. "Still the same as before." The marks had saved Julie's life three times, from Koriniha's knife, a flying undead's claws, and even the fangs of her vampire mother, but there was no such thing as *gifts* when the Old Ones were concerned. Everything from them came with a price. We just didn't know what that price was going to be yet. "We've been trying to find more information about the Guardian, who he was, where the magic comes from, maybe even how to get rid of it, but no luck yet."

One of the Haights was telling a story about parking his truck on a blood fiend when the hostess led another big group into our section of the restaurant. There were a dozen of them, they were all male and all dressed the same, in matching tan cargo pants and tight black polo shirts that showed off that they all really liked to lift weights. Every last one of the newcomers was casually scanning the room for threats. It was obvious that the half of them that couldn't sit with their backs to the wall were made slightly uncomfortable by that fact.

They were Monster Hunters. A Hunter gives off a certain vibe, and these men had it. Wary, cocky, and tough, they were Hunters all right, they just weren't as *cool* as we were. VanZant scowled at the gold *PT*

Consulting embroidered on the breast of every polo shirt. "Oh, no ..." he muttered. "Not these assholes."

"Friends of yours?" I whispered as the hostess seated them a few feet away. I noticed that most of them were studying us the same way we were studying them. Apparently my table gave off that Hunter vibe too. There was a little bit of professional curiosity and sizing up going on from both sides.

VanZant wasn't happy to see them. "They're a startup company headquartered in L.A. They've been around about a year. Loads of money, all the newest toys. They're professional, but ..."

From the look on Green's face, he didn't like PT Consulting much either. He spoke a little louder than he probably should have. "Their boss is a real prick and they've been weaseling in on some of our contracts. They'll swipe your PUFF right out from under your nose if you aren't careful."

A few of them seemed to have overheard that, and there was some hushed conversation from the other table as they placed their drink orders. "Easy, Green," VanZant cautioned his hotheaded friend before turning back to me. "PT Consulting is prickly. They've got this modern *bushido* code of the warrior culture going on. They take themselves real seriously. Their owner is a retired colonel who got rich doing contract security in Iraq. When he learned the real money was in PUFF, his company switched industries, lured away a bunch of MCB with better pay, and set up shop in my backyard."

"You don't sound like a fan ..."

"He gives mercenaries a bad name, and MHI is mercenary and proud. I'd call him a pirate, but that's an insult to pirates."

"Prick works," Green supplied again. "Thieving pricks, the bunch of them."

I noticed a couple of angry scowls aimed in our direction from some former Monster Control Bureau agents sporting PT shirts. They recognized us too. It probably didn't help that I was wearing a T-shirt with a big MHI Happy Face on it. *Oh well, not my problem.* I just wanted to enjoy my second plate of steak, sushi, and six species of shrimp.

The oldest of the PT men got up and approached my end of the table. He was probably in his early fifties, but built like a marathoner, sporting a blond buzz cut and suntan lines from wearing shades. His mouth smiled, but his eyes didn't. "Well, if it isn't Monster Hunter International. What an unexpected pleasure to run into you gentlemen here. Evening, John."

VanZant nodded politely. "Armstrong."

Armstrong scanned down our table, sizing us up. Unlike his company, my guys were dressed randomly and casual, except for Cooper and Nate being dressed fancy so that the single young guys could try to pick up girls later, and the Haights looking like they were on their way to a rodeo. Armstrong saw Gregorius sitting toward the middle and gave a curt nod. "Hey, I know you from Bragg...Sergeant Gregorius, right? I didn't know you'd joined this bunch."

We had recruited Gregorius after the battle for DeSoya Caverns, where he'd been attached to the National Guard unit manning the roadblock. Apparently he knew Armstrong in a different professional capacity, but judging from the uncomfortable expression on Gregorius' face, he shared VanZant's opinion of the man. "Evening, Colonel. Wife didn't want me sitting around the house retired and bored. This sounded like fun."

Armstrong's chuckle was completely patronizing. "I didn't recognize you with that beard. You look like Barry White. Staying busy, I hope," he said as he scanned over the rest of us. He paused when he got to me. I was pretty sure I'd never met him before, but I am rather distinctive-looking and had developed a bit of a reputation in professional Monster Hunting circles, some of which was even factual. So it wasn't surprising to be recognized. "You're Owen Zastava Pitt, aren't you?"

"In the flesh."

"I'm Rick Armstrong." He said that like it should mean something. *Rick Armstrong.* Now that was a proper superhero secret-identity name. "I'm CEO of PT Consulting." I stared at him blankly. I looked to Trip, but my friend shrugged. "PT Consulting..."

"Potato Tasting?" I guessed helpfully.

"No. It's—"

"Platypus Tossing?"

"Paranormal Tactical," he corrected before I could come up with another.

"Nope." I shrugged. Armstrong seemed let down, but tried not to let it show. What did he expect? I was too busy battling the forces of evil to pay attention to every new competitor on the block. Julie took care of the marketing, I was the accountant. "Doesn't ring any bells."

"Oh, it will." He smiled that fake little smile again. "I'm sure we'll have some teaming opportunities in the future."

I didn't know this Armstrong character, but something about him simply rubbed me the wrong way.

Plus, VanZant's opinion was trusted, and if one of our team leads said that they were assholes, that was good enough for me. "You should leave me your card, you know, in case we're too busy doing something big and important and a little case pops up that we don't have time to pay attention to." I can be a fairly rude person when I just don't give a crap.

"Well, MHI is *established . . .*" Armstrong said, meaning *old*. So that was how it was going to be. "But we're the fastest growing Hunting company in the world. We've got experienced men, a solid business plan, financial backing, the best equipment, and top leadership."

"Nifty. I should buy some stock."

"Speaking of leadership, there's a rumor going around about MHI's." The way he said that sounded particularly snide.

"Oh?" I raised a single eyebrow. This conversation was cutting into my precious shrimp time. "What about our leadership?"

"Word is that Earl Harbinger's been off his game lately. I heard he disappeared for a few months, came back depressed and missing a finger. Rumor is that he had something to do with that incident up in Michigan. You know, that *mine fire*"—he made quote marks with his fingers—"that killed half a town in their sleep, or so the MCB said. I'd hate to think that was one of his cases that went bad."

Sure, Earl hadn't been the same since Copper Lake, but that was none of Armstrong's business. I didn't know all the details about what had happened in Michigan, but I knew enough to know that Earl wasn't *off his game,* he was *angry*. A government agency that he didn't want to name had put his girl-friend into indentured servitude.

"Maybe Harbinger's thinking about hanging it up? That would be *such* a shame. A real loss for our whole industry."

"I'll be sure to pass along your concern. Because, wow, if Earl Harbinger were to retire, who would men like you look to for inspiration?" I gave him a polite nod that I intended to say *shove off, dirtbag*. "See you at the conference."

"Tomorrow then. Looking forward to it. I've got work to do. You boys have a nice supper." He went back to his table to say goodbye to his men. I swear half of them had to resist the urge to salute.

"I *hate* him so much," Gregorius said softly, but didn't elaborate further.

"Well, you do sorta look like Barry White," Cooper told him. He flinched when Gregorius thumped him in the arm.

Soon enough our conversations had picked back up, and if anything, were even louder than before. Milo called my cell to tell me that he would be here soon, and that he and some of the Newbies he'd picked up at the airport would be joining us for dinner. I'd met the crazy elf girl, Tanya, when she'd impersonated an elven tracker to tag along on one of our jobs. She and Edward had saved some kids that had blundered into a pocket dimension filled with telepathic fey monsters. She was the first elf MHI had ever hired, which I still wasn't convinced was entirely a smart move, but Milo assured me that she would easily be able to pass for human in public. The other Newbie was named Jason Lacoco, a name I recognized as the Briarwood

Hunter Earl had recruited during the Copper Lake incident, but who I hadn't met yet. I told Milo I'd have the hostess pull up another table.

By the time I put my phone away, Green was telling a very animated and inappropriate story, and using a cream puff for special effects purposes. Most of my group was laughing loudly at him. The PT men were all stoically chewing, glaring his way occasionally. Apparently the modern warrior code meant you weren't supposed to carry on in such a manner in public.

I was filling plate number three with nachos, potstickers, and mozzarella sticks when Nate came up beside me. He had been sitting at the far end of the table, so had missed my chat with the PT leader. "Hey, Z. I need your help with the black-shirt dudes."

"What do you mean?"

"They keep eyeballing us."

"It's because we're so damned handsome, Nate. They just can't help themselves."

"You say so, but they seem *angry*."

I looked over as Green downed another beer, belched loudly, and then wiped his mouth with the back of his hand. I couldn't hear what he was saying, but Trip seemed distressed and everyone else was amused. Trip, ever the voice of reason, seemed to be trying to get Green to quiet down. VanZant's seat was empty. He'd probably gone to the bathroom and left our drunken vice cop momentarily unsupervised. A few of the PT consultants were looking fairly belligerent at this point. "Is Green trying to pick a fight?"

Nate sighed. "He's still mad about a job his team did all the dangerous work for, but PT swooped in and claimed the PUFF at the last minute. Green was personally out twenty grand and one of their team almost got drowned by a giant squid in the process."

"So you don't need my help with Pontoon Tactical, or whatever their name is, you need help controlling some of our men. Look, why don't you go tell Green to chill out? You are a Shackleford. This is your family's company." I know Earl was expecting a lot from Nate, as he was the one expected to carry on the Shackleford family name. That was a lot of pressure, especially since his big sister pretty much ran the nuts and bolts of the operation already. Nate was tough and enthusiastic, but still trying to figure out his place in the company. The tall young man looked sheepishly at his shoes. "But you won't . . . Because you don't want to come off as the boss's grandson and annoying wet blanket on everyone's good time . . ."

"Reverse nepotism is a hell of a thing. I'm still low man on the totem pole. I say anything and I'll just come off as a whiner trying to throw Julie's weight around."

"If you imply Julie is heavy, she will shoot you." I knew that wasn't what he meant. Besides, Julie was in great shape. My wife was a 5'11" Amazon warrior southern belle art-chick sniper. "And you know she doesn't miss much."

"You know what I mean," Nate pleaded.

"Ask Holly. Nobody will mess with her."

"Are you kidding? I think she finds the whole thing amusing. Please, Z, I don't know all these guys very well, but they respect you."

"I'm no team leader." Some of us had headquarters duties above and beyond being on Hunter teams, but as far as the actual MHI org chart went, I was only the finance manager. Which put me at about the same level as our receptionist, only Dorcas had been around longer and was scarier.

"You're also the God Slayer."

Valid point. Travelling to another dimension and blowing up a Great Old One did earn you some cool points with this bunch. "Leadership sucks sometimes, Nate. You're going to have to get used to it." His older sister would have simply kicked everyone into line, but the youngest Shackleford hadn't found his groove yet. He'd been a Hunter longer than I had, but it was tough to grow up in the shadow of legends. "All right, fine. Just let me grab some more fish sticks."

By the time I'd plopped back down in my seat, I could tell that Green had clearly egged the two nearest PT Hunters on to the point that they were itching for a confrontation. The man certainly had a gift. I could sense there was ugly in the air. Normally that wouldn't bother me too much, but we were supposed to be professionals, we were outnumbered, and I was pretty sure that I recognized one of the PT men from watching Ultimate Fighting on TV.

"Z, that one dude keeps looking at me!" Green exclaimed, voice slurred. "He must think I'm sexy!" Then he looked over at the Ultimate Fighter and licked a cream puff suggestively.

The Ultimate Fighter got up quickly, and Green, being stupidly fearless at this point, did too. Trip intercepted Green, and one of the PT Hunters grabbed the Ultimate Fighter's arm. I, and my tray of goodies, stepped between the two sides as I tried to play peacemaker. "Whoa! Easy, man."

The Ultimate Fighter bumped me and I got Thai peanut sauce on my shirt, and most of my food landed on the floor. It says something about how much I've matured over the last couple of years that I didn't knock him the hell out for wasting such precious cargo. About half of the PT Hunters got up quickly. On my side the Haights and Gregorius jumped up, looking eager, while the rest of my side had that inevitable resigned look of *I'd better help my idiot friends* on their faces. Say what you will about Hunters, they always have your back. "Everybody, relax. No harm meant. My friend's just had a few too many."

Trip dragged the sputtering Green back into his chair. Luckily, Trip was the stronger of the two.

I tried to defuse the situation. "I've seen you on TV, right? Light heavyweight. You were great. I love that stuff—"

"Keep your idiot on a leash," Ultimate Fighter snarled as he was guided to his seat. "Uncivilized Alabama rednecks."

I thought that Green was a Californian, but saying so probably wouldn't have helped matters. In fact, I think Nate was the only native Alabaman at the table, and he was well spoken and wearing a tie. I sat down. "Green, you dumbass. Chill the hell out already or I swear I'll break *another* one of your bones."

"Sorry, Z. It isn't my fault they're such jackasses. I was just telling everybody about how PT is a bunch of no-good, backstabbing, lying cheats, and Armstrong is a thieving sack of—"

"Dude, use your *inside* voice," Trip suggested as he studied the table of muscle and testosterone growling at us. "I don't want to get beat up."

Green giggled. "I'm not worried. We got Z. Just hide behind him. That was my plan. He's *huge*."

"Thanks," I muttered. "I'll remember that when I'm getting my teeth kicked in."

A server came by, and I quickly apologized for the mess and slipped her a twenty. Luckily nobody had called security, and it looked like everything was going to be cool. VanZant got back, saw that some of the staff was cleaning up my spillage and everyone looked tense, and asked what he'd missed. I jerked a thumb at Green. "I think he needs to sleep it off."

VanZant shook his head sadly. "He gets spun up sometimes. I've got him. Come on, man. Why don't you go splash some water on your face or something." He dragged Green up by his collar.

"But I didn't finish my creampuffs!"

"My apologies, Z. He is a really good Hunter when he's sober."

Crisis averted, I went back for replacement food as VanZant led our most inebriated Hunter away. I caught sight of a small man with a gigantic red beard waving at me from the entrance, and so I pointed Milo in the direction of our table. The last of the MHI dinner party had arrived.

Plate partially reloaded, I was preoccupied with using tongs to pick up some crab legs when somebody bumped into my arm. Another solid fellow had been reaching under the sneeze guard at the same time. "Pardon me," he said politely.

"Sorry about that," I answered as I moved a bit to the side. "Didn't see you. Easily distracted by crab legs, you know."

"Thanks." He scooped up several pounds of crustacean and dumped them onto his plate. Crouched, he still barely fit under the sneeze guard. He straightened his back and towered over me. I'm 6'5", was wearing thick-soled combat boots, and he still had me beat by a few inches.

"If you've seen that show about how hard these are to catch, that just makes them taste even better..." I trailed off. The man seemed strangely familiar. Probably thirty, he was thickset, with biceps like hams stuffed under his black T-shirt. His enormous head was stubbly with short, dark hair, and there was a crease running down the middle where he'd had a severe skull injury or maybe brain surgery. Beady eyes narrowed as he got a better look at me. One of his eyes wasn't pointing in quite the same direction as the other one. A look of confusion crossed his wide, flat face.

Where did I know this man from?

Of course I hadn't recognized him at first. He'd aged. After all, it had been several years, and he hadn't had that scar on his head nor the bad eye. Plus the last time I'd seen him I'd been kneeling on his chest and dropping elbows against his bloody and unconscious face until his eye had popped out and his skull had broken in half.

"*You!*" we exclaimed at the same time.

His tray hit the floor with a clatter. The other patrons around the seafood area were suddenly quiet. The giant's mouth turned into a snarl and his hands curled into a fist. "Son of a bitch!"

The final illegal, underground money fight I'd ever participated in had been against this monster. All I'd known going in was that he was a killer, a prison-hardened, brutal machine of a fighter, and then he'd beaten the living hell out of me until I'd finally taken him down, lost control, and nearly beaten him to death. I'd never even known his name.

I took a step back. He was right to be mad. I'd lost it. It was the worst thing I'd ever done. "It was an ac—"

"Accident?" Veins were popping out in his neck. "I was out, and you didn't stop hitting me until they dragged you off! You put out my eye!"

"Sorry." *Man, that sounded pathetic.*

"You ruined my life!" And with a roar, the giant charged.

I lifted the metal serving tray like a shield just in time for his fist to bend it in half. The tray went flying and a waitress screamed. Dodging back, I thumped hard into the table with the ice swan. An instinctive duck kept my head attached to my body as the giant threw a massive left hook that decapitated the swan. Then he lowered his shoulder and rammed into me, taking us both onto the table. The ice swan toppled, hit the floor, and exploded, sending bits everywhere. The table collapsed beneath us and we went rolling off in separate directions.

There were a few seconds of shocked silence, and then fight-or-flight kicked in for everyone in the buffet. For the regular people, it was flight from the two very large men crashing about. Sadly, flight wasn't the normal first reaction for a Hunter. There was a battle cry from near the exit. "That PT guy hit Z!" Green shouted as he shoved his way through the people. *The man who had attacked me was wearing a black shirt*... Green sprinted across the restaurant yelling, "Fight! Fight!" Then he dove and tackled a random PT employee who was getting a piece of pie from the desert bar.

"No! It's not them." I got up, but the giant was

already coming my way again, and then I was too busy protecting my vital organs from his sledgehammer fists to communicate.

The occupants of the MHI table had all stood up to see what was going on, and so had the Paranormal Tactical crew. The two sides looked at each other for just a moment...and then it was *on*. The last thing I saw was one of the Haight brothers clubbing a PT Hunter in the jaw, because then I had to concentrate on my own problems.

The giant was coming my way, hands up and loose, protecting his face. Even enraged, he was moving like a pro. The last time we'd squared off had been a close one. This was the toughest human being I'd ever fought, at least now that I knew Franks didn't count as human.

"I don't want to fight you," I warned.

"Should'a thought of that before you tried to murder me."

He came in quick, but this wasn't a ring, and I wasn't fighting fair. I kicked a chunk of ice and he instinctively flinched aside as it zipped past him. I yanked a cloth off a table and threw it over his head like a net. I'd like to say that I did it dramatically and all the plates and pitchers stayed in place, but they didn't, and most of them shattered on the ground. Temporarily entangled in the tablecloth, he couldn't defend himself very well, so I charged in swinging. I slugged him twice in the stomach, and when his hands went down, I reached up and tagged him with a shot to the mouth.

But then he threw the tablecloth back over me, and I think it was an elbow that got me in the side of the head. I was seeing stars when he slung me around and put me into the meat area. Ham broke my fall. The meat-slicing buffet employees ran for their lives. Getting up, I hurled a pot roast at the giant and he smacked it across the room.

We clashed. There wasn't any finesse at all; it was just a slug fest. We went back and forth, trading blows. Too busy trying to protect my face, I got hit in the ribs, which sucked, and then he nailed me in the stomach, which really sucked, and suddenly I was regretting the several pounds of food I'd just consumed. His shoe landed on a piece of ice, and as he slid off balance, I snap kicked him hard in the thigh of his grounded leg.

He went to his hands and knees. "Stay down!" I ordered.

The restaurant patrons were evacuating. Green had someone in a choke hold and another PT man on his back. I'd forgotten that VanZant had used to be a champion welterweight, and he was knocking the snot out of a PT man twice his size. The Haights seemed to be having a jolly time, until one of them got hit with a chair. Gregorius was wrestling a PT Hunter next to the soda machines. Ultimate Fighter had Cooper in an arm bar. Albert, despite the cane and leg brace, was a shockingly tenacious fighter, and he was facing two PT Hunters at once, which apparently Trip didn't think was very sporting, because he slammed one of them *through* a corner booth. Even Holly had gotten into it. A PT man hesitated, not wanting to strike a girl, until she groin-kicked him like she was punting a football.

Turning back to the giant, I didn't see that my opponent's hands had landed on another serving tray, which he promptly swung and clipped me in the temple. That one rocked my world. I landed flat on my back. The giant came over to stomp me, but Nate body-checked him into the soft-serve ice-cream machine. Too bad the Shacklefords were from Alabama, because the kid showed a lot of promise as a hockey player.

The vanilla spigot had broken off, and soft serve came spooling out. "Got no problem with you," the giant said through gritted teeth. "Just him. Get out of my way."

"You mess with MHI, you mess with all of us!"

The giant cocked his misshapen head to one side. "What? *MHI?*"

Nate tried to punch him, and though he was fast and relatively skilled, the giant was simply out of his league. He effortlessly slapped Nate's hands aside, grabbed my brother-in-law's tie to hold him in place, then slugged him. One, two, three solid hits before Nate's brain had even recorded the first impact. Nate went down, out cold.

That really pissed me off, and I came off the floor, ready to kick some ass.

Hotel security guards were pushing their way inside. Since the restaurant rotated on a platform, the whole place was shaking badly under the stampede. The other ice sculpture fell and broke, and somehow somebody had managed to throw something hard enough to break one of the chandeliers. There was some screaming as Green got pepper-sprayed, and more screaming as Lee shoved a rival Hunter into the chocolate fountain.

One of the PT men got in my way and I dismantled him. I didn't have time to dick around with these chumps when there was a real enemy to fight. I stepped into the clumsy swing and drove my forearm and all my mass into him so hard that he went spiraling over a table. Another of the black polo-shirted Hunters had gotten between us, so the giant simply picked him up and tossed him over the sushi bar, not even bothering to slow his pace. We met in the middle and proceeded to beat the crap out of each other.

He was fast for a big man, and so was I, but he had a reach advantage, so I had to keep moving to stay ahead of him. I wasn't used to being the smaller and lighter fighter. We locked up on each other as we hit the far end of the buffet, both of us throwing knees and elbows. Between the two of us we probably weighed close to seven hundred pounds, and the furniture broke around us like someone had turned loose a herd of enraged wildebeests. I didn't realize we'd gone too far until my shoulder hit the cold glass of the restaurant's bubble. The glass cracked.

I caught my boot against the railing, heaved the giant back, and managed to hit him with a staggering overhand right. That slowed him down.

"Lacoco! Stop! Z! Owen! What the heck? Quit hitting that Newbie!" Milo was running our way, just ahead of a bunch of casino security and a Las Vegas police officer. "You're on the same team!"

The giant must not have heard Milo's words, because he bellowed, launched himself into me, caught me around the waist, and we hit the interior window. The glass shattered around us and then we were falling, *briefly*. We hit water, but it wasn't particularly deep, because right after the water came tile. And the tile was *very* hard.

Groaning, I lay there, flat on my back in half a foot of water, covered in sparkling shards, the wind knocked out of me, staring up at the hole in the buffet's glass wall one story above, as cold water from a dragon-headed fountain spit on us. The giant was on his side next to me. He had a few nasty cuts on his face and arms from the glass. I probably didn't look much better. I realized then that his not-quite-in-the-same-direction eye was fake, because it had popped out and was sitting at the bottom of the pool between us.

A huge crowd of gamblers and shoppers were standing there, gaping at us. Many of them started taking pictures.

At least the fall had finally knocked the fight out of him. The giant looked over at the MHI Happy Face on my tattered shirt with his good eye and groaned.

"Jason Lacoco?" I gasped.

"Uh-huh . . ."

"Owen Zastava Pitt." I coughed. "Nice to meet you. Welcome to Monster Hunter International."

Then several police officers converged on the fountain to arrest us.

CHAPTER 2

"This sucks," Trip said as he studied the cement floor of our cell. I had lost count of how many times he'd said that already.

The two of us had been separated from the others not too long after getting our mug shots taken. I suppose it was good policy to not put too many members of the same rumble into the same cell afterwards. Sure, it was an ugly place that smelled like barf and was filled with losers, but it wasn't *that* bad. "Come on, dude. *Way* nicer than the last jail I was in." I slapped my bench. "See this? Not a single scorpion in sight."

"We're not in Mexico, and your mother-in-law probably isn't going to show up and murder all the guards, either."

True. All things considered, though, despite having just been in a fight, both of us were relatively unscathed. My abs hurt and Lacoco had clipped me a few times, and I had a terrible headache from landing in the fountain, but overall I was doing fine. "Just trying to keep things in perspective is all."

"You're not helping." Trip lowered his voice enough that the dregs of society we shared the holding area with wouldn't overhear. He looked around nervously. "I've never been arrested before. I've never even got a speeding ticket! I've got a spotless record."

"Had," I corrected. "Does it matter? All the goody-two-shoesness in the world didn't keep the Feds from beating you like a piñata that one time anyway...And look on the bright side, now you'll have way more street cred with the gnomes."

From what we could put together about the chaotic aftermath of the events at the Last Dragon Buffet, most of my dinner party had ended up in jail. A few had been taken directly to the hospital, but Trip said that he was pretty sure he saw Tanya escape through the kitchen. Elves were sneaky like that. Matters had been complicated when the responding officers discovered that almost all of us had been carrying at least a gun, and in some cases, two or more guns. The cop patting down Cooper had nearly had a coronary when he had found the first hand grenade.

I couldn't speak for Paranormal Tactical, but on our side the concealed weapons were perfectly legal, with all the paperwork done and fees paid. If a Hunter knew he was going to be somewhere, he was going to make sure he would be there armed, and the peculiar legalities of our career field allowed us quite a bit of leeway when it came to determining what exactly constituted *armed*.

Despite the thirty-six handguns, thirty-two knives, four wooden stakes, three collapsible batons, two frags, a block of C4, Lee's sword cane, and the piano-wire garrote collected by the Las Vegas PD, not a single weapon had been introduced into our brawl by either side, unless you counted the chair that somebody had whacked Shawn Haight over the head with. The good stuff was in case of monsters, not people...Though I felt sorry for any bozo who might decide to try to mug a Monster Hunter.

A jailer stopped at our cell. "Jones and Pitt." There was a buzzing noise, a loud click, and our cell door rattled open. "You're free to go."

That was quick. We had only been here for a few hours and hadn't even been questioned yet, let alone brought in front of a judge. "Really?" The assorted hoodlums, drug dealers, drunk drivers, and johns that were sharing our holding area looked at us with no small amount of jealousy. "Already?"

"It's your lucky day. This way."

Earl Harbinger was in the waiting area. Hands shoved deep into the pockets of his leather jacket, which was what he did when he needed to keep his hands occupied because he was somewhere where he couldn't smoke. I'd like to be able to say that he seemed relieved to see us, but on the contrary, my boss was rather perturbed.

"Hey, Earl. Thanks for—"

He cut me right off. "You have any idea how many favors I had to call in to keep anyone from pressing charges on you idiots?" The more annoyed Earl was, the more southern he sounded, and right about then, he sounded like he was ready to fry up some catfish and watch some NASCAR.

I looked to Trip, who shrugged. "Lots?"

"Lots? Funny, that's the exact same word the casino's

lawyers told me when I asked how much the damages were going to be."

"That bad?"

"Wait until you see the invoice. It's the size of a phone book." Earl rolled his eyes. "I thought charging us for an ice sculpture that was gonna melt anyways was a bit of overkill. They've got nothing on the law though. MHI has done jobs for the city before. They still owed us for taking out one of the nastiest ever vampire infestations a few years back, so they didn't bend us over too bad, but the next time Las Vegas needs our services, we're basically working for *free*. You know how much that offends me in principle? Ruthless bargainers there. I've got Julie and Eddings working up the new contract now."

Eddings was our team leader in Las Vegas, and from what I had heard about him, he wasn't going to like working pro bono. "I'm really sorry, Earl."

"And I was lucky to wiggle out that easy. I ever tell you how much I despise Nevada's jackass senator? The minute he heard there were Hunters on the hook he came sniffing for a deal. Only time he's worried about a budget is when it comes to screwing over Hunters. Cutthroat rat bastard. I think we dodged a bullet. Lucky for us the casino management is dead set on Ick-mip being a success, which would be tough with two dozen of the attendees in jail."

"I appreciate you getting us out."

Earl snorted. "I didn't spring you out of the goodness of my heart, Z. Don't think I did this because we're related now, either. I figure, pretty as Julie is, she could find a replacement husband in a couple days. Week tops."

Sometimes it could be difficult to have the toughest Hunter of all time as your great-grandfather-in-law, but I had helped fight a demon inside his brain once, so we'd bonded. "I love you too, Earl."

"Smartass." Earl looked toward the main hall. The rest of us were being brought out, and Earl nodded at VanZant when he arrived. "Hell, if I wasn't so worried about maybe needing y'all on short notice and hamstringing a quarter of my teams, I would've been happy to let the system take its time, and we'd just post bail when they eventually got around to it. But I got word Paranormal Tactical was trying to cut their own deal, with *my* clients, and *that* I will not tolerate."

VanZant came over. "Admit it, old man. You're just mad because we had a fistfight and nobody invited you. I seem to remember a time that me, you, and Sam remodeled a bar in Wyoming."

"First time I'd ever beaten a man with a taxidermied moose head." Earl had known VanZant for a long time and finally cracked a smile. "All right, you got me there." The two very experienced Hunters shook hands. "Where's your boy? The one that, from what I heard, started this mess." Green came around from behind his team lead, bruised, haggard, nauseous, and seeming rather deflated. "You, I ain't done with . . . And you'd damn well better not throw up in the rental van."

Eventually, everyone that hadn't been taken to the hospital was present. Holly had also managed to avoid being arrested, which wasn't particularly shocking. "I think I chipped a tooth," Lee complained as he felt around inside his mouth with his tongue. "Heh. Worth it, though."

"That was awesome when you put that guy into the chocolate fountain," Trip told him. "Bet that burned."

"Not as awesome as when you body-slammed that one dude." Lee and Trip fist bumped.

Harbinger scowled and both of them shut up. "Not that I don't like the idea of kicking all our competitor's asses as a business model, but I don't like the reality of it costing me so damn much. Y'all better start praying the zombie apocalypse starts soon, because you're going to need that much PUFF money. The bill for this fiasco is coming out of your pay." There was a collective groan at that. "Collect your crap and let's get back to the hotel."

I waited until everyone else was heading for the sign-out desk. There was a big box of evidence weapons to be sorted through, and Green, having had the sense to leave his gun in his room after he'd raided the minibar, had been the only one of us unarmed. I motioned for my boss's attention. "Hang on a second, Earl. We need to talk."

"This better be good news, because so far I ain't happy about the less-than-illustrious start of this conference."

"We've got a problem with one of the Newbies." I didn't know all the details of what had happened in Michigan, and Earl had never wanted to elaborate much, but I knew that Jason Lacoco had been involved in that incident. Somehow he had gained Earl's respect, and that was a tough thing to do.

"Near as we can figure, the elf is still hiding somewhere in the casino. Tanya will come out when she thinks the coast is clear. Trailer park elves are sneaky like that."

"Not her. Lacoco. He started the fight. Not Green."

"He's at the hospital." Earl looked at me funny. "Needed stitches from opening a window with his face. How'd Jason start it?"

"I didn't know who he was, never knew his name, but..." I pointed at one of my eyes. "The glass one?" Then I jerked a thumb at my chest. "Yeah, that was from me, illegal fight that ended badly. Turns out he's still holding a grudge."

"*What?* Why the hell—"

"I didn't know. It was a long time ago. When Lacoco saw me he lost it and tried to hit me. Green thought he was with the other guys, PT jumped in, and it just all went to hell from there."

"Damn it." Earl rubbed his face in his hands. "That would've been mighty nice to know beforehand. I probably would've arranged an introduction that didn't involve quite this much destruction. Well, now we've got one more example of why we really need to hire an HR person."

"That would be an interesting questionnaire. Check this box if there are any members of MHI in need of your vengeance."

"Jason's a good man, Z. Solid."

"He's a killer."

"And you ain't?"

Earl had me there. I hadn't just killed monsters since I'd taken this job, though I hadn't lost much sleep over the members of the Church of the Temporary Mortal Condition that had wound up on the wrong end of Abomination. "Lacoco's served time."

"I'm aware. He also risked his life to save a town from an army of undead werewolves and had the balls to hit me with a fire ax. You'll pay him the same amount of respect you would any other Hunter, and I'll tell him to do the same to you. I won't tolerate any unnecessary bullshit. Understood?"

"No. I don't," I answered. Earl glared at me. He was the boss, and though I'd earned my place in our organization, it would be stupid to argue with him. "Okay fine, understood. Maybe if you'd said more I wouldn't have got caught by surprise. When are you going to tell us the rest of the story about what happened in Michigan?"

A dark look crossed his face. "Never." He turned and walked away. "Let's go."

Despite the fact that we'd wrecked a chunk of the place only a few hours before, the Last Dragon staff welcomed us back with nervous smiles. Apparently their management had been satisfied enough by Julie's contract to forget the whole thing ever happened. It's amazing how fast things are forgiven when absurd sums of money and favors are exchanged. This must be what it is like to be one of those rock stars that destroys hotel rooms and drives cars into pools. Normally I could ask Mosh about that sort of lifestyle, but considering my brother's current circumstances it would probably only make him angrier.

I really should go see my brother while I'm in town...

Before dropping us off, Earl had told me that he would speak to Lacoco once he got back from the hospital. Barely knowing the man, I didn't know how that was going to go over. It wasn't like I had any personal beef with Lacoco. What had happened before was stupid, and it was my fault, but it had been years ago. I'd only known the other fighter by reputation, and it was a bad enough rep that though I had felt awful for nearly killing the man, at least I had known that it couldn't have happened to a more deserving person. But Lacoco still held a grudge. He was lethal and mad at me, which was a terrible combo. Even if he promised Earl that he would play nice, we were in the kind of business where training accidents happened. Lacoco had already gone to prison once, and whomever he'd killed the first time around hadn't even smashed one of his eyeballs into jelly and cracked his skull open. I would do my best to avoid him, but I would have to watch my back as long as he was around.

We were a motley bunch, ripped clothing, some black eyes, busted noses, split lips, and sour dispositions, and we were the ones that hadn't needed medical attention. In the lobby, a few men in black suits watched us with thinly veiled hostility. The suits were too expensive for them to be MCB here for the conference, so that meant that the high-end hotel security had gotten the memo and were keeping a special eye on us. Dinner had been six hours ago, so we were all too exhausted to even make eye contact with well-dressed guards as we piled into the elevator to go back to our rooms. Security had to be hating life, especially since Cooper and Lee were still grumbling loudly about how the police had confiscated *some* of their explosives.

The view out the crowded glass elevator was very nice, since the interior of the hotel was one gigantic open space for most of the interior. They were still painting and decorating the top floors. Despite being huge, the hotel itself was like a ghost town. The ICMHP attendees were the only people staying here. There were a few hundred guests, but that wasn't much considering just how vast this place was. The new hotel's staff was still learning on us. You might as well work out the bugs on people that were here for something top secret, who wouldn't be allowed to give bad reviews afterward. We liked to think of ourselves as celebrity guests, but realistically we were probably more like test subjects.

They had stuck most of MHI on the sixteenth floor. I was the last one off the elevator. The room I was sharing with Julie wasn't too far down the hall. I said good night to the others and ran my key card through the machine. I was surprised that despite the very late hour, my room was packed with Hunters, most of whom laughed at me when I entered. A few of them took up a chant. "Rocky! Rocky!"

Julie was there with the others. Julie was dressed for business, not the armored, hair tucked under a helmet so it wouldn't blow in front of her scope, prescription goggles, sniper-rifle-wielding outfit; but the other, conservative, yet attractive business look, hair down, normal glasses, hot-librarian look that she used for schmoozing with officials and bureaucrats. Both of her modes made MHI lots of money, but tonight only one of them had helped get me out of jail. My lovely wife folded her arms and clucked disapprovingly. "See? You always overdo it at the buffet and then regret it later."

"Why's everyone having a party in our room?"

She came over to inspect my face. "Not too bad. By

your regular standards, you got off easy. I can barely tell you were in a fight at all. Usually you look like hamburger," Julie said with a smirk, then gave me a kiss. "Earl rip you a new one yet?"

"Started to, but this one wasn't my fault. Long story." I raised my voice. "Aw, come on, guys. It isn't funny." My fellow combatants heard the commotion and followed me in from the hall. Now the suite was really packed. "Seriously, I've had a crappy night. Everybody beat it."

"And miss the fight?" Julie took me by the hand and led me over to the TV. Someone's laptop had been hooked to it. It was showing what was obviously a security-camera video from dinner. The video was right at the point where Lacoco and I hit the window; it shattered dramatically around us, and we plunged out of sight. The assembled Hunters had a great chuckle at my expense.

Holly was sitting on the couch and running the computer. "Hey, Z."

"How'd you get out?"

"Escaped through the kitchen...Here, watch. We've seen this five times now. It never gets old." She backed it up and started over. The file began at the point where Lacoco and I bumped into each other at the crab legs. "The look on your face when the big PT guy hits you with a tray is priceless."

"What? He's not—shit. How did you get—"

"Melvin," Holly explained. "Somebody told the troll back at base, so he showed some initiative, broke into the casino's systems, and lifted the video. Piece of cake for him. We've got the buffet from three angles. Don't worry. I told Melvin that if he stuck this on

YouTube I'd kill him. He's still scared of me." She saw the very embarrassed Trip standing behind me. "Hey there, Slugger. At one minute and ten seconds in, you totally wreck some dude. Epic face-plant. I didn't know you had it in you. On the other hand, we've got Cooper there getting his ass handed to him by that square-jawed good-looking one..."

Cooper was trying to get to an angle where he could see the TV in the crowded room. "Hey, he was really strong, okay? I thought I did pretty good."

"Video don't lie, Coop. I was waiting for him to start hitting you with your own arm and repeating *why do you keep hitting yourself?*" Holly looked up. "Oh, hey, Albert! You guys need to see this. On camera two you can totally see Lee trying to drown some poor bastard in chocolate. The chocolate smackdown is *amazing*. We should totally sell this online."

"Having an IT troll is great," Lee said. "I'd buy a copy. This is better than pay-per-view."

"Sell enough, we might recoup the ridiculous cost of that ice swan," Julie suggested.

"Speaking of ice, I could use some for my back... So really, everybody get out."

The audience booed. "Come on, Z. Can we watch it one more time?" Holly begged.

"*Fine.*"

There was a chorus of *yay* from the Hunters. I sighed. My people were completely incorrigible.

The dream began in the desert.

The wind was dry and cold. The sun was weak and bitter. Around me was a sea of sagebrush and there were brown rocky mountains not too far away. I was

standing in a flat, open area, in the middle of a lifeless circle of hard dirt about a hundred feet across.
The sagebrush grew right up to the edge and then
stopped. There were buzzards circling overhead, but
none of them would fly over the dead circle.

In the middle of the dead circle was a depression
in the dirt. The frozen ground burned under my bare
soles as I approached. It was as if the dirt had collapsed, revealing a sinkhole, but as I got closer, I could
tell that this was no natural occurrence. Something
had dug this place up. Rotten wooden braces shored
up the edges of the hole, and a metal ladder, now
mostly turned to rust, led down into the darkness.

Then I was at the bottom of the hole. A single
shaft of sunlight, swimming with dust, followed me
down. The shaft terminated where it was black and
deep, and now there was metal beneath my feet.
There was a hatch.

It had been sealed for a very long time.

Yet, there was something new. Metal had been
exposed through the dust. *Scratches.* A design had
been etched into the metal of the hatch. And as I
watched, the scratches began to glow, growing brighter
and more vivid in the darkness.

When recognition came, when I realized what the
mark was, I bolted awake.

The last thing I remember from the dream was
that stale air had come hissing out from around the
hatch as the container had unsealed.

Julie found me on the balcony, staring at the gaudy
lights of Las Vegas, wondering why I'd had a dream
about the evil symbol my father had warned me about

last year. She left the sliding glass door open and the air conditioning poured out behind her. Good old Vegas, middle of January and somehow it was eighty outside. She leaned on the balcony next to me and didn't say anything for a time. Julie knew me too well. "You okay?" One gentle hand stroked my arm.

I glanced over. She was as beautiful as the day I'd met her. The breeze blew her long dark hair into her face, and she absently gathered a bunch of it and stuck it behind one ear. She'd left her glasses inside, which meant that she hadn't joined me for the view. The city gave her a bit of a neon halo.

"Couldn't sleep," I answered simply. "Bad dream."

"Bad dream . . . or *bad* dream?"

That was a fair question. I did have a bit of a history with that sort of thing; dark premonitions, ancient prophecies, other people's memories, and that sort of thing, all as a result of my peculiar station I held in the order of the universe. It wasn't exactly a picnic. "Normal kind." *I think.* "Don't worry about it."

"Worrying comes with the territory when you're married to someone like you. Can't blame a girl for asking. So what was it?" she asked. I shook my head. "Come on . . ."

"There was this thing buried in a desert. Old, not ancient, but way older than us. It had a hatch like a submarine on it. I don't know . . . something was living inside, but it was coming out. The mark that Dad drew for me, it had been scratched on there."

A scowl crossed her perfect face. "You think it's time?"

A year ago my father had finally told me about his past, about his *mission*, about the reason he'd been such a harsh taskmaster to his sons. He believed that his time was up a long time ago, his life miraculously returned, all so he could prepare one of his sons for something vital. He'd known something bad was coming for most of his life, the end of the world, he'd called it, and he'd done his best to make us ready. One of us had to die to save the world. The events since I'd joined MHI had confirmed to him that I was the one the mysterious Others had been waiting for. He'd told me that when that certain symbol began to appear, the time had come. The rest of his story was on a letter, sealed in an envelope, and locked in a safe, left there after I'd refused to read it. Dad sincerely believed that once I knew the whole story his life would end.

That was one hell of a burden to put on a son.

"Naw. Probably not. Just me worrying about stuff is all."

"Your dad has been calling a lot lately."

"He's trying to get me to come for a friendly visit. We both know he's going to ambush me somehow, trying to get me to 'man up' so he can get all self-righteous and die a proper martyr. Then I'm supposed to go all kamikaze on *something* to save the world again. I don't think so... You know what pisses me off? He got shot in the head once and that makes him the expert? I do this for a living."

Julie chuckled. "You know, most couples in their first year of marriage are talking about things like whether they should buy a house—"

"Which is why I married a chick who already owned a sweet mansion."

My attempt at levity failed. "—Or if they should start having kids."

That was a sad subject for us. I looked back at

the city. "Yeah, well..." As long as Julie bore the Guardian's mark, we were scared to even think about the possibility. We didn't know exactly what they had done to her, besides keep her alive a few times when she should've died, but to what purpose? We knew so little about the Guardian, and the only other person we'd ever met with her same curse, the man that had shared it with her in fact, had been instantly skinned alive by a minor Old One when it had taken that power away. We didn't dare risk passing that on to a child. "Hell. I don't know. I just wanted to get some sleep."

"You're watching for a mystery symbol so you know when some new asshole intends to start the apocalypse, and I'm trying to learn how to get rid of these," she rubbed the magical black marks on her neck, too hard. "And worrying about mystical Guardians and magical time-destroying artifacts, and what to do when Mom inevitably tries to murder us again. The most experienced Hunter we've got is preoccupied listening for rumors of a red werewolf, and we're at a conference with the people that shut us down. A little insomnia is understandable."

I put my arm over her shoulders and pulled Julie in close. "I do love how you always manage to look at the bright side of things."

We stood there together for a time, me looking at the pretty flashing casino lights and Julie looking at what I could only assume from the strength of her prescription as a bunch of colorful blurs. Regardless of how strange our life was, as long as we had each other, everything was going to be fine. "It's four o'clock in the morning. I'm going back to bed," she finally told me. "Registration starts at nine."

"I don't think I can fall back to sleep just yet."

"I said I was going back to *bed*, not back to *sleep*." Julie grabbed a handful of my shirt and pulled me along. "Sleep is for quitters."

CHAPTER 3

The first annual International Conference of Monster Hunting Professionals was held at the same time as the shooting industry's big trade show, SHOT (Shooting, Hunting, Outdoor Tradeshow). That had been a good call on the organizer's part. First off, since we were in a business that officially did not exist, at a conference that didn't exist, talking about things that didn't exist, it provided a crowd of tens of thousands that we could easily blend into. Second, it killed two birds with one stone. For those of us that didn't particularly care to listen to panels about laws, regulations, and the latest trends in *blah blah blah*, we could sneak down the street to play with all the latest guns and toys. Many of us had gotten memberships for both events. Milo had a federal firearms manufacturer's license, and both of us had come armed with MHI corporate cards and a stack of purchase orders. You know ... Just in case ...

I had been told that there was a certain secret underbelly of the SHOT Show for Monster Hunters. Many of the companies in the gun and gear business knew about us and loved us because we had lots of money and burned through equipment rapidly. So if you wore your company logo or managed to talk to the right sales rep at the right place, you could get peeks behind the curtains at the good stuff that wasn't available to the public. With hundreds of us from around the world all converged here, that meant there would be even more super-secret cool-guy stuff to play with. Plus, Milo had told me that there were usually tons of free samples.

As a lifelong gun nut, this news had made my year, and I was so excited to make it over to the SHOT Show that I could taste it. I had already color-coded a map with companies that I needed to hit up, and I had even built a spreadsheet for all of the things we needed to buy. Guns, ammo, new types of armor to experiment with, knives, explosives, and Milo *really* wanted a killer robot.

Unfortunately, since I was now management, protocol demanded that I put in some face time at ICMHP first. So here I was, map, spreadsheet, and purchase orders ready to go, and I was roped into attending the opening ceremonies instead. Acres of guns calling my name right across the street, and I was stuck schmoozing.

Now, there were plenty of panels I did want to attend, though most of those were scheduled in the evenings. I couldn't wait to hear the nitty-gritty about some of the rare types of monsters that had been encountered and what had proved most effective in destroying them. There was even a Q&A session for the team that had taken down the infamous Glasgow mega-snake. They could keep the laws and ethics nonsense panels. I was in this for the things that would make me a more effective Hunter. The last thing I wanted to do was listen to a lobbyist for equal rights for vampires or some bullshit like that.

After Julie and I had come down the elevator, we signed in, got name tags, and were hustled through the registration area of the Last Dragon's conference area. There were all sorts of attendees, academics, lobbyists, salesmen, government types, but mostly Hunters, more Hunters than I'd ever seen, Hunters from all over the world. Hell, according to Julie this was the greatest concentration of Hunters anyone knew of. None of us were dressed for battle and nobody was wearing their war face, but you could tell they were Hunters. You could just smell it on them. These people had seen things that even I hadn't seen. It was kind of exciting, yet also strangely intimidating, and for the first time I felt myself becoming really excited for this event.

This morning there appeared to be a few MCB working in conjunction with casino security. I spotted Agent Archer from across the room, and he gave me a brief nod of acknowledgement. I hadn't seen my former bodyguard since New Zealand. It appeared that the efficient agent was the man in charge of coordinating with the local security. I felt pity for any reporters that tried to make their way into this particular shindig.

As we were riding up the escalator into the conference center, Julie tapped me on the shoulder. "Look who's here."

I followed her pointing finger. "Well, obviously it wouldn't be a party without Agent Franks." The hulking agent was standing off to the side, watching the passing crowd of Hunters with dispassionate eyes, probably deciding which ones were the greatest threats and in what order he would eliminate them if necessary. Though the hall was crowded with guests, they seemed to instinctively part around Franks, like seals with a killer whale in the surf. He was a one-man wall of intimidation. And they didn't even know that he wasn't really human.

"Lovely."

"Don't misunderstand him. Under that violent, frightening, remorseless killing machine exterior, he's got the heart of a saint...Or two. Probably two hearts. I'm going to say hi."

"Knock yourself out, hon."

Franks saw me coming. His lips parted in what was either disgust or annoyance, but it certainly wasn't a smile. I waved happily. "Franks, buddy! How you been? You're looking well. Are those new ears?"

"Pitt..." Franks didn't seem to appreciate me talking about his secret in public.

The taciturn monster Agent Franks and I had an odd relationship. We had killed a great Old One together. Normally that would be a wonderful way to make friends with someone, only I don't think Franks had friends, nor did he want any, and if he got the order, I had no doubt he would shoot me dead without the slightest hesitation and then not feel even a glimmer of remorse. At best, Franks respected me a tiny bit more than he did most people, but as far as I could tell, he thought of most people as insects, so that wasn't saying much. "How you been?"

He looked around the crowd and grunted.

"Me too, thanks for asking," I said. Franks scowled. That was usually what passed for conversation with the man made out of spare parts. "So what brings you here?"

"Orders."

I could almost have sworn that he sounded bitter about that. "Myers around?" Franks raised a single eyebrow, as if to say *you haven't heard?* The fact that I understood that gesture told me that I had spent entirely too much time around Franks. "Wait. What happened to your boss?"

"They'll announce it." He really didn't sound happy now. Another agent came up next to Franks and whispered something to him. "Reporter or protestor?" Franks listened as the agent kept whispering. Not that he actually displayed any emotion; having something to do seemed to cheer him up, or maybe I was just projecting, like when you have a conversation with a plant. "Someone is trying to get in without a badge." He began walking away.

"Well, don't kill anybody."

Franks paused for a second. "Why not?"

"Uh . . . Never mind. See you around, Franks."

I followed the crowd. Luckily there was a table of coffee and snacks, so I grabbed a couple of doughnuts on the way in. The opening ceremonies were being held in a gigantic ballroom. A stage and podium had been set up in the front, and the rest of the room had been filled with chairs. My wife spotted me and waved. She'd saved us a few seats.

Earl was shaking hands with some old acquaintances. He joined us a moment later with "I hate these sorts of things."

We sat toward the back. Julie was wearing a conservative dress that just screamed business, Earl was in his leather jacket like normal and extra irritable because there wasn't a smoking area anywhere nearby, and Nate was in a suit and had a bandage on his nose from last night. The poor kid looked rough, but that was understandable since getting hit by Lacoco was like getting hit by a truck. There were other members of MHI in the mass of Hunters filing in. Many of us had been smart enough to skip this part to go look at guns. I didn't see Lacoco, which was probably a good thing, and I had no idea if Tanya the elf had ever turned up either. Obviously, Skippy and Edward, who had been working our last case with us, didn't like crowds and had volunteered to stay with the chopper at the airport. That was unfortunate, because if we'd had Edward's Orc Fu at the buffet fight we would've totally kicked ass.

Julie had been doing this for years and Earl had been doing this for a *really* long time, so between the two of them they knew almost everybody and kept up a running commentary as the other participants came in. "Those are the boys from Tokyo. They positively own the giant monster business. I'll have to introduce you. They're all right."

"Good to see French Hunters made it," Julie said. "Is that Jean Darne's son?"

"I think so . . . I should probably avoid him. He might be a little sore since I beheaded his daddy."

"You did his dad a favor," Julie said. "I'll talk to him later. I can relate."

"Be good to keep up friendly relations." Earl nodded. "Those French Hunters are all right."

There was a sudden flood of matching black polo

shirts. They had even choreographed their arrival, with Armstrong in the lead. "Hey, Prehensile Tails got out of jail too."

"I thought it was Panoramic Toast." Even Julie had decided to join in.

Earl gave Paranormal Tactical Consulting the once-over. "Well, now it's obvious why you kids wanted to hit them so bad. They look like assholes."

That went on for some time as Earl grouped all the newcomers into one of two categories. They were either *assholes* or *all right*. Because of his extraordinarily long career, Earl was like an encyclopedia of everyone in the business, and if he didn't know them personally, they were more likely to fall into the asshole category. For Earl, everyone from the government automatically went into the first bucket until proven otherwise. By the time the lights dimmed we had seen Hunters from fifteen different countries, sometimes more than one team from the same country, with Earl praising one bunch and cursing the next.

My phone buzzed with a text from Milo. *Dude. SHOT is awesome. Our ammo mfg is loading our 30 cal silver bullets in 7.62x39 and 300 win mag now! I got free samples and a hat!* That simply wasn't fair.

It took another fifteen minutes for everyone to come in. Many of the latecomers looked hung over and tired, but such was the nature of Vegas. A spotlight turned on over the speaker's podium and the MC came out wearing a tuxedo. "How long is this going to take?" Earl leaned across me to ask Julie.

She had thoughtfully grabbed a schedule. "Let's see . . . Welcome, intros, some announcement from the MCB, a couple of keynote speeches . . . About two hours.

Then the luncheon, then the panels start...And you two had damn well better be attending the ones I'm on. The keynote address is at six."

Earl and I groaned simultaneously. "I'm gonna need a smoke." Earl got up to sneak out.

"Bring me back a plate of those little sausages and some cheese balls, would you?" I asked.

Regardless of what business you're in, these sorts of things were always the same. Introduce yourself. Applause. Introduce everybody else. Applause. Tell a lame joke. Applause. Thank everyone and their dog... I mean, come on, the people in this room kill supernatural beings for a living... How could you possibly make that tedious? Yet somehow, they did. The master of ceremonies was long-winded and I was quickly bored. It didn't help that Milo kept texting me every so often about something else that I was missing. *Z! I met Ted Nugent and got his autograph! He was cool.* Followed ten minutes later with *Found secret killer robot company! Going for a test drive! LOL!* If I hadn't known Milo was such a nice guy I would've sworn that he was tormenting me on purpose. *Picking up more awesome free samples! 20mm cannon!* The number of bodies crammed in made it too warm, and per Julie's insistence, I'd worn a tie, which made it more stuffy, all of which made me want to take a nap.

When the MC introduced the guests of honor, he mentioned that an invitation had been extended to Raymond Shackleford the Third, owner of Monster Hunter International, but that he'd been unable to attend due to health reasons. Which was partially true, with the other part being that he'd simply thought the whole thing had sounded boring and being a guest of honor was pretentious. When they said the boss's name, all of the members of MHI, myself included, gave him a standing ovation. I was happy to see that several members from some of the foreign teams stood up out of respect too. They should. He was a living legend.

"Aw, Grandpa would've really liked that," Julie said.

That part was interesting, but then it was back to thanking the generous organizers of this illustrious secret gathering and all that jazz. I hadn't gotten much sleep, so I think I might have nodded off for a minute or two when Julie elbowed me awake.

"Huh? What?" *Had I been snoring?*

"Did you catch that?"

"What?" And then I noticed that there was a general murmur going through the audience.

"The next speaker is the new director of the Monster Control Bureau, and it *isn't* Myers."

Dwayne Myers had been running the MCB since right after I'd first been mauled by a werewolf, but he had only been the *interim* director, pending congressional approval. The previous real director had been run out because of some scandal. Myers had been running things for so long that I had always just assumed he would end up officially in charge. Myers was a complete jerk, but he was also a ruthlessly efficient jerk. I perked up. Hunters had no choice but to deal with the MCB, so this announcement could go either way.

"What's his name?"

"Douglas Stark. Sounds familiar, but I can't remember from where. Ringing any bells?"

"Never heard of him." I looked around for Earl, since he knew everybody, but he wasn't back yet. "A new guy, huh? How bad could he be?"

"Never say that about the MCB," Julie hissed. "You'll jinx us!"

The MC got out of the way and a stocky man with bulldog jowls entered from behind the curtains. He walked across the stage with a swagger, took his place at the podium to sporadic and lackluster applause, reached into his suit, took out a piece of paper, cleared his throat, and began to read his speech. "Thank you, Ken. Thank you, everyone, for the warm welcome." The dozen or so MCB agents that were actually clapping stopped. "I'm Special Agent Doug Stark and I am *honored* to be a guest here at the first annual International Conference of Monster Hunting Professionals. It is my goal to usher in a new era of cooperation between public sector and private sector Hunters."

"That'll be the day." Earl slid in next to me. He had neglected to bring me more snacks. "Why's that jackass talking?"

"That's the new MCB director."

"You're messing with me . . . Oh shit, you're not. *Him?*" Earl's eyes narrowed. "God help us . . . I should've killed that son of a bitch when I had the chance."

After Director Stark's incredibly self-aggrandizing speech, we broke for lunch, and the first thing Earl did was track down and corner Agent Franks to get an explanation. I followed along, mostly because I wanted to see what happened when the unstoppable force ran into the immovable object. We found the big agent in the hall outside the main room, frowning at the multitude of passing Hunters, surely bummed that he wasn't allowed to hit them. "Franks. We need to talk."

"Harbinger." Franks didn't seem surprised to see us. "Pitt."

"What the hell happened to Myers?"

"I'm unable to comment on personnel matters." He said the words like they were memorized. I had a sneaky feeling that would be the standard line from any member of the MCB.

"Come on. We both know this is a bad call. I can't stand Dwayne, but he's a strategic genius compared to Stark. What did they do with him?"

The wheels turned, but apparently Franks had something to gain by not being a totally uncooperative dick. "Transferred. Agent Myers is over the Special Response Team." To the best of my knowledge, the MCB's Special Response Team were the ones that came swooping in with all of the big guns. It was a job that seemed a little too *militaristic* for Agent Myers.

"That's a demotion. Why in the world would they do that? Are their heads that far up their asses over there? Stark's a coward and a moron. We both know that."

Franks looked around to see who was listening, and for the very first time ever, I think he might have been *uncomfortable*. "I'm unable to comment on personnel mat—"

"Cram your personnel matters. You unable to comment about what happened in Copper Lake? Or the Arbmunep? Or Lord Machado? Or all the other shit popping up around the world since then? Things are speeding up everywhere and your boss was throwing a fit about it. I know about you stopping something big in California recently."

Franks scowled, suspicious. "He told you?"

"A little, because as much as me and Myers hate each other, that son of a bitch at least knew what was at stake. We had an understanding. Something's coming. We can all feel it, and they put fucking Stark in charge? The man spent half a werewolf siege trying to throw children out of a bomb shelter so he could take a spot. What is *wrong* with you people?"

Franks glanced around again, apparently didn't see any of his men, then surprisingly, reached into his suit and shut his radio off. "Agent Myers was . . . opinionated."

"Dwayne rocked the boat."

Franks shrugged. "Over my pay grade."

I couldn't help myself. "You get paid? I figured you were in this for the perks."

Franks had a real talent for ignoring me. "Agent Myers had some . . . disagreements . . . with the administration. Agent Stark . . ."

"Is a bootlicking bureaucrat paper shuffler who'll roll over and do whatever he's told."

"I am unable to comment on personnel matters," Franks said again, but I could've sworn that one sounded like a *yes.* "Agent Stark was cited for valor for stopping an outbreak in Michigan." It was so very hard to tell when Franks was being sarcastic. "He likes you, Harbinger." *Okay, that time I could tell.*

"I bet he does . . . I'm the one that broke his fat nose. So someone in the government wants their strongest entity for dealing with the supernatural neutered and out of the way." Earl leaned in really close and looked Franks square in the eye. "Unicorn is calling the shots again, ain't they?" Earl said that with a lot of venom. *Unicorn?* I didn't think he meant like an actual magic horse with a horn. *Who the hell was unicorn?*

Whoever Unicorn was, Franks didn't like hearing that word. Franks took an uncomfortably long time responding. "This conversation never happened." He reached into his coat, turned his radio on, and went back to scanning the crowd, ignoring us completely.

Earl stomped off and I followed him down the hall. "What's he talking about? Uni—"

My boss silenced me with a hard look. "Not now." This had to be related to what had happened in Copper Lake, but Earl was in such a sour mood that I didn't dare bring it up.

Julie and Nate were at the luncheon, mingling and being social with some of our competitors. The two of them saw the look on Earl's face and immediately knew something bad had happened. "You okay?" Julie asked as she excused herself from a red-faced Englishmen with a really big mustache.

"We'll talk about it later, but right now, do me a favor, talk to as many of the overseas Hunters as you can. I want to know what kind of activity they've been seeing lately, and especially if it seems to be on the rise."

"You want me to spread the word?" Julie pulled out her iPhone. "There's a mess of us here."

"Get Holly. All she has to do is smile and any man will tell her whatever she wants to hear." Earl thought about it for a second. "On second thought, ask everybody you think can play it close to the vest and talk to our competitors without getting into fistfights." He glanced at me as he said that.

"In my defense, I didn't fight anyone from PT. I fought one of our Newbies."

"Skip Paranormal Testicles or whatever the hell their name is. I want to know about outside the country, areas where we don't have a lot of contacts especially, and I don't want this getting back to the MCB that we're asking."

"You think something's up?" Nate asked. He had a nasty black eye and a purple lump on his head from yesterday.

"I'm looking for a pattern. Myers was worried the last time we talked, enough that his superiors were getting sick of him. If he was bugging them enough to get himself demoted out of their hair, then something must be up. But play it careful, there might be some other forces at play..." Earl trailed off, worried. "Keep it professional. Not everybody here likes us. We're more successful than they are. Jealousy breeds contention."

"And don't forget we're also the reason all the other US Hunters got put out of business for a while too," Julie muttered. The aftermath of MHI's hundredth-anniversary Christmas party and Ray Shackleford's craziness had gotten private Monster Hunting banned in the US for several years. "It's easy to hold a grudge against the people that got your job declared illegal."

"I'm on good terms with the old school. I'll take the Russians and the Japanese. Julie..."

"I'll talk to Pierre Darne," Julie volunteered. "I really should anyway."

"Call Albert in, too. I think he speaks Chinese. Their team seems okay, but their government-provided translator is a prick. Oh, yeah, and Priest knows the South Africans. I think he's talking to them now. And, Z..." Earl faced me.

"Who do you want me to schmooze?"

"Nobody you might piss off. I didn't hire you for your diplomacy, and you tend to say things you shouldn't, so just play it cool."

"I do okay—"

Earl cut me off. "I've got one word to sum it up for you ... gnomes."

Crap. He had me there.

We broke up and moved off in different directions to mingle. I had no idea what Earl was concerned about. I could be social with the best of them. After all, these were fellow Monster Hunters, men and women with a higher, nobler calling. Defenders of the innocent, protectors of the good. Like Agent Stark had said, this was a new era of cooperation. This should be a piece of cake.

And then the crowd parted and I was standing in front of three men from Paranormal Tactical, and judging from the scrapes and Band-Aids, they had been at dinner last night. All three of them gave me withering death glares. Earl had wanted discretion, I really didn't want to go back to jail, and I was already paying for that frigging swan, so I turned and kept walking ... only to have the chief jerk himself, Armstrong, step in front of me. I recognized the muscular man standing behind him as Ultimate Fighter, and despite beating the hell out of some of my guys—Melvin's video confirmed at least two—he didn't have a scratch on him.

"Owen. I'm surprised to see you here. I heard you took a nasty spill." The unctuous bastard just oozed sincerity. "Landed in a fountain, if I heard right."

"No biggie, Rick. The tile broke my fall."

He looked over my shoulder at his men. "I hope

you boys are getting along better after last evening's unpleasantness."

"Boys will be boys."

"I hear you there." Even his laugh was annoying. It's weird how some people can be perfectly polite, yet still be complete asshats at the same time. "It's understandable that your men needed to blow off some steam, especially with all the stress MHI is under."

"What stress?"

"MHI isn't used to competition. You've got us taking business from you out west, the Vermont Stump Jumpers in the northeast. All these hungrier companies, and MHI is so old-fashioned and stuck in its glory days. It's got to be tough for you."

My gosh, I hated this guy. I watched Ultimate Fighter. He seemed wary but relaxed. They weren't stupid enough to do anything here, what with all of the hotel security being keyed up, not to mention Agent Franks. This was simple Type A personality posturing. *Screw it.* "Yeah, it is tough being the biggest and best in a world of fly-by-night wannabes, but you get used to it."

The friendly facade slipped just a little. "Some say the Shacklefords are dinosaurs."

"Like a Tyrannosaurs Rex." I laughed in his face. "Oh, I'm sorry..." I gestured at his men. "Was I supposed to be intimidated?"

"Everybody knows the sun is setting on MHI." Armstrong folded his arms. "But I didn't come over here to trade barbs, hotshot. I've got something for you. Mr. Durant, if you would..." He stepped out of his way and Ultimate Fighter took his place.

I sized him up. He was much smaller than I was,

but this dude was cut, and judging from the videos, not somebody you wanted to tangle with. "So, I'm guessing you're supposed to be PT's tough guy."

He handed me an envelope. I took it without even thinking. "Everyone needs a hobby. I happen to enjoy competitive mixed martial arts. However, as a member of the bar, I'm also Paranormal Tactical's legal advisor. I'm serving in the latter capacity today."

He was remarkably well spoken for a man who had choked Cooper unconscious. "You're an attorney?" I opened the envelope, looked inside, read, blinked, reread, and still couldn't believe my eyes. "This is a restraining order..."

"Oh, you thought that you were the only ones that could call in favors on short notice. Last month we helped out a judge with a bad case of hobgoblins." Ultimate Lawyer nodded at the other PT men. "You've been served in front of witnesses. Since we now fear for our safety, any MHI staff that was involved with last night's altercation are required to stay at least one hundred yards from any employee of Paranormal Tactical Consulting at all times. The lawsuit paperwork for the injuries sustained by our employees during your company's reckless and negligent rampage will be delivered to your Alabama office by certified mail."

The order looked legitimate. It even had each of our involved Hunters' names on it, except for Holly's, because she'd managed to avoid getting arrested. I couldn't believe this. Slugging each other was one thing, but lawyers? That was just plain nasty. "You son of a bitch."

"One hundred yards, Pitt. Better start walking," Armstrong suggested.

"You haven't seen me shoot, asshole," I muttered. "You should've asked for a thousand."

He started to say something else, but luckily another person interrupted our conversation. "Owen Zastava Pitt?" A thin, tanned-as-leather young man pushed past the three PT goons. "Is that you?" He sounded Australian.

"That's me." I shook his hand with my right while I crumpled the restraining order in my left, glaring at Armstrong.

The Australian shouted at his friends. "It is him!" Then he went back to pumping my hand up and down. "The primary on one of the biggest bounties ever, well, how do you do?" The other Australians followed along, and pretty soon I was shaking hands and getting slapped on the back by a bunch of friendly tough guys from a small company out of Melbourne. The PT Hunters were forced out of the way. The interlopers even wanted to take their pictures with me. "What happened in New Zealand? We snuck a look at that great big fucking insect tree they built the silo over and it's ugly as they say. So, the rumors about you blowing up an Old One, true?"

"Sort of." I glanced over at my new enemies and shrugged. "Celebrity. You get used to it...Come on, we need to go to the other end of the hall before I can tell the story. These morons just served me with a restraining order because we kicked their asses in a friendly little fistfight."

"Really? Just for that?"

"It was even a fair fight."

The Australian scowled at them. "What cocks."

"I know!"

CHAPTER 4

Twenty minutes later, the tie was undone, sleeves rolled up, stuffy decorum had been ditched, and I was at the far end of the hall, surrounded by a crowd of Hunters as I told them the story about facing off against the Dread Overlord in its home dimension. After the Australians had drawn attention, I'd picked up a mess of assorted Europeans, some Brazilians, two guys from India, and an absolutely stunning woman from South Korea. Apparently, obliterating a great Old One with a doomsday device designed by Isaac Newton was so awesome that it transcended all cultural and language barriers, plus it helped that I did great sound effects.

Careful to leave out the classified or embarrassing parts, such as me being the Chosen One and surviving zombie bites, Agent Franks' real identity, the fact that the MCB had been infiltrated by a death cult, or that the Condition's necromancer had once been a member of MHI, it still made for a pretty nifty story. Plus it had been a while since I'd had an audience where

it was legal for me to actually tell it to. Everyone at
MHI had already heard it a dozen times.

Earl and Julie came by at one point, with Earl just
shaking his head in amazement. I wasn't getting the
information that he wanted, but I was certainly suc-
ceeding as MHI's goodwill ambassador. Offending the
gnomes and getting beat up that one time had been
an aberration on my diplomatic resume. I could be
perfectly decent at networking when I put my mind
to it. Julie seemed rather proud of me, and gave me
one of those wifely *I knew you could do it* smiles.

I folded the restraining order into a paper airplane
and sailed it over to Julie without even interrupting
my narrative. She caught, unfolded, and read it while
mouthing something that looked suspiciously like
ducking mother truckers, but I'm not very good at
lip reading. Julie immediately whipped out her phone,
surely to call MHI's own attorneys. Our little spat with
PT was about to get even uglier. You did not want to
play business hardball against Julie.

I was surprised when Agent Archer had joined
my crowd, though he had probably been sent over
to make sure I wasn't giving away any state secrets.
So I pointed him out as one of the heroes of the
Arbmunep fight, not that I had any idea what he
had actually done during that particular fight, since
I'd been rather preoccupied at the time. The young
agent's cheeks grew red with embarrassment, but since
I'd now singled him out as one of the good guys, he
was pretty much trapped into agreeing with me about
how stupendous everything had been.

I finished the story with, "And the worst part,
since the Dread Overlord wasn't actually on Earth,

we didn't get to put in for the PUFF bounty!" Most of the Hunters laughed, while a couple of translators hurried to finish the story, and then their charges laughed too. A few of the Hunters didn't join in, and these were the ones that thought I was full of crap. I couldn't particularly blame them, since if I hadn't witnessed the mountain-sized squid god, I wouldn't have believed myself either.

One German in particular was looking at me like I'd pushed his grandmother off her walker. "You speak about creatures of unbelievable horror so flippantly, I wonder perhaps if you have ever actually seen one." He was of average height, fit but not big, probably forty, with a neatly trimmed beard and a very stern demeanor. "A great Old One is nothing to joke about. Even speaking of them draws their ire."

"You think talking about them makes them angry, try hitting one with an alchemical super weapon. I don't think we've met . . ."

He immediately handed me a rather nice business card. "Klaus Lindemann. I am the commander of Grimm Berlin." That was one of the companies that Earl had referred to as *all right*. Several of the other Hunters had apparently heard of the German team as well, because there were some impressed-sounding whispers from the crowd. I stuck the card in my pocket. "I intend no disrespect—"

"That's normally what someone usually says right before they disrespect you," I said as I handed him one of my business cards. OWEN Z. PITT. COMBAT ACCOUNTANT.

"Yes . . . but your tale is absurd."

"You don't have to take my word for it."

Lindemann sniffed. "I did not intend to."

"Agent Archer!"

The Fed jumped, not used to being pointed out in a group of Hunters. He swallowed hard, and Archer was one of those skinny types with the pronounced Adam's apple, so his discomfort was extra obvious. "Yeah?"

"Sorry about blowing your cover." Several of the Hunters laughed at that, since the guys with black suits and earpieces were obviously MCB. It didn't matter what country you were from, every Hunter knew about the MCB, if not personally, then at least by reputation. "Care to tell our honored guests about how me and Franks blasted the Dread Overlord?"

Archer was like a deer in the headlights. I knew from experience that he was pretty decent at lying to the press, but this wasn't a bunch of ignorant dupes to be led around by the nose. These folks made their livings killing things that weren't supposed to exist. "I ... uh, can neither confirm nor deny ..." He looked around nervously at all the waiting Hunters. "There's an official MCB press release concerning the events in New Zealand ... and ... Shoot ... That's all I can say."

"Thank you, Agent." Just having the official type corroborate that *something* had happened was even better, because now their imaginations would fill in the blanks. It gave my story a certain air of legitimacy. "It was really neat. Giant alien death tree and crazy cultists. You guys would've loved it." Archer realized too late that since he hadn't simply shot me down, he had sort of verified my story to the others, which I'm positive hadn't been his assignment. The young agent tried to be discreet as he fled the crowd, probably worried that his superiors were going to chew him a new one.

"It's real enough," an Englishman told Lindemann. "The New Zealand government has a mutual assistance treaty with the BSS." His tone suggested that their feelings about their British Supernatural Service were equivalent to our opinion of the MCB. "Their Select Group were carrying on about one of our contracts at the time, but they left in a hurry to help damage control. Word from a chap on the inside was that they had to hide a big one."

"I've seen the aftermath of this Arbmunep beasty," the leader of the Australians said. "The whole area's been cordoned off by military research. There's a new building on the spot. Looks rather like a very unnecessarily big silo, and they won't say what's inside."

Lindemann adjusted his sport coat. "So it seems that something extraordinary did occur in New Zealand." The admission seemed to pain him. "I stand corrected, Mr. Pitt. You have my apologies."

"I know what's in that silo. They're studying the Arbmunep. From what the cult leader told me, there are more of those things buried all over the world." Earl had wanted us to gather intel, so it was worth a shot. "And that's not the weirdest thing we've seen lately. MHI has had a few really odd cases over the last few years . . . Mr. Lindemann used the word extraordinary. I'd say that fits. What about you guys? Anything extraordinary in your neck of the woods?"

One of the other Europeans, a stout older man, leaned forward and said something to his translator. The translator hurried and spoke. "Like this thing that came from underground, there are things beneath

Serbia. Tunnels from the middle of the world. The . . . diggers?" The older man repeated himself. "The diggers of the holes are coming into the light. These are new things, but legend says they have been here before."

"Us too," said a bulky man with spiky black hair. "I am from *Orzel Biaiy Wojskowy Zawierajacy Kontrakt* . . . White Eagle Military Contracting of Poland. Over last two years, we have seen many things come from below. Monsters came out of ground, revealed entrance to tunnels beneath Lodz. Things were . . . how you say . . . *hibernating*. For a very long time, but they woke up and now they are gone."

Several others began to speak at once, talking about strange new monsters awaking and dragging themselves out of the earth. My Portuguese sucked, mostly because I'd learned it magically from a five-hundred-year-old dialect, but I could've swore one of the Brazilians said something about whole *towns* going missing. His translator was still trying to catch up when one of the Indians began telling us about how their government had forbidden his company from investigating a village that had been mysteriously depopulated on the border with Pakistan. Both countries were blaming the other, but the initial army scouts had reported finding freshly dug tunnels that led to what appeared to be the ruins of a city deep beneath the surface.

That had only been two months ago.

"It seems that many things long buried wish to be found again," said the woman from South Korea. Her melodic voice cut right through the chatter, catching all of our attention. Her English was measured and carefully pronounced. "We were cautioned by our ambassador not to speak of it, but I believe we may have a related issue. In our region there was a disturbance on the ocean floor." I hadn't noticed that we'd been joined by one of the translators from the People's Liberation Army. He snapped something at the woman from Korea, and though I couldn't understand a word of her response, I'm pretty sure her sharp response basically told him to go screw himself. The government interpreter ran off, probably to tell on her.

"Pay no attention to him. There was an incident which was embarrassing to his country's navy. Our two governments had an agreement not to speak about this, but from what I am hearing now, I believe this should be known to all of you."

"Your government? You are private or government?" the big Pole asked, suspicious. MHI really did a have a lot in common with our competitors.

"I am privy to some things. You could call me a consultant," she answered innocently.

"Consultant? More like secret agent ninja," one of the Australians whispered to me. Apparently he was familiar with the woman.

"An anomaly appeared on the ocean floor, in over two thousand meters of water. It rose from the mud overnight."

"Anomaly?" I asked.

"A city." When she said that it stunned the whole group. "It is two kilometers across, and sonar indicates that there are approximately twenty structures, the tallest of which was over a hundred meters."

"Deep Ones, maybe?" the Pole asked.

"Far too advanced for such creatures. We do not know what inhabited it, but we were warned to be on the lookout, since it appeared that the inhabitants abandoned the city as soon as it rose from the mud. We do not know where they went. The beggar's navy, pardon me, North Korea lost a spy ship over the disturbance, and then the Chinese navy lost a submarine to an unknown force while investigating. They then destroyed the city to keep it from falling into the hands of the Americans."

"When did this happen?"

"Two weeks ago."

Her comments caused quite a bit of commotion. "Holy shit!" I exclaimed, and that was one of the most coherent comments of the bunch.

Earl's hunch had been right. There was a pattern emerging, and it was scary as hell.

I wasn't the only one with crazy news to report. The South Africans had confirmed to Priest that there had been reports of isolated villages being found totally emptied of people, cooking fires still burning, vehicles still running, all with signs of tunneling nearby. Lee had managed to get a similar story to that of the Korean woman out of one of the Chinese Hunters about the underwater city. National security was one thing, but most Hunters realized that there were some threats out there a lot bigger than any one country. The PLA interpreter was going to have a cow, but none of us gave a crap about their lost submarine, when we were more worried about what had destroyed it. Julie had gotten rumors of strange new activity in the Paris underground from the French, and Earl had heard that one of the Russian companies had lost an entire team to an unknown entity that had begun terrorizing a mine in Siberia.

Earl had ordered us to meet back in his room. A

cartoony world map had been bought from the hotel gift shop and affixed to the wall. Pushpins were stuck into various locations as more Hunters reported in. Over the last hour we'd gone through a fifty-pack of pushpins, and there were still more stories coming in.

"How could we have not heard?" Julie asked in amazement. "This is staggering."

"It isn't like we all hang out together, and you think our government-mandated secrecy is bad, we're nothing compared to some of these places." Earl read a message off of his phone, shook his head sadly, and stuck another pin into a comically distorted Mongolia. "More tunnels . . . Of course we've heard of some of these, but we always thought of them as random monster attacks, outbreaks, craziness . . . But this . . ." He stepped away, as if he was trying to see the whole picture.

The three of us studied the map. I couldn't put my finger on what was troubling me. "Rates have been up before. When I first got hired we were at an all-time high."

"Sure, but that was stateside, and mostly because of the private Hunting ban. It was individuals, monsters here and there, the natural growth of a predatory population that had lost the best thing that kept it in check. These, on the other hand . . ." Julie stroked her neck thoughtfully. "These are oddball events with bigger repercussions, and all over the last few years. MHI alone has faced two since then that if they'd gotten out—"

"Three," Earl corrected. "Copper Lake was another tip-of-the-iceberg-type event. If I hadn't shut that down quick, it could've turned a lot worse. Ours were all connected, though. Machado was being used by the Old Ones, then Hood was working for the same Old One, and his daughter was somehow involved in Copper Lake."

"But that was after we killed their god, Earl! That's hard for a religion to bounce back from."

"Christianity seemed to do all right," he said.

"That's because it didn't stick...So, three events related tangentially to the minions of a specific Old One, but he, it...whatever, is toast. So do we think something like him is pulling these strings? These new events, they're like ours, little things that could spiral out of control in no time."

"A few," I answered. "But there are so many where we don't know what happened. People missing, or some type of creature shows up and then disappears, and most of them with an underground connection."

"Like they've been sleeping for a long time and they're all starting to wake up. But why, and where are they going? So we've got a rash of two types of events, things waking up, and other things poking us with a stick. *Testing* us." Earl muttered, staring at the map. "These aren't outbreaks...This is a mobilization."

"Of what?"

"I don't know, but this is what Myers was seeing. And now I think I know why that son of a bitch was suffering from insomnia. Hell, makes you wonder what else he knew about and couldn't tell us."

"You should call Dwayne," Julie suggested.

"Got his number?" It was a testament to how troubling the situation seemed that Earl wasn't joking.

"So have we decided all these things are connected?" I asked, already knowing the answer, but hoping to be wrong. "We making this official?"

"I just don't know how... We'll need to talk to everyone, get as many Hunters on the lookout as possible," Earl ordered. "Shouldn't be a problem, though. From what I saw, word's already gotten out. Most of us are a suspicious bunch by nature. After the bunch with Z started swapping stories, all the sharp Hunters know something's up. I wouldn't be surprised if there are ten maps just like this one in this hotel by now."

"Thank goodness for this conference or we might not have put things together..." Julie trailed off.

"What?" Then I realized what she'd thought of. "The conference."

"Thought of that already," Earl said. "The timing seems a little suspicious to be holding the first annual one of these things. Almost like they wanted all these different bunches of Hunters to put their heads together."

"One hell of a coincidence. Did the MCB want us to figure this out on our own?" Then I shook my head and answered my own question. "That doesn't make any sense. They didn't put this on, but if they were trying to keep these trends secret, why allow the conference to take place at all? Why not just send us all an email and say, 'Attention, Hunters, be on the lookout for an invasion of mole people.'"

"Maybe it isn't the MCB pulling the strings..." Earl said.

"Who then?" Julie asked. "Ick-mip has private organizers, but there's no way they'd be allowed to do this without government approval."

"Nobody. Never mind." Earl looked around. Then picked up the notepad from the nightstand table and scribbled a brief note. *Not now. Room might be bugged.*

Julie and I glanced at the walls nervously.

Earl nodded, deadly serious.

What the hell had we gotten ourselves into?

The mood at ICMHP had changed drastically over the last few hours. Earlier it had been a sort of festive environment. Now half the crowd was somber, as they realized that they weren't alone and things were messed up all over the rest of the world too, and the other half was really excited, because they'd come to the same conclusion and were now figuring out how they could make money off the situation by blowing things up. Hunters are proactive like that.

I caught a couple of the panels that sounded interesting, where the topics were about the technical end of Hunting. It turned out that the German, Lindemann, was a former member of the elite German counterterrorism unit GSG-9, and a walking encyclopedia of how to kill dangerous fey. That panel alone was worth the price of admission. Sure, he had insulted me earlier, but at least I had been insulted by the best. Then I went to one of the boring policy ones, but my wife was on the panel so I had no choice. She spent most of it arguing with some idiot professor who was advocating fair trials for intelligent undead. After that was another one on PUFF filing and how to get timely payments from the Treasury, but I snuck out after fifteen minutes of listening to information that I already knew about.

The conversations in the halls were different than before. Stupid Hunters didn't live long, and we worked in a business that fostered a healthy sense of paranoia. The guests knew that something was up, and many of them had come to the same conclusions that we had. The conference was rigged. The timing was too suspicious. The official policy makers hadn't wanted the world's Hunters to know what was going on, but someone else with sufficient pull had arranged to put us all together where the subject would surely arise, but they weren't direct enough to simply come out and say it.

The keynote address was next. When I had read the description earlier, and it said that it was going to be the MCB director discussing policy, I hadn't expected there to be much turnout. But now with all of the fresh new conspiracy theories floating around, there was already a crowd formed outside the banquet-hall doors waiting for the keynote to begin. Unfortunately, some of the men loitering around the hall were PT douchebags, which meant that I needed to hang back in order to not violate the restraining order. But since I really wanted to hear what Stark was going to say, I'd just waited until the lights went down before sneaking in. The room was packed, so I didn't think anyone would notice me. John VanZant, who was also named on the restraining order, was standing in back too. Agent Franks was the last one in, and he just stood there, glowering.

A moment later Director Stark walked out to the podium to sporadic applause. A bunch of unfamiliar bureaucrats came in behind him and sat on folding chairs at the back of the stage. I found it amusing that Stark already had a *posse*. Myers had got by with just Franks . . . And then I realized how odd it was that the MCB's single most famous asset had been stuck out here in nowhere land and not in prestige seats. Was there a reason for that? I looked over at Franks, but his expression was as inscrutable as ever.

The first few minutes of the keynote were more prewritten nonsense. The only interesting bit was about how the United States government would be awarding several large new contracts for monster-related facility security. The accountant part of my brain filed that away, but the Hunter part really wanted to know about this strange underground invasion. Stark changed topics, but now it was more blather about synergy and mission statements. The audience was becoming tense. Now that they knew something was happening worldwide, the Hunters were eager for answers. They wanted meat, and they were being given fluff.

"Tell us what you know!" a man shouted from the center of the room. I couldn't make out who it was, but I was impressed a bunch like this had been patient this long. Stark pretended that he hadn't heard and kept reading. Then another Hunter to the side yelled something similar, then another Hunter in back raised a rude question, and the bureaucrats behind Stark began to shift nervously.

Stark reached up and adjusted his suddenly too-tight necktie. It must have been constricting his considerable bulldog jowls. "Easy, everyone. I don't know what you're carrying on about."

"Lies." That accusation caused some shifting and looking by the MCB in the audience to see who'd said it. Earl Harbinger saved them the trouble of searching, because he simply stood up so everyone could see him. "We know about the pattern. We know about the attacks. Don't waste our time."

Stark blanched when he saw who it was. I don't

know what their history was, but it was plain to see that Stark didn't like, and was a little frightened of, Earl Harbinger. What was it with Earl and collecting personal grudges with MCB Directors? "You need to quiet down or I'll have security remove you."

Security? Franks sighed dejectedly. *Sweet.* I would pay good money to watch Frankenstein and the Wolfman fight. That would be some Clash of the Titans level awesomeness right there. Earl sat back down, but I could tell that he wasn't done yet. Once Earl got to pushing he wasn't going to quit until he got what he wanted.

"Now where was I?" The vibrating of Stark's pocket was picked up over the microphone. He tried to ignore his phone and kept on reading from his increasingly pointless speech.

Agent Franks lifted one hand to his earpiece, scowling. His blunt features twisted into a dangerous scowl, then he walked quickly from the hall. The three government men sitting on the stand behind Stark all reached into their pockets at the same time. The lights of the phone's displays could be seen across the hall. The G-men exchanged glances, and then two of them stood up and quickly walked off stage. The other agents providing security all began speaking softly into their microphones. Phones began buzzing all across the auditorium, except for a few MCB men who had forgotten to put them on vibrate, and those began to ring. Every single MCB in sight had just gotten a call.

Something was going down.

A murmur rose from the audience. Agent Stark continued reading from his prepared remarks and let the call go to voice mail, but after a few seconds his pocket began buzzing again. He finally looked up from his paper, scanned the audience, saw all the display lights and realized there was a problem. "Better answer this. Probably the wife." He laughed nervously, covered the microphone with one hand, and turned away to take the call. Stark listened and didn't make a sound for probably thirty seconds. It was very awkward.

When he turned back around, his eyes were very wide. "Well, uh...Let's see...Important business. You'll have to excuse me for a moment." He took a few halting steps, realized he should probably say something else and came back to the microphone. "I'll be right back. There is nothing to be concerned about. Please remain seated." And then the Director of the MCB fled the podium.

The audience murmur evolved into the suspicious muttering of several hundred Hunters. The final government man on the stage looked around, realized he was all alone, then got up and hurried after his boss. A minute passed, but no one came out to fill the void. It was the middle of the keynote address and the spotlight was completely empty. Now we knew something really interesting had happened.

"Bring out the dancing girls!" one of the Australians shouted. There was general nervous laughter.

My phone vibrated. I pulled it out, expecting a text from one of my teammates. Hopefully someone had been able to overhear one of the MCB and had an idea what was going on. But the number was listed as Unknown.

Would you like to know what is going on? Meet in room 212. You have 5 minutes.

That seemed odd, but it wasn't until I looked up that I realized the really weird part. There were about fifty other Hunters scattered across the room reading their phones too. I recognized most of them as team leaders or managers from the various companies. Van-Zant, who was standing only a few feet away, showed me his phone.

We had all received the same message.

CHAPTER 5

"You think this is a trap?" VanZant asked as we got on the escalator. He glanced back at the crowd behind us. "We're about to put the world's most experienced Hunters in one room."

"That's whatever room *I'm* in, John," Earl Harbinger retorted.

"I'm just saying it's a tempting target."

"If it's a trap it's got to be one of the most convoluted things I've ever heard of. You think we're gonna open the door and get pounced on by shoggoths?"

"Shoggoths don't really *pounce*," I said. "It's more of a squishy lumbering motion."

Earl had briefed VanZant and the other team leaders about the pattern we'd discovered earlier. "If this is an invasion, now would be a really convenient time to eliminate a shitload of the opposition's brainpower in one move."

Earl stroked his chin thoughtfully. "If that was the case, it'd be smarter to blow the whole hotel up. Get us all." He looked down the escalator. Since we'd been toward the back we'd gotten out first. Just from our company I could see Julie, Cody, Paxton, Eddings, and Priest. That was a big chunk of MHI's leadership. In addition, I recognized many familiar faces from today's schmoozing, including owners and commanders from most of the different companies. Everybody wanted a piece of this puzzle. Say what you will about Hunters, we were a curious bunch. "You've got a point."

"I was a soldier, Earl. I still try to think like one. If we'd caught this many Taliban honchos in one place I'd have dropped a mortar round on it faster than you could blink. Assuming I could actually get permission, of course."

"Fair enough. Split off at the top. Stop every other one of our people. Hang back just in case."

"Roger that," VanZant nodded. "We're the cavalry."

Earl leaned in and lowered his voice. "Especially stop Julie. Tell her it's my orders."

"Why?" I asked. "She's not going to like getting left out."

"Julie stays outside. If it is a trap, I'm almost indestructible and you're replaceable. If MHI lost her we'd be out of business in no time. She's the only one of us that can negotiate a contract worth a damn."

Sure, a chivalrous husband would've stuck up for his wife, but life's too short to pick a fight with Earl Harbinger.

"Julie only gets the best contracts because she's cute," VanZant said as we reached the top. "The rest of us are a homely bunch." He stepped off to the side and had disappeared into the casino's crowds within seconds. It is easy to be inconspicuous when you're short.

Room 212 had been one of the panel rooms earlier. The long table in front had been removed and someone had rolled in a television. The chairs were still in neat rows, with a single sheet of paper neatly folded in the center of each one. I picked one up. The photocopy only had a few lines on it. "The number ten million, a phone number and . . ." *A bunch of numbers and letters.*

"Coordinates," Earl looked over my shoulder. "To the northeast of here."

He was really good. "That's what I thought," I lied.

It wasn't that big of a room, and our competitor's leadership filled it quickly. Many of them appeared nervous. A few of the younger ones were trying to play it cool as they patted theirs sides to make sure their guns were still there. Most seemed curious. The older and more experienced Hunters looked annoyed, having gotten tired of playing games a long time ago. The big Pole from White Eagle squished in next to me. He was wearing way too much cologne. Many Hunters remained standing, and a few of our guys stood right next to the door.

The TV came on by itself, displaying a close-up of a deathly pale, very thin, totally bald man wearing persimmon-colored sunglasses and a white dress shirt that was nearly the same color as his skin. "Good evening, Monster Hunters. Welcome to Ick-mip." Earl tensed so violently that my chair shook. I looked over to see that my boss's teeth were clenched, his lips pulled back in snarl of hatred. "I am Mr. Stricken," the TV said.

"You albino motherfucker," Earl growled.

Stricken smiled. "Pleasure to see you too, Mr. Harbinger."

That confirmed a few things. Stricken was on a live feed, we were on camera, and they knew each other. The sunglasses swiveled to the side as Stricken studied something. "Before I continue, please shut off all your electronics and recording devices...Yes... Third row...Ms. Kim. Shut it off temporarily or I shut you off permanently. If I see so much as an electrical blip in that room it'll put me in a really foul mood. And please close the door." Stricken appeared to be watching another screen. "Were you born in a barn? Shut it or this meeting is adjourned."

I turned to look. Cody was closest. Our New Mexico team lead hesitated. He was an old friend of my father, the man that had saved my brother's fingers, and one of our wiser, more experienced, and cautious men.

"This isn't a trick. If I wanted you dead, I would've poisoned your breakfast..." Stricken said as he looked to the other side and read something. "Which was a jalapeño omelet at Denny's at six forty-five this morning. Well, you're an early riser, Mr. Cody. Now close the door. I will not tell you again."

"Do it," Earl ordered. Cody pulled the doors closed.

"Thank you." Stricken launched right into his message. "At twelve hundred hours today there was a monster-related event in a small town in northeastern Nevada. Due to the isolated nature of the location, law enforcement officials didn't discover the aftermath until a few hours ago. The scene has been contained, but the MCB was only recently made aware and has gone on full alert."

So that was what had interrupted Stark's speech.

"How bad?" a man that looked suspiciously like Buddy Holly asked.

"Ten confirmed dead, fifteen missing, Mister..." Stricken's head shifted to the other side as he studied a different monitor. "Wylder, Team TALON...Heh... That's a clever acronym. Allow me to clarify, Mr. Wylder. It was a more of a truck stop with some trailers around it than an actual town, but it's gone now. Those not ripped limb from limb vanished without a trace. We're not sure exactly how many, because the containment team is still finding pieces and trying to figure out which pieces go in which body bag. Do not interrupt me again."

A young man sitting a few rows ahead of me stood up. "Who are you?"

Stricken waited a moment for the information to load. "Pierre Darne...I knew your father. You take directions as well as he does, as in not at all. What part of 'don't interrupt me' did you fail to grasp? I know there's a language barrier here, and English is your third language, but I'm about to offer you a very lucrative business proposal, so you can either sit your ass down or get the hell out of my meeting and wait for the official MCB press release."

Darne reluctantly returned to his chair.

"I represent a special, multiagency task force within the United States government."

Earl snorted.

"We would like this particular issue dealt with as quickly and quietly as possible. The provisional PUFF bounty for this particular one-of-a-kind entity is listed as the first line on the sheet left on your chair." I looked down at the $10,000,000.00 and gave a low whistle. "For our foreign friends in the audience, those are American dollars, which must come as a letdown to those of you still collecting bounties in pounds, but at least they're not pesos. If you go to the PUFF website you'll see that this new bounty was posted in the last fifteen minutes with all of the applicable information to be filled in later."

The big Pole leaned across me to ask Earl, "Is he telling truth?"

"He's from the government, all right," Earl said, which didn't really answer the question.

"Some of you may be wondering if this is legitimate. Understandable. When this meeting is over I'd like everyone present to check their *personal* bank account. A good faith payment of ten thousand dollars has been placed into each to compensate you for your time. Think of it like a gift basket, only without the mixed nuts. But more importantly, you will be able to confirm that the money was wired there by the United States Treasury's Perpetual Unearthly Forces Fund. That should confirm I am who I say I am."

He hadn't really said *who* he was at all, but if this Stricken could get the PUFF to move that quick, the dude had some pull. Getting them to process something as simple as a zombie kill required processing reams of paperwork.

"More importantly, my task force has oversight over the requests for proposals on several new, very lucrative US government contracts. You heard the new MCB director. I'm talking about several worldwide markets, too. Whichever company manages to complete this particular assignment will...let's be honest, *win* many of these contracts."

That caused a stir. Big government Monster contracts were always worth a fortune, with a company being paid merely to be on call in case something happened at a certain facility, which rarely did. For example, MHI had a contract with the Department of Energy for a few of their sites, including one contract at Los Alamos that dated back to the forties, interrupted only while we'd been shut down. To any Hunting company, contracts like that were like an endless cash dispenser, and when they did come up, the competition was fierce.

Being the accountant that I am, I turned to Earl excitedly. We were talking about astronomical sums of money, but the look in his eye told me that none of that sounded in the least bit appealing to him.

"What is the monster?" the German, Lindemann, asked. Stricken looked to his monitor. "I will save you the time, Mr. Stricken. Klaus Lindemann, Grimm Berlin. We get the point. You are well informed. I too, enjoy being informed. So please, do tell us what is the nature of this creature?"

Stricken smiled, and there was something inherently *wrong* about that expression, like the muscles of his gaunt face weren't used to making friendly shapes. "Your reputation precedes you, Mr. Lindemann. The threat is of an unknown type and number. There are no witnesses. The only intelligence we have is where it last struck, the coordinates of which are on your sheet."

The German spoke for all of us. "It would seem that if the type is unknown, then this bounty seems suspiciously excessive. Normally, such a payment is reserved for the most lethal of beings."

Stricken's smile vanished as quickly as it had appeared. "Like I said, your reputation precedes you. So full of annoying questions... Participate or not. Your decision. The rules of the contest are as follows. Whoever kills this thing first collects the money, wins a bunch of contracts, and gets to brag that they're the best. I want it dead and I want it dead now. I do not give a shit how you do it as long as it gets done fast. The rest of you can cry about it to each other in the hotel bar later. When it's dead, call the provided phone number and everything will be arranged."

"This is not fair," shouted one of the Europeans. "We were not allowed to bring most of our equipment into the country!"

This time Stricken didn't even bother to look up the man's name. He pointed at himself. "Does this look like the face of a man who gives a flying fuck about the concept of *fair*? Improvise, asshole. The world's biggest arms expo is being held down the street. You'll think of something. What the hell are you waiting for? The clock is ticking."

The Hunters looked at each other, confused.

"What's wrong with you? It's a race. Act like it!" Stricken shouted. "Go!"

Uneasy, several Hunters rose. The early standers sized each other up, wheels turning, because no matter who you were, ten million dollars was a lot of money, and to some of these smaller companies, a single decent contract could guarantee their future, and so the rush began. Several of the Hunters went for the exit at the same time in a big ungainly clump.

"Monster Hunter International, stand down," Earl said with the utmost calm, knowing that every one of his people would comply instantly. "We ain't going nowhere."

However, most of the room ran for it. Cody had to get out of the doorway to keep from being trampled, as men from five different companies tried to push the doors open at the same time. The burly Pole didn't want to try to squeeze past me, so he kicked his chair over and went out that way. Some of the smarter commanders simply pulled out their phones and alerted their subordinates, rather than trying to fight the mob. I spotted Armstrong shoving his way out, but he was too busy thinking about how to spend that much PUFF money to notice me violating his restraining order. The violent, struggling clot of Hunters finally broke loose, and they spilled out into the hall as Stricken's image continued to watch the monitors with approval. There was something about his smile that was simply unnerving.

Lindemann stopped next to Earl. Unlike many there, he didn't seem ruffled in the slightest. "This man Stricken, you are certain he is with your government?"

"He ain't from the nice part," Earl said.

"I was not aware that there was a nice part," Lindemann chuckled. "If you would excuse me then, gentlemen." He calmly walked down the now clear aisle.

"I believe that man intends to win," I said.

"My money is on him," Earl answered. "But you never know. Maybe one of the new ones will surprise us."

"It's a shame to have outsiders handling work on our turf...Oh man, they're foreigners doing the jobs Americans don't want to do. That's *so* tacky."

"Trust me on this one. We don't want any part of Unicorn business."

"Wait...So that's *Unicorn?*"

"Special Task Force Unicorn."

"They like MCB?"

"Not in the slightest, but not in any of the good ways. MCB is to hide monsters from people. STFU is to *use* monsters against people. I'm surprised to see the rat come out of the walls."

Stricken was still watching his monitor, waiting, as the last of the experienced Hunters left and all that remained was MHI. "Harbinger, I'm surprised. You don't strike me as a man that likes losing."

"I especially don't like to lose people," Earl said, sounding strained.

"Me either, which is why I want this mission wrapped up rikki-tic. Who else do you have there? I can see you left half your leaders outside just in case. Clever . . ." Stricken's glasses moved to the other side and he read. "Pitt, Owen Z. . . . Now you're an interesting case."

I didn't know anything about this man, but I knew I didn't want him paying any attention to me. "Not particularly."

"Keep telling yourself that, kid. I've got some blank spots in my file about you. I really don't like having blank spots. Incomplete reports keep me up at night." I was so glad Myers had shredded his paperwork about me after the Arbmunep.

"One of your pets go off the reservation again?" Earl challenged.

Stricken chuckled. "No, this isn't one of mine. My current roster is very well behaved, plays well with others, follows orders, regular upstanding citizens deserving of future PUFF exemptions. I couldn't ask for a better strike force of supernatural killers. Oh, why the sad face? Come on, Earl, still bitter? She's almost halfway done, just over one year left, then time's served, she's free to go."

Earl was leaning forward, holding onto the back of the folding chair in front of him. The metal beneath his hands creaked and bent as his knuckles turned white. "I've already cleaned up one of your mistakes. The suckers can handle this one. You wouldn't be coming to us unless you want somebody else to bleed on your behalf."

"You've got me all wrong." Stricken clucked disapprovingly and shook his head with theatrical sadness. "As one professional to another, I'll level with you. This isn't one of mine, but it was one of the task force's teams that responded to investigate. Intel said this should've been a cakewalk, turned out it wasn't. That team has gone missing."

"Surprised you care."

"There're always more things looking for a PUFF exemption to replace them." He shrugged. "But I do hate losing valuable assets, especially pretty redheads."

The metal in Earl's hands snapped in two.

"See you around, Earl. Enjoy your conference." Stricken reached toward the camera. The screen went black.

"No!" Earl stood, flinging one hand outward and sending four chairs clattering across the room. "Son of a bitch!"

A picture appeared on the TV screen. Three figures were walking down the lowered back ramp of a gray C-130 cargo plane. Behind them was a high desert scene, brown sagebrush dusted with dirty snow. They were dressed in multicam and combat gear, carrying rifles. There were two men in front and an attractive woman in back. Her red hair was rather striking in a shot so filled with bland, dusty colors.

"Heather..." Earl whispered. He walked forward, as if in a daze, staring at the TV screen. After a few seconds, the picture disappeared and the TV changed to silent static. "Damn it!" Earl smashed his fist into the TV and knocked it flying from its stand to explode into pieces against the far wall. Earl stood there, back to us, shoulders hunched, fists clenched.

"Earl?" Cody asked. "You okay?"

"Team leads, collect your men. We're going hunting," he snapped. "Move out."

The team leads obeyed and immediately hurried from the room. I stuck around. The team leads had all been briefed on his condition, but they hadn't seen it up close like I had. Earl was breathing hard, head down, staring at the broken TV. I'd seen him change before. I recognized the signs. I could feel the energy in the air. Stricken had enraged him so suddenly that it had provoked the beast within...

I reached to the compact STI .45 that was concealed in a tuckable holster on my belt. We both knew the drill. Earl was squared away, more so than any other werewolf, but letting a werewolf change inside a place crowded with innocents was simply unthinkable. I didn't want to shoot my friend, didn't think I'd need to, but those were his orders, and I wasn't going to take any chances. *Come on, Earl.* "You okay?" I asked after a few seconds.

He turned around. His respiration had slowed. His eyes were the normal blue rather than the dangerous gold. Earl turned, in control again, dragged a shard of glass out from between his knuckles, and tossed it on the carpet. "Will be, as soon as I snap Stricken's neck. Let's get to the airport."

CHAPTER 6

Our Mi-24 Hind screamed over the Nevada desert, the ground a dark brown blur beneath us. The pilot's area was separated from the passenger compartment, so I had no way of looking at Skippy's instrumentation to guess just how stupidly fast we were flying, but I could tell you this: we were going *really* fast. All orcs were supernaturally good at something. Skippy's particular gift was breaking the laws of physics with a helicopter.

Those of us on Harbinger's team had spent a lot of hours in the Hind, but none of us had ever been aboard with Skippy pushing it like this before. Earl had told Skippy that there was a race, and it was very important that we win this particular race, so Skippy had cranked the stereo to eleven, put on some heavy metal, and kicked our chopper in the butt, dedicated to not bring dishonor to MHI.

"Is it supposed to rattle like that?" Trip asked through clenched teeth.

"Washing machines don't rattle this much. What do you think?"

Milo was sitting across from me and must have caught the look of distress on my face. "Impressive, huh? There's no way this baby is supposed to go like this. Maximum speed is only around two hundred. We're beating that by a good bit. Not too shabby, considering she's older than some of you guys." Milo patted the bulkhead tenderly. "And to think, it wasn't that long ago that she was in two pieces!"

Skippy had put a lot of hours into fixing up his beloved steed after the Arbmunep had knocked it out of the sky. He'd tested it around Cazador and assured us that everything was fine, or as he put it, the engine spirits were pleased. Though we'd all been nervous riding in it, the helicopter had seemed to run okay on our most recent case, but we hadn't been racing with it, either.

"Not helping, Milo. Not helping at all." Holly's voice didn't sound happy over the headset. Since the gunner's seat was rather cramped, she was the thinnest one here, and had expressed interest in learning how to fly, Holly was riding forward. She had the best view, but I imagined that it was a lot like having the front seat of a roller coaster.

"Are you kidding? When an orc fixes something, it stays fixed. They're like wizards with duct tape. Magical duct tape wizards, right, Ed?" Milo reached over and thumped Edward on the shoulder. The orc tilted his goggled head, apparently confused by the red-bearded human touching him. After a moment, Ed went back to looking at the window and listening to the talk radio streaming on his earphones. "Well, Ed is more of a duct tape samurai, but you get the idea."

All of our rivals were racing for the same place,

but as far as I knew, we were the only Hunters with a helicopter. It was still almost three hundred miles to the site, and our pace wasn't exactly set for fuel efficiency, so we needed to stop and refuel once along the way. MHI owned a decent-sized airplane, but it was parked uselessly in Alabama. We were also the only company with Hunters stationed in Salt Lake City, which was the closest metro area, but unfortunately all of them had been attending ICMHP too.

Earl Harbinger had decided to cover all the bases, so he had paid a ridiculous sum to hire a Gulfstream on short notice. It is amazing how fast you can get flight plans altered when you carry a suitcase full of money everywhere you go. Interestingly enough, another prop plane had taken off on an emergency flight a few minutes before we'd gotten to the airport, hired by someone they had described as a business-like German man.

The group on the Gulfstream would beat us there by a good margin, but we wouldn't be too far behind. We had no idea how hard the creature was going to be to track, so the air cover could potentially come in handy. Behind us was a convoy of vehicles, MHI-owned for some, and rentals for our Hunters that had flown in. Obviously, most of us at the conference were travelling light, but Eddings, the Las Vegas team lead, had one hell of a well-stocked armory in their office that was hidden in the basement of a pizza place.

Nearly thirty members of MHI and an unknown number of our rivals were on their way to northeastern Nevada. "This many Hunters will be overkill." I tried to lighten the mood. "It's probably just a troll angry that he lost his internet connection."

Holly wasn't buying it. "That kind of PUFF money, Z, it's more likely Godzilla."

"Or Dracula riding Godzilla," Trip said.

Since we had a race to win, Skippy had requested that we travel light. Milo had been bummed when he hadn't been able to take his heavy *free samples* from the show, but Skippy had said they could load them up for the ride home. Milo was simply too excited to play with them to wait for UPS to ship them back to Alabama. So we had two orcs, four humans, and a small load-out of weapons and ammo, with me being the biggest piece of cargo. It was hard to tell when Skippy was unhappy, what with the mask and all, but he had grumbled something about me being "big, like ox make us slow," but how that evened out because "blood of great war chief bring good luck." That was the sort of thing that replaced complex aviation calculations when you were an orc. Because I was related to a rock star, it meant we could go faster.

Thinking about my brother gave me a twinge of guilt, and I promised myself again that I'd go visit him before the conference was over. With the blow his career had taken, he was reduced to working in Vegas, playing shows that would've been far below him a couple of years ago. The whole thing was my fault, and Mosh had been avoiding my calls. I was worried about him.

There was a sudden bang. I grabbed onto the overhead straps as the chopper lurched.

"What was that?" Holly asked, alarmed.

"No problem. No problem," Skippy's gravelly voice came over the intercom. "Tail rotor break." He pronounced it *row-tor*.

"Break? What do you mean *break?*"

"No...is good break. Skip mean...break *in*."

"That sounds bad, Skippy!"

"No...The spirits that live in tail rotor...happy together now."

"You said the spirits were happy before we flew last time!" Trip exclaimed.

"No. Engine spirits happy. Tail rotor spirits...not so much. Very angry tail rotor."

"Last time I checked, you need a functioning tail rotor to fly a helicopter."

"No. Not to fly. Only not to spin around. Like circle...Until hit ground. Explode!" Skippy made the horrible wheezing noise that passed for orc laughter. "But rotor happy now! Yay!"

"We're so gonna die," I muttered.

"No. No," Skippy insisted. "Gretchen sacrifice chicken for us. Skip knew. Rotor spirits come 'round."

Flying with Skippy had been a lot easier back before he was willing to talk to me so much. Now that we were part of the family and he'd opened up about his piloting and maintenance methods, it was frankly unnerving. But the rattling did seem to taper off a bit. Trip began to breathe again. Edward lifted one hand, extended his pointer and pinky fingers and threw the horns, then went back to his talk radio. Milo grinned. "See? Told you so! Orcs are great at fixing things...And I'll admit, I did help a little." He sounded rather proud of himself. "I sort of had to. Orcs think welding is black magic."

And to think, Julie had been upset that Earl had wanted her on the jet, a new vehicle which was serviced by actual mechanics, not a thirty-year-old Soviet flying

tank that had been out of service for the last year due to
a terrible crash, kept together by a mystical orc, whose
wife, the medicine woman, had shaken some chicken
bones over it to pronounce it fixed. My *poor* wife.

Since Julie was our best shot with a rifle, she usually rode in the chopper anytime there might be a
need for air cover. It was kind of odd that Earl had
ordered her to go with him, but he'd seemed rather
overprotective of her lately. Now that Earl had finally
relented and told us the rest of the story about what
had happened in Copper Lake, I thought I could
understand why. He had filled in the rest of the
details during the ride to the airport. Earl had been
afraid to let anyone else know about Special Task
Force Unicorn, but with Stricken showing himself to
so many Hunters, the cat was out of the bag.

Why that cat had decided to let itself out was
another question...

At least we knew why Earl had been extra sullen
since he'd gotten back, with his girlfriend being drafted
into a covert group of government-sponsored monsters
doing who knew what. Earl wasn't even able to contact
her. He had to go to sleep each night without knowing if she was alive or dead. I'd be pissed off too.
And now with Heather Kerkonen in danger, assuming
Stricken was telling the truth, Earl had launched us
on this mission for personal reasons. I was more than
glad to go into harm's way to help a friend, but ten
million bucks was a very nice added incentive.

Once the Hind's shaking had subsided enough that
we could actually read without our eyeballs jittering
out of our heads, Milo pulled a map out from his
armor and held it between me and Trip. He pointed

to where we were heading. "This is the spot of the last attack." He moved his gloved finger. "This is the closest airfield to the target. They're a couple hundred miles an hour faster than we are, but they'll still need to procure ground transport. Ticked as Earl seemed, I figure that won't take too long . . . He's liable to hijack somebody. They should be on site at least half an hour before us."

"Cops and MCB are already there, so whatever it is has already moved," Trip pointed out.

"I know, and I'm going to be really upset if I'm missing SHOT Show and this thing has just up and flew away, or ate a big lunch and now it's going back to sleep for another hundred years, so we waste our time screwing around in the desert while it hibernates and dreams happy monster dreams. That happens *all* the time . . . I don't get to test drive killer robots very often."

All Hunters hate going into a situation without good intel. There was no doubt Stricken knew more than he told us, and whatever he wasn't saying was certainly bad news. "If this thing is on the move, and if it really is ten million dollars worth of nasty, then someone else is bound to run into it."

Holly couldn't see the map, but she could listen to our conversation. "I've been flipping through the radio and the police bands. If I hear anything I'll let you know."

"We might get lucky. All the Hunters in airplanes will get there fast to the wrong place, and everybody else in a car will be too slow, but if the creature makes a move in that window, we'll be in the right position to catch it. They're too fast or too slow, we're just right."

"We can be Team Goldilocks!" Milo exclaimed.

"I like it," Holly said. "*Goldilocks*. It has gravitas."

I ignored them. "If it shows up somewhere else, we'll be the first to swoop in on it."

"Us and the MCB," Milo said. "A bunch of them bailed out of the conference too. Just because Stricken sent all the Hunters doesn't mean that MCB answers to him."

"Maybe they do." Since Myers was gone and Agent Franks wasn't being shown much love, I had my suspicions about who was actually calling the shots. "MCB will be too busy keeping snoopers out of the area and lying to the press." I didn't know if my guess about their internal politics was right or not, but I really didn't want to get in Franks' path if I could help it. "If only we had a clue what it was, we might be able to figure where it was heading, how fast, or if it'll just hunker down. Anything interesting on the map?"

"Nothing major in the area... Pretty desolate. Some little towns here and there. Not very much farming, some mines. It snowed a few days ago, and the desert gets really cold, so there probably won't be campers to pick off. It would be nice if it was cold-blooded and sleepy... You go out further, Wendover is north. Lots of nothing to the west. I hope it doesn't go east."

"Why?"

"Dugway Proving Grounds, where the Army stores all of its nastiest chemical and biological weapons. North of that is the test range where the Air Force does bombing practice. The whole thing is bigger than some states. I'm guessing a Russian attack helicopter flying over will raise some eyebrows. I don't think Skippy wants to get shot down."

"Skip no like crash again. Just fixed Hind. Crash bad."

"Regardless of where it's going, I'm worried about what happens when we find it," Trip said. "That gigantic dollar figure making you guys nervous? That's more than master vamp money. What the heck is this thing?"

"Beats me, but I do like the idea of sleeping on a gigantic pile of money," Holly answered.

"You totally should try it. It's awesome. I sleep like a baby." I could get away with saying crap like that in this crowd. Even by MHI standards, I had been the primary on some very impressive bounties, but my closest friends knew that I'd donated most of my Lord Machado money to the families of the Hunters that had died at DeSoya Caverns. Not that I was hurting financially. I'd married a Shackleford.

We stopped at the small airfield along the way and paid way too much for avgas. The only employee had been excited to see us. Our brutal chopper was a lot neater than his usual Cessnas and crop dusters. Even with the red-and-white pseudo-civilian paint job, the Mi-24 still looked dangerous, and therefore interesting. Busy day too, he told us, since a plane full of Germans had landed, topped off, and departed only ten minutes before we'd arrived.

That didn't make any sense. Why would Lindemann stop early to top off the tanks? The kid said that they were flying in a PAC P-750, which Holly said should have given them plenty of extra range to get to the site. Now Earl would beat Lindemann there for sure.

Unless Lindemann had an idea of where the monster was heading...

I mentioned that once we got back into the air. My

personal theory was that maybe Stricken had given the Germans intelligence he hadn't shared with the rest of us. He'd told Earl about Unicorn's missing team and no one else. Stricken had called this a contest, but as he'd admitted himself, he wasn't the type of man that cared about concepts like *fairness*.

"Maybe Lindemann has a psychic on his team," was Trip's guess.

"That's stupid."

"Says the psychic."

I rolled my eyes. "I'm *not* psychic."

"Can you read minds?"

"Come on, Trip, we've been over this a hundred times. Only in very specific circumstances, after being exposed to a specific artifact of the Old Ones, and the effects don't seem to last for very long. I haven't read someone's mind in like forever. And it isn't mind reading, it's just particular memories."

"Psychic."

This was an argument I was never going to win. Trip still believed it was a gift from God. Yeah, I suppose it sort of was a gift from a god, just not *ours*.

"Maybe he's got someone that can do magic," Milo supplied.

"Possible, but also stupid."

"Obviously, because that would be *so* unlikely, as we're riding in a helicopter with orcs," Holly said. "Hell, Earl's even got a magic-using elf girl with him—"

The helicopter jerked harder this time, slamming all of us back into our seats. Only this time it wasn't a mechanical effect, but rather because Skippy had freaked out on the controls. "Elf! *Elf?* Harb Anger has filthy *elf?*"

"Bad move, Team Goldilocks," I shouted at Holly.

"Crud. Sorry, Skippy." Holly had forgotten about the animosity between elves and orcs. They'd been at war since the dawn of time, with both sides blaming the other for all manner of atrocities. Earl deciding to hire one of the trailer park elves was a subject that he'd been planning on broaching to Skippy's people gradually.

"*Elfs?*"

"Oh crap." Milo grabbed his headset. "Listen, Skippy, it isn't like that."

"Tribe not . . . not *good* enough? Urks brave for Harb Anger? Elfs are evil—filth—*grugnulish!*"

I had picked up a handful of orcish, but I didn't know that word, though it was obviously not meant as a compliment.

"Wretched pack of pig dogs . . ." Milo clarified the Orcish profanity. "I wouldn't say a *pack*. We just got the one. Easy, Skippy. Inferior elf magic can be useful for lesser things that we would *never* bother a noble orc for. It was Earl's call. He was planning on telling you."

"Harb Anger . . . wise chief." Skippy made a grumbling noise, but he wouldn't be so easily placated. "Keep elf *grugnulish* . . . away. Elf no corrupt tribe!" Skippy continued to mumble for a bit, then he changed the CD to rage-infused Scandinavian death metal and somehow made the stereo go even louder so he wouldn't have to listen to us. We'd hurt his feelings.

"Way to go, Holly," Trip said. "We weren't supposed to mention Tanya."

At that, Edward, who hadn't shown the least bit of reaction to his older brother's fit, leaned forward and removed his ear buds, head turned quizzically to the side, apparently interested for the first time.

"It's cool, Ed. Same one you met before in Indiana," Milo said soothingly. After Earl had been conned into hiring the elf girl for a temp job, it had been Edward who had gone into the pocket dimension with her. It had been a rescue mission, us trying to get to a couple of lost children, but no humans could get past the telepathic assault of the creatures inside. The elf girl's stupid bravery had been enough to convince Earl to grant her wish and let her have a shot at becoming a Hunter. Ed had seemed happy because he'd gotten to dismember some giant fey monsters. Mission accomplished by the magically immune elf and orc, and MHI had gotten paid, so it had been a good day all around. "No need for...slashy slashy," Milo pointed at the two sheathed swords balanced between Ed's knees. "You two seemed to get along okay."

Edward seemed to ponder that for a minute. The only thing visible beneath the baggy black balaclava were two unblinking yellow eyes. As usual, Edward was a complete cipher. Then he simply put his earbuds back in and returned his attention to the window. Ed always seemed to be in his own little world right up until the time to get his slice and dice on.

With Skippy still occasionally muttering orc profanity into our headsets, we passed the time by running through possible scenarios and coming up with plans and backup plans. Normally this would be the part where I'd nervously triple-check my gear, but there wasn't enough room to safely maneuver guns inside the crew compartment, and besides, Skippy, who frowned on the idea of someone negligently putting a round through his precious chopper, was already in a bad mood.

"That was Julie on the radio. The jet has landed." Holly said. "One of our Utah guys arranged for a truck to pick them up. Earl's group will be on their way to the attack site in a few minutes."

My watch said we were still at least half an hour out. "What's the ETA for—"

Holly cut me off. "Hang on. Got something . . . Highway patrol is going nuts . . . Shots fired. Officer down . . ."

We all perked up. *Could this be it?*

"He's injured, says he can't tell what it was, but it's huge . . . Some sort of animal . . . Bug . . . Something. He's panicked."

Trip got excited. "Bet that's our monster!"

"Drewbeck Road in . . . Where's Lutz?"

Milo got the map out in a jiffy. "South of the attack site, not too far west of where we are now."

"Skippy, hang a left!"

Holly wasn't much of a navigator, but Skippy got the idea, and I had to grab onto the straps again as Skippy banked us hard to the side. Sideways turned to down and all of the unsecured gear cases slid across the floor. "Easy there, Airwolf!" It would be nice for Skippy to say *hang on* or something before doing something crazy.

Milo began reading off numbers and Skippy corrected course. The light in the crew compartment changed as we flew toward the rapidly setting sun. "Be there . . . ten minutes." The Hind began to rattle harder again as we shed altitude and gained speed. "See stupid elfs do that."

"Cop's radio went quiet," Holly warned. "I'll alert Julie."

There's a certain feeling that comes with the beginning of a new hunt. Excitement, tension, nervous energy, and yeah, even fear... It's kind of addictive. I could feel it and I could see it on the faces of my companions. Except for Ed, who didn't seem to care one way or the other. "Let's blast this thing fast and save them the ride."

"Think we should use the door gun?" Milo asked.

We still had a few minutes of daylight left, and after that we could always switch to night vision. "You ask that like there was any possible way I'd say no."

Milo gave me a thumbs up, and went to unzipping the case that held the FN 240 machine gun. Trip opened an ammo can and lifted out one end of a belt of silver 7.62. We'd wait until we slowed down before opening the door to place it on its mount. It was cold outside, and I could only imagine what a two-hundred-mile-an-hour wind chill would be like. Between Milo's belt-fed and one of Julie's custom M-14s she'd left aboard if we needed a precise shot, we could rain down some hurt from the sky.

"Airplane above. Go same place as us," Skippy said. "But go faster." He sounded offended by that.

"Skip's right." Holly said. "Somebody just blew right past us."

"Can you tell who it is?"

"No idea."

"More Hunters?" I looked to Trip and Milo, but neither one of them had a clue either. "They must have heard the same distress call. Maybe they're going to land in a field or something."

"It's a really rocky area," Milo said. "Is it like a bush plane?"

"No, Milo. It's a big, twin engine prop plane," Holly said. "And they're leaving us in the dust."

"Propel-or," grumbled Skippy. "Faster than Hind . . . but *boring.*"

"They're way ahead now, hard to see them with the sun. Skippy, I'm borrowing these binoculars."

That was the same type of plane the German team had rented. "Lindemann." I know that we weren't in this for Stricken's stupid race, but I couldn't help feeling angry. I'm competitive like that. Money is money, and this was MHI's territory. "They're probably going to land on the road."

"Ooh, he's good." Milo whistled. "I wonder how much he had to bribe the rent-a-pilot to try that."

Holly came back over the intercom. "Okay, I can see a sign for a garage ahead. Couple structures. No other buildings for half a mile. There's the flashing lights from the police car right in front. I don't see anything else around. There's lots of big rocks and the road is curvy. I'm not seeing any long flat spots."

"It'll take the Germans a pass or two to find a place to land. We can still get in there before they do."

"On the bright side, if they do pull it off, maybe they'll be able to help that highway patrolman in time," Trip said.

Leave it to Trip to be the voice of compassion. I'd been so distracted at being beaten by our rivals on our own turf that I hadn't even thought of that unfortunate man. The sad truth of this business was that more often than not we got there to clean up after the monsters had done their thing, and actually rescuing people was rare. "True. But I still want to beat these assholes on principle."

"Uh...guys?" Holly sounded surprised. "The Germans have gotten out."

"*What?*"

"They've jumped. When I looked up I saw somebody fall out the door."

"Parachutes? That crafty bastard." Well, now I could see why Lindemann had been getting so much admiration from the international Hunters at the conference. Lindemann hadn't just rented a plane, he'd rented one used by skydivers. They probably even had all of the equipment right there ready to go at the airport. That's also why they'd stopped early to gas up. Simply get to the general area and wait for the target to show. "Why didn't we think of that?"

"None of us know how to jump out of airplanes?" Milo asked rhetorically.

Boone and Gregorius both had Special Forces backgrounds, so had Cody, but he was too old for that kind of thing now. So they'd all been jump qualified at one point, but they were all either with Earl or in the convoy coming up from Vegas. The only other member of MHI I could think of that would've been ready to do that was Sam Haven, who had been a SEAL, but he was dead. As far as I knew, none of the rest of us were prepared to get out of a perfectly good aircraft while it was still in the sky. "Valid point."

"I can't see...Whoa...He's going to hit! Wait. There's a chute. Holy shit. It opened right before the ground. There's another one. They're landing right on top of the place."

"Okay," said Trip. "That's pretty tough."

"The ladies love Klaus," Milo added. "And it sure isn't because of that accent... All shouty and stuff."

"Please, not another word about your man crush on Klaus." I had to hand it to Lindemann, that was a clever move, but would it be ten million dollars clever? We could still get this thing first. They were on foot, had to be lightly armed, and we had mobility on our side. "Okay, Skip. The German team is on point. Let's back them up. Bring us in to provide cover."

The three humans in the back unstrapped from our seats and clipped safety carabineers to the ruggedized straps on our armor. The attached bungee cords would keep us from falling out the door and to our deaths if Skippy had to maneuver suddenly. We each checked the man next to us to make sure he'd been properly secured. Edward, as usual, didn't care, as orcs didn't really like to pay attention to things like safety. If things got nuts, Ed would stay inside by the sheer power of his badassitude. When everyone was ready, Trip yanked one side door open and I got the other.

A blast of freezing wind struck us. *Damn, it's cold.*

Milo and Trip went to work moving the heavy 240 into place on the left. Taking Julie's rifle, I threw the single-point sling over my head and right arm, because if I dropped her four-thousand-dollar gun out the chopper she'd murder me.

I stuck one leg outside, braced my foot on the step, and leaned out. The skin of my face was exposed, and it immediately stung from the cold. You didn't think of Nevada as frigid, but in the high desert in January, it was nasty. "Wow! That's refreshing." I rocked in a twenty round mag, pulled the bolt back and let it fly, chambering a round of silver .308. Then I was really glad for the sling, because it let me free my hands to dig around in a pouch until I found my ski mask. I fumbled it on, then got my headset back on over my head.

Trip had gotten the same idea as me and was putting on his mask too. He was from Florida, and normally started shivering at sixty degrees, so he was hating life right about now. Now we matched Ed. Milo, who was from Idaho and seemingly immune to cold, slapped the feed tray down and ran the charging handle of the machine gun. "Left side ready!"

The pouches on my armor were filled with 12-gauge magazines for Abomination. I had one sack of mags for the M-14 on the floor, so I stuck my inside boot through the strap to keep it from sliding away. "Z, ready on the right."

"One minute," Skippy roared, so of course that meant it was time to change the music. I don't know if it was a coincidence, or out of spite because we'd hired an elf, assuming Skippy even understood concepts like nation states, but his choice of *Mein Herz Brennt* by Rammstein was rather suspicious.

I flipped up the scope covers. I still had a few minutes of light, so I was going to use them as well as possible. I was no Julie, but I wasn't too shabby with a rifle, and I'd shot this particular heavily modified Troy chassis enough times to know it was a tack driver. It was probably better to start with the scalpel before going to Milo's meat cleaver. "Give me an angle, Skippy."

The chopper turned a bit, and the tall sign of the gas station came into view. We were only fifty yards off the ground by the time we crossed the road. The gas station was an ugly building, with a grimy little convenience store attached to a cinder-block garage. The garage door was open, and there was an older car parked inside with the hood up. There was a single gas pump, not even covered by an awning. Twenty yards behind the garage was an old single-wide mobile home. The whole area was lightly dusted with snow.

"The Germans are all in the parking lot." Holly said. "Friendlies are dressed in gray-and-black camo."

"Got them." There were five figures crouched behind a tow truck. Colorful sports parachutes had been quickly abandoned, and the wind was dragging a few of them down the highway like rainbow tumbleweeds.

The police car was parked right next to the garage. The driver's side door was open and I could see a pair of legs hanging out. As I watched, two of the Germans got up and ran for the police car while the others covered them. Their guns were aimed at the gas station, so I put the rifle to my cheek and glassed the windows to see what they were looking for. I turned the focus knob on the Leopold scope until the picture was crystal clear. A huge shadow zipped across the interior of the convenience store before ducking back down. "What the hell was that?"

"ID?" Trip shouted.

I wasn't sure what I'd seen. It had been broad, at least four feet across, couldn't tell how tall, and dark in color. It had seemed . . . bristly. "Beats the hell out of me, big, but it moves fast." I kept scanning. The interior of the shop was trashed. Shelves were knocked over. Some of the windows were broken. Something was spilled on the counter. I couldn't tell if it was blood.

The Hind was still moving, but slowly, gliding over

the road. The gas station was in the middle of a small valley. There were hills all around, but there was a clear area for at least fifty yards in every direction. If the thing ran for it, there was nothing for it to hide behind besides sagebrush and rocks smaller than it had been. Unless it was bulletproof, we had it cornered. I turned my view back to the Germans.

The two runners had reached the highway patrolman, and one was dragging him by the arms while the other was walking backwards behind them, eyeing the building. Suddenly the front window of the store shattered outward, but I couldn't see what had caused it. The Germans rushed back behind the tow truck, but held their fire.

"What did that?" Holly asked.

"Can't tell..." I searched through the scope. I followed the sparkling trail of broken glass away from the station. Something had been hurled through that window, and I found it on the police car's hood. "Wait. Got it...Oh hell."

"What?"

It was hard to tell, because it was so red and mangled, but I was pretty sure I knew what I was looking at. "I think that's a human torso."

Something shifted inside the store, knocking over another shelf.

My inclination was to assume there were no survivors inside, hose the place down, then torch it to be sure. But I couldn't see what Lindemann could see. Maybe he was going to try and reason with it or some nonsense. You never knew. Theoretically, I was in command, but Milo was far more experienced than I was. Earl had left me in charge because Milo wasn't comfortable with the whole leadership thing, but that didn't mean I couldn't pick his superior brain. "How do you think we should play this?"

"Gas pump is far enough away we should be able to destroy the building and not blow us all up. But..." Milo stroked his long red beard thoughtfully. "Klaus has boots on the ground. Let him make the call."

I could see one of the camouflaged individuals pointing and giving orders. A split second later, all five of them rose and opened fire on the building. The remaining windows shattered. The glass cases inside came apart. One German rose and chucked something into the open garage. Lindemann's men all ducked as one. A sharp explosion later, a cascade of dust and smoke belched out every opening. A lone hubcab went rolling across the parking lot.

"You know, I'm starting to like these guys," I said.

The Hind's nose was pointed at the building as we slowly drifted across the parking lot, and with Milo and me hanging out by the bungee cords, we could both shoot forward. "They don't get to have all the fun." Milo let the 240 thunder. Every fifth round was a tracer, and Milo shredded the facade of the convenience store with a continuous stream of red flashes. Cinderblocks puckered, spat, and then broke. Milo kept working the muzzle side to side, absolutely wrecking the place.

"Hee hee hee... Pretty." Skippy, for one, liked the tracer's effect.

Once Milo had run through his two hundred rounds, he immediately yanked the cover open, just as Trip pulled over a fresh belt. "It's cool, but I wish we would've brought the mini-gun. Six thousand rpm is so much niftier. In fact, I picked up a brochure for this new model today—"

While Milo carried on about justifying the purchase of another mini-gun, I was still watching, waiting. The place had been shredded, but there was no sign of the creature. It had to have been hit. The question was if we were dealing with something that particularly cared or not.

During our shooting spree, the last slice of orange sun had disappeared. Shadows were lengthening, but too early for night vision. It was a good thing the Leopold gathered so much extra light. I could still see pretty well through it. There was a flicker of movement from inside the destroyed garage. I shifted the scope over just in time to see that something bristly and black was pushing past the car. "Garage!" My finger went inside the trigger guard and flicked the safety forward.

The M14 barked. Shooting while hanging out a helicopter isn't the most solid of positions, so the scope rose with the recoil. I brought it back down as the shape moved past the car. I fired again, certain that I got it, but my third hurried shot punched a hole in the car's front fender. I only got the briefest look at the creature, but it seemed insectlike, with long, terrible legs, and a body coated in thick, bristly hair. Only it was the size of a horse.

The monster scuttled around the corner of the building and was quickly out of sight. Four of the Germans went running after it. Their muzzles flashed as they got a clear shot.

There was a strange vibration on my chest. It took me a moment to realize that it was my phone. It was bad timing. They could leave a message.

"Owen, answer your phone," Holly ordered from up front.

"How—"

"Because one of the guys on the ground is making exaggerated phone motions like we're playing charades and pointing at us."

"Oh . . ." It took me a second to get to the right pouch. There was no way I could hear over the roar of the rotor, but apparently Lindemann had thought of that as well, and sent me a text.

Under control. It is ours.

"You greedy son of a bitch. Lindemann wants us to back off."

Want to help? Police needs med evac.

I let out a long sigh of disbelief. "Skippy, can you land us close to that tow truck?" Skippy grunted an affirmation. I told the others what the message said. We'd just been monster blocked.

I'd unclipped and was ready to hop out by the time our tires hit pavement. Klaus Lindemann was waiting for me, wearing an odd suit of mottled gray-and-black body armor, with just a bit of a confident smile on his face. He was holding a G3K in one hand and my business card in the other. *So that's how he'd had my number.* "I had hoped you were aboard. Thank you, Mr. Pitt, for your help," he had to shout to be heard over the chopper. "However, we were first. We will take it from here."

"My ass you will."

"Your ass I will take from here?" Lindemann asked, totally sincere. "I am afraid I am unfamiliar with that expression."

My crew knew what to do, and they'd all bailed out

right after me. It took Holly the longest to get extricated from the front cockpit, but as our best medic, she went right over to the wounded man while Trip and Milo covered her. Edward sauntered over to stand behind me, still tucking swords into various places.

"We're not here to poach your bounty, but you don't know what that thing is. We're coming with you."

Lindemann paused to listen to his own radio. "It does not matter what it is, because it is disabled and soon to be dead. My men have it."

"Z!" Holly ran over. "The cop's in bad shape. Several bad lacerations and a shitload of blood loss. He needs a doctor *now*."

"We applied a tourniquet," Lindemann said. "The wound on his leg was very severe."

Too bad Gretchen hadn't come with us. Even if there was an ambulance on the way, we were in the sticks, and Skippy was still the fastest way out. "Load him in the Hind. We don't know what hit him though . . ."

"Don't worry. If he starts to change into something I'll toss him out the door." It was hard to argue with Holly's brand of ruthless enthusiasm, plus Trip was already carrying him to the chopper, regardless of whatever I would've said anyway. "So unless he turns into a werebird, that should do the trick." Holly went back to her new charge.

"I will make sure MHI is put in for an assist." Lindemann tried to soothe me.

It didn't work. "Damn right you will." I walked back to the Hind, put Julie's rifle back and took out Abomination. As nice as Julie's rifle was, having my fat, mean, full-auto 12-gauge Kalashnikov with its silver inlaid bayonet and hefty grenade launcher was strangely comforting. "Because I'm going with you."

"That isn't necessary."

"Maybe it's got a friend." I turned away from Lindemann. Milo had come up behind me. "Get him to the hospital and update Julie. Trip and Ed are with me." Edward patted a sword hilt to demonstrate he understood.

Milo nodded approvingly at Lindemann. "That whole parachute thing was pretty nifty."

"Thank you." Lindemann gave a little bow. "You must be Milo Anderson, the Edison of Monster Hunting, the DaVinci of creative destruction, or would that be destructive creation. Your work is legendary."

I swear that Milo blushed. "Oh, totally exaggerated."

"Give me a freaking break." I was still in a bad mood about losing out on a ridiculous bounty by a matter of seconds. "Come on."

Lindemann, Trip, and I made our way around the garage as the Hind lifted off and sped away with the rest of my team. It always seems extra quiet after you've been listening to the Hind and Skippy's music when it was suddenly gone. The windswept desert was eerily still.

"Klaus Lindemann, this is Trip Jones," I said, gesturing at my friend as he pulled off his ski mask. It was a lot warmer without the airflow. Trip shook Lindemann's hand. "One of MHI's best."

"Now you're just sucking up," Trip replied with a smile.

"And this is Edward." Of course, his mask stayed on. I hadn't thought about how to introduce our orc, since it was supposed to be a secret that we had them.

Thankfully, in the near darkness, the green skin and yellow eyes didn't stand out as much. Ed didn't offer to shake hands. "He's our . . . administrative assistant."

"I see . . ." Lindemann said, studying Edward and his many edged weapons, but not commenting further.

The creature's trail was easy enough to follow in the snow, having left a chaotic pattern of two-inch-circumference holes in the snow. The boots of Lindemann's men had obliterated many of the tracks. I recognized the little pockmarks in the snow as spots where hot brass had hit and immediately melted through.

"I can assure you, gentlemen. I would not cheat you out of the assist money. We run a scrupulous operation at Grimm Berlin. Mr. Harbinger, I have no doubt, would assure you of our integrity."

"He's spoken highly of you." Well, he put them in the All Right category instead of the Asshole category, which was about as good a compliment as you could get from Earl Harbinger. "I don't doubt you. More than anything I'm curious to see what all the fuss is about."

"Ah, well in that case, we are in agreement." There was a small wooden shed with a bit of light seeping out around the edges of the door, but we could see from the tracks that the monster hadn't gone anywhere near it. Stepping over a chicken-wire fence and making our way through a dead vegetable garden, we found the other four Hunters at the side of the old trailer house. They were standing in a semicircle, rifles shouldered, weapon-mounted flashlights illuminating one spot on the ground at the end of the trailer. One of the Hunters called out in German, then immediately began to rattle off a bunch of information to his boss.

"They swept the house. Empty. There appeared to

be a single occupant. An older man. The mechanic. Certainly the corpse that is now decorating the policeman's automobile."

As I made my way around the Hunters, I finally got a good look at the creature.

"That's it?" Trip was incredulous.

It was a giant spider. Or what was left of one. It had been riddled with bullet holes. It was hunched up on itself, its exact shape hard to see. Trip's reaction was understandable. Sure, a tarantula the size of a loveseat was terrifying, but not ten million dollars terrifying. By our standards, something like this wasn't that abnormal, and depending on the size and severity of the infestation, was worth a few thousand bucks, tops.

"I do not understand," Lindemann said. He barked a command at one of his men, who leaned into his rifle and cranked off several shots. The bullets struck, splattering the snow with bits and pieces of fuzzy meat. It didn't even twitch. Certain that it was dead, Lindemann walked right up to it and shoved it with his boot. It rolled over on its back. The eight legs splayed open, revealing the damaged underbelly. Yellow guts rolled out into the snow. "Curious."

He was thinking the same thing I was. "This is too simple. One of the guys from my Newbie class got a dozen of these things with a homemade bomb."

Too bad Albert Lee wasn't here. He was an expert on giant spiders, but then again, our librarian had rapidly become an expert on everything. Lee had even instituted a companywide program of our Hunters turning in mandatory after-action reports for every case, all so he could catalog monster behaviors, reactions, and vulnerabilities, then analyze the results, and file them for future reference. It was a really good idea, but I'd hated writing reports at first. It felt too much like school, but after Lee had given me crap for being needlessly stuffy and doing things like never using any contractions in my early reports, I'd loosened up, and now writing about my cases came more naturally.

One of the other Germans spoke English. "Could there be more of these around?"

"For that sort of bounty, there would have to be a colony of them..." Lindemann said. "Which one of you dropped the spider?"

"It was me," said another of the men, surely speaking English for me and Trip's convenience. These Europeans were so helpful like that.

"Good work, Hugo. We shall stuff it and make a toy for your children to play on. It will look rather nice in your flat. That is all such a meager beast is useful for." Lindemann kicked the monster again for good measure. "What game is this Stricken playing at? Why waste all of our time for *this*?"

"I survived the Stuttgart Massacre," said Hugo. "I saw horrors you cannot imagine. The chancellor herself personally presented me with the bounty payment and certificate of appreciation. I hate to think we will make far more money for shooting a large bug than for surviving hell on earth. It makes no sense."

"I intend to collect the bounty promised," Lindemann vowed. "There is much the American government does that makes no sense..." he looked at me. "No offense."

I snorted. He wasn't going to get an argument out of me on that one. "MCB will be coming from the first attack site soon. Cops will be on the way too."

"Take photos," Lindemann directed. "I have heard rumor that the Monster Control Bureau will destroy evidence to keep from paying bounties." That was a new one on me, but two digital cameras were flashing within seconds. These guys were certainly efficient.

Trip took me aside. "Something's fishy."

"I know. This is too easy." I wasn't about to say anything about Earl's girlfriend in front of the Germans, but there was no way a single giant spider took out a werewolf.

"A very wise man once said there ain't no such thing as a free lunch. This seems suspiciously like free lunch territory to me." Trip looked over at the trailer. "I'm going to poke around."

"Take Ed. Keep him away from the Feds too. Myers' whole provisional *don't ask, don't tell if you're an orc* might not be in effect anymore." I wish I had thought of that before keeping Edward here. "Where'd he go anyway?"

Trip pointed. Edward had walked over to the dead spider and was examining it. He drew one of the many knives strapped to his body, squatted down, and sawed off the last few inches of one of the legs. He speared the chunk of leg, dropped it into a cloth, wrapped it up, and stuck it inside his coat. "What's wrong, Ed?"

Edward looked at me, seemingly confused. He struggled to find the words. His English wasn't nearly as good as his brother's. "Spy-der . . . Not real."

"Looks real to me," Trip said. "What do you mean?"

"Not real." Edward shrugged. "Fake." Our orc patted his coat. "For show." Then he wandered over to inspect the nearby shed. Curious, I followed him.

Ed held up one hand, motioning me to stop. In

one sharp movement he drew one of his swords. Trip and I instinctively shouldered our guns and pointed them at the shed. Lindemann caught the movement and raised his H&K. The three of us fanned out. Edward looked over at me and nodded, then he ripped open the door.

It was a chicken coop.

The light I had seen earlier was a single large bulb designed to keep the birds warm. There were a few straw-covered shelves where the chickens made nests and laid eggs. Edward looked around inside, then sheathed his sword. Trip and I slowly lowered our weapons. Edward picked out a large white chicken, reached down, and scooped it up.

The bird seemed rather nervous. "Edward, why do you have a chicken?"

Edward tucked the chicken carefully under one arm. "Sacrifice . . . For tail row-tor spirits." Then he walked toward the trailer. It took the befuddled Trip a second to realize that was where he had been heading to begin with and he followed along.

Lindemann paused by my side. "Your *administrative assistant* is an odd sort."

"Chicken theft? That's totally going on his next evaluation."

CHAPTER 7

While Trip checked the trailer, I investigated the shop. Between the German's explosive device and Milo's mad minute, every light in the place had been busted, so I used my flashlight to maneuver. We had really trashed the garage, and everything that could break, had. I poked around behind the tool chests and shined my light down into the oil pit, but the only other spiders I could find were the normal, itty-bitty kind, and even then, chucking a small bomb into an enclosed space did wonders for cleaning out the cobwebs.

The bathroom hadn't been cleaned for years, but it didn't matter anyway, since the toilet had been pulverized into porcelain shards by a few 7.62 rounds. The water tube had been severed and was spraying the grimy remains. Through the now broken door, the small convenience store was in even worse shape. It had been a dark little place to begin with, and the only thing left on the shredded walls was a girly calendar from the nineteen-eighties. A rack of engine oil and antifreeze had been completely obliterated, and the nasty puddle filled most of the tiny space. Broken glass crunched under my boots as I circled the counter, where I found the rest of the proprietor.

I had to look away, and considering what I do for a living, that's saying something.

Something moved in the entrance. Startled, I spun around and lifted Abomination.

It was only a man. I quickly turned Abomination's muzzle aside. "Don't sneak up on people like that." Even with my flashlight pointed to the side, plenty of light bounced back for me to see that he was young, probably in his late teens or early twenties, Asian, fit, with a short, neatly parted haircut, no armor, but dressed in unfamiliar olive drab fatigues. The style of his clothing tipped me off. Some of our rival Hunters had arrived. "Who are you?"

The young man stared at me and didn't answer. Considering all of the foreign companies Stricken had unleashed on this place, he probably didn't speak English. I had met a lot of people today, but I didn't recognize this one. "You speak English? Who are you with?"

"With? I'm with . . ." He blinked a few times, confused, then rubbed his face, like he was just waking up. "I don't know. Nobody, I guess. I've got to find her."

His English was fine. "Who are you looking for?"

He moved slowly, unsteady, as if really seeing the destroyed store for the first time. He looked past me and saw the pile of limbs and organs that had recently been a person. "It's happening again."

"What are you—" Then I realized that he was unarmed, or at least with nothing that I could see. Because of the military cut of his clothing, I'd assumed he was a Hunter, but why come here without a weapon?

Was he a local who'd just blundered in? But he didn't seem shocked or disgusted to see the body, just disappointed. "Who are you?"

"Z?" I turned to see Trip coming through the doorway from the garage. "Who're you talking to?"

I turned back around and the young man was gone.

Running for the entrance, I stepped in the puddle of oil, slipped, and nearly went down, but I skidded along and made it to the door. I stepped outside, looked both ways. He was gone. Ten feet into the parking lot and I could see around the police car, and...

Nothing.

"You okay?" Trip asked as he followed me outside.

"I was just talking to a guy. He was right *here*. Asian kid, about this tall." I held one hand out at shoulder height. I turned back around, but the cold desert was empty. "I thought he was one of the other Hunters." Nervous, Trip took his night vision monocular out and used that to scan the parking lot. I looked behind the tow truck but the stranger was gone. "Weird."

"If we had a normal job, I'd laugh it off and say you imagined it, *but...*"

"Flexible minds," I repeated MHI's unofficial motto as I rubbed my face with one glove. I could've sworn I'd been having a conversation with a real person. Maybe Lacoco had hit me harder yesterday than I'd thought. "Hell if I know." Trip looked like he was eager to show me something. "What've you got?"

Trip held up a DVD case. "You love B-movies. Seen this one?"

"*Terrorantula?* Nope." The cover shot was a girl in a bikini being menaced by a bad CGI spider. I flipped it over and read the back. "Shocking tale, special effects masterpiece . . . a mutant spider terrorizes a camp for wayward girls. Rated R for horror, violence, language, and nudity. *Terror. Tarantula. Terrorantula.* I'll have to add it to my Netflix queue."

"The DVD was still in the machine. I think this was our victim's entertainment last night. You seeing what I'm seeing?"

I looked at the picture again. "No way . . ." It did have an uncanny resemblance to the dead thing next to the trailer, though the real one was scarier.

"That's what I said. Coincidence?"

"If he watched *Jaws* the night before and got eaten by a shark while surfing in the shark-infested ocean, that would be a plausible coincidence. But *Terror-friggin'-antula* in the middle of Nowhere, Nevada, which isn't exactly known for giant spiders? What are the odds of that?"

"We'll have to ask Lee. Dude dreads giant spiders. I bet he knows right off the top of his head, but odds? Astronomical?"

"Trip, I know it offends your tender Baptist sensibilities when I use profanity, but what the *fuck* is going on here?"

Trip pointed to the north. "Choppers inbound. We can always ask the MCB."

The Monster Control Bureau arrived a few minutes later, blasting in with two Blackhawks and a single Apache helicopter and doing their whole usual dramatic entrance, slide down the ropes and yell at everyone bit. I warned Lindemann and his men about what to expect, so we were prepared to go peacefully. The MCB response wasn't nearly as ham-fisted as I was used to, and the responding agents didn't even make us lay face down in the snow while screaming commands at us. I suspect that was because Agent Archer was the first one down the rope and he recognized me right away. Lindemann started to explain what had gone down, but things got really complicated when several Nevada Highway Patrol cars came in, sirens blaring, and the Feds started fighting with the locals, who were really pissed off and anxious to find their man in distress.

The MCB kept the cops away from the giant spider, but they allowed me to at least tell the cops that we'd airlifted their buddy out. However, they did it with an agent standing in my shadow to make sure I didn't say anything about any monsters. *Monsters? That's crazy talk!* Things began to calm down when the responders got word that Holly had radioed their dispatch and reported that they were on the way to the hospital.

After that, the scene became a circus. Several bullet bikes were stopped at the south roadblock, ridden by Hunters who'd snagged the fastest thing they could in Vegas. Paranormal Tactical arrived next in several SUVs with tinted windows, having broken a lot of speed limits to get here. From a distance, I witnessed Armstrong arguing with Agent Archer when the MCB wouldn't let them through the barricade. Earl's group that had come in the jet arrived from the opposite direction, riding in two borrowed pickups. They got stuck at the roadblock on that end. I sent Trip and Edward to meet them. Trip snuck the DVD with him, and Edward still had his kidnapped chicken.

I had somebody else I wanted to speak with first.

Agent Franks was inside the store, squatting next to the body, examining the carnage. Two other agents were taking pictures. I figured that since they hadn't thrown me out yet—since officially I'd been here for the assist—talking was worth a shot. "Looking for any useful replacement bits? His left foot still seems to be in pretty good shape."

Franks stood and glared at me.

"How's that work, though? Do you have to try to find new feet in the same size? Because otherwise buying shoes would be a real pain the ass. Excuse me, I'd like these, but in a size ten for the right and a size thirteen for the left. I bet the shoe store hates you."

"Escort Pitt from the premises," Franks told his men, then went back to his examination. "If he resists, shoot him in the face."

"Well, that's fairly specific." Before the first agent could reach me, I quickly said, "I wanted to talk about a mythological horse."

Franks held up one hand. His men paused. "Leave us." The agents knew better than to question Franks, gathered their cameras, gave me the stink-eye, and walked out, making quite a bit of noise on the broken glass. "What do you want, Pitt?"

"Your radio on?"

Franks moved his hand over and shut it off.

"Stricken? Know him? Really white fella, kind of scary. Controls a shadow government agency and throws millions of dollars at monsters worth a couple thousand bucks. Ringing any bells?"

"Ought to ring your bell . . ." Franks muttered, not bothering to look at me. "I know of him."

"I haven't had the pleasure of meeting him in

person either, but you know about this job he sent us all on . . . Did you hear the part where he said one of his teams went missing?"

Franks stopped poking at the body for a moment to shake his head in the negative.

"Interesting, don't you think? Assuming he was telling the truth, a Unicorn team, including a werewolf that Earl Harbinger insists is remarkably talented, went missing. You heard about any more of these spiders?"

No response. I took that as another no.

"You'd think they'd stick out, rampaging and all. So just this one little critter takes out a strike team made up of PUFF-exempt monsters, massacres a truck stop full of people, then runs thirty miles an hour to come down here to eat this guy. Odd."

"Your point?"

"Just wondering. Is the MCB as in the dark about this as we are?"

"I see fine in the dark. You don't. You still owe me a kidney."

Accidently shoot a guy once and he never lets you live it down. "I've got the organ donor sticker on my driver's license. I'll make sure to put you in my will. *Agent Franks gets my kidneys.* I hope you're not in a rush to collect."

Franks stood up. "Keep pushing and find out . . ."

"Stricken is who got Myers demoted. Right?"

Franks stepped over the body and began walking to the garage.

"Franks, wait." Luckily, he paused, because I probably couldn't have stopped him if I'd wanted to. "Myers is a scumbag, but we both know that everything he did, no matter how stupid or ineffectual it was, was to defend this country. This new guy, I don't know what his deal is. All I know is something strange is going on. Not just in this particular case, but all over the world. Myers knew that. He could see the pattern. I know you can, too. Now you've got a puppet for a boss and a shady character calling the shots. We've both been to the other side. We know what's out there. I don't want them—"

"Do you *ever* get to the point?"

I suppose by Franks' taciturn standards I'd just given a speech. "Okay, fine. I'm offering my help."

Franks seemed to think about it at least. "Noted..." Then the big agent simply left the room. The two agents that had been waiting a polite distance away returned to take their photographs.

So much for trying to be nice. Not that I particularly wanted to throw my lot in with Franks, but this whole situation was making me uneasy. Change was in the air, and not in a good way. Distracted by thoughts of the day's odd revelations and new questions, I walked down the road in the dark, making my way to where the rest of MHI was parked at the police barricade. It was time to go home; well, Vegas was close enough to home for now. At least it was warmer there. After the stomach-churning ride up here, I was happy to volunteer to drive a car home. Hell, I'd walk.

The sound of shouting stopped me in my tracks. It wasn't fearful or surprised shouting, which were the sorts that Hunters tuned into the fastest because it usually meant that something was coming to eat you, but rather this was officious and angry shouting, which wasn't as dangerous, but nearly as interesting.

I stopped to listen, and when I couldn't hear exactly what was being said, I put in my electronic hearing protection and cranked the volume all the way up.

Two figures were standing next to the garage under the few remaining lights of the elevated sign. I was standing in the center of a dark road, so I could see them a bit, but they couldn't see me at all. The hulking one in all the body armor was obviously Agent Franks. The thinner man in the trench coat was unfamiliar, but he was the one doing the shouting.

"—stuff it! I don't care what Myers would've done. Myers is out. This is a Task Force mission now! If you don't like it, call your new boss. Stark will tell you the same thing. Stay out of our way."

"Sir," Franks didn't so much as raise his voice, but he still managed to sound dangerous. "With all due respect—"

The other man was oblivious to just how lethal Franks could be. "I don't want your opinion, Agent. MCB is glorified crowd control and I don't see any witnesses here for you to intimidate. Man your little roadblocks and write your press releases. If we need a trigger pulled, we'll call you. Until then we'll do the heavy lifting."

Franks wasn't deterred. "This smells like Decision Week—"

"The Task Force will make that determination after we inspect the evidence. Not you. Mr. Stricken wants you back in Las Vegas. You're too stupid to make policy decisions."

I was shocked that Franks didn't simply reach over and pull the man's arms off. I wasn't aware that you could insult Franks that directly and live. But Franks stood there, absolutely motionless and just took it. How powerful were these Unicorn people?

"Director Myers was deluded. The president made his call. They keep you around to kill things, Agent Franks, not for your brains. You're a relic. You're a monster that's been given too long of a leash. Your handlers have given you too much leeway for too long. You'll shut up, get in line, and do what you're told. Get that through your thick, armor-plated skull, and we'll all be better off."

"You need me," Franks said, so quietly that I could barely pick it up.

"If it was up to me, we'd dismantle you and bring back the Nemesis Project." The stranger was actually stupid and prideful enough to laugh at Franks.

Franks' manner changed. Just a little shifting of his stance, but I could sense the sudden danger from where I was. Franks had just switched from Obsequious Government Employee Mode to Kill Your Ass Mode. *This ought to be good.* The new guy must have caught the subtle difference too, as the laughter quickly died. The agent gently placed one large hand on the stranger's shoulder.

"Mr. Foster . . . I've been ordered to tolerate you people. If you ever mention Nemesis around me again that tolerance ends, along with your life." He said it in such a way, so casually, that there was absolutely no doubt he was telling the truth. "Tell Stricken that I'll follow the president's directive, but the next STFU toady that annoys me leaves in a bag." Franks must have given a little squeeze because Foster yelped in pain. "Understand?" Foster nodded vigorously and scurried away. It was amazing how fast roles could reverse with good old-fashioned threats of serious bodily harm. Franks turned, looked right at me, and began walking my way, taking long, angry strides.

Uh-oh...

I thought about running, but if he was mad at me, it wouldn't have done any good. I stood my ground. "Franks."

He stopped in front of me. "Pitt." It was obvious that he'd known I was listening. Well, he had just said he could see in the dark.

"So, what's Project Nemesis?"

"Classified."

"Decision Week?"

"Classified."

"Okay then..." We both stood there awkwardly for a moment. I looked around the desert, stuck my hands in my pockets, and began to whistle.

Franks seemed pained. "Still want to help?"

That had to have been difficult for him. "Sounds like you're thinking about doing something through unofficial channels."

He shrugged.

"Depends. Will the president be upset?"

"I've killed ogres smarter than this administration," Franks answered unexpectedly. Rather than wait for my answer, he began walking toward one of the parked MCB helicopters.

It was a difficult and dangerous choice. Get involved in power struggles that were way over my head and maybe get some answers, or stay put and miss out on information relating to some very strange and potentially world-altering events. I really didn't have a choice. Being a Monster Hunter isn't just a job for some of us, it's a calling. I was a meat shield for the entire human race. Innocent people were alive because of the hard choices I'd made and the risks I'd taken. It was a track record that I'd like to keep.

I'm such a sucker. I followed him.

"Where are we going?"

"Classified."

It was shaping up to be a long night.

CHAPTER 8

I left a message with Julie telling her that I would be out of pocket for a bit, couldn't say where I was going, how long I'd be gone, but not to worry, I'd explain later, and that I'd find a ride home. It says a lot about our relationship that that wasn't a particularly strange call by our standards.

The MCB Blackhawk was downright plush compared to my usual ride. Okay, it was still pretty Spartan, but I didn't see anything wrapped in duct tape. Agent Franks sat across from me. Of course, he didn't feel like talking, and he just sat there with an F2000 rifle resting on his lap. The pilot and copilot were the only other people on board. Franks had given them a few instructions and we'd taken off, heading east. I couldn't tell what direction we'd gone from there because it was dark and the rare lights out the windows didn't reveal any landmarks.

My few attempts at conversation had ended in some variation of "Classified" or a blank stare. I swear that sometimes he was like this just to piss me off. Franks acted like he had an exact number of words allotted to him every day, and that he'd be heavily penalized if he went over his limit. Sadly, he saved most of his complete sentences for threatening people, and managed to accomplish most of his communicating through scowling, blinking, and radiating malice.

I knew his secret. The thing that we all knew as Agent Franks had been the inspiration for the fictional Frankenstein's monster, and had been around for a very long time. His creator, the alchemist Konrad Dippel, had died in the seventeen-hundreds, so Franks had to have been first stitched together sometime before that. His very existence piqued my curiosity, but it was all for naught.

"So, Franks. When did you come to America?"

"Classified."

"You weren't..." I tried to think of the right word. "*Born* here. Why'd you immigrate?"

He stared at me for a second. "Classified."

Sweet. I had gotten *both* possible responses to a *single* question. I was making real headway here. After that achievement I decided to take a nap.

A change in air pressure woke me up. Franks didn't appear to have moved an inch, but my watch told me an hour had passed.

"ETA, five minutes," Franks stated. "When was your last psychic episode?"

It took my sleep-addled brain a moment to process that. "What?"

"When was your last psychic episode?" he repeated.

He wasn't supposed to know about that. Franks had been my bodyguard during the incident with the Condition and my last exposure to the Old Ones, but I'd done my best to keep it from him, though he'd certainly been around for enough to know that I wasn't ordinary. "No. I'm not—" but he just kept staring at me with those remorseless, merciless, borrowed eyeballs of his. "Fuck you, Franks. *Classified*."

He tilted his head to the side, probably deciding how to kill me without messing up his nice helicopter. "If I cared, I would've did something last year."

He had me there. Myers had been eyewitness to me being bitten by a zombie and not dying. If the MCB gave a crap, they had more than enough to lock me up for *study and evaluation*. Besides, Franks didn't seem too particular about that sort of thing. He only cared if oddities like me were useful for completing his assignments. But damn it, I didn't want to tell him anything. "Fine. But you answer some of my questions, I'll answer some of yours." That wasn't very likely. I was safe.

Franks stared at me. Back to square one.

I looked out the window. There were more lights below us, big orange security lights in a gigantic grid pattern. There were lots of fences and strange, squat white buildings. None of it was familiar.

Franks cleared his throat. I turned back to him. "I came for the war."

Franks was going to talk? *No way*. He wasn't going to get off that easy. "Which war?"

"The first one."

I thought about that for a second. "America's first war or . . ."

"I was a Hessian."

It was so out of left field it took my brain a moment to run back through its trivia vaults. "A Hessian? Like,

the Germans that fought in the Revolutionary War...
Whoa...Man, that's crazy. No way." Franks' expression said *Yes. Way.* Logically, I knew that Franks was
much older than that, but that certainly put things
in perspective. "Wait. The Hessians worked for the
British. You switched sides? Why?"

"Benjamin Franklin asked nice."

"Ben Franklin! Really? That's amazing. You knew
the guy that invented electricity!"

Franks raised an eyebrow. You can't *invent* electricity.

"You know what I mean. I can't believe you met
Ben Franklin." I waited for him to continue, but he
just went back to glowering at me. That meant it was
my turn. Assuming he was telling the truth, and of
the many horrific things that Franks was, I'd never
taken him for a liar, that was an astounding amount of
information. No doubt if I ever shared it with anyone
he'd break me in half. I had no choice but to talk.

"Okay then...My last incident was right after the
Arbmunep battle." I didn't think I needed to disclose
that the last experience was reading his superior's
mind and discovering that Agent Myers had once
been involved in some horrific, illegal, and amoral
things during his contractor days. Specifically, he had
been complicit with Ray Shackleford IV in allowing
Martin Hood to animate the dead in order to collect
PUFF on them. It was embarrassing for Myers, not
that I cared, but more embarrassing for MHI and the
Shackleford family name, and that I did care about.
"Nothing since then."

"Nature of the ability?"

"It's happened half a dozen times, tops. Began
with Lord Machado, aggravated by exposure to their

artifact...which I hope you bastards have locked up nice and safe somewhere."

He tilted his head the other direction.

"Memories. I can view memories." Franks' eyes narrowed suspiciously. "Not yours. Ever. Trust me. I don't want to see what's in there. It's only happened with physical contact. It seems like they have to be thinking about that particular memory, and I have to really want to know." There was a lot more to it than that, like my experience inside the mind of Carlos Alhambra or when I tried to help Earl against the demon Hood had put into his head. But screw Franks. He'd known Ben Franklin and wouldn't talk about it. If he got to have such awesome secrets, so did I. "That's pretty much it."

"Hmmm..."

Franks thought about it for a long time, so long in fact, that I'd thought he was done. I went back to looking out the window. Judging by the vehicles below, we were over some sort of sparsely populated area of a military base, with only a few random, mysterious buildings here and there, with lots of wide open desert between them. Milo had mentioned that the attack site had been west of the vast Dugway Proving Grounds, so I guessed that was where we were now.

"When we get there, tell me if you feel anything."

"What is *there* specifically?"

"We're not sure." Shockingly enough, Franks didn't elaborate. Then we landed in the middle of a field.

After flying over miles of government facilities, I would've expected to have arrived at *something*. But there was nothing but sagebrush and snow outside. A single yellow pickup truck was stopped nearby with the headlights on.

The Blackhawk's door slid open, and standing there was a vaguely person-shaped thing in a gigantic yellow rubber chemical suit. I could barely see the shape of a face behind the glare of the plastic face shield. Considering Milo had told me that this was where the Army buried all of their chemical and biological weapons, meeting somebody wearing a big scary apocalypse suit wakes you right up.

He, she, it—damned if I could tell—handed a big rubber bag to Franks. "Agent Franks? We were told to expect you. Put these on." It was a man, and his voice came through a speaker on the bottom of his helmet.

Franks unzipped the bag, revealing more chemical suits. "Why do we need these?" I asked nervously.

"Who is this?" the stranger asked.

"Consultant," Franks answered.

"He hasn't signed a waiver. If he dies it isn't my problem. He'll need to sign a waiver."

"He was never here," Franks said.

"Neither were the other multitudes traipsing through my facility all day. Same rules apply. If he leaves your side, my men will shoot him."

"Understood."

The helmet turned to me. I could mostly only see my own reflection. "Stay close to the agent or you will be shot."

"Got that the first time. So, why do I need the suit?"

"Nerve gas. If you stray off the path, you will be shot." The night suddenly seemed extra chilly. "Nerve gas?"

"Nerve gas. If you cross the fence—"

"Yeah, yeah, I got it, cross the fence, get shot."

"No. If you cross the fence, the nasty shit that's buried over there will burn right through your respirator and you'll be having a seizure in ten seconds and dead in under a minute. My men won't have to shoot you, but you'll want them to. Get your suits on and meet me at the truck." The rubberized man waddled away.

What have I gotten myself into?

Franks tossed me the helmet. "Hope that fits."

"Up yours, Franks. I hope yours doesn't."

Franks nodded. "That would be unfortunate. Nerve gas tickles."

The fence wasn't as impressive as I thought it would be. It was made of weathered old wooden posts and three rusting strands of barbwire. It didn't look like it would stop an aggressive cow, let alone terrorists.

"This section we unofficially call the Scary Zone. Most of the rest of the base doesn't even know this section exists or what my people do. Some of the things buried here date back to the forties, when we really didn't know a lot about storing biological agents, and everyone was in a real hurry. Many of the records were lost, so what exactly is here, and where and how it's stored, is questionable at best. Should be pretty safe now, but one time I saw a coyote cross this fence. He made it a couple hundred yards out into the Scary Zone, started to foam at the mouth, then just fell over, dead. Didn't so much as twitch," said the man in the lead, who still hadn't bothered to—and probably never would—introduce himself. "We run a much tighter ship now. If anything looks even sort of suspicious we lock this place down tight, nobody in or out until we're sure everything is accounted for. But storing things properly back then was a little more . . . wild west."

There was a four-wheeler-sized path between the

sagebrush and the fence. The snow had been churned into a sandy mush from many recent sets of footprints. Walking was difficult in the rubber suit. The full-face helmet obscured my peripheral vision. The booties were floppy and clumsy. I would imagine that this thing would be stifling hot most times, but since it was just above freezing with an icy wind, it was nice and toasty. My breathing sounded like Darth Vader. I kept as far away from the barbwire as possible because I really didn't want to rip my suit.

There were flashlights set in the tops of the helmets, and the light bobbed up and down as we went at least half a mile down the path. We'd only seen a few other staff, who had also been wearing big suits, and none of them had any identifiers on them. I hadn't seen any of the people who were supposed to shoot me if I wandered off, but I had no doubt they were out there, watching us with high-powered rifles and night-vision devices. I was not going off the path. *No, sir.* Place like this, you could get retina cancer just from glancing off the path too hard.

"This particular storage unit wasn't cataloged. It didn't show up on any of our maps or tables. The units around it all date from 1943 to 1945, so that's our approximate time frame. Somebody stuck it in the ground and didn't so much as make a note. No idea what project it originated from or what the nature of the unit was. I hate, hate, *hate* when they do that."

"Have you been down yet, Major?" Franks asked.

"Hell no. Not going to, either. Once you people say the case is closed, we're going to cover it back up and stick a sign on it that says 'Do Not Touch.' I don't want any of my people involved with it. We'll stick to safe things, like anthrax. I thought we had all of these damned Decision Week leftovers cataloged by now. Last time MCB was out here was when a hard rain revealed one of their experiments. A deer was exposed to it and grew tentacles instead of antlers. Tentacle deer . . . The Army doesn't pay me enough to deal with that kind of shit."

That was the second time I'd heard mention of Decision Week tonight.

"Who else went in?"

"Just the team from your agency, couple of hours after we sounded the alarm. They poked around, took some pictures, decontaminated, and flew out."

Franks stopped. "Which team?" I bumped into him. Rubber squished and squeaked. It was very awkward.

"Two men, one woman. Good looking redhead, that one . . ." the Major stopped when he realized Franks wasn't moving. "Let me guess, not MCB? Their credentials said MCB and they had all the right approvals. So, far as I'm concerned, that's who they were, and I don't ask questions."

So the missing Unicorn team had been here already. That was news to Franks.

The major began walking again. "Heh, you black helicopter types, always with the games."

"It's no game," Franks muttered.

"My job is to watch things so awful that a single vial could kill a city. Anything less than that sounds like games to me."

"You know, Franks, all of this being manipulated and lied to, now you get to know how Hunters feel about you guys." It felt good to laugh at him. "Sucks, don't it?"

His helmet rotated toward me. I couldn't really see his face, but I could still tell he was contemplating throwing me over the death fence to look for foaming coyotes. But he didn't—probably decided I might still be useful—then it was back to waddling.

Several small red flags had been stuck into the ground, and the major took a right when he reached them. There was no real trail here, but the feet had made a path through the snow. The sagebrush grabbed at my clumsy booties and tried to trip me. I was glad when the major led us onto a clear spot where the annoying knee-high bushes were missing.

"Motion detectors went off at oh-four-hundred yesterday. Our responders found this hole and we lowered a camera to find the seal broken. Since there were tracks leading out, but not in, that's when we called your agency. Tentacle deer was enough for me. It's your problem now."

It seemed strangely familiar, this cleared area... and then the hazy, half-forgotten dream from the night before came rushing back and my knees turned to jelly.

I had seen this place before.

Slowly turning, I confirmed that the open spot was a perfect circle. The brush hadn't been cleared at all, it simply wouldn't grow above what was buried beneath.

In the dream, there had been a hole in the middle, with a rusty ladder leading down to a hatch that was never intended to be unsealed. I was scared to look, because to confirm it was to confirm my worst fears. I hadn't volunteered to be the Chosen One, or poster boy, or whatever the hell I was, for a bunch of dead Hunters and the combined forces of good, and I dreaded when they tried to tell me something.

Experience taught that when I dreamed about a case, it meant that bad things were on the horizon. For a moment, I couldn't spot the hole and I felt nothing but relief, but then I realized it was just a trick of the light. There was a depression in the snow. The footprints led right to it.

The major pointed one black rubber glove at the hole. "There's your containment unit."

"Shit."

"What?" Franks asked.

If the dream had been prophetic, sent by Mordechai or Bubba or whoever, then at the bottom of that shaft would be scratched the symbol I'd been terrified to finally find in real life...the mark that belonged to a being that would bring about the destruction of mankind. The mark that would end my father's life. "Nothing."

I didn't need to see his face behind the mirrored visor to know that he didn't believe me. Franks waited.

"I've seen this place in my dreams."

"You didn't mention precognition." Franks sounded accusatory. "You're a terrible psychic."

"Uh, well..." the major coughed. "I didn't hear that at all. I'm going to go wait by the fence." He waddled off.

"I can't go down there, Franks. It's dangerous." Franks reached for his side instinctively, then realized he couldn't reach his pistol through his suit. "No. I think the danger's gone. I just can't. I can't see...Look, if the dream was right, there's a mark down there. It'll kill—I can't explain...My father... It's complicated."

The faceless suit watched me.

"It's not like that, Franks. I can't go down there."

"Hunters make everything complicated."

The story came spilling out. "My dad was supposed to have died a long time ago, but he was kept alive by, I don't even really know by who... all to prepare me for the end of the world. He warned me about a mark, and when I see it, then I know it means the end is here. He's supposed to deliver a last message to me, but then he'll die. I saw that mark in my dreams last night, scratched into whatever is at the bottom of that ladder. If I go down there, I'll know it's started. I'll have no choice. I'll have to hear him out. When his mission is over, his borrowed time is up and he dies. I can't kill my father, Franks."

Franks was puzzled. "Will the world end anyway?"

"I..." *Probably.* Dad certainly thought so. The war was coming, no matter what. "I just can't."

Franks looked at me, then the hole, then me again. It would have been easier if he'd called me a coward, but he simply went over to the hole, found the ladder, and began climbing down without me. Franks' headlamp disappeared, then I was alone, standing in the blighted circle as the cold gradually leeched through my suit.

Dad was mad at me. He'd accepted his death, and couldn't understand how come I couldn't too. He had been preparing for it his entire life. I had only been kicked in the face with it recently. Finding out that I was the one who was supposed to fulfill his life's work had been a relief for him, a burden lifted. The selfish old bastard had been glad to dump it all on me, and now he couldn't grasp how come I wasn't eager to simply hear his message and end his life.

The hole taunted me.

I had seen too many things to doubt his story. I'd faced alien gods and ancient horrors. I'd swam through another reality and been inside the blank gray hell of a mind torn to pieces by a demon. If Dad said he'd been given his life back and sent on a mission to help me head off the apocalypse, then I believed him.

The decision would have been an easy one if his life hadn't hung in the balance. I was sick and tired of being manipulated by forces beyond my understanding. It was even more obnoxious to discover that they'd been manipulating my family long before I'd even been born. I'd dealt with the other threats on my own terms and I'd made things work out. Just because Dad was convinced he had to do it the way these mysterious Others wanted and throw his life away in the process didn't mean that was our only option. Screw the Others, whatever they were. I'd do this my own way. Maybe I could handle this and not involve him?

The dream had been a clue. Someone had wanted me to find this place. The stories from the other Hunters about the pattern . . . Could it be this mysterious foe that Dad had been sent back to warn us about? If so, then me not fulfilling my duty would only make things worse. This was bigger than me, bigger than my father. I had to face this. I had to know.

That still didn't make it easy.

"Damn it, Dad." I went over and aimed my headlamp down the hole.

The ladder was narrow and rusty. In reality, I could only smell rubbery, recycled air, but I could've sworn that an odd scent came up the shaft, dust and age.

Franks' light was moving around at the base, about twenty feet down. I swore again and started down carefully, the ladder creaking and shedding red. At least if I slipped, I'd have the honor of taking Franks with me.

The walls were dirt, shored up with rotting wooden beams. There should have been cobwebs or bugs, roots, some sign of life, but the shaft seemed unusually sterile. The shaft opened up in the last bit, enough that I could squeeze in next to Franks. He didn't even bother to greet me. The floor under my squishy booties was metal.

The air was heavy. I was having such a hard time breathing that I thought my respirator had malfunctioned. I forced myself to look down. Sure enough, just like the dream, there was a hatch.

But there were no scratches. There was no mark from my father's mysterious antagonist. The metal was covered in dust, only recently disturbed by footprints, but undamaged. I began to breathe again. The dream had shown me this place, but it had also showed me the mark, glowing in the darkness.

What did it mean?

The hatch was open just a crack. Franks reached out and touched the rusty wheel, but it turned freely, having been broken loose recently. I shuffled out of the way as he lifted it. Hinges screeched in protest and the lid thudded into the wall. Another ladder led down.

"You first," Franks ordered.

"Why?"

"I'm important."

"Screw you, Franks. You're the one with replaceable

feet. You go first." I got tired of looking at my own reflection. "Fine. Jackass."

I started down. The metal shell was several inches thick. My headlamp illuminated the far wall only a few feet away, with each rung of the ladder casting huge black shadows. This ladder was far more sturdy and the trip much shorter. I reached the floor quickly.

It was a circular space, like standing at the bottom of a metal water tank. I estimated that it was the exact same diameter as the dead spot of desert above. I moved aside as Franks dropped down the last few feet.

Between our two sets of headlamps, the entire room was illuminated. "Cozy."

There wasn't much inside. Only a stainless-steel operating table off to one side, bolted to the floor, with some tall metal boxes behind it. I began to shiver uncontrollably. The room wasn't refrigerated. There seemed to be no power supply. So why did I suddenly feel incredibly cold?

The construction of the boxes seemed old-fashioned, with big plates held together with strips of sheet metal and rivets. One side was open, and the interior was packed with copper wires and glass tubes, the contents of which had long since evaporated. There had been batteries at the bottom, but they had melted into a greenish-white acidic sludge. There were no signs or labels on the machine, but there were a few obvious spots, discolored and free of dust, where nameplates had been torn free and taken away very recently. There was a dusting of brass shavings on the floor, gleaming and new compared to everything around it.

"Looks like your Unicorn pals did some cleaning."

"They're not *pals*," Franks muttered.

A bundle of wires led from the machine, and I followed it back to the table, where it split apart into dozens of individual strands, each of them terminating in two long needles. They were spread haphazardly around the floor, but it *felt* like they had all been jammed into a body at one point, from one end of the table to the other. I picked up one wire and examined the end. The tip of the prongs was stained with a dry, black substance. I dropped it, not wanting to find out if it was the sort of thing that would eat through a chemical suit.

The table wasn't shaped at all like the kind of thing you would tie a giant spider to. Rather, it was man-sized and man-shaped. There was far more going on than some simple arachnid. Leather straps hung from the edges of the table. Franks picked up one strap, and it was so dried with age that it cracked in his hand. A very long time ago, someone or something had been strapped down to this table and stuck full of needles leading back to a machine that did who knew what, then buried and forgotten.

My teeth were chattering. "What's the deal, Franks?"

"You getting anything?"

"Angry." I gestured at the machine. "What does the MCB know about this?"

He shrugged. *Nothing.*

"Yeah, well, Stricken sure knows more than he's telling. Maybe I should go ask him."

"Your funeral." Franks went back to examining the table.

"Who is this Stricken guy supposed to be that even you're afraid of him?"

"I'm scared of no man . . ."

"What's Nemesis then?"

Franks paused. That word seemed to make him angrier. "Getting anything yet?"

"I'm not a supernatural Geiger counter, Franks. It doesn't work like that."

He mumbled something to himself about useless Hunters and continued looking for clues. I went back to the machine, but its function was beyond me. Whatever it did, judging from the condition of the batteries, it had run out of juice decades ago, but the thing on the table hadn't moved until recently. *Why?*

I looked to the ceiling for the first time. The hair on the back of my neck stood up. It was *wrong*. The top of the space was the same seamless metal as the floor, but there was an odd pattern of discoloration around the hatch. "Franks..." I reached up and found the switch for my headlamp. "Kill the lights." It went dark. The glass lamps in our helmets faded slowly orange. Then the tank was pitch black. I stood there, respirator laboring, skin burning with cold, and waited.

The light was faint at first, so weak that I thought I'd imagined it, but then it began to grow, glowing with the muted color of aged bone. The light took on a sick green tint, and then I could see it clearly.

It was the symbol.

The mark had been placed above. It had seeped through the metal of the tank until its malevolence could be felt inside. It had been placed there to wake up whatever had been strapped to that table. Somehow I knew what it had been like here, asleep, waiting, between worlds. When suddenly the sick light had intruded, forcing itself into the safety of the tank. And *it* had awoken.

Suddenly weak, my knees buckled. In the darkness I floundered, panicking, until I struck the ladder and held on. The sweat running down my body turned to ice.

"Is that it?"

I couldn't respond. The feeling of terror that clenched my insides was more than just my own. It was a residue, a shadow of the fear left behind by the occupant of the tank. I tried to move, but it was as if I was frozen to the ladder, and if I let go the darkness would swallow me. The tank was closing in on me. I had to get out.

Something inhuman screeched in my ear.

I flinched away from the noise as there was an impact against my suit. The rubber squeaked as I was shoved against the ladder. Off balance, I landed on my back, the air tank clanging loudly against the metal floor. "Help!" Another hit bounced off my face shield hard enough to drive the back of my head against the ground. I got my hands up in front of me, but through the clumsy gloves I could only feel *cold*. "Get it off!"

The light from Franks' helmet was sudden, searing, and I was looking up into the emaciated face of something hideous, blue, and dead. It screeched again, opening a mouth full of rotten, broken teeth. Ice crystals fell and stuck to my face shield. Then just as suddenly, it was gone and Franks was standing over me.

The thing slammed into the far wall with a bone-jarring crunch. The light flashed wildly as Franks went after it, and I caught a brief glimpse of a skeletal form, with skin like parchment stretched over bones, and a wild mane of white hair. Then the light swung the other way as it came off the wall and launched itself at Franks.

The unnatural terror that had felled me was gone. I could move again. I fumbled for my own headlamp as I rolled over and stood up.

Franks had caught the screaming thing, used its momentum against it, spun it over one shoulder and hurled it against the steel table. It didn't seem to feel a thing as it pushed itself off, but I intercepted it and kicked one leg out from under it. Freezing cold burned through the rubber booty and into my foot.

It felt no pain and got right back up. I planted one big rubber fist into the side of its head. It stumbled a bit, but then Franks was on the other side and he slugged it back toward me. Fists aching with cold, I hit it, then he hit it, the skinny thing rebounding back and forth between us as we played undead tetherball. We were both clumsy in the suits, but we were both really good at beating things to death. It screeched again, then Franks knocked its jaw clean off. My next hit sent it spinning over the table where it fell to the floor on the other side.

Two headlamps bounced as we both went after it, ready to stomp the unlife out of the horrid thing. There was nothing there. "What!" The floor was nothing but a tangle of stained copper wires. Breathing hard, I whipped my head around, searching... "Where—"

Franks was scanning too. "It's gone."

Gone? "What the hell?" It hadn't gone up the ladder. We were in a solid metal tank with only one exit. The burning cold in my extremities began to subside, replaced by the hot flush of adrenalin. "Let's get out of here."

For once, Franks didn't disagree.

❖   ❖   ❖

The desert night that had seemed so bitterly cold before seemed welcoming after the unnatural chill of the tank.

"Where did that thing come from?" The two of us were in the dead circle, scanning the desert with our headlamps. "What was that?"

"Ice ghoul," Franks said. "Mummified undead."

"They common around here or something?"

"Only in polar latitudes."

Dugway, Utah, wasn't pleasant by any means, but it certainly wasn't the arctic. "They teleport?"

"No. Glorified tough zombie on ice."

Now I was really confused. It hadn't come down the ladder. It had appeared out of thin air, jumped on me, got the hell beat out of it, then disappeared. "I've never even heard of those before."

"Rare. Haven't seen one since . . ." Franks trailed off. "Interesting . . ."

"What?"

"Classified."

After all that . . . "Screw you, Franks! You rotten son of a bitch! Take your stupid 'classified' and shove it up your—"

"Everything okay, Agent?" the major had waddled back to the circle.

"We're done here."

"And the containment unit?"

Franks took one last look at the hole. "Bury it."

CHAPTER 9

I had been taken in the back of the pickup to a portable shower, sprayed with foam, scrubbed with brushes, then taken out of my suit, sprayed with hot soapy water, then sprayed with freezing water, then given my clothing, armor, and weapons back. Since there was no indication of any actual chemical or biological agents in that particular containment unit, and there was no sign that any of the surrounding units had been breached, it was probably overkill, but I liked not puking blood or having brain damage, and wanted to keep it that way.

While I was getting washed, rinsed, and repeated, my mind was on the symbol. No matter how much I'd hoped otherwise, I'd known this day was going to come. Everything my father had lived for was to prepare me for this. He had drawn that symbol in the dirt of the Cazador compound to show me what to look for and given me a letter to fill me in and absolve him of his last responsibilities. The letter was still unopened, sitting in one of my gun safes back in Alabama. He was certain that as soon as I read it, his borrowed time would be up. Dad thought I hadn't read it because I was a coward. Maybe he was right, but I didn't want to just murder the stubborn old bastard. How would it happen? Would he keel over the minute I read it? That was a hell of a thought, because I didn't have much choice now.

Franks met me at the Blackhawk. It was all warmed up and ready to go. "I've been ordered back to Las Vegas."

I climbed in after him. "Any new word on the attack?"

"Grimm Berlin got the bounty. MHI got the assist. Congratulations." Franks actually sounded bitter. "Case closed."

A few minutes later we were in the air. By that point I was too tired to even try wheedling any further information out of Franks. I knew it wouldn't do any good. He seemed even more reclusive than normal. I used the rest of the flight back to get in another nap. Hunters get so used to working stupid hours and being exhausted that most of us develop the ability to sleep the instant the opportunity presents itself.

"Wake up."

The neon brilliance of Las Vegas was outside the window. I stretched. That had been a solid power nap. Franks was holding something out for me. It took me a second to realize it was an open laptop. He pressed it into my hands, took the audio line out of his headset and plugged it into mine. I flipped it around so I could see the screen.

Special Agent Dwayne Myers, former interim head of the Monster Control Bureau, had aged a lot over the last year. His hair had thinned further and turned whiter. He'd lost some weight, and it wasn't like Myers could afford to lose much weight to begin with. Thin, tired, face lined with stress, and dark circles under his eyes, Myers was looking haggard. "Pitt. This is a secure video conference, but I need to keep this brief. I will deny this conversation ever took place."

There was a short list of people I trusted. Myers wasn't on it and never would be. This man had been prepared to nuke Alabama in order to do his duty. He had ruined thousands of lives in his mission to keep monsters secret from the public, including my own brother. Myers wasn't the type to let things like collateral damage get in the way of doing his job. He'd used me before and would burn me the second that it became convenient. "What do you want?"

"I take it you're aware of my demotion."

"I'll admit, I cheered a little when I heard. I haven't got the invitations made up for the party yet, but I did order the cake."

"Amusing, but I wouldn't be so quick to celebrate. I take it you haven't dealt with my replacement yet. No? Well, you are in for a real treat, and I don't mean the cake. This is a courtesy call. Agent Franks has made me aware of what you've discovered—"

"Oh, good. Maybe you can fill me in, because he hasn't made me aware of shit." I looked over the top of the monitor as I said that. Franks ignored me.

"I'm afraid that there are some certain specifics which can't be shared relating to government programs—"

"Like Nemesis?" It never hurt to go fishing.

Myers frowned. "For one. Regardless of what unfounded rumors you've heard about that, just be aware that as long as I or Agent Franks is in any sort of position of authority, that project will never be implemented."

"Because I'll kill anyone who tries..." Franks muttered under his breath.

"As to our current business, I have no more information about today's case than you do. That is not why I'm talking to you now. I need you to deliver a message to Earl Harbinger."

Myers hated Earl. I'd be surprised if the message was anything other than *drop dead*. "What's the deal?"

"Tell him that what we spoke about in Copper Lake, I believe it's happening now. I don't know what's coming, but MHI and everyone like you out there needs to be prepared. If I learn of anything that may help, I will pass it on. MHI must be ready to act."

"Myers, we were born ready. Our greatest impediment to actually doing our jobs is you assholes screwing with us and keeping us in the dark. Franks told you about the symbol we found?" The image of Myers nodded. "Do you know who it belongs to?"

"No, we do not."

That felt like the truth. "Have you seen it before?"

Myers didn't answer.

"I thought so. Where?"

"Everywhere. It has been showing up over the last few years with ever-increasing frequency. My sources told me that the Hunters at the conference were talking about many of those same instances today."

I swallowed hard. My father's symbol and the pattern of new monster appearances were related. "Myers, listen—"

"I'm out of time, Pitt. Just know that things aren't

what they seem. Changes are being made in how the government does things, about how we combat the forces of the unnatural. I did not...*agree* with some of these new policies. No matter what you think of me, you know everything I've done has been to protect America. I took a solemn oath to defend this country. I will continue doing that to the best of my abilities, no matter how dark things become, no matter what, I will fulfill that oath or I will gladly die trying."

Myers was beginning to scare me. "I'll tell Earl."

"Good luck, Mr. Pitt." The image went black.

Franks snatched his laptop back and immediately began scrubbing files.

I called Julie from the airport. She was glad to hear that I was back safe, but I was afraid to tell her anything specific over the phone.

"That thing my dad wanted us to watch for? It's here. And tell everybody that it's involved in what we figured out earlier."

There was a long silence. "That's not good..."

"We'll make it work."

"We always do."

All of this secret squirrel nonsense was making me even more paranoid than usual. I told her I'd catch everyone up when I got back to the hotel, but there was something else that I needed to take care of first. I ended the call with a heavy heart and a nervous stomach.

My greatest worry was what to do about my father. My opportunity for procrastination was over. I needed to learn what he knew. His letter was safe at the Shackleford mansion. I could call him on the phone, but I needed to do this in person. Mom and Dad lived hundreds of miles from here, and the selfish, weak, human part of me was thankful that seeing them right this minute was impossible. I'd faced all manner of evil, but I didn't know if I had the guts to do this one simple task.

I needed to talk to someone who would understand. I needed to talk to family.

The hazardous materials folks at Dugway had given me a large nylon bag to put my armor and weapons in, which enabled me to make it through the airport to hail a cab without causing any freak-outs or calls to the police. I'd already gotten one tour of the Clark County jail, didn't particularly want another. I gave the cabbie Mosh's address and then went back to wondering how I was going to tell my little brother that I had to end our father's life.

Las Vegas was a nocturnal city by nature, so despite it being late, the traffic still sucked. The cab ride gave me even more time to think, which was the last thing I had wanted to do.

My brother was on the opposite end of the strip from where MHI was staying. This casino was older, more run-down, but he was living there for free as long as he played a few solo shows every week. There was a huge publicity shot poster of him at the entrance, looking all steely-eyed, with his shaved head and really long goatee, wearing a leather vest that showed off his muscular arms and intricate tats. The interior of this casino was dim, smelled like cigarette smoke, and was filled with old people playing nickel slot machines. I asked a cocktail waitress who was too worn down by life to be wearing an outfit that skimpy for directions. Tonight's show was almost over.

The stage was in a bar in the back of the casino. Once I got past the pings and whistles of the electronic slots, I followed the sounds of a guitar. I paid the cover charge and got my hand stamped by a fat man at the door. I was glad to see there was still a pretty good-sized crowd. It was nothing like the mob he had been able to draw before, but the hardcore loyal fans hadn't abandoned him. I made my way in, squeezing past a lot of men wearing spikes and chains and women with too little clothing and lots of extra piercings.

The song was a new one. Low key...*sad*. I didn't think I'd ever heard him sound like that before. I'd heard him play loud, boisterous, frantic, often angry, but never depressed. This was a new development.

I spotted Mosh in the back, on the stage, all alone except for a stool, some pedals, a microphone, and his guitar. I was glad that it was dark and the lights were shining in his eyes. I was worried seeing me in the audience might have screwed him up.

My brother looked rough, worn down, tired. I was used to seeing him with a certain boundless enthusiasm, especially when he was playing. The look on his face was one of concentration, of frustration, not that zen look of *this is what I love* that he used to have. He'd been the best in the world at something, only that had been ripped away and stolen. The fun was gone.

He still sounded great. He'd never been proud of his vocals, but I'd always thought he had a good voice. Considering that he'd lost most of the feeling and dexterity in his fret hand, his playing sounded remarkably solid. It took me a second to realize what was different. He'd switched sides. He was playing the frets with his right hand. He'd re-taught himself how to play as a left-hander.

Mosh finished his sad song, looked up from his guitar, said "Thank you, Las Vegas." And then walked off the stage before anyone even realized they were supposed to clap. There were cheers and a chant for an encore, but there weren't going to be any encores tonight. My brother was done. Life had kicked his ass. When the lights came back on over the disappointed crowd, the stage was empty.

It was a real bummer of a finale.

A security guard wouldn't let me backstage. There was no need to complicate things so I didn't push it. I knew where he was staying. It had taken Melvin less than five minutes to get the room number for me.

There was another poster of Mosh in the elevator. This one was more recent than the older publicity poster in the entrance. I know it isn't cool for rock stars to smile in pictures, but here he just looked grim. No surprise. This was the best job he could find after getting kicked out of the band that he'd founded and dragged to the top. They'd said they didn't need his baggage. They were idiots. Sure, I was biased, but Mosh was a musical genius, brilliant performer, and sharp businessman. He had built Cabbage Point Killing Machine. They were nothing without him.

"Quit staring at me," I muttered at the poster.

Even though they'd been surgically reattached with *relative* success, having his fingers cut off by the cultists had ruined him. His guitar playing had gone to hell, and his life had followed along. Myers' cover-up had pinned the blame for the destruction in Montgomery on my brother's supposedly drug-addled misadventures. His name was mud, even by rock-star standards. Trashing a place was one thing, having several innocent people die because you'd gone crazy with the special effects and crashed a tour bus into a fuel tanker was something else entirely. He'd avoided criminal charges—only because the MCB didn't want anyone saying anything too crazy in court about two rampaging oni—but the avalanche of lawsuits had bankrupted him. Their record label had gotten sick of the bad publicity, and now CPKM was floundering along with a new guitarist who couldn't hold a candle to my brother.

So Mosh was reduced to washed-up celebrity status, playing at a shitty casino to pay the bills, and it was entirely my fault. When they couldn't get at me, the Condition had targeted my family instead. I was the one they'd wanted, but Mosh had paid my price. It made me wish that I could bring Hood back from the dead so that I could kill him over again. Only this time I would make it hurt more.

I got off the elevator at the penthouse suite, still going over what I was going to say. *Hey, dude. Sorry knowing me absolutely ruined your totally awesome life. Oh yeah, and now I've got to kill Dad. So how you been?*

The hotel had probably been very nice when Sinatra was still singing here, but it hadn't been remodeled since then. The carpets were dingy. The wallpaper was cracked. I'd heard they were talking about knocking it down and putting up a new casino on the valuable real estate. Many of the traditionalists wanted to save this place out of a sense of nostalgia. Those people probably hadn't been inside recently, because this dump was ready for the wrecking ball. I knocked. Nobody answered the door. He probably wasn't back yet, so I settled in to wait.

Just what I needed, more time to think.

Ten minutes later the elevator returned, and when the doors slid open, my brother came out with a girl under each arm. The women weren't exactly dressed for the church choir, were medium attractive, seemed a little tipsy, and Mosh already had lipstick smears all over his neck. Even being a washed-up rock star had its perks.

"Hey."

Mosh looked up from his distractions and saw me. Surprise registered on his face for just a second before he forced a smile. "Hey, bro." The greeting was awkward. "What're you doing here?"

"In town for a convention . . . I'm staying at the Last Dragon." I nodded at the party girls. "Bad time?"

His thick eyebrows drew together into an angry V. "It's all bad times now." His left hand was resting on one woman's bare shoulder and his fingers twitched inadvertently. "Ever since . . . you know . . . Ladies, this is my big brother Owen. I owe him *so* much."

"Your brother?" Even the groupies sensed the sudden tension. "You guys do look kind of alike."

"He looks more like Mom," I said. "Sadly, I take after our Dad."

"I always was the *lucky* one."

This had been a bad idea. I looked at the ugly carpet. "You know, I'll just come back later."

"Naw, it's cool," Mosh said, sounding resigned. "I can't avoid you forever."

"We've got some more girlfriends downstairs. We can call them and throw a party," suggested one of the aspiring brain surgeons. "Your brother's sort of cute."

Now she was just lying. I was a lot of things, but *cute* wasn't one of them.

"Don't waste your time. My brother here's not the party type. Owen is married to an absolutely stunning, beautiful, loving, completely homicidal woman. Did you girls know that my brother is a professional Monster Hunter? For real . . . He kills monsters for a living. Dude's like a superhero. He's killed werewolves, zombies, vampires, you name it."

"Mosh, please . . ."

"Nuh-uh."

"No way." Giggle.

"Yeah, way. All that stuff is real. See, but this one time Owen pissed off this ancient squid god from outer space. That's how I really lost my fingers. Asshole death cultists kidnapped me and took them off with a hacksaw blade. That bus accident was just a bunch of lies. Huh, Owen? Tell them."

MCB would drop him like a hot rock if he kept this up. "You trying to get in trouble? You know how the system works."

"The system? Oh, yeah, I know all about the *system*. The system is why I'm here now. Yeah, ladies, monsters are real. Straight from your worst nightmares, things you can't even imagine, but my big brother *protects* us from them. Huh? Tell them, Owen. Let us hear your tales of glory."

"Shut up."

He pointed at the nylon bag I had over one shoulder. "You got Abomination in there? Going to go save the day, dispense some *monster justice*? That's what really happened in Montgomery. This giant red monster and his purple bitch sister, they killed those people, not me."

One bimbo was giggling hysterically, but the other one was actually paying attention, eyes wide, looking between me and my brother. She actually seemed rather perceptive for someone with a nose piercing.

"You keep talking like that in public and the MCB—"

"The MCB will what? Ruin my life?"

"They'll *end* your life, dumb shit."

Mosh let go of the girls. He couldn't hide the anger anymore. "You—"

"We need to talk." I cut him off. If he wanted to have a fight, we should at least do it someplace private. "It's important."

"Oh, really? Whose life are you planning to wreck this time?" Mosh sneered.

"Dad's."

He stopped, closed his eyes, took a deep breath, then rubbed his face with both hands. Knowing Mosh, he'd either calm down or take a swing at me. I got lucky. Once he composed himself, he addressed the groupies. "Diane, Cindy . . ."

"Cathy."

"Yeah, whatever. I've got to jet. Family business. Sorry." He pulled two red tickets out of his vest. "These are good for drinks on me at the bar downstairs. Enjoy yourselves. I'll catch you ladies after another show."

The groupies made disappointed noises. "Do they validate parking?" Cathy asked, but Mosh was already steering them back toward the elevator.

He roughly bumped into my shoulder as he passed. "Thanks for ruining my evening." He unlocked his door, I followed him inside, and he slammed it shut behind us. "You're an asshole."

"I didn't mean to interrupt your *date*."

"How'd you find me?"

"Your show isn't a secret. Big sign out front. I even saw your face on a taxi."

"How'd you know my room number?"

"If you would've returned my calls, I wouldn't have had to have my IT troll hack into the hotel computer."

Mosh just shook his head, stomped across the suite, and flopped onto the couch. "Make it quick. I'm busy."

I took in the surroundings. The place was a mess. Mosh had never been what I would've described as tidy, but this was the room of someone who just didn't care. There was a pink bra hanging from the ceiling fan. Discarded takeout boxes were piled on the counter, and the coffee table was covered in many empty and partially empty liquor bottles. "This place doesn't have maid service?"

He put his gigantic leather metal-studded boots on the table. "I put out the sign. Do not disturb. Been disturbed enough lately." Mosh sighed. "Sit already. You standing there just pisses me off more. All looming like that."

Abomination's bag went on the carpet. I sat on the loveseat across from him. "You're just bitter that I got the tall genes." I had him by a few inches.

"You got the stupid genes too...What do you want?"

"I've been trying to get a hold of you." This was worse than I'd expected. Him sitting there glaring at me wasn't helping. We hadn't talked much lately. He'd been pretty charged up at first, thinking he was going to overcome adversity and all of that type of thing. He had even joked around about applying for MHI, but then the constant smears, negative publicity, and avalanche of lawsuits had slowly ground him down. "I've been worried."

Mosh snorted. "I'm a nobody musician. I'm a has-been. Why worry about me? You're Mr. Dangerous. You're the Chosen One."

"Yeah, it's a real picnic. Look, man, you know I'm sorry about—"

"I don't want to hear it."

We sat there in an uncomfortable silence. There was an acoustic guitar leaning on the arm of the couch. Mosh picked it up, and began to strum it absently.

I looked at the bottles. There were a lot of them. "Drink all that yourself?"

"None of your damned business. Is this an intervention? Is that why you're here, Owen?"

"Two things . . ." I would tackle the easy one first, I'd get to killing Dad in a minute. "You dropped off the face of the Earth. You haven't talked to anybody. We're worried—"

"I'm fine." Pitts are such terrible liars.

"I know you've been through a lot. I can help out."

His face turned red. "I don't want your money."

He had taken that entirely the wrong way. "That's not what I meant." Mosh watched me for a bit, trying to decided if I was intentionally trying to offend him or not, then turned away from me and started playing a song, something familiar, from when we were kids and he'd been taking classical lessons. It sounded amazing. Almost as good as before. "I heard you play tonight. You sounded good."

"It was pathetic."

"Naw, it was great."

"You're deaf. Always have been. It's from all that shooting. This? This is trash. This is embarrassing."

The tune he was playing now was incredibly complicated, and his fingers were flying back and forth with blinding speed. It was amazing, and he was doing it all with the wrong hand. I didn't try to talk, I just listened, hoping that he would open up. I watched the scowl of concentration on his face grow deeper, and then I understood what was wrong.

It was beautiful, haunting, better than anything almost anyone else would ever be capable of producing, but it wasn't *perfect*. He wasn't now, and probably never would be, as good as he'd once been. And that was killing him.

"I'm impressed," I said quietly.

Mosh struck one last harsh, discordant note, then took the acoustic guitar by the neck and swung it against the table. Bottles bounced across the room. The guitar flew away in pieces. He stood up, fists clenched, veins popping out in his neck, and shouted, "I don't want your pity!"

I got up and got in his face. "Then stop being pathetic."

Mosh's teeth were clenched and I got ready for him to hit me. "You ruined me, Owen! Is that what you want to hear? You want to rub it in? I had everything. Now I'm nothing, and it's all your fault!"

"I know." I had also tried to trade my life for his, but now wasn't the time to bring that up. "I was the target, not you. I'm sorry."

He glared at me for a long time, nostrils flared, and I wondered if that was how I looked when I got mad.

"I'm sorry," I repeated.

"I wish it was that easy. It's not just you." Mosh broke away and began pacing. "*They* wrecked me. They wrecked my name. They wrecked my career. Everyone thinks I'm a scumbag. Sure, I've done some crazy things. I've had some fun. But I never hurt anybody. Now everyone thinks I'm the kind of guy that can just negligently kill a bunch of people, but I'm not going to go give some public, weepy apology for something I didn't do, so now, even worse, I'm a heartless bastard negligent murderer. MCB's happy. The bunch of lying bastards."

"That's what the MCB does," I agreed.

"Like you can talk. You're a liar too. You lie about everything you do! Your whole life is one big lie." He continued pacing and yelling at me, calling me every name in the book, but I just took it. He needed to get it out. I could tell he was starting to cry a bit, but trying to hide it. "You play their game. You take their money. How are you any better than them?"

I didn't have a good answer. Like he'd believe me if I told him I'd do this for free anyway. I shrugged. "Someone has to do it."

"Thought so." Once he'd railed against me and the government, he got to the Sanctified Church of the Temporary Mortal Condition, the entity that had physically dragged him into this world to begin with. "And the cult. They're still out there. You know it, I know it." The pacing stopped. "It was awful. They tied me to a chair. Then that evil psycho British chick sawed my fingers off! She laughed while I screamed! She thought it was *fun*. She thought it was fucking hilarious."

He had never talked about the actual act before. I hadn't known that it had been Lucinda who had done the actual dirty work. I'd managed to kill almost everyone else involved, but she'd managed to get away. Copper Lake had proved she would continue to be a thorn in our side. "She's evil. She helped murder half a town in Michigan last winter. Next time we run into her, she's dead. I promise."

"You know the worst part . . ." he sniffed. "After they beat the hell out of me, but before they took my fingers off, she asked me for my autograph. I thought she was just a kid. I thought, what's someone like her doing here? Wanted me to sign a CD, believe it or not. Said she was a big fan."

"Did you?"

"I was too traumatized not to. I bet she just sold it on eBay." Mosh laughed hard, then wiped his eyes. "Look at this dump! This is my life now. As soon as I make a dime somebody else sues me for it, and all I can do is say yes, you're right, no contest, Your Honor, because if I don't, if I tell the truth, then the MCB shoots me. You don't know what it's like. I had everything! Nice house, nice cars, beautiful women. Everything."

"So they took your Ferrari—"

"It was an Aston Martin!" he corrected me quickly. "It was a Vanquish and it was *sweet*."

"And you can be a big crybaby about it and drink yourself to an early death or you can cowboy up and move the hell on."

"Up yours . . . Move on, doing what? You trying to recruit me again?"

I shrugged. "Why not? It's important work. You know what's really out there now."

"I wish I didn't."

"If wishing worked, you'd still have your Aston."

Mosh picked up the remains of the broken guitar. "I'm not like you, Owen."

"No, you're not. First off, you're better looking. But really, Dad taught you the same things he taught me. Hell, Mosh, my current teammates were a high-school teacher and a stripper. Growing up in Pitt family boot camp makes you Chuck Norris in comparison." That was a complete lie, since Holly was the hardest mortal human I knew and Trip was as reliable as the sunrise, but I was trying to build my brother up, not tell him that my teammates would eat him for breakfast.

"You were the tough one, not me."

Now it was my turn to laugh. "I'm the one that fell into line and did exactly what Dad told me to do. You're the one that had the guts to do your own thing. That makes you brave. I didn't stop listening to him until after you'd told him to get lost and followed your own dream. Standing up to Dad? Screw fighting monsters. *That's* tough."

Anger temporarily spent, Mosh seemed deflated. He returned to the couch. "It's been one hell of a year."

"I can't argue with that." *And now here comes the hard part.* "Speaking of Dad..."

He knew the basics about Dad's letter and his cryptic warnings, but not the specifics. Mosh was suddenly suspicious. "What? Is it that thing in his head?"

"Sort of. The symbol he warned me to watch out for. I found it tonight." I told him briefly about the containment chamber, but didn't give too many details. If he was stupid enough to haphazardly mention the existence of monsters in front of some random bimbos, talking about the Scary Zone was sure to put him on

Agent Franks' to-do list in no time. I had no idea how
many witnesses Franks had actually murdered, or if
his epic intimidation skills usually did the job, but I
had no doubt if Mosh kept talking about monsters,
one morning he would *accidentally* cut his own head
off while shaving.

"So what does this mean? Is Dad going to just . . .
croak?" He focused on a stain on the carpet and
randomly rubbed at it with his boot. "Why does this
have to be our family?"

I wish I knew. "It's way bigger than us. I've got
no choice. I have to find out."

"He'll die."

"I know, but if I don't, and something he knows could
mean the difference between winning the apocalypse or
not, what am I supposed to do? If I don't do anything,
everyone dies. Does Dad seem like the kind of guy to
exaggerate about it being the end of the world?"

He looked up from the stain. "You're supposed
to be the Chosen One. You've done everything they
wanted. Can't you cut a deal with them?"

"I don't even know who *them* is."

"Find out then!" Mosh's rage came back with a
vengeance. "Find out, tell them you'll kill whoever this
new guy is, but they have to leave us alone! It's all
about you, but it's everyone around you that suffers.
Me, now Dad, even your wife—Yeah, I heard some
of your people talking after your buddy Sam's funeral.
Even Julie, she's got some kind of evil curse on her."

I lowered my head. "It's not like—"

"Fuck you, Chosen One. It's all about you, but it
was those poor orcs that got their village burned down
and their kids murdered."

He was right. Didn't mean it didn't hurt to hear it. I got up. "We're done."

"Run away then, hero." Mosh stood up too. "You're just going to let Dad die for you, too."

"I'll do what I have to."

"You always say that. That's so simple when it's everybody else doing the suffering. You get to save the day but ruin everyone around you. You're cursed as bad as your wife. Maybe when she dies because of you, you'll understand how the rest of us—"

I punched him square in the mouth.

Mosh caught the edge of the coffee table, took out the remaining bottles, tripped and landed on his butt. I stood over him, fists clenched. He started to get up. "Don't..." He saw the look on my face and knew he'd pushed the last wrong button. "Just don't."

My brother wiped the blood from his split lip with the back of his hand. "Get out."

The sack of guns and armor went over one shoulder. At the door, I took one last look at my brother, sitting on the floor of a ratty hotel room. Cheeks burning, hand stinging, I made it into the hall.

That hadn't gone well at all.

CHAPTER 10

The mood back at the Last Dragon was considerably brighter than at Mosh's place. The first thing I heard when the elevator opened on my floor was dozens of voices, awful drunken singing, and loud music.

Is that . . . polka? Sure enough, somebody had put on polka music to celebrate Grimm Berlin's victory. Lindemann's team was in the hall, each of them holding a gigantic beer stein, singing badly in German, while two athletic young women that I was fairly certain weren't Hunters danced around in full-on Oktoberfest lederhosen outfits.

Hugo, the Hunter that had finished off the giant spider, saw me, slapped me on the back, handed me a plate full of chopped sausages speared with toothpicks, then shouted *assist!* The other fifty or so people packing the hallway did so too. Apparently news of MHI's semi-useless gun run on the gas station had spread.

Lindemann's team was flush with cash from their big win. The various other Hunters packing the halls may have been disgruntled about losing, but the Germans had bought the booze, so everyone was happy. The bratwurst was actually pretty darn tasty, and I hadn't eaten since lunch. After a few seconds everybody went back to singing and ogling the dancing girls, so I was able to make my escape.

Apparently most of the Hunters attending the conference had been concentrated onto a few floors of the hotel, and there appeared to be half a dozen room parties going on. Doors open, groups of Hunters inside, some parties louder than others, ranging from drinking games—Green seemed to be holding his own against a big Russian—to some old cranky bastards playing poker. There were a lot of strangers present, and many of them were really good-looking women.

The first other MHI Hunter I spotted was Holly Newcastle. I almost didn't recognize her, since she'd done her hair and makeup and put on an outfit that was a lot tighter and more revealing than the body armor I was used to. Since she was almost like a sister to me, it was easy to forget that Holly was smoking hot. "Z! You're back."

I had to lean in to hear her over the noise. My career had left me with a bit of hearing damage. "Who are all these other people?"

"The babes?" She grinned. "I called some of the girls that I used to work with." I'd almost forgotten that this was Holly's hometown. "I told them that there was a party with a bunch of attractive, buff, and recently filthy rich German guys at it, which explains the Oktoberfest outfits. But they brought a few friends, who brought a few friends. You know how it goes... Say what you will about Hunters, but they do know how to have a good time."

Constant fear of imminent death will do that, I suppose. Cooper wandered past, chatting up a cute girl in a UNLV T-shirt, making up a story about the bruises on his face he'd picked up from Ultimate Lawyer, and when he saw me and Holly he gave us a thumbs-up and a goofy smile. It just wouldn't be a gathering of Hunters without hedonism and bad decision-making. "Where is everybody?" I asked. Holly jerked her head toward Earl's room at the end of the hall. "And why are you all dressed up?"

She smirked. "You realize this is our first night off in weeks? We're in sin city. I've lived here, worked here, but I've never been here and *wealthy* before." That was true enough. Hunting was a very lucrative business when done correctly. "I'm going to see how the other half lives. I'm going to gamble stupidly and not care, get comped fancy drinks with umbrellas in them, and meet handsome men with normal jobs. I'm going *out*. I'm going to have *fun*."

"Blowing up monsters *is* fun."

"You workaholics are all the same. Julie's with Earl and some of the others, still talking business. Trip's in heaven. He found a couple other kindred nerd spirits and they're upstairs playing role-playing games. I tried to get him to come with me, but he's too churchy. I think Vegas scares him. He might actually have fun or something. Milo's doing something to the chopper. Us saving that cop was good PR. The conference management actually gave permission for Skippy to land on the helipad on the roof. He was really pumped. Said he'd never landed on a big glowing shiny building before. Where'd you go?"

While she'd been talking I'd been eating the rest of the little bratwursts. I talked with my mouth full.

"Hung out with Franks in a chemical-weapons dump. Wrestled a ghoul. Busy night. I'll tell you about—"

"Later, Z. After the drinks with tiny umbrellas and lots of blackjack." Holly patted me on the shoulder and sauntered off.

Earl's door was blocked by the gigantic figure of Jason Lacoco, one of the only people present taller than me. He was simply standing there, thick arms folded across his chest, watching people with his one good eye. A woman approached and asked Lacoco something. He pulled out a tiny notebook, looked at it, confirmed she was on the list, stepped out of the way to let her pass, then went back to standing and glaring. Having been a bouncer myself, I recognized the stance. Lacoco was on guard duty.

I hadn't spoken with Lacoco since the buffet fight. The man was a convicted murderer and a thug. I had no idea what Earl Harbinger had seen in him, but I had to trust my boss's instincts. Earl did have an eye for talent, me, despite my early mistakes, being a perfect example. I wasn't looking forward to talking to Lacoco, especially since I was on such a roll with the whole interpersonal communication thing tonight, but I needed to report.

"Jason," I said to the giant. His misshapen head swiveled toward me. His shoulders were so big he didn't seem to have a neck. His lips parted, showing his teeth, but he stopped whatever words he'd been about to say. This man hated me.

He exhaled. "Harbinger's expecting you."

"Okay . . . I've been wanting to talk . . ."

"I've got nothing to say to you."

"Listen, Lacoco. We're both Hunters. We're on the same side. What happened before—"

He stepped out of the way and didn't say another word.

Well, at least we hadn't hit each other. By tonight's standards I'd call that a win. From the look in his real eye, I could tell that the two of us weren't done yet. I went inside.

Earl's room was just as packed as some of the other rooms that were holding parties, but this was no party. Apparently this had become the official command center for all the Hunters Earl had deemed "all right." Julie was in front, doing what she did best, coordinating, leading, and picking brains. Most of the MHI team leaders were present, as were several men and women that I recognized as management from some of the other companies. Lindemann was there, as was the large Pole from White Eagle, the woman from South Korea whose name I hadn't gotten yet was off to one side speaking to the head of the Japanese contingent. There were at least twenty people crammed into the suite. A few of the smaller American companies were represented, but I didn't see anybody from Paranormal Tactical. Good thing, because I'd simply *hate* to violate my restraining order.

The cartoon map that we'd stuck to the wall earlier now had a lot more pins in it. The smoke detector had been pulled out of the wall and craftily disabled in a way so as to not set the rest of them off. Earl wasn't the only smoker present. I swear, are there any Europeans who don't smoke? The room was swimming in fumes. Luckily the balcony door was open or my asthma would have been killing me.

Julie excused herself from the Australian boss when she saw me come in. I was sure glad to see her. "You're back." She gave me a hello kiss. "And you taste like bratwurst...Where have you been?"

"I went to talk to Mosh."

"From what you said on the phone, I figured that was what you were doing." Julie was truly fond of my brother and was genuinely concerned for his well-being. "How'd that go?"

"Not good. I wound up slugging him in the mouth."

"Really, Owen?" Julie put her hands on her hips. "Really? You know *tough love* is just an expression, right?"

I shrugged. "I'll tell you all about it later." Well, since she wouldn't approve of my actions, nor did I like to bring up her condition, I'd tell her *something*. "Has everyone heard about the symbol I found?"

Julie nodded. "As much as we could share without getting into all the *complicated* stuff."

"Appreciate it." I had enough problems without all these strangers knowing about the odd things that I'd accomplished. As Stricken had said, there were blank spots in my file, and I wanted to keep it that way. "So what's going on now?"

She pointed at the map. "We've made a gentlemen's agreement with about half the companies at the conference. We're going to share more information, especially about anything suspicious relating to this pattern. Lee got volunteered to coordinate and set up a sort of information clearinghouse. I think maybe we've even laid the groundwork to actually work together in the future. When the next event occurs, we're going to be ready to strike fast, anywhere in the world, and get some answers."

"Really?" That was good work for such a short amount of time. "Impressive."

There was a sudden bang as something hit the linoleum in the kitchenette, and then two men were shoving each other against the fridge. I recognized one from the company out of Tel Aviv, and he had a thin man with curly black hair in a headlock. "Isn't that the dude from Cairo?" The two of them were forcefully separated by some of the other Hunters.

"Damn it, Mustafa. Starting shit again? I warned you to be on your best behavior," Earl roared from across the suite. "Jason! Toss his ass out." Lacoco immediately came into the room, grabbed Mustafa by the belt, hoisted him off of the floor, and carried the sputtering Egyptian out into the hall.

"Eh . . . Maybe *impressive* isn't the best word." Julie said. "We still need to get the bugs worked out."

Since Earl had gotten everyone's attention anyway, he decided to address the entire room. "All right, Hunters. Today's been an educational day for us all. We know we're facing something big, but we'll just kick its ass back to hell just like every other bunch of supernatural yayhoos that have tried this sort of nonsense before. We've got a lot of work to do, but we've laid the foundation . . ." It was fascinating to see that even with a bunch of people that only knew Earl by reputation, he still somehow ended up being in charge. They were all listening intently and nodding along. Earl simply had that effect on Hunters. "But now I'm sick of y'all, so get the hell out of my room." There was general laughter, and then some more after the translators caught up. "Klaus here won the lottery today, so the drinks are on him." Lindemann did a little bow to the crowd. "No. Seriously. Beat it."

After the place had cleared out, I found Earl Harbinger back at the map. His whole manner had changed.

When he had the crowd, he had been in leadership mode, confident, assured, even a little cocky. Now Earl seemed distracted and dour, with half his attention wandering back to the map. "Don't fret over getting beat by Klaus. Trust me. Men like him were why World War II took so damned long to win. What've you got for me, Z?"

I quickly gave him a rundown of the night's events, the spider, and the empty containment unit. "Do you know what Decision Week is? I heard it mentioned a couple of times. I think the tank at Dugway was left over from it."

"Decision Week, huh? Cody around?" Earl looked to Julie.

She shook her head. "He's playing poker with some of the old-timers."

"That's where I should be . . . loafing around with the retirees . . . Decision Week is ancient history. I know a bit about it. It was a weapons program that went wrong back during the war."

"Why's it called Decision Week?"

"That's when the Manhattan project decided to go with atomic weapons instead of demons . . . Atom bombs are much safer. Desperate times called for desperate measures. They dabbled in all sorts of things, magic, transdimensional forces, fey, you name it, they fiddled with it there, until they had a few experiments get out of hand and lost a whole mess of scientists. MHI helped in the cleanup at Los Alamos. I was overseas at the time, so didn't participate. Way before his time too, but that's Cody's team contract, and he still takes care of the mad-science-related problems, so has studied up on the details."

"He might look like an old lumberjack, but Cody's

got two hard-science doctorates," Julie said. "If a monster seems to violate the laws of physics, he probably has an equation to explain why and how, and trust me, he'll write it on a dry-erase board and try to explain it to you."

"We'll bounce this stuff off him, see if any of it sounds like something he's heard of... Most of the stuff that our boys snuck out of the Los Alamos cleanup that wound up in the archives was way over my head, but Cody's read up on it. Continue."

I did. Earl didn't seem particularly surprised about the message Myers had wanted me to deliver. Every now and then he'd stop and ask a question or clarify something. I knew what Earl really wanted to ask about, but he refrained. "And sorry, Earl. Nothing at all about a red werewolf. She'd been there, but no idea where they went after Dugway."

"I figured as much..." He finally turned around and ground his cigarette into an ashtray. "Either Heather's team disappeared into the desert without a trace or Stricken was just yanking my chain, manipulating us for who knows what." Earl sighed. "Well, to hell with Stricken. To hell with Myers. To hell with the bunch of them. They take and take and take some more... Hunters bleed, and sacrifice, and die, all for a world that doesn't give a shit about us. They just assume we'll step up because we always have. Maybe one day we just won't bother."

I'd never heard him speak like that before. Earl Harbinger would never quit, never give up, the idea was inconceivable. My wife looked as concerned as I felt. "Earl, if there's anything we can do..."

"I'm just beat is all. We'll talk about it some more in the morning. Good night, Z."

CHAPTER 11

Julie awoke with a gasp. It immediately startled me wide awake. My hand landed on the long slide STI .45 resting on the nightstand. "What?" The alarm clock read 4:12 A.M. "What's going on?" It took me a second of fumbling in the unfamiliar hotel room to get the lamp turned on.

My wife was sitting up in bed, breathing fast, scanning the room nervously. Sweat was running down her neck. "Nightmare . . . I think." She found her glasses, put them on, then stopped, puzzled. She placed one hand against the black lines on her neck, then snatched it back as if she'd burned herself. She looked at me, eyes wide with surprise. "Something's wrong. Something's here. I can feel it."

"What?"

"It's like an alarm is going off on my skin." She sprang out of bed, whipped off her nightgown, and began pulling armor out from under the bed.

"Crap." None of us understood how any of this metaphysical stuff worked, but we knew some of the

Guardian's abilities had been passed on to her. If those evil lines were saying something was wrong, she didn't have to tell me twice. "Crap, crap, crap." I rolled out of bed and started getting dressed. I always left my clothes where I could find them fast, even in the dark. "What is it?"

"I can't tell." No matter where we were, or what we were doing, Julie always kept a loaded rifle under the bed. This one was her *Inside Gun*, a heavily customized Springfield SOCOM with a short sixteen-inch barrel and a red dot sight. It was a stubby version of her regular rifles. She had it out and leaning against the nightstand before she'd even started putting her socks on. "I just feel like something really bad is here."

"And people keep calling me the psychic," I said as I tied my boots. "Should we wake everyone up?"

"Give it a second," Julie said. "My neck's stopped tingling. Maybe it's nothing."

I kept gearing up, all the while hoping it was a false alarm. If Julie was wrong, maybe it had only been a bad dream caused by the celebratory bratwurst. Nothing would happen, we'd eventually go back to sleep, and laugh about it in the morning. Well, probably not laugh, since being marked by magic related to the foul Old Ones was never a laughing matter, but at least we would go back to sleep. Then I realized how freaking *cold* it was.

"Feel that?" Julie asked, and I could see her breath come out as steam.

"Yeah . . ." I read the numbers on the thermostat. The digital display said it was sixty-eight. Then it blinked and showed the time as 4:15, then it blinked again. Twenty-four degrees. "Holy moly." There were a few times in my life when I'd experienced this kind of rapid, unnatural temperature drop. None of them had ever been indicators of upcoming good times. "We've got incoming."

"Incoming what, though?" Julie said. "Here, buckle me." I helped her with her harness while she pulled out her phone and started typing. "I set up a company-wide alert earlier, just in case." My iPhone was sitting on the table, and it began to vibrate as it received her message a few seconds later.

"Clever. You're cute when you're paranoid."

"And freezing. Stupid magic warning thing should've told me to pack a sweater."

I was still buckling and checking mag pouches as we entered the empty hallway. Julie had just put her earpieces in. "Radio check. This is Julie, who's with me?" I hadn't gotten mine in yet, so I wasn't sure who responded, but she gave me a thumbs-up. She had somebody. "Gather in the halls. If you know where other Hunters are sleeping, wake them up... Yes, Green, wake the foreigners too. No, I'm not yelling." She rolled her eyes. "No. I don't know what it is... What's the temperature like on your floor? Okay." Julie looked back at me. "Fifteenth floor is good. Seventeenth floor is comfy... Sixteenth floor is unnaturally cold. It's here with us. Repeat, unknown entity seems to be on the sixteenth floor."

"Son of a gun," I muttered as I pulled back the charging handle on Abomination and chambered a round of silver buckshot. "Figures."

"Okay, Hunters above and below. Stop the elevators and seal the stairwells. There are... five stairwells and two—no, three elevators. Don't forget the freight one.

We are not letting this thing get away." She signaled for me to get my radio in, and while I did so she watched the hall. "Watch your shots. There are a lot of innocents here."

I got my earpieces in place, and all sound took on a slight bit of distortion from the electronic amplification. They weren't crystal perfect, but I could hear my teammates and protect my hearing from gunfire at the same time. I touched Julie's arm to demonstrate that I was good to go. She nodded. The door across from us opened and Trip came out, wearing the top half of his armor, but only a pair of basketball shorts and flip flops. "Late night?" I asked Trip. "Did you level up your paladin?"

"Paladin? No. I was playing Warmachine. There's no . . . Never mind . . . How the heck did you get dressed so fast? My gosh. Do you sleep in this stuff?"

Our hotel deal had been mostly for rooms with two queen-sized beds, so Milo was Trip's roommate. He came out a moment later, slapping a magazine into an M-4. His beard was particularly puffy and terrifying when it hadn't been groomed yet. "What've we got?" He too, had only gotten part of his gear on.

"Dude . . . You have flannel footy jammies?"

Milo looked down. "Yeah, aren't they nifty? Shawna got them for me for my birthday."

"Shhh." Julie held one finger up to her lips. We fell silent. She pointed down the hall toward one of the other doors. I couldn't tell what she was seeing. She keyed her microphone. "Something's going on in 1613. Checking it out."

I leaned in close to my wife. "What is it?"

"Look at the carpet."

I'd been studying the door. I hadn't noticed the floor. The carpet around 1613 seemed darker. I took another step and the carpet squished damp underfoot. As I moved, the light glistened off of what appeared to be water running out from under the door.

Milo had noticed it too. "Wet and cold monster stuff," he whispered. "We'll see who's laughing at my warm footy pajamas soon enough."

"Wake up whoever's next door and let's get them out of there. This might be ugly," Julie suggested. Milo took one side and Trip took the other, knocking loudly, as me and Julie slowly approached 1613. "Whose room is this?"

I'd walked right past this after leaving Earl's last night. This had been one of the party rooms. "One of Grimm Berlin's, I think." The stuff trickling out from under the door looked like normal water, nice and simple, like maybe the toilet had backed up. Nothing supernatural at all, except the carpet was already coated with a sheen of ice.

Nate Shackleford had come around the opposite corner. Julie signaled for her brother to knock on the doors on that side. Jason Lacoco arrived a moment later. *Great.* Not my first choice of who I wanted at my back if something went down. There was some angry swearing in Spanish as Milo roused the first of the other occupants.

There was a loud grinding noise from inside the 1613, like someone was dragging a piece of heavy furniture. All of the Hunters in the hallway tensed.

Julie got back on the radio. "Earl, something's going down. We're going in."

"Hold on. I'll be there in a second," Earl responded.

There was a shriek of terror on the other side of the door. "Someone's hurt. Going in now," Julie shouted. I tried the doorknob. It was so cold I could feel it through my glove. Of course it was locked and needed a key card.

"Somebody else go, then. Julie, stay put. It's too dangerous."

"What?" Julie's mouth fell open. "You...what?" I was as stunned as she was. Julie wasn't exactly some delicate flower. She was always wherever it was the most dangerous. She'd been hunting monsters since she was a teenager. Earl had never coddled her before. My wife's surprise turned to fury. "Sorry, Earl, you're breaking up."

"Hold on! That's an order."

"What's his problem?" She let go of her mike and looked at me. "Kick it."

"Love to." The lights would probably be off inside, so I turned on Abomination's flashlight. Julie moved out of my way, covering me with the Springfield. I raised one size-fifteen boot and let it fly. The hotel door was really solid, but I was big, excited, and the deadbolt ripped right through the jamb. The door flew open with a bang, with me and Abomination one step behind it.

I skidded to a wet halt. Too surprised and confounded to move forward. "Fuck me..."

The water wasn't from an overflowing toilet or a busted pipe...It was from the *river*. The fifty-foot-wide, gray, frothy *river* that I was standing on the grassy bank of. I looked down. The tan hotel carpet simply terminated in a straight line and on the other side was dead winter grass. I looked up. There was ceiling, regular old, textured white ceiling... and then it, too, ended in a straight line, and past that there were *stars*. It was a wide-open night sky, and it sure as hell wasn't in Las Vegas. To the side, there were no walls, there were *trees*. Inside room 1613 was a river and a forest, at least as big, if not bigger than the entire casino we were supposedly in.

The hotel room wasn't simply gone, it was like it had never been here, and I'd stepped through that doorway into a whole new world.

Julie was right behind me. She collided with me. "What the—" I could hear Milo, Trip, and Nate behind us. They could all see it too. I hadn't just lost my mind. "Back up. Back up!" Julie ordered. I was glad to get back on the carpet.

"I just looked inside the room next door. There's no giant forest in that one," Milo said. The space which should have held that room was a copse of dense, gnarled, gray trees. "This is *bad*."

As bizarre as this was, I'd seen something similar a couple of times, extra-dimensional spaces grafted onto an earthly entrance. "Pocket dimension?"

"They don't normally appear out of nowhere," Julie said.

"Got a better explanation—" There was a scream to my right. The coat closet opened and the source of the scream nearly got ventilated by several very jumpy Hunters. A woman fell out amidst a clatter of clothes hangers and the ironing board. "Help! Help me! It got him!" She was hysterical.

"Who's she?" Julie asked, Springfield shouldered, ready to blast the stranger.

I recognized the silly, skimpy, and now soaked and

Larry Correia

muddy Oktoberfest outfit. It was one of the dancers. "She's from the party. Trip, grab her."

Trip took her by the arm and helped her up. She was hysterical. "It's coming back. It's coming back!"

"What's coming back?" Julie asked calmly.

"It. Hugo called it *Nachtmar* before it . . . it got him! The metal with the worm in it, and the bones, and, and . . ." She pointed at the river and screamed incoherently.

Something had appeared in the swirling, muddy water. At first it was just a dark spot, easily lost between the currents, but then it was heading our way, slowly, deliberately. A sharp point appeared. The incoherent screaming was getting on my nerves. "Get her out of here, Trip!" The point grew into a single black horn, then the water split around a wider shape made of decaying metal. It was moving along the riverbed, climbing out of the water, gradually coming right at us. "We've got company."

The others had crowded in around me in the narrow space between the coat closet and the bathroom. There was a clatter as guns were readied. "Hold your fire," Julie ordered. "We don't know what we're dealing with."

More of the head broke the surface, revealing a metal helmet, decorated with spikes and antlers and horns, but much larger than it needed to be to fit a human head. With each step it would bob into the water, then come back, and a little bit more would be revealed. There was a slit for the eyes, but only a cold blackness behind, there was a gash for a mouth, stained with rust. More spikes appeared as broad, razor-studded shoulders emerged. It was like a medieval suit of armor, only misshapen and twisted, broken, reformed, and then *sharpened*. Another step and its chest came out, the metal rent open, revealing white humanoid ribs, tangled with rotten fabric and frayed rope. Behind the ribs was a heaving, pulsing, translucent gray *sack*, like an unnatural organic engine.

Waist-deep in the river, it lifted one gauntleted hand to display the jagged remains of a great sword. The other hand rose, holding the severed head of the German Hunter, Hugo. It showed the head to us, displaying it like a trophy.

"I'd say we know now," I shouted.

"Fire!" Julie commanded.

I put the holographic reticule of my EOTech on the monstrosity and let Abomination roar. The other Hunters did the same. The muzzle blast from so many guns in such close proximity was brutal. The armored monstrosity shuddered and wheezed as hundreds of projectiles slammed into it. Holes puckered in the metal. An antler snapped off. Bullets hit the gray organic mass inside, but rather than puncture through, they impacted, deformed the surface, but didn't penetrate. A terrible shriek came from the monster. I kept pulling the trigger, hammering alternating rounds of silver buckshot and heavy slugs into my target until the firing pin landed on the empty chamber with a sharp *click*.

It reeked of unburned powder and fear in the narrow space. As the guns fell silent and everyone scrambled to reload, the creature began walking slowly toward us again. Hugo's head was discarded and swept away by the current. "The door's a choke point. Fall back," Julie said.

The weight of the Hunters around me broke and moved away. "I got this," I said as I broke open the new grenade launcher mounted under Abomination's handguard. Milo hadn't been able to come up with a steady supply of the Russian grenades, so I'd switched to an American-made M203. Normally, firing a grenade launcher at a target inside the same hotel room would be suicide, except this hotel room was now the size of a park, and the metal monstrosity was just far enough away that I could blast it and not be hit myself with shrapnel. I dropped a hefty 40mm shell in and slid the launcher shut.

BLOOP. The grenade hit the creature square in the chest and detonated in a flash of smoke. The explosion knocked it back into the river with a ponderous splash.

"Suck it!" Nate shook his fist. "How you like us now?"

The thing thrashed and clawed its way out of the mud. Metal creaked as it stood back up. It had shrugged off a direct hit from a 40mm. As disturbing as that fact was, the other dozen or so horns, antlers, and points popping up in the water behind it was much worse. It had brought friends.

"Fall back!" Julie shouted as she rocked another mag into her rifle.

I lumbered out of the room, yanking open a grenade pouch on my armor. Trip and Milo had taken up positions on either side of the door, and after I passed by, they started shooting.

Nobody in the hotel had slept through that. Hunters from all over the world were coming into the hall, trying to figure out what was going on. Lindemann pushed past the crowd, armed with nothing but a pistol and wearing one of the hotel bathrobes. "That's Hugo's room. What is going on?"

"Unknown monsters," Julie said. "Looks like a pocket dimension opened up inside."

"I must retrieve them—"

I blocked his way. "Hugo's dead."

"No. It can't be." Lindemann was shocked. "You are certain?"

I nodded. "It chopped his head off."

"I must see." He swatted my arm away with surprising strength. He reached Milo, and when he saw what was inside, began swearing vehemently in German. It was hard to hear him between the gunshots. He turned to Julie. "It is the beasts from Stuttgart!"

"What?"

"We have fought these before. The Stuttgart Massacre, but this is impossible."

Earl Harbinger arrived. "I told you not to go in!" Earl snapped at my wife, but rather than continue on that futile path, he got right down to business. "What've we got?"

Julie began to explain. When Trip and Milo ran their guns dry, Lacoco and Nate took their place. More Hunters were filing down the hall with heavier weapons. I have no idea how the big Pole had managed to get a PKM into the country, but I was glad to see a belt-fed. Word of what was happening had spread quickly. The rooms on either side were secured, the alien forest that had somehow invaded our hotel hadn't spilled through the walls. Instead, a single, maybe five-hundred-square-foot room was holding several acres of forest.

Lacoco was firing a Remington 870 as fast as he could pump the action at the cumbersome monster. When he clicked empty, I grabbed him by the shirt and yanked him away before he even realized he'd run dry. He snarled at me but I shoved him aside. Personal beefs could wait. This was business. "Move your ass, Newbie!" I shouted as I took his spot. "Reload that gun!"

Half a dozen silver slugs later I got my first indication

that shooting these things wasn't completely futile. The original monster had been practically chewed into scrap by our small-arms fire, and collapsed in a clanking and wheezing heap twenty feet from the door to our reality. The metal shell had been hammered so badly that it was simply not capable of further movement. "Good news! They can be stopped."

"Bad news is that I see at least ten more coming," Nate warned.

The gray, seemingly bulletproof tumor that had been stuck inside the chest cavity of the first creature slid out into the grass. The disgusting blob was alive, and squealed in an obnoxious high pitch as Nate hit it with several rounds of .308. The slug was the size of a calf, and it oozed and rolled itself back toward the river, leaving a steaming trail of blood and mucus behind.

"Oh, that is just nasty," I growled as I launched another grenade into the approaching wall of iron. "The slugs in the torso are driving the suits. Next!" I shouted as I moved away.

The big man from Poland took my spot. He hadn't even bothered to put on a shirt before coming to fight. The tattoo of linked ammo he had around one big bicep matched the belt hanging from the Russian machine gun at his side. His booming laugh made me think of a pirate captain. "I got out of bed with many beautiful women for *this*?" He fired from the hip, working the PKM side to side. Despite the lack of aiming or fire discipline, he wasn't missing, and there was a continuous stream of clangs as bullets struck metal. The dude was good with a machine gun.

Earl was shouting orders. Lindemann interrupted him by tugging on one sleeve of his Minotaur-hide jacket. "Harbinger, listen to me. This is impossible. This cannot be happening."

"Get a hold of yourself, Klaus, your boy is dead—" The German leader hadn't struck me as the type to go into denial, especially at a time like this.

"I mean that this is an impossibility. This is some sort of magic trick. I know these beasts. We destroyed them years ago. They only come from one very specific place in my country. They cannot simply appear here."

"Well, they have."

"So it appears." Lindemann didn't sound convinced. "*Something* is here."

"Assuming these are your old pals, how do we kill them?"

"The suits are mecha-magical constructs. The creatures that live inside them are the intelligence and source of power. They are vulnerable to heat. They can only survive in cold and moist environments."

"They aren't going to like Vegas much," I said.

"Anybody got a flamethrower?" Earl shouted. The call was repeated, but sadly, even Hunters aren't prone to drag along anything that heavy, awkward, and potentially lethal on vacation. Plus, checking a flamethrower onto a commercial airliner is a pain in the ass. "Damn it. Find me some incendiaries. Make some Molotovs. Z, hold that doorway no matter what!"

The better-armed Hunters had formed a line to take a turn. Despite the language barrier, everybody had caught on pretty quick that we did not want whatever everyone else was shooting at in 1613 to get out. "Got it." A quick glance confirmed that the monsters were getting closer, but they were having to funnel toward us, and as the armor-piercing rounds took them down, they were being forced to clamber over the fallen. We were chewing them to bits.

But there were still more coming out of the river...

"Here! These should help." Esmeralda Paxton squeezed past the line of Hunters with an armful of liquor bottles and a set of curtains over one shoulder. She flipped open her knife and began slashing strips from the curtains. She handed me a bottle and a rag.

"Will this stuff burn?" I smelled it. *What was that, ninety proof?* "Gah, never mind." I stuffed the strip of curtain into the neck of the bottle and swished it around until it was soaked. I didn't smoke, but anybody who might need to set something or someone on fire should always carry a lighter. Before I could get mine out of my armor one of the Europeans reached over, flipped open a turbo lighter, and ignited the rag. "Thanks." And to think that I'd complained about all those annoying smokers earlier.

I hurled the Molotov through the doorway. It shattered against one of the fallen monsters and ignited its carapace. The creatures around it shrieked and pulled away. The alcohol burned far too quickly and the monsters were back on the move. "More!" I turned back to find that the Hunters without rifles or shotguns had formed an assembly line, cutting, stuffing, and lighting. A flaming bottle was waiting for me. Another two shooters cycled through as I took the second Molotov and chucked it at a different creature. It only burned for a few seconds of painful wailing. The dampness of the invading forest and less-than-ideal incendiaries was thwarting us. Two enterprising Australians had wrapped their curtains around lamps to make bundles and poured whiskey all over them.

I got out of the way as they lit them and tossed the blossoming fireballs into 1613. The slugs made a chorus of painful shrieks.

We were the very model of efficient monster killing.

"Coming through! Make a hole! Bomb coming through." Lee and Cooper were shoving their way down the hall, one dragging something big, the other pushing. The crowd parted and it was revealed to be the housekeeping cart.

Earl looked up, recognized his former Explosive Ordnance Disposal tech and his former Marine demolitions specialist, and smiled. "This should be interesting. Clear a path!"

Seeing who was involved, I was suddenly very nervous. The two of them stopped a few feet away. From the look of the cart, they had raided the janitor's closet for cleaning supplies. Lee began pouring a big jug of a clear liquid into the trash can. Cooper dumped in a five-gallon bucket of something red. Lee began to stir it with a mop handle. The two explosives experts seemed positively giddy. That was a bad sign. "Somebody order fire?"

"Everybody except the next shooters fall back!" Earl shouted.

Milo came over, read the label on one of the empty bottles, and nodded approvingly. "Ooh, good idea. Hey, did you guys notice all this laundry soap?"

"Brilliant!" Lee exclaimed as he snatched up a box.

"Fall *way* back!" Earl clarified.

"Don't worry. This should mostly just stick and burn rather than explode." He sounded very excited, and if Milo was excited, then we should probably evacuate the city. "Mostly."

If this was going to be it, I wanted to be where it was most dangerous, so I cut in line to be the last shooter. Lacoco took the other side. The nearest creature was only ten feet away, and as it took another halting, clanking step, I realized that the carpet in front of me was receding, almost as if the dead grass was consuming and replacing our reality. The bathroom was gone. There was a tree where the coat closet had been. Their world was growing. "Hurry it up!"

The housekeeping cart rolled on squeaky wheels until it was between me and Lacoco. Everybody else retreated. Cooper reached into his cargo pants and came out with a white phosphorus grenade. "My only one. This is our initiator." My team was the only one that had arrived directly off a mission, and with the corresponding armament. The rest were supposed to be on vacation. *How much deadly crap had Cooper stuck in his luggage?* "You'll probably want to chuck this thing as *far* as you can." He really emphasized the word *far*. "Ready?"

I looked at Lacoco. "Yeah." He put his shotgun down and took hold of one side of the cart.

The nearest monster was lifting a gigantic spiked mace over its antlered head. It would be on us in seconds. I grabbed the other side. The cart came off the ground easily enough. "Far as we can. Gotcha."

"Everybody take cover!" Earl warned.

Cooper yanked the pin on the hand grenade. The spoon popped off and he dropped it into the garbage can of chemical sludge with a *plop*. "Do it."

We hadn't exactly rehearsed this. There was no *one, two, three,* or an organized *heave, ho,* or any of that jazz. The fuse on a hand grenade is measured in a few short, very angry seconds. Lacoco and I both roared and flung the housekeeping cart as hard as we could. It sailed past the nearest monster, the lifeless helmet turning to watch it pass by, but then that was all I saw as Cooper reached out, grabbed the door, and yanked it shut.

"Get down!" Diving as far as I could, I hit the soggy carpet and covered my head.

FOOOOOOM!

The entire world shook, and the explosion was so loud that my hearing protection shut itself off for several seconds. The lights went out.

Somebody was coughing. Then I realized it was me. It was raining dust. Powerful flashlight beams appeared from both ends of the hall. Then something cold and wet was running under me. I rolled over and was glad to see that a pipe had busted in the ceiling and water was squirting into the hall, rather than it being the invader's river water. The door to 1613 had been blown out and smashed through the opposite wall. Two feet of wall on either side of the door had been turned into splinters, and drywall chunks and the soggy carpet had been peeled back and shredded.

I wasn't the only one coughing. The hallway was filled with a noxious smoke. I couldn't see into 1613 at all. A shape leapt through the smoke and ran into the blast area. "Clear!" Earl called out from inside the room.

"Clear as in they're all dead?" I shouted back.

"Clear as in they're *gone*. Status?"

"Good," I answered as I extricated myself out from under a few feet of building materials.

"I'm okay." Lacoco came out of the smoke covered

in dust and a trickle of red rolling down one cheek. He reached down for where he'd left his shotgun, but that whole section of wall was gone. He looked around and swore.

I shouldered Abomination, which was still faithfully tethered to my armor. "You'll want to put a sling on that. Losing guns gets expensive."

"Go to hell," Lacoco told me.

Cooper walked up, proudly surveying the damage. Lee joined him a second later, laughing his ass off. They high-fived each other. The fire alarm was an annoying *beep beep beep*. Thank goodness the sprinklers didn't go off, because that would have extra sucked. Hunters appeared through the haze, converging back on 1613. Earl walked out of the chaos, waving his hand in front of his face. "It's over," he assured everyone.

I breathed a sigh of relief. Julie reached my side and began running her hands around my head and neck. It wasn't out of tenderness, though. She was looking for injuries. Being right next to an explosion was always a bitch, and bleeding to death while you were in shock was always a possibility. Someone else was inspecting Lacoco. "I'm okay," I assured her.

"Uh-huh . . ." Now she was checking my arms for blood. "Keep talking. How's your head?"

"I told you I'm fine."

"What's the anniversary date of the first time we met?" she asked.

That was a terrible question to check for traumatic brain injury. "Uh . . ." I sucked with dates. "It's on the calendar?"

"Hah, gotcha," she grinned. "Owen's good."

"What happened to *mostly* fire, Milo?" Earl asked.

Milo peeked his head around the corner of the next room. "That was way more explodey than I expected. What brand laundry soap was that? Oh . . . wait a second . . . I was thinking of something else. Never mind."

The smoke cleared out quickly because there was a strong breeze. And when we could see again, the source of the breeze was fairly obvious. The pocket dimension, if that was what it had been, was gone. Room 1613 was back, but it was *toast*. The Cooper-Lee-Anderson insta-bomb had removed the windows, most of the back wall, and the balcony from 1613. The lights of the strip were bright through the gaping hole in the side of the hotel. The walls were shredded and blackened, the ceiling hung in tattered strips. The furniture was mangled.

Ten Hunters in various states of dress and preparedness swept into the room and secured it. There were no signs of the monsters, of the river or the forest, and especially no sign of Hugo. I walked to the edge of the remodeled outer wall and looked down. The balcony had landed in the pool. It was a good thing nobody had been swimming this early in the morning. There were a lot of flashing lights in the parking lot below as police cars and fire trucks arrived.

Trip joined me. He whistled at the destruction. "Between the buffet and this, I'm thinking we're not getting invited back next year."

CHAPTER 12

"Other than the water that leaked out, there's no evidence it was ever here. A whole forest comes out of nowhere and takes over. Monsters that shouldn't exist kill a Hunter and then disappear into thin air... I've never heard of anything quite like that before." Julie told the assembled decision-makers.

I was sitting on the burned remains of the hotel bed. Ten minutes ago it would have been in a magical river. "You're a master of understatement."

Lindemann was in the center of the room, picking through the debris. "There is no sign of Hugo. Damn it." He kicked the remains of a chair. "What is going on here?"

No one had a good answer for that.

The room was packed with lead Hunters from various countries. Many of our own experienced MHI staff were out running interference. We knew how to deal with American law enforcement much better than anyone else. The fact that there was an MCB contingent already in town was sure to complicate matters. They would probably be here shortly.

"We're missing a few Hunters, but those that are gone were seen leaving the party, some alone, some with new friends. None of the other companies seem to be missing anyone. So it seems that everyone is accounted for except Hugo," Julie explained. "Surrounding rooms weren't affected, just this one. But how and why? The only witness said Hugo called it *Nachtmar*."

"It means nightmare. That word will do as well as any other," Lindemann said. He tossed a chunk of broken wood into a puddle. "Fitting."

"You knew what these things were, Klaus?"

"They were the cause of the Stuttgart Massacre..." Most of the European Hunters began nodding and one of them crossed himself. "Grimm Berlin lost nearly half of our men."

I was unfamiliar with the event. Julie leaned over and whispered to me. "It's their equivalent to the Christmas party. Bad op."

Lindemann seemed haunted as he continued to poke through the debris. "The monsters had been created in a necromantic ritual several hundred years ago, designed to be immortal soldiers for Emperor Maximilian by a mad alchemist named Schreiber. Only a few were activated in that time, but the denizens that were grown to give them life proved to be far too bloodthirsty, and the rest were hidden away and buried, hopefully to never be used."

"I remember hearing that Maximilian's iron army was one of the mystical things the Third Reich was searching for." Earl should know. He'd been there, and had probably gotten that information firsthand, but since only a handful of us knew who he really was, that went unsaid.

"Which they never found, thankfully. It wasn't until ten years ago, when a new canal was being dug in the city and their chamber was accidentally flooded. The water released them from their slumber. The *Bundeswehr* asked for our expertise in the cleanup. Only the beasts escaped the tunnels and entered a neighborhood. It was...*horrific*...We destroyed them all, wiped them out completely, but in the process Hugo and I were all that survived from our team."

"That's why you said these things were impossible."

"The artistry of those creations is like a signature. Those were Herr Schreiber's work. There is no way that such a particular design could be recreated so accurately, so far away, and in such different circumstances. The alchemical methods were lost hundreds of years ago. It would be like us discovering a Wendigo in Italy or a mermaid in Mongolia. These were special, one of a kind, regional monsters. No, something else is afoot here."

"We should interview the woman Hugo was with," Pierre Darne suggested. He was a young man, but struck me as a competent leader, maybe a little nervous, but trying to hide it, sort of like Nate in that respect. He kept his manner professional, though I did notice that he wouldn't make eye contact with Earl Harbinger. Pierre even looked a bit like his deceased father, tall, thin, handsome, and with an aristocratic sort of air. "Perhaps she saw how it began?"

"She was pretty freaked out, though." I glanced at Trip. He was far more compassionate than most of us. If anybody could handle a shell-shocked stripper it was Trip. Holly was one of the Hunters that had gone out for the night and hadn't returned yet, but I could only imagine that she'd just slap the hysterical girl a couple of times and tell her to get a hold of herself. "You got this?"

"I've got it," my friend answered before walking out.

"So this is why government man pays ten million American dollars for a simple spider," the big Pole said. "I think maybe this case is not so simple after all."

Earl was nodding in agreement. "It has to be connected. That stupid critter didn't kill all those people today and disappear an entire Unicorn strike team."

"Unicorn?" several of the Hunters asked at the same time.

"Special Task Force Unicorn . . ." Earl answered. "Stricken's bunch. Shit. Forget I said that name. You don't want to go around repeating it. Real low-profile bunch. They're the ones that do the things you don't ask about. They make MCB look like Boy Scouts."

"How do you know this?" asked a muscular Greek Hunter who had come to the battle wearing nothing but his underwear.

"Never mind that." Earl was obviously regretting mentioning the name. "That's not important right now."

"You were so enthusiastic earlier about sharing information, but it seems you're the one keeping secrets from the rest of us." The Greek Hunter approached Earl. "MHI thinks they're better than everyone else. You're wrong, Harbinger. I think you are in league with the men from your government. I think you knew about this event beforehand."

One of the Chinese took the opportunity to jump in. "It was your men that sounded the alarm. How do you explain some of them already being armed and fully equipped so quickly?" He gestured at me and Julie.

"I sleep this way." I answered. "Doesn't everybody?"

The two questioners glowered at me. I couldn't help it. I was born to be a smartass.

Julie however, was a peacemaker. "I woke up from a bad dream. I had a real bad feeling is all, and I thought I heard something out of place. So we geared up. That's it."

"Convenient." The Greek Hunter walked threateningly toward Earl. "You take all of us for fools?"

"Them? No. You?" Earl took his time shaking a cigarette out of a pack and lighting it with his MHI Zippo. "Maybe . . . Back off, kid."

"I should give you a beating, Harbinger."

I didn't know who knew about Earl's secret here, but there were definitely rumors floating around about how dangerous he was. Many of the Hunters in the blasted room got sudden excited looks on their faces that read variations of *oh, no, he didn't* or *this ought to be good.*

Earl simply blew smoke in the angry Hunter's face.

"Sit down, idiot," Lindemann shouted before the Hunter could take a swing at my boss. The German came over and shoved the Hunter back. "You are no match for him, and your stupidity is wasting our time." That seemed to cow the man. He may not have known Earl, but all of the Europeans knew the man from Grimm Berlin. Lindemann turned back to Earl. "I lost a brother tonight, Harbinger. I would appreciate you focusing on the task at hand."

"Sorry, Klaus. Accusations get my dander up."

"Dying pointlessly has the same effect on me. What else do you know?"

"Hugo was the one that killed the monster today, and now this . . ." Earl waved his hand around the blasted room. "I think he brought something back with him from the desert. I just don't know what, but I bet I know who does. I think Stricken set us up."

"Stricken," the Pole spat. "I will gut him like pig."

"Get in line," Earl said. "I should've considered this possibility. Today's case wasn't about a single creature, it was related to some kind of phenomenon. I assumed whatever it was had been left out in the desert, not dragged back here with us. This is my fault. I shouldn't have made assumptions. I was distracted."

"That doesn't matter now," Pierre Darne said. "My concern is that this may happen again."

"It's possible. One of my men travelled with Agent Franks from the Monster Control Bureau to where the creature originated from. Knowing what we know now, I think he might have experienced something related. Owen, report."

"Can do." I gave them the quick rundown about what I'd seen in Dugway. It only took a few minutes. I could tell that many of them were angry that they hadn't heard this several hours ago, but we hadn't known then that the damn whatever-it-was was here with us at the time.

"The ghoul . . . It appeared, attacked, and then was gone," the Pole stated.

I knew where he was going. "Sounds familiar, doesn't it? What happened here was far more elaborate. The thing that jumped on me only lasted for a few seconds, and there was only the one." If my fists weren't still sore from punching it I could almost have dismissed it as a figment of my imagination. "Tonight was a whole lot nastier."

"I have a theory . . ." Julie began.

"I've got my own theory." The Greek Hunter had decided he wasn't finished and stormed back to the center of the room. "A portal appears and kills off MHI's competitors. Then, since they were the only ones that were prepared, MHI banishes the creatures, saves the day, and I'm sure will claim the bounty. They are heroes. Their competitors are gone. It is all too convenient."

There was a lot of murmuring at that. Most of the other leaders seemed annoyed or incredulous, but a few looked intrigued at the idea. "That's ridiculous," I said, sick of his crap. "You seriously need to shut the hell up before you get hurt."

"You're not in charge here. I don't have to listen to you."

"Well, I'm wearing an automatic shotgun while you're just wearing tighty-whiteys, so you might want to start."

There was a reason that Julie was our negotiator. She stepped between us. "I can assure you MHI had nothing to do with this." Despite being frustrated, she was still trying to hold together the fragile alliance she'd helped form earlier. "If we were trying to get our competitors killed, why'd we sound the alarm and start an evacuation?"

"I don't understand your plot yet, but it wouldn't be the first time MHI has opened a portal. The bastard Ray Shackleford did it once." He said, glaring at Julie. "It wouldn't surprise me to find out that his daughter followed in his footsteps."

Wrong answer. My wife lost it. Julie extended her fingers and ridge-handed him in the throat. The Hunter opened his mouth, but all that came out was a long wheezing noise. Julie stepped back as he reached for her, but you don't go very far without much oxygen. He doubled over, clutching his neck as his face turned red. He'd gone full-on purple by the time he laid down on the floor and concentrated on not passing out.

He was still breathing, just not well. "Wow . . ." I said. "What's that little tiny fragile bone in the neck called?"

"The hyoid. Don't worry. I pulled it. He'll be fine, but the next person that brings up my parents won't be." Her accent tended to get a little stronger when she was under stress but trying to hide it. Julie looked around the room, seemingly calm. "Anybody else want to accuse me of witchcraft? Because we can get that nonsense out of the way *real* fast." The Hunter from China was quiet as Julie stared him down. "Good."

The big Pole boomed out his pirate-captain laugh. "I think our friend here needs some fresh air." He grabbed the downed Hunter by the ankle and dragged him effortlessly toward the door. "And maybe also a medic."

Dominance established. "As I was saying before I was interrupted, I've got a theory . . ." Julie checked to make sure nobody else was going to say anything. Nobody was that stupid. "I think the spider, the ice ghoul, and these armored things were all caused by the same phenomenon. One of our men found the video the victim in Nevada had been watching before he'd been killed. It was called *Terrorrantula*."

"I love that one!" The Australian leader proclaimed. "It was mostly sheilas running around with their clothes off, but there was a giant spider in it. Not a very convincing one, but I see where you're going."

"Giant spider shows up in Nevada to somebody that probably had giant spider on the mind. Hugo kills the spider, and then monsters from his past appear in his room. My husband saw a specific type of ghoul, and even though he wasn't familiar with it, Agent Franks seemed to be. Four events, three of which we know the victims had some knowledge of the thing that manifested. We don't know what killed the other victims at the first attack site, but I'm betting whatever it was came from one of those people's imagination or memories."

Pretty and smart, plus a mean sucker punch. I'd married up. The Hunters exchanged glances, there was some mumbling, but nobody could outright reject what she'd said. It was a bizarre idea, but this was a bizarre business. "That's quite the theory," Pierre Darne said. "All conjecture, but slightly more likely than MHI trying to sabotage their competitors." He held up his hands defensively and smiled. "Only joking, Julie. Please do not hit me."

"Oh, Pierre, you're far too charming. Anybody have any better ideas?"

Nobody had any. The Chinese Hunter then asked, "Assuming you're right, then the question becomes, what's causing these events?" *Oh, now he's rational and non-accusatory.*

"Or if it is going to happen again? Hell, who are we kidding? With our luck, when *will* it happen again?" I said. "Holy shit, if we're talking about monsters appearing out of people's imagination, can you think of a worse place to be than around a bunch of Hunters?" That was a sobering thought.

There was a sudden commotion at the entry hole. "Harbinger!" VanZant burst into the room.

"What is it, John?" Earl checked his watch. "Feds here? Took 'em long enough."

"Yeah. We've got Feds." VanZant was out of breath. "But they're not coming inside. They've formed a perimeter around the parking lot and ordered all the first responders back. Nobody in or out. There's an MCB agent with a bullhorn saying anyone that tries to leave the casino will be shot."

"What?" I got off the bed and went to the remains of the balcony. Far below, the flashing police lights had formed a line and were blocking the strip. Men in blue windbreakers, surely MCB, were ushering people from the parking lot and stringing up caution tape. "What're they doing?"

"They're surrounding the place." Earl's voice was completely flat. "We've been quarantined."

"Do not come any closer," the man said, his voice amplified over a loudspeaker on one of the police cars. I couldn't see very well since there were a lot of spotlights pointed at me. I could safely assume there were also guns pointed at me. "The disease is not dangerous, but it is very contagious. Stay calm and stay in the casino. Do not panic. You will be safe inside the casino. Representatives from the CDC will be here shortly with medicine."

Man, that was lame. "Cut the crap," I shouted back. "I'm with MHI. Let me talk to Franks or somebody in charge."

"Go back inside for your own safety. The disease is not dangerous, but—"

"Oh, come on! It isn't a disease, it's a . . ." I was the only person standing in the parking lot. There weren't any bystanders to spill the beans on monsters. There were probably Las Vegas cops in range of my voice, but it was hard to tell with the lights. "You know what it is. See this?" I gestured at my armor. "Who else dresses like this? I know you're watching me through a scope. Crank up the zoom." I pointed at my happy-face patch. "See? I'm MHI. I know what's up. Let me talk to Franks or Archer or somebody that has a clue. We've got a situation in here." I began walking toward the cars.

"If you come any closer we will use force."

"Just get Franks."

"I'm warning you. Don't come any closer."

"Listen, asshole—" I jumped when the bullet struck the pavement three feet from my boots. Fragments pelted my armored shins. "Shit! Okay, okay, I'm going back inside." Turning, I walked back toward the front entrance. "Son of a bitch."

There still hadn't been any official word from the government as to why they'd locked us in here. All we knew was that they'd worked fast, completely containing the casino in less than half an hour from the initial alarm. The agents that had been staying here had been seen receiving calls and practically running out of the place. Someone had given them an order to pull out within minutes of the event. Who that someone was, and what they knew, was still a mystery.

My radio hissed in my ear. "Told you that would happen."

She had warned me this wouldn't work. "Thanks, dear. Any luck?"

Julie and a few other Hunters who had brought sniper rifles had gone up to the roof to get a better picture. "None of our regular MCB contacts are answering. They cut the landlines a few minutes ago. I wouldn't be surprised if they get a jammer here soon and shut down everything else. I think they're instituting a complete communications blackout. I got off a message to Grandpa in Alabama, so at least somebody on the outside will know what's happening."

"Aw, hell. I'll be there in a second." I took one last look at the outside. As far as I could tell, the authorities had locked this place down tight. Other people had tried to leave from some of the other exits, but they'd been turned back too. Some of the anti-Hunting activists had even been turned back with a tear-gas canister, and a Hunter from Jai Jiwan Security from New Delhi had a nasty welt from a rubber bullet. The fact that they'd launched a real bullet in my general direction wasn't a good sign that they were getting *more* patient.

The main lobby of the Last Dragon was in complete pandemonium. In addition to the hundreds of Hunters and assorted hangers-on that were here for ICMHP, there were also a bunch of hotel employees and some construction workers who were still finishing the upper floors. There were also a handful of non-ICMHP guests trapped, people who had been in the casino gambling when everything had been locked down. Luckily there weren't that many of those at four in the morning, comparatively speaking, but it was still another hundred or so angry and frightened people that had no idea what was going on. A large percentage of them had gathered in the lobby, trying to figure out what was going on, or to loudly demand that they get to leave. I heard that an armored car was blocking the exit ramp of the parking garage and a couple from Florida had popped their tires driving over a set of spike strips and then been herded back inside by men with guns and gas masks. They were especially pissed off.

I felt really bad for the hotel employees. It was the night shift that had been stuck here, and they didn't know any more than the guests. I walked past a few managers that were being browbeaten by angry customers. Since none of the people that had instituted the quarantine were actually in here with us, and there wasn't anyone effective to yell at, they were shouting at whoever looked like they might have some authority.

"You there, security guard. I demand to speak to your supervisor!" A large old lady rolled up to me on her mobility scooter. "This sort of treatment is completely unacceptable. I want to speak to him immediately."

I looked down at my armor. It had started out coyote brown, but a few years of abuse, tears, rips, burns, stains, and replacing various ruined parts had left it a mottled modular mess of different-colored pouches and stab-proof sheets, some of which I'd color-corrected with spray paint. Hell, I was wearing a kukri that was damn near a short sword. Even after repeatedly hosing down room 1613, I still had sixty rounds of 12-gauge in a drum and four magazines, a few 40mm grenades, two handguns, and six spare magazines of .45. As a big dude, when I was geared up, I looked particularly enormous. I would have to be the most heavily equipped security guard in history, but in our current circumstances, it was as reasonable an assumption as any. "Ma'am, I don't work here."

"You're not security?" I shook my head *no*. "Police?

The army?" Still no. She looked very displeased. "What are you?"

"I like clothes with lots of pockets."

She made a noise that sounded like *harrumph,* then gunned her little scooter away, searching for someone else to feel her terrible Lark-powered wrath.

Earl had commandeered one of the ICMHP conference rooms to serve as Hunter Central. Trip met me on the way in and tossed over Abomination. If I had been wearing it when I'd tried to talk to the cops, it probably wouldn't have been a warning shot. Earl was at the opposite end of the room, talking to a small group of people. "What's going on?"

"He's talking to casino management, trying to get them up to speed."

"What's he telling them?"

Trip smiled. "Surprisingly, a lot." Normally we tried to keep things on the down low as much as possible to keep the MCB off our backs. "Earl seems really dead-set on protecting everyone he can. Not that he hasn't always been willing to risk his life to protect the innocent and things like that. But I think he's changed . . . It's like he *cares* more." Trip, the stalwart goody-two-shoes of our organization, seemed really pleased by this development.

"I take it you approve?"

"Well, yeah . . . I just hope Earl Harbinger isn't getting soft in his old age."

We both laughed at that absurdity. Earl Harbinger made Clint Eastwood look like Mr. Rogers. As a general rule, the more a situation sucks, the more humor you can find in the little things. Then I had a very somber thought. "Last night when we thought it was just a stupid spider in the desert, Earl could tell himself that his girlfriend wasn't really missing. But after what we just saw..."

"I don't know, man. If it was something like what appeared to the German, then she might be gone. I talked to the girl that was with Hugo. She said he jumped out of bed screaming *Nachtmar, Nachtmar,* and then one of the big metal things just rose up out of floor and started hacking him with a big rusty sword. That's all she could get through, before she just kind of stared off into space repeating *so much blood* over and over."

"That's an awful introduction to this world."

"I don't know of any good ones. As for Earl's girlfriend, werewolf or not, if that's what happened to the Unicorn team... He seems to be focused on working right now, but whatever we're up against, if it killed someone Earl cares about, I almost feel sorry for the thing. Almost."

I'd prefer to have another great Old One gunning for me than an angry Harbinger, and if what was going on wasn't caused by something that could be killed, then I would really hate to be Stricken. "Speaking of merciless badasses, you heard from Holly yet?"

Several MHI employees had been out when the monsters had appeared, including some of our most experienced people and our entire Las Vegas team, who had actual houses to sleep in, but Holly was the only member of my team outside the quarantine. "I left her a message but she didn't answer. I'll try again." Trip pulled out his phone, then frowned at it. "That's not good. I've got no service."

My phone was also showing no signal. I checked my

radio. "Com check. Can anybody hear me?" Nothing but static. "They're jamming us. Damn it, Julie called it."

Trip put his phone away. "I figured you'd be used to that by now."

"She likes to remind me. What do we have to work with?"

"About half the companies have thrown in with us. The other half are off doing their own thing. Some of them were staying at other hotels, so we've got about three-quarters of the conference attendees here. Of the half that are with us, half of those actually like us, and the other half know that since we've got more locals we have the most ammo. Milo and some of the Australians are putting together an equipment inventory. Those guys over there..." Trip nodded toward another group that had come up with a map of the hotel, "are dividing everyone up into two-man teams and figuring out how to patrol this whole place."

"Assuming the *phenomenon* happens again..."

"We get on it fast. You want to let it spread out and get really big before we find it next time? Didn't think so. That group over there is collecting all the brainiacs. They're trying to figure out what's happening and how to stop it." There were a dozen Hunters in that group, including Lee, Paxton, and Cody from MHI. Cody was actually writing equations on a dry-erase board. Julie hadn't been kidding about him. "Another group is acting as go-betweens with the non-Hunter guests. Turns out one of our guys, Tyler Nelson from the New York team, knows all about the psychology. He said he would get them calmed down. He helped talk down Hugo's girl too."

"Nelson? Any relation to the Doctors Nelson?"

"Their grandson," Trip said. "Small world, huh? Following in the family footsteps, got a degree, practiced, then got bored. Now if I ever have kids I'm going to encourage them to do something safe."

"Look how well accounting worked for me..."

"Hey, do what you need to do fast, because we're going on patrol in ten minutes. We're going to clear this place, room by room. Shoot. I just realized without radios that is going to get a lot more complicated."

"Don't worry." I patted Abomination. "We've got other ways of making noise."

I hit the smart group first. Not wanting to interrupt, I hung back and listened. The debate was rather heated and they were trying to decide if it had been a pocket dimension, a portal, or a something I'd never heard of involving a whole bunch of PhDs' names stuck together. Back in school, I had test scores high enough to get a MENSA invite, but this stuff was *way* over my head. Cody saw me and gestured for me to approach. He pointed a dry-erase marker at my heart. "You. Earl said Franks mentioned Decision Week?"

"He did, to someone I think was from STFU. Then the major at Dugway talked like the containment unit was left over from it."

Cody turned his dry-erase marker on a bald Israeli. "See? I told you this had Decision Week stink all over it." The burly, bushy-haired Vietnam vet turned back to his dry-erase board and began writing more numbers and symbols. "So, the question now is, whose work are we dealing with? Weiskopf? Silverman? He loved summoning things from Planck space. God help us if it was Hampson and his neurobiological demon bondings. Yuck." Cody shuddered.

I sure hated to interrupt all that calculus. "Is this like what they did during Decision Week?"

Cody laughed. "Decision Week wasn't the project. It was the end *result*. The name comes from the week that everything in Los Alamos went batshit insane and the high command *decided* that atomic weapons were less dangerous. They pushed the boundaries of science until they blurred into magic and then into something beyond that. It was madness."

"But does any of this sound familiar?"

"Z..." Cody put the cap back on his marker and turned around to face me. "They tried everything out there. It is so damn top secret that even though I've worked on the DOE contract for the last twenty years, I don't know a tenth of what laws of the universe they violated."

"I've been a scientist most of my life. I believe in the pursuit of knowledge above all," said an unfamiliar man with a proper British accent. I realized that he was one of the academics from the ICMHP curriculum. At least some of the non-Hunter guests weren't totally useless. "But what they did there? Bugger that. I'd rather go back to rubbing two sticks together to make fire."

"They poked God in the eye," said the Israeli. He made a two-fingered poking motion, like unto the Three Stooges. "*Poink*. He was not amused."

"Desperation makes you stupid," Cody said. "They'd been working for a while before Decision Week happened. Nobody knows what set it off. Several of the experiments went horribly wrong all at the same time. Reality was ripped to shreds. Men mutated. Turned into insects, incorporeal wraiths, you name it. Some were found with their bodies partially fused into solid objects. Portals were opened to who knows how many dimensions. Ancient gods were communed with, Aztec to Zulu and everything in between. Brilliant men were driven mad. A Nobel Prize winner grew an extra eye in his forehead. Some minds switched bodies. They had this one janitor, his tongue grew its own mouth, complete with tiny little shark teeth, and then started communicating...in *Latin*. A better question, Z, is what *didn't* happen at Los Alamos."

Lee was taking rapid notes. "Tongues with teeth? That's *awesome*."

"Not for the fellow whose tongue began talking to him, I'd imagine," Paxton said. Even in her armor she still reminded me of a Cub Scout den mother. Even the werecat on her team patch was cute.

Cody continued, "Our problem now is deciding which, if any, of those harebrained experiments we're dealing with here. All of the experiments were potentially war-ending weapons, but some turned out to be far more dangerous than others. None of the possibilities are good, and this quarantine indicates that the government has decided this is one of the bad ones, but obviously not the worst."

"How can you tell?"

Cody shrugged. "They haven't bombed us yet."

I was sorry I asked. Before I could say anything else, someone bumped my elbow and moved into the brainiac circle. It was Edward. I was shocked to see that Tanya, Princess of the Elves, was right behind him. Surprisingly enough, Edward was standing right next to an elf, and nobody was getting stabbed. From what I understood of those two groups' history, that was really good. I looked around to make sure Skippy wasn't here too, because seeing those two together would cause him to lose his mind. Luckily, no Skip. Edward, as usual, was entirely covered, wearing mirrored shades and a ski mask. As a Newbie, Tanya hadn't been issued armor yet, and was wearing a too-tight tank top and jean shorts. Apparently she was pretty confident she was going to pass training, since she'd gotten the MHI logo tattooed on her ankle. With her hair hiding her pointy ears she could at least pass for a human being, but she really didn't look like she fit in with this crowd.

Even though he'd already gotten my attention, Ed bumped my arm again. It was odd to see the orc so willingly enter a room full of humans. "What's up, Ed?" I looked at the non-MHI Hunters. "This is Edward, my administrative assistant."

"Tell them, Ed," Tanya said. She put her hands on his shoulders and shoved him toward the table. Still no stabbing. I was impressed. Edward grunted at Tanya to quit bugging him, then reached into his black coat and pulled out a cloth. He set it down on the table and gently unrolled it for all of us to see. The smart Hunters leaned in.

It was a fuzzy little lump of pointy flesh. "That's from the spider?" Lee asked, instinctively moving back from the table. I remembered Ed chopping the end of the limb off and his cryptic words about it not being real. The orc pointed at the thing, as if to say, *see?*

"What? I don't get it?" Cody said.

"Ed says it's fake. It ain't real and stuff," Tanya explained.

Curious, Lee overcame his dislike of giant spiders

and came back over to squint at the piece of leg. "Hmmm... You know, there is something weird. I'm no biologist..." Albert Lee knew more about giant spiders than the rest of us, since they had been his initial exposure to the world of monsters, had killed a bunch of his friends, and nearly cost him his life. "The hair is wrong. This is like fur. The ones I've killed had bristles. And the bottom is wrong. This is like a spike. The other ones had a sort of pad."

Ed shook his head in the negative and grunted angrily. A knife materialized in his hand. I knew from experience he usually had a dozen of those stashed. He pointed the tip at the leg and made a poking motion. I tried to see what he was getting at. There was a bunch of sand that I hadn't noticed in the cloth before, but other than that, it looked like the end of a spider leg, only it was about the size of a hot dog. Then Ed took the knife and began mashing the leg violently with the flat of the blade.

It crumbled into sand.

"What the hell? Can I see that?" Cody took the knife from Edward and scooped up some of the dirt. Half of the sample still looked like the leg, black, hairy, and distinct, but at the edge of where Ed had smashed it, it simply turned into brown sand. "I'll be damned."

"The magic on it has worn off. He showed it to me first," Tanya explained proudly.

"Fake... Moosh," Ed explained. He looked around at the humans, seemingly embarrassed to have said anything. By Edward's standards of communication that had been a doctoral dissertation.

"Good work, Ed," I told him.

The brainiacs were intrigued by this new development. "Z, is this what the soil in that area looked like?" Paxton asked.

It was hard to tell. It all looked like sand to me, and much of it had been covered in snow. "Pretty close, I guess."

The smart Hunters began to jabber excitedly. Cody gave Edward his knife back. "Ah ha! Matter organization at the origination site! That narrows down the possibilities." He uncapped his marker and went back to his board. "If the pocket dimension—"

"It ain't no pocket dimension," Tanya cut in, putting her hands on her hips. "Duh."

"What do you mean?"

"They gotta have a focal point to anchor on Earth. They can't just pop up. It takes days to stick one on. And I looked all over that blown-up room, and there ain't no focal point nowhere."

"How do you know?" asked the Englishman, eyeing her suspiciously.

Tanya was trailer-park elf royalty and proud. She snorted, indignant to be questioned by *commoners*. "I don't need fancy schooling to know about magic." She went up to the board and snatched Cody's marker away. "Now this is what it looks like when you connect an *eskarthi-dor*, which is the right name for it. Y'all have been saying it wrong." She drew some quick symbols. "See? That's what the anchor looks like. That thing that popped up before wasn't no *eskarthi-dor*, but I can probably figure up what it was fast enough." She looked at Cody's equation, shook her head disapprovingly and rubbed out a number with her thumb and replaced it with a triangle. "People just don't understand magic right. Wish I could call momma. She'd know what this was, no problem. Ed, be a love and fetch me a Mountain Dew. I need to do some figuring."

Ed looked at me, shrugged, and then wandered off to find her a Mountain Dew.

"Diet, Ed!" Tanya shouted, not looking away from the board. "Gotta watch my figure."

Cody tilted his head to the side and studied the interloper as she continued writing strange Elvish symbols. "And you must be Tanya."

"Yup. The one and only greatest wizard that's ever lived."

"I believe that," Cody muttered to me, then raised his voice. "Well, you do know *some* magic, which means you know more than the rest of us. Welcome to the smart team, Tanya...Now give me my marker back. You have to earn your own dry-erase marker."

CHAPTER 13

Trip and I went on patrol. We were one of ten different teams out looking for early signs of trouble. Most of those had a casino employee or two with them to keep them from getting lost in the confusing place. Earl had directed the two of us to the camera room to try to coordinate some more help.

It had been an hour since the quarantine had started, but the Feds still hadn't tried to communicate with us. Phones, radio, and internet were all down. Cable TV still worked, and as we passed a big screen above one of the bars, I spotted the front of the Last Dragon. "Hey, that's about us."

The man being interviewed was a tough guy in a suit with a short haircut, which pretty much screamed MCB. "You know, that guy looks like he's in really good shape for a CDC spokesman." Trip found the remote on top of the bar and turned the volume up.

"There's no need for alarm. Everything is safe and contained. One of the guests at the casino showed symptoms of a very rare type of African hemorrhagic fever."

"Is that like Ebola?" asked the nervous reporter.

The agent looked right at the camera. "Yes. Exactly like Ebola. Which is why we suggest that everyone stays well back from the containment area. It is *very* contagious."

"Is there any danger of it spreading?"

The MCB agent gave a fake laugh. "Oh, no. Everything is perfectly safe and there is no danger at all to the city of Las Vegas. The people inside may be inconvenienced, but our doctors are testing them now. Once we are certain that no one else is infected then they will be released. The whole procedure should only take a few days at most."

"Great. We've officially got Ebola." If the hundreds of innocent people trapped in here hadn't been freaked out before, they would be now. I looked over at Trip. "How much you want to bet somebody at the MCB is getting screamed at for forgetting to shut the cable off into here before that aired?"

The TV turned to static. "Jinx. Way to go, Z."

"Sorry."

We continued walking through the oddly lit neon wonderland of beeping and clicking slot machines. It felt odd being so empty of people, but the entire casino floor area had been closed off. There had been some argument about what to do with everyone stuck here. Some of the casino staff had wanted to try to stick to business as usual, but Earl had been rather persuasive that that was an incredibly stupid idea. Since word had arrived from their management that they were to cooperate with us, they had acquiesced.

Some of the Hunters had thought it was best to keep everyone in their rooms, while others had thought it was best to try to put everyone into a few big areas so they could be watched. Both methods had their pros and cons, and depending on what we were dealing with, either one could potentially be the best or worst possible thing to do. If we were dealing with something like a fast-spreading mutating plague or undead outbreak, then keeping people separate behind locked doors and controlling choke points made a lot of sense. In a situation like that, sticking everyone in one place could potentially create a zombie army in a matter of minutes. On the other hand, keeping them in small groups made them virtually impossible to defend, and would be terrible if the phenomenon could simply pop up wherever it felt like, which is what had apparently happened in Hugo's room. It wouldn't do any good to be isolated behind a locked door if the thing he had called *Nachtmar* could simply float up through your carpet and chop you to pieces.

The decision was a moot one anyway, since very few of the bystanders that had been trapped here were inclined to listen to us, and the place was a huge maze of interlocking rooms and confusing corridors, so if somebody wanted to wander off it wasn't like we could really stop them. It's a free country. Most of the trapped non-Hunters and employees were clustered in the common areas, some whining, others nervous, though nobody had panicked yet. The Ebola announcement would probably change that, and it would more than likely really suck for Nelson and Hunters that had volunteered to herd sheep.

Meanwhile, the Hunters had thrown politeness out the window and were all openly armed, and many of them didn't speak a lick of English. Not to mention that this was Nevada, and the SHOT Show was in town, so many of the stuck gamblers were probably concealing guns too. I was all in favor of people packing heat, but we didn't want anyone to get jumpy and decide that my side were the bad guys here, so MHI was encouraging the other Hunters to be polite.

Hotel security had still been consulting their manuals to see if there was an official policy about what to do in a situation like this by the time we had a small private army wandering their halls looking for monsters. So security had shut down the gambling areas and locked up the money. Now they were mostly protecting the vault and trying to keep their trapped tourists calm. They'd been told to defer to Earl's judgment, a wise choice. The only services trying to conduct business as usual were a strategic few of the restaurants, open for breakfast, because people full of bacon are less likely to riot.

Not too bad of a reaction considering we had only been quarantined for an hour. It had been one heck of a crazy day and the sun wasn't even up yet.

"I think this is it," Trip pointed at a door that was nearly invisible under the strange lighting. There was a swipe pad for a key card. He tugged on the door, found it locked, then knocked and waited.

A few seconds later it was opened for us by a middle-aged, overweight man in a wrinkled gray suit, who blocked the way and regarded us suspiciously. He was wearing a big gold name tag that read MITCH. "Who're you?"

"We're from MHI," Trip said.

"Let's see some ID," he demanded.

Trip looked down at his body armor. "Seriously?"

"These particular circumstances aren't exactly in the handbook, okay? Gimme a second . . . Fine. Management warned me you were coming. This is on them if you do anything stupid. All right. I'm the night-shift surveillance room supervisor. This way."

We entered a very normal corridor that could have come out of any office building in America. "How'd they tell you we were coming? I thought the phones were down."

"There's an internal switchboard and operator. We can still call from room to room, but we can't call out," Mitch explained. That was good to know. I'd have to make sure to alert Earl and spread the word. "I saw you coming. I see everything here. Management said I was supposed to fully cooperate with you." He took note of Abomination and Trip's KRISS submachine gun. "Rules say no unauthorized weapons in the control room. *That's* in the handbook."

"I'm not feeling real rulesy right now, Mitch."

"We're trained professionals," Trip said. "We're perfectly safe."

"Friggin' management . . . I get fired if I don't follow the handbook but they just toss order right out the window at the first sign of trouble. Management just picks and chooses which rules to ignore and then everything turns to chaos, and you watch, because then it goes on *my* evaluation . . . Chaos, I tell you."

"Total chaos. Complete pandemonium, I know, but here's the thing, you can have my full-auto shotgun when you pry it from my cold, dead hands. Apparently your management is on my side in this argument, so quit dinking around and let's go."

"All right, fine. Guns, guns, guns. You better be on

your best behavior." The chunky man turned and led us down the hall. "What's going on?"

"Have you seen the news?" I asked.

"Before it went out, we were. It isn't Ebola," Mitch said. "I know that much."

"What do you know?"

"Damned near everything."

"That's unlikely," I whispered to Trip.

"Whatever it is, we don't need outside contractors to handle it. We've got our own security force here. My guys can handle anything."

"Well, apparently *management* disagrees with you there, Mitch."

Muttering profanity, Mitch swiped his card and led us through another door into a large room. Two uniformed security guards watched us suspiciously and put their hands on their holstered pistols, but since we were with Mitch they hesitated. Trip gave them a friendly wave. "Morning." Past the guards were a bunch of employees watching dozens of computer monitors. Each monitor was divided into four separate camera views, and they switched around every few seconds.

"That's a *lot* of cameras."

"Thank you," Mitch answered with pride. This was obviously a man who *owned* his job. "Hey...wait a second, dreadlocks. I recognize you now. You two were with that bunch that trashed the buffet."

"It was all a misunderstanding," I said.

"We looked great on the security video, though... I mean, we probably looked great on video." Trip corrected himself. "I can only assume. Obviously."

"Freaking management." Mitch grumbled. "They said we were supposed to be nice to you conference attendees. At least the polo-shirt bunch had the common decency to move to a hotel across the street and out of my hair. If it was up to me I would've pressed charges and never ever let any of you back on the property."

"But then we wouldn't be here to save the day now."

"Freaking management." Mitch gave the sort of resigned sigh that only a truly disgruntled employee that knows he's smarter than his bosses can make. "Come on." Mitch took us to the first couple of computers. "These banks cover the street. How many people you got out there now, Mickey?"

The employee manning those computers looked over and did a double-take when he saw how Trip and I were dressed. "I lost count when the National Guard showed up."

Mitch continued his tour. "Most of these cameras are of the casino floor, these show the shops and plaza, here's the conference center, and we can cover every corridor and elevator in the hotel. I saw you all running around on sixteen earlier. We called the police and sent up a security team, but they got turned away by some of you assholes who wouldn't let them up the stairs—"

One of the uniformed security guards butted in. "They don't pay us enough to argue with a bunch of crazies with machine guns."

"And then *this*—this travesty." Mitch pointed at one of the four squares on the screen. It was black. "Can you believe that?"

"There's nothing there," Trip pointed out.

"Exactly. You people *broke* one of *my* cameras."

"That's what happens when you set off a homemade

bomb in an enclosed space while trying to stop an invasion of metal Teutonic slug monsters. Hell on the hardware." I cracked my neck. "Speaking of which, you guys got any Tylenol in here?"

Mitch must not have caught the slug monster part. "That camera was very expensive."

"Put it on my tab with the ice swan. That damned thing cost more than my college education."

"Oh, I will. You just wait until you see your final room bill."

"Don't finalize that bill just yet. We might not be done wrecking your stuff..." I raised my voice and addressed the whole room. "Attention, everybody, I'm Owen Pitt. This is Trip Jones." Earl had warned me that I should keep this on a need-to-know basis. The less these people knew about monsters, the less likely the MCB was to ruin their lives afterward. They only needed to know enough to not get themselves killed. "We're consultants and we're here to help you through this situation."

"Management has specified that we need to give these men our cooperation." Mitch's tone left no doubt as to his opinion of that decision. "*Full* cooperation."

"Which means we're pretty much in charge," I said. Mitch looked at his shoes and grumbled some more. "On the bright side, if something goes horribly wrong we're the ones that get blamed and sued, and you probably won't get fired." That seemed to cheer him up. "But we're going to need your help."

"What's going on?" asked one of the employees. "Something bad?"

"Bad? What gave it away? Okay, seriously. This is going to sound weird, but it's the truth. What I'm about to tell you must be kept secret. You can't tell anybody. Not your family, not your friends, nobody, or the government people outside will shoot you. I'm not kidding..." Many incredulous looks were shared by the security room night shift. *Here goes nothing.* "We think there's a dangerous supernatural entity loose in your casino." There was some nervous laughter. It gradually died as my expression didn't change. "Yeah. Sorry to break it to you. It killed several people in northern Nevada yesterday and murdered one of your guests this morning in room 1613."

A long, awkward silence filled the room. "That's nuts," Mitch finally said.

"You know what? Go ahead and roll with that. We're crazy, so just humor us until we're done." I didn't want to waste my time debating the skeptics. "We still need you to do your jobs and keep your eyes open, and most importantly, keep a cool head."

"Cool head?" That had offended Mitch. "We're professionals. We handle criminals daily. We can spot pickpockets and cheats smoother than the guy in this place's magic show. There haven't been any rappers shot in *my* casino, because we see trouble before it happens. We can handle this. This isn't nothing but a chance to get some overtime for my boys."

"Good. Keep that positive attitude." *You're probably going to need it.*

"What's this *supernatural entity* look like?" asked one of the techs incredulously.

"We don't know. It's able to change shape," Trip said as I moved down the line of monitors, looking for suspicious activity. "So we'll need to know about anything that seems out of place."

Seeing this many different angles really drove home just how huge this facility really was. Starting at the top, there were a few different views of the roof where Julie's group of marksmen were keeping an eye out. A black shape that had to be Skippy had a panel open on the tail rotor of our chopper and was beating something with a hammer. That just filled me with all sorts of confidence.

"Provided Skip doesn't break anything, we can still fly out of here if we need to," Trip said quietly to me. "Unless the MCB has a surface-to-air missile down there . . . Which they probably do. Never mind."

Beneath the roof level and helipad was the hotel, all twenty luxurious stories, eight cameras per floor. The upper floors weren't done yet, but cameras were already installed there. There were no cameras in the rooms, but every hall was covered. I counted all of our small Hunter teams going room to room. They'd knock, talk to the occupants if there were any, then move on. I spotted the other patrols in the gambling area, the concourse, and the shopping area. All were accounted for. I addressed the security personnel with my authority voice. "Keep an eye on those patrols. If any of them disappear for more than a couple of seconds, sound the alarm. If any of them look like they start freaking out about something, sound the alarm. Hell, if you see *anything* weird, sound the alarm. Then I want you to use the switchboard and call the conference center so we can get my people on it fast."

"If we see something strange, we can ring the closest patrol and warn them," suggested one of the men.

"Good call. Do that too. I'll make sure they know to answer." I decided to try and placate Mitch. He needed to feel important. "I can tell you run a tight ship here. You men are our first line of defense. All of these innocent people are counting on you. The faster we react, the fewer of them die. With you as our eyes, I know we can get through this alive."

The employees exchanged nervous glances. Apparently my words of encouragement hadn't helped any. When it came to motivation, I was no Earl Harbinger.

"Friggin' management." Mitch wandered over to the coffee machine, still muttering angrily to himself. The angry banging told me that he was taking out his frustration on the coffee maker. "Want one?" Mitch called to us. "How do you Ghostbusters like your coffee?"

"Without spit in it?" Trip whispered to me before answering him. "Five sugars."

"Jeez, Trip, why don't you just melt some candy bars in it? None for me, thanks."

One of the techs spoke up. "Hey, boss, I've got something coming up the main valet parking circle."

Me and Mitch bumped shoulders trying to see the monitor. He spilled coffee on my armor. The screen showed a small, tracked remote-control vehicle driving from the police line toward the front door. "What is that?"

"It's a bomb-squad robot," Mitch said. "We had a threat a few months ago and the cops used one of those little guys to blow up a suspicious package someone left on the concourse. Turned out it only had sandwiches in it, but you never can be too careful."

There was an unfurling spool of wire on the back of the little robot and a package dangling from its single arm. "Have your operator warn the conference center. The Feds want to talk."

❖   ❖   ❖

We took one wrong turn and ended up in an entirely different section of the gambling floor. It didn't help that this place had been designed to be confusing, so that anyone attempting to leave would get turned around until they just gave up and gambled until they died. By the time Trip and I had sprinted back across the casino, the robot messenger had already arrived.

Several Hunters were keeping the furious crowd away from the entrance. The robot was rolling on its little treads back the way it had come. Cooper was guarding the front door. The former EOD man waved goodbye at the departing robot. "Carry on, noble PacBot."

"Friend of yours?" Trip asked. At least he could talk. He was in a lot better cardiovascular shape than I was. I was busy catching my breath.

"I carried one of those heavy little buggers on my back for a lot of long foot patrols in Afghanistan," he answered. "Pain in the ass to drive with only a little screen in a pair of glasses and a Playstation controller. Still, I think we should buy a couple. I bet I could stake a sleeping vampire with one."

"Where's Earl?"

Cooper pointed down. "Follow the cable."

The robot's delivery had been taken into a side room for privacy. I made sure to close the door behind me. There were already several Hunters inside, most of them leadership from different companies. A desk had been cleared off and a laptop was running in the middle of it. The computer was plugged into a cable that led directly back to the roadblock. The hard line enabled us to bypass the jamming.

The initial communication must have been something, because Earl was yelling at the computer. "Damn it, Stark. Don't be an idiot!"

"What'd I miss?" I whispered, but the nearest Hunters shushed me. I pushed between bodies until I could see the jowly face of the new MCB director fill the screen.

"That's the deal, Harbinger. Take it or leave it."

"My folks will stay and we'll take care of this thing, and I bet most of the other companies would volunteer too, but for the love of God, let us evacuate the others. They've got nothing to do with this. They're sitting ducks in here."

Stark's chins trembled. "Well . . ." he looked to the side as someone off screen addressed him. From the background, I was guessing that he was in some sort of armored vehicle, probably right outside. "I can't allow that. My hands are tied."

"How many innocents are you willing to let die this time? You want another Copper Lake on your hands?" Earl's voice was low and dangerous.

"No, of course not." He sputtered. "That's exactly what I'm trying to prevent. This entity can't be allowed into the city."

"You learned what it is, didn't you? What's in here with us?"

"I can't say. That's classified." Stark kept glancing nervously to his left. "You've got twenty-four hours to get a confirmed kill on this thing, or we'll be forced to take drastic measures."

"Drastic? You intend to burn this place down with all of us in it, don't you?"

"I did you a favor getting that much of a delay

approved. I put my neck on the line for you. You were lucky to get twenty-four hours." Stark was turning red. "You don't know what you're dealing with."

"Then tell me!"

"I . . ." Stark glanced left again. "I can't."

"If you can't, then put somebody on who can."

"I'm the final authority on this mission."

"Bullshit. You're a lap dog for Special Task Force Unicorn. Put Stricken on."

Stark blanched when he heard those words, but he tried to recover. "I'm the head of the MCB. Don't question my authority!"

Earl's voice turned into a low growl. The assembled Hunters all took an unconscious step away from him. "*Now.*"

Stark hesitated, glancing to the side one last time. He listened quietly, then, resigned, shuffled out of view without another word. A moment later he was replaced with the narrow, unnaturally pale face of Mr. Stricken, who seemed to fold his long body into the space. His odd-colored glasses hid his eyes. "Harbinger," he greeted without emotion.

"What've you done to us, Stricken?"

"I merely offered you a lucrative business opportunity. I thought it was some Decision Week dreg that needed a fast cleanup. It wasn't until a couple of hours ago that I was briefed on the particularly nasty nature of this case. If I had been aware of the threat level sooner, I would have dealt with this matter internally. If you have anyone in there who isn't already familiar with the basic facts of that incident, send them out of the room now. They'll thank me later."

None of the Hunters moved.

Earl controlled his seething rage long enough to ask, "What've you locked in here with us?"

"Let's see . . . Locked in there with you: Ick-mip guests of a non-militant persuasion, approximately one hundred and forty. Staff, one hundred and twenty-two. Monster Hunters, two hundred and fifteen from fourteen different companies. One crew of sheetrockers, some union electricians, and we're trying to get a handle on gambling addicts that were dumb enough to be there at four A.M., but I'm estimating that around fifty, and an unknown number of co-eds and party girls who crashed Grimm Berlin's celebration, and last but not least, one extremely dangerous science experiment."

"Capabilities?"

"Unknown."

"Weaknesses?"

"Unknown."

"What do you know?"

Stricken's smile was totally devoid of human warmth. "Most of the records pertaining to this particular experiment have been destroyed or buried deep, even by my admittedly high standards for secrecy. However, it has been brought to my attention that some of the original Decision Week scientists are still alive and may have firsthand knowledge. We are contacting them now."

The Unicorn man was a seething bundle of lies, but that part sounded plausible. "There's a reason you locked this place down so quick when you found out it had followed us here. There's something else. How do you know this thing is so dangerous?"

"My first responders retrieved some physical evidence from the containment unit."

Earl looked to me and I nodded.

Stricken's laptop was rigged to watch the entire room. We should have known. "Pitt... I'm not surprised. So that was you in Dugway with Agent Franks."

Denying it would only waste valuable time. "There were some tags missing from the old machine."

Stricken chuckled. "Interesting. I was wondering who that second man in the photos was. It was hard to tell with those chemical suits on. It figures. I'll have to have a few words with old Frankie about the necessity of maintaining security protocols."

"You do that." If we were lucky Franks would lose his temper and beat Stricken to death, hopefully before he got to me for inadvertently ratting him out.

"My team did recover some items. One of the others had a project identification number. Setting internal matters aside for now, and getting back to your original question, we were able to track the identifiers back to one of the most exciting and secretive weapons projects in history. I'm assuming you already knew that, though. Of course you do, because Agent Franks couldn't keep his big fat stupid mouth shut. Interesting fact, did you know that they ranked all of the World-War-II-era experimental weapons systems on a scale from one to ten, with one being the least, and ten being the most potentially destructive and disruptive to society?" Stricken waited.

"Werewolves were a two," Earl whispered.

"To put the projects in perspective, the atomic bomb, which, as you are well aware, was the final choice of which avenue to pursue, began at an estimated number four and ended up as a number five. Anything over that was considered unreasonably dangerous. Of the supernatural options that were explored at Los Alamos, the plan to bomb Germany with a zombie virus was a steady number eight. Zombifying Japan was only a seven, but that's because it was an island and zombies can't swim for shit. Anything dealing with the Old Ones was considered too dangerous to contemplate unleashing without significant backlash, and got an automatic ten."

"Get to the point," Earl said.

"As new projects were introduced or more was learned about their potential, the projects were moved up or down on the sliding scale. This particular project began as a lowly number two, but after one single field trial was moved to a *thirteen*. We're talking about the judgment of men who thought enslaving demons was simply another way to expand the scientific frontier, yet something about this particular project scared them shitless. Luckily, this was not one of the projects that got loose during Decision Week. They destroyed the records and the evidence was buried, until now."

"Why didn't they just kill it?"

"I don't know. Maybe they didn't have the technology. Who knows? If I find out, I'll let you in on the secret. In the meantime, as for your request to let the innocent bystanders out, I have to deny that request. The phenomenon has some incorporeal nature, otherwise it wouldn't have been able to follow Hugo Schneider back to Las Vegas. For all we know, it's *inside* one of you."

The Hunters all shared an uneasy glance. It was certainly possible, but *who?* "You know anything else?"

"I know you're probably fucked, but you'll go down fighting. That should buy my organization time to learn more. My superiors have granted me some leeway. If you can't provide me a permanent solution by this time tomorrow morning, we'll raze the casino to the ground and salt the earth. If we think it might escape, that timeline will speed up rather dramatically. My number-one mission parameter is to maintain secrecy at all costs. My secondary parameter is to protect the city and as much of the population as possible. They go hand in hand. The higher the body count, the harder it'll be for Agent Stark and his remarkable PR department to make this all neatly go away. Let's make the best of our brief time together. Anything else?"

"I've got manpower but we don't have much in the way of equipment. How about you send your robot back over with a trailer of ammunition and medical supplies."

"Harbinger, Harbinger, Harbinger . . ." Stricken's laugh was cold. "Come on, buddy. I'm going to give the order to burn you out of there tomorrow morning. I know how you people think. The last thing I want to do is arm you better! Put yourself in my shoes. I'm under no delusions that you're going to find a way to beat this thing when the best minds of the greatest generation couldn't. But we're in Vegas, so I'm in a gambling mood. I'll put a little on my long shot, i.e., you, but I've got to hedge my bets. If that's all, I've got work to do."

"And Heather's team? Did they really disappear, or were you using her to motivate me to do your dirty work?"

Stricken stroked his chin thoughtfully with his eerily long fingers. "I told the truth that time. There's still no sign of them. She's MIA."

Earl hung his head for a very long time. The Hunters were so quiet you could have heard a pin drop. "Stricken?"

"Yes, Harbinger?"

"This isn't over between me and you."

"I would expect nothing less. I'll be in touch." The screen went black.

CHAPTER 14

One of the first keys to survival in a bad situation is organization, or as Earl liked to say, "Keep your shit together and you're less likely to choke."

Milo had completed his inventory of all our available equipment. It wasn't nearly as good as I'd hoped. Sure, all of the Hunters had been armed, but very few had been loaded for bear. My team was the only one that had come in directly from a mission with a full load-out. Our Hunters who had road-tripped in had quite a bit of gear, but the ones who had flown in were minimally armed, though after the lesson of the Christmas party, you'd be hard pressed to find an MHI member who travelled anywhere without at least two guns and their armor. The Hunters from other countries were worse off, with most of them having been dissuaded by all of the bureaucratic hoop-jumping, though many of them had found some crafty way to arm themselves locally immediately after Stricken's challenge. A few had even been able to do it legally.

We had no heavy weapons. We had almost nothing

left as far as explosives. The ammunition supply would be sufficient for maybe one decent engagement, and we were sorely regretting all the silver .308 we'd wasted on a nearly empty gas station. Cooper had been given the assignment of improvising some explosives, so he had drafted a few other Hunters, some of the staff, and even one of the strippers Holly had invited, and was teaching them how to make IEDs. Hotel security had one arms locker that they were very proud of, but which was relatively lame by our standards. Mitch had claimed its contents for his staff who were guarding the casino's vault.

Trip and I had gone back out on patrol. There weren't nearly as many of us wandering around now. Rumors were spreading like wildfire amongst the trapped guests, and it had started getting really heated. One tourist had lost his temper and taken a swing at one of the Brazilian Hunters, who had promptly choked the fellow unconscious. It is never smart to get into a wrestling match with a Brazilian. That had gotten a few more people riled up, and so now all of our more diplomatic Hunters were occupied babysitting.

This whole situation was really bugging me, but there was one thing in particular that was eating away at my calm. We took the elevator up to the roof to check on my wife's team. Team was a real overstatement, since basically Julie had grabbed anyone who had brought a rifle with a high-magnification scope and stuck them where they could get the best view. I knew she had collected four people, two who didn't speak any English, and an orc that wouldn't leave his helicopter.

We'd procured a key card from Mitch that let us access the areas that were normally restricted. It was windy and surprisingly cold on the roof. The morning sun was a pale globe over the desert. Las Vegas was a different animal in the early sunlight; a big, lethargic, sleepy, decrepit, sleazy animal that had stayed up too late drinking the night before and woke up grumpy. Since the Last Dragon was one of the tallest buildings in the city, Julie had a commanding view of the strip from here.

I spotted my wife at the far corner of the roof. She had her back to us, and was braced against the railing, watching something far below through her scope. I wanted to talk to her alone. "Do me a favor and check on Skippy," I told Trip. "See if there's a phone up here and he knows to answer it if it rings."

"Does Skippy even know how to use a phone? Guess I'll find out."

Julie heard my approach and quickly turned to see who or what was coming towards her. Relief flooded her face. She was just as jumpy as the rest of us. "Hey. Glad you're here."

"You should keep somebody close by to watch your back," I chided her. "Remember what happened to Hugo."

"I'm not stupid," she answered as she slung her M-14, her manner suddenly defensive. That usually only happened when I was right, which wasn't very often. "I've been doing this longer than you have."

"You pulling rank on me, dear?"

Julie frowned. That had been a cheap shot, though as MHI's business manager she did outrank MHI's accountant. "I've only got four people and a really big area to watch."

"Then I'll go ask for some more," I answered gently.

"Fine." Julie relented. "Sorry, I'm touchy is all."

"Me too." I took a spot next to her at the railing. Looking over the side made me dizzy, but it didn't seem to bother her any. Her dark hair was loose and blowing in the wind. There was something I was worried about, but I wasn't ready to broach the topic yet. "Anything new and exciting?"

"There are snipers on the casino's other rooftops. They're watching us right now." I looked around but couldn't see anything. "Don't bother. They're pretty well hidden. Down here," Julie pointed to the right, "is the pool and the gardens. You might want to have the staff lock those doors, because people are still wandering out there looking for a way out, but I'm not seeing any of our patrols, so I don't think we knew that part was still open. Oh, and I know where Presumptuous Trout went."

"Huh?" It took me a moment to realize that Julie had decided to jump on the bandwagon and start making fun of Paranormal Tactical too. "Those jackasses? Where?"

She nodded at the barricades on the street. "Stricken has hired some contractors to work security."

"Son of a bitch." I didn't have the scope, so would have to take her word for it. "What douchebags."

"The word that came to mind for me was *whores*. Other than that, from here I can see in the windows to the conference center and walkway over the concourse. I saw Earl walk through there a minute ago, looking madder than usual." Somebody had already given her a brief summary, but I told her all the details from the grim conversation with Stricken. "So do you think the science experiment in that containment unit was the thing that's supposed to end the world that your dad has been trying to tell us about?"

"I don't know for sure, but it doesn't *feel* like it." Sure, the symbol had been there and all, but it had felt new, whereas the occupant of the unit had been there for decades. It was more like the symbol had been used to wake it up. "Here's hoping it's not. We're not ready. But honestly, it's the instigator, but I don't think Hugo's *Nachtmar* is it."

"Good. I've got plans. I'm getting my hair done next week."

"Thanks for not yelling at me for procrastinating murdering my dad to prevent Armageddon."

"Don't beat yourself up. We don't know what's going on yet, and besides, your dad's probably delusional." Julie quickly changed the subject because we both knew he probably wasn't. "It's been pretty quiet up here. The only things I've seen through the windows down there are people angry about being stuck in quarantine."

"How can you tell?"

"On twenty power I can't exactly read lips, but I can certainly read body language. The situation's getting rowdy in there, which is why I didn't ask for any more help up here. I figured we needed all the Hunters we could get inside."

"Speaking of being needed inside..."

"I knew you'd get around to asking that eventually." Julie knew me far too well. "You want to know why I volunteered to be out here, on lookout duty that anybody else could do, instead of being my usual diplomatic, take-charge self, herding cats downstairs?"

"Pretty much."

My wife leaned on the railing and watched the barricades. She took a long time answering. "Because I lost my temper and hit that stupid Hunter."

"Personally, I thought that was awesome."

"Yeah, you would, Mr. Solves All Problems with Bludgeoning."

"That's actually my Indian name. I'm one sixty-fourth Cherokee."

"You don't get it. I'm supposed to be the rational one. I'm supposed to be the calm one that makes good decisions. If you lost it on that guy, nobody would've been surprised. I'm supposed to be good with people."

"You do have a bit of a reputation. Julie's the brains. I'm the one that's good at lifting heavy things and reaching items on the top shelf."

"When he accused me of being like my dad...I don't know. I just...Well, that wasn't me."

"Your dad was tricked into doing some awful things. Of course you got mad. You're only human. One cheap shot deserved another. Dumbass got what he deserved."

She reached up and rubbed her neck absently. Her voice was so low I could barely hear her over the wind. "Maybe."

I reached out gently and caught her wrist. "Cut that out."

She realized what she'd been doing and slowly put her hand back on the railing. "Stupid things...I guess I'm just extra sensitive about doing things out of character. I'm afraid they might, I don't know, *change* me. They're not inert. They've saved my life, but they've never talked to me before."

"Talked?" That was alarming.

She shrugged. "No words or anything like that,

but the marks woke me up. They warned me about the monster's presence this morning. I could tell they *wanted* me to be ready."

I didn't know what to say. "Julie..."

"Look at the timeline. I had to have woken us up the instant the *Nachtmar* appeared. It was like... I don't know, like it was aware. Like it wanted me to go fight. They're telling me things now. Are they progressing? Changing?" So far there had only been benefits to the Guardian's magic, but in this business we had plenty of examples of how *gifts* from the other side worked out, and they seldom ended well. "I don't know. What does it mean?"

I could sense her distress. I put my arm over her shoulder, pulled her close, and rested my lips on her forehead. "It means we're lucky to have you."

"Thanks."

"Everything would've been a whole lot worse if we'd been caught with our pants down. Even then, only half of us actually had pants. Except for Milo's footy jammies. I still don't know what the hell to think of those."

That finally made Julie smile a tiny bit. She put her arm around my waist and the two of us spent the next minute in silence watching the army below that would be killing us in twenty-three hours. "I'm just scared is all."

"That's normal."

Now she did laugh, but it was a bitter one. "Now being scared about being quarantined with a monster would be normal. That doesn't bug me in the slightest. All these people in danger, and I'm scared about being cursed. Go figure. Maybe I'm selfish."

"Says the woman who risks her life daily protecting the clueless. Look, I'm okay with selfish. Selfish keeps you alive longer, and I want you around for a long time."

"I suck at being selfish." Julie sighed. "Have them send somebody up to replace me. I'll go herd cats."

"Thanks, hon. Just promise me one thing."

"What?"

"Keep me in the loop about this stuff. If anything else weird happens, I want to know right away," and as I made that request, Julie stiffened against me. "What? I just want to help."

"Nothing." Julie slowly relaxed. "Anything else happens, I'll tell you, I promise."

Trip held up one fist, the signal to halt. I froze in place. "You hear that?"

The two of us were on the empty shopping concourse. The only sound I was picking up was the burbling noise of a nearby fountain. "What?"

"A phone," Trip exclaimed as he took off running. Everybody could hear better than me. I followed along, and a second later I could hear it as well. The ringing was coming from inside an information kiosk. Trip didn't bother trying the door, and instead vaulted over the desk, knocking over a display of postcards and brochures of local attractions in the process.

"They're going to charge us for those too." I took up a defensive position next to the counter and scanned for threats while Trip looked for the phone.

"Bingo." Trip came back up with a red headset. "Hello?"

If this was the security room warning us about

something they'd seen on their video cameras, I couldn't see it from here. As far as I knew, we were the only two in the entire shopping concourse, and this place was as big as a good-sized mall, only fancier. The palm trees' leaves were swaying a bit from the air circulation. An ornate clock was ticking above. The ceiling was decorated with enough murals that it made the Sistine Chapel look dumpy. This was the section where the filthy rich came to buy absurdly bejeweled watches and designer shoes that cost more than normal houses. Come to think of it, I was actually in that sort of income bracket now, but mentally I would always be too much of an accountant to shop in a place like this.

"Yeah . . . Uh-huh . . . Okay. Got it." Trip looked at me. "Mitch says we've got suspicious activity ahead to the right."

That was back in the still ridiculously expensive but not completely unreasonable section. "Define suspicious."

"One of the security alarms went off."

"Tell Mitch that if he sees us start shooting to send backup."

Trip did so then hung up the red phone. "Come on."

Sound echoed for quite some distance in the huge space. As we ran toward the disturbance there was a sudden crash and the sound of breaking glass just ahead. It really made me wish for my radio. *Stupid jamming.* I reached the corner and signaled for Trip to hold position while I risked a peek. With Abomination at my shoulder, I snaked my way forward until I could peer between the leaves of a potted plant at the source of the noise.

One of the shops—an art gallery—had a broken window. The easels immediately inside had been knocked over. Glass was scattered across the tile. I couldn't see what had caused the disturbance. It could be our monster, or it could be one of the guests had decided to do some looting. If it was the former, this could get nasty, if it was the later, it really wasn't a problem.

I looked back at Trip and signaled for him to leapfrog forward. I pointed Abomination at the shop as Trip ran past and slid behind a concrete planter. I waited for him to get his KRISS pointed at the shop, then I moved up and past him to crouch behind a bench, ready to blast whatever scaly horror showed its hideous face.

A tense minute passed. If this was our mysterious entity, would it work the same way as it had in 1613? Was it spreading while we hesitated? Should we rush it? But the decision was made for me. There was a clank of metal on metal, and a black shape moved inside the shop. "Hold your fire," Trip shouted. There was a gleam of reflected light as something glinted off of mirrored goggles. "Ed? Is that you?"

Edward the orc cheerfully waved one gloved hand when he saw me aiming Abomination at him. He walked through the mess, hopped down from the display stage, and walked through the broken window. He had a small painting tucked under one arm.

Befuddled, I put Abomination's safety back on and stood up. "What're you doing here?"

He proudly held up the painting. It was Elvis Presley on black velvet.

"Ed! There you are!" A high-pitched female voice came from the other direction. "What've you done?" Tanya ran down the hall toward Ed. The orc presented the painting of Elvis to her. "Oh, you big dork! We're gonna get busted."

"What're you *both* doing here?"

"We were on patrol!" Tanya exclaimed. "I told Ed I really thought that painting looked totally rad and how it would look awesome hanging in my room. Oh, we're now gonna get arrested. Way to go, Ed." It was hard to tell with the mask, but I think that hurt his feelings. "We've got to run for it before the cops get here. Ed don't understand human ways and I'm too pretty to go to prison!"

I rubbed my face in my hands. Trip began to laugh. Tanya was starting to panic and Ed was just confused. "Okay, okay, everybody relax. Tanya, chill. Ed, put that picture back. I knew I shouldn't have let you take that chicken. It was like your gateway drug... And who in the hell thought it was a good idea to send an untrained Newbie and an orc out on patrol?" Tanya wouldn't make eye contact and seemed intent on studying her shoes. "Tanya?"

"Nobody... Cody said the Smart Team needed to take a break from all that thinking, but I kinda still wanted to help the regular Hunters. Everybody else is pitching in. So me and Ed, we went out looking for the monster."

I looked at Ed. "And you went along with this brilliant plan?" Ed shrugged. If these two were hanging out together, Skippy was going to lose his freaking mind.

"Are you even armed?" Trip asked her. She was only wearing a snug tank top, so if she was concealing a handgun she was a lot better at it than I was, and I had a lot of practice.

"Well, kinda... When I thought Ed was going to get arrested, I sort of... well, ditched my stash." She walked back the way she'd come from, disappeared behind a few trees, and then came back with her *stash*, which consisted of a compound bow and a quiver of broad-head hunting arrows. The bow still had a price tag hanging off of it. "We passed a sporting goods store back there. They didn't have no guns, but I saw this and I sort of... You know... Harbinger always says to improvise, adapt, and survive! I'm like totally improvising! I'll pay for that window. I ain't paying for this one though!"

"You stole that bow?" Trip was mortified.

"Borrowed," she corrected me. "After we kill the monster I'll give it back. I figure I'm doing them a favor. If it got used by a badass Monster Hunter they can sell it later for a whole lot more. I'm talking premium. Who wouldn't want it then? And I know how to shoot a bow super good. Back in the Enchanted Forest we poach—I mean, we *legally* hunt deer and stuff all the time."

"Well, she is an elf," I told Trip. "The bow seems strangely appropriate."

"Now that's just racist stereotyping," Tanya sniffed. "I'm offended."

"You can file a complaint with the Trailer Park Elf Defamation League when we get out of this." Another phone began to ring. This one was a courtesy phone mounted on the wall near the bathrooms. I went over and answered it. "Hello?"

"Are those friends of yours?" Mitch snapped. "If so, all that damage is going on your bill."

At this point I didn't know if any of us would still be alive to pay it anyway. "Yes, they're with us. It was a misunderstanding. I'll keep an eye on them."

"What is it with you people and breaking every—" I hung up as Mitch continued to squawk.

"Okay, Tanya. You two need to stick with us. Ed,

despite being totally clueless, I trust. You . . . not so much."

She folded her arms indignantly. "Harbinger said I'm—"

"Harbinger gave you a job because the rest of us know jack and shit about magic, and he thinks you could come in handy, and we don't have to pay a fortune to your mom in consultant's fees. Some day you might be a full-fledged Hunter, but in the meantime you're a Newbie who doesn't know anything. Got it?"

"Yes, sir," the elf muttered.

"Stick close to us and do exactly what we tell you." The phone rang again. "Damn it."

Trip was still getting a kick out of this. "Mitch is probably calling back with your new balance. That Elvis painting was easily the most expensive thing here."

I flipped him off as I put the phone to my ear. "This is Pitt. What now?"

"Oh. My. God . . ." Mitch was breathing heavily. "I can't believe it. It pulled their arms off. It's hacking at them. There's blood and guts and blood and blood and brains everywhere. Oh, God. I don't know what it is."

"Slow down. Where?" Trip noticed the sudden shift in my demeanor and signaled Edward, who immediately drew one of his swords.

"Concourse B, second floor. Go back to the Squishy Yogurt, up the escalator, hang a left, and go down the long red hallway. They're in the nightclub. You're closest. Oh God, one of them is still alive but it's sawing on him *right now.*"

"Send help. We're on our way." I hung up the phone and hoisted Abomination. "It's back."

CHAPTER 15

Mitch's hasty directions got us there fast. The long red hallway he'd mentioned was one of the places where the casino connected to the shopping area. In the middle of it was one of the Last Dragon's three nightclubs. The double doors were open. The lights were off inside. The four of us paused in the hall to ready ourselves. We had no idea what was in there, and I *hated* that. "Wait for backup?" Trip suggested.

"That's the smart thing to do," I agreed. Then there was a bloodcurdling scream of agony from inside. The sound made all the hair on my arms stand up. Someone was still alive. "So much for smart. Tanya, stay put. Edward, keep an eye on her."

"I can help—"

I cut her off. "You are. We'll flush it out. You're cutting off its escape," I lied. There was no time to screw around arguing with an obstinate Newbie. "When help comes, send them in, but I need you to *guard this door.*"

"Can do!" She saluted me, just like she'd seen on

TV. Hunters don't salute. Edward, baffled by that uncharacteristic display, did the same thing, only more awkwardly. "We'll kill the shit out of it!"

Trip had taken cover at the corner of the door. He had point. "Ready."

"Do it." He swept around the corner, the brilliant beam of the Streamlight mounted on his submachine gun cutting a swath through the shadows. I followed right behind him.

Back when we were on the Amazing Newbie Squad, Trip had been a mediocre shot, with only barely passable proficiency. He'd come a long way since then, and the two of us had practiced this sort of thing hundreds of times. Now he was smooth, moving down the entryway of the nightclub crouched and quick, gun butt tucked into his shoulder, eyes flicking back and forth, ready to react instantly to any threat.

Something had gone down in here. A few lounge chairs had been flipped over. A table was broken. A picture frame had been torn off the wall. Trip came to a stop and held up one hand. He took a knee to inspect something. It was a bloody combat boot. Trip flipped it over with the long sound suppressor screwed onto the end of his gun. There was still a foot inside of it. A trail of blood droplets led away from the boot. We moved on with increased urgency.

I looked behind the bar. *Clear*. Trip stuck his flashlight inside the coat check. *Clear*. I couldn't find a damned light switch anywhere. Trip looked at me and pointed two fingers ahead. I nodded. He moved silently onward.

There was a large opening where the lounge fed into a far bigger room. I had to blink as my vision adjusted.

Black lights. Everything in the room that was white took on a glow. Since we were dressed in browns, greens, and grays, the only thing that stood out on us was our teeth and eyes. In the new light, I could see a white mist curling around the floor. The blood trail disappeared into it. There was a fogger running inside. Trip reached the edge, risked a quick peek, then pulled back. He signaled for me to come up and take a look.

The dance floor was huge. The interior was dome-shaped, tapering to a point at the top. There was a whole second level of catwalk, with a smaller dance area and more bars and lounges. The floor was a milky soup of glycerin fog. The illumination shifted and changed as the lights moved around above us on automated tracks. There was a hiss that made me jump, but it was coming from a nearby speaker. Music began to play, some obnoxious repetitive techno bass mix. It was deafening.

Something had just turned all these things on. That something was in here with us.

Trip thumped me in the arm to get my attention and pointed at something on the second-floor catwalk opposite of our position. There was a black figure silhouetted in the lights. I aimed my EOTech at it but held my fire because I couldn't identify what it was. The lights shifted around on their tracks and then we could see.

"That's Green!" Trip exclaimed.

Our fellow Hunter on the edge of the balcony, hanging over the dance floor. His arms had been extended and lashed down to the metal handrails with extension cords. His shaved head was stained red, hanging down, chin against his chest. His MHI-issued armor had been rent open in places and was soaked with blood. His legs were dangling in space. I realized with a shock that one of his feet was missing, and blood was drizzling from the stump. *What the hell had done that?*

The mangled Hunter stirred, lifting his head weakly for only a moment before letting it loll forward. "He's alive." Green's lips moved as he said something, but we couldn't hear him over the music.

"We've got to get him." Trip began moving, but I reached out and grabbed him by the armor.

"It's a trap." I pointed at the fog.

Trip had to shout in my ear to be heard over the noise. "We can't leave him. He's bleeding out."

"I know." We had to move fast. I scanned the fog. I couldn't see anything, but there was a knot of dread in my stomach. It was waiting for us. I knew it. But if we didn't tourniquet that leg soon, Green was done for. It might already be too late, but we had to try. There were three sets of circular stairs to the next level. Two close, one on each side, only thirty feet away. There was a third at the far end, near where Green was suspended. "Follow me. Watch the floor."

The fog parted around our boots and drifted up to our waists. The room was unnaturally cold, but nothing came out of the floor to murder us. We reached the stairs and started climbing, but we had been so intent on something hiding on the floor that we hadn't expected a threat to drop from the tangle of cables and scaffolding near the ceiling. I caught a glimpse of tattered fabric fluttering in the black light as it leapt from its perch. Abomination rose and I was able to fire a single round before the thing hit the stairs.

It was like having a blanket thrown over my head. I was engulfed in darkness. Multiple hard limbs swatted and thrashed around me. It might have been making a noise, I don't know, the music was so loud I could barely hear myself. I tried to shove it away so I could turn my shotgun against it, but it threw itself against me. Something cold and metallic scraped against my face, and then jabbed hard into my neck guard, trying to pierce my throat. I lashed out, but it was like punching a sheet hanging from a clothesline. It hit me back, and beneath that snapping piece of fabric was something as hard as an iron bar.

Its momentum took us both over the railing and we fell into the fog. I hit on my side. The blanket lifted as I rolled away. My attacker went the opposite direction.

Trip was still on the stairs, gun raised, searching for a shot, but it was already gone. "Go save Green!" I bellowed. I came up with Abomination in one hand, flashlight cutting through the mist. Something shifted just ahead of me and I cranked off a round of buckshot in its direction. "Go!"

Trip probably hadn't heard me, but he caught the gist. He leapt up the stairs three at a time, heading for our dying Hunter.

The music was thumping with electronic beats. Whatever was here with me was low to the ground, completely covered by the fog, but I knew it was circling, looking for an angle of attack. I took a step backward and collided with the stairs. The mist shifted and I fired again. It was moving with frightening speed. I briefly caught sight of two black points rising and falling, like the elbows of somebody scurrying along on their belly, but then I lost track of it completely.

I had to get out of this fog. I went around the railing, got one boot on the bottom step, but then it came out of nowhere and hit me again. *So fast.* I was jabbed in the lower back, but the point didn't penetrate my armor. I swung around to shoot but it latched on and pulled me down. The next thing I knew I was sliding along the floor on my back. It came around and was on top of me in a flash of black and glowing white streaks. It was like a collection of ratty blankets draped over a coat rack. One limb rose above the fog, spindly white fingers curled around the handle of a jagged knife. It stabbed downward but I was just able to get my armored forearm up in time to knock it away from my face. The knife rose and fell, ripping and slicing, trying desperately to pierce my armor, seeking my flesh.

The fabric puckered and flexed as bullets struck the creature. The lump of a head turned up and away from me. A round struck something solid beneath the rags and I felt the vibration. The thing leapt effortlessly away and drifted back into the mist, rags fluttering. It disappeared before I could get Abomination around. I looked over to see Trip halfway down the second-floor catwalk. The suppressed subgun didn't make enough noise to be heard over the music but I could see a match flicker of light at the muzzle and the brief glint of ejected brass. Trip had just saved my life. I got up as he kept firing into the mist behind me. Trip lost sight of his target, snarled in frustration, and started running toward Green again.

Stupid fog. I moved toward the stairs. It was still out there, waiting. I couldn't hear its approach over the music. I couldn't see a damn thing. I was like a swimmer bobbing on the surface of the ocean being circled by a great white shark. I caught the flash of reflected light out of the corner of my eye just in time to duck to the side. The thrown knife spun past where my head had been. I fired repeatedly, spacing the shots about a foot apart, hoping to clip the damned thing.

The stairs were right there. I got on them and made it out of the mist. I climbed as fast as I could until the fog was several steps below me. I was breathing hard, and the sudden heat on my cheek told me I'd been cut. There was still no sign of the threat. I risked a glance at Trip. He'd untied Green and was lifting him over the railing. I looked back just in time to see a chain come sailing out of the mist.

It struck me in the calf and wrapped around my legs like it had a mind of its own. There was a sudden jerk as the chain pulled tight and my feet came out from under me. Falling, I crashed hard against the stairs. It dragged me down. *Thump thump thump.* I managed to get my left hand onto one of the steps and clung to it for dear life. The chain jerked hard. It pulled me off the stairs and my fingers burned as I struggled to hold on. Crying out in pain, I could feel the chain fraying through my armor. I lifted Abomination with one hand, pointed it down the length of chain, and fired wildly until my shotgun was empty.

The chain unclenched, fell away, and zipped back into the fog, as fast as it had come. "What are you?" I shouted uselessly.

The creature lifted itself completely out of the fog for the first time. At first it was simply a black rectangle, but as the lights shifted I could see it was shaped like a man. Incredibly tall and thin, contorted and spindly.

I couldn't see much else of its actual form, since its body was entirely wrapped in dirty rags hanging in strips. The white bits of fabric glowed under the black lights but most of it was sick and dirty.

It lifted its arms from inside the folds of its body. One drew a butcher's knife. The other was holding a meat cleaver. Another pair of arms rose beneath that, this pair holding a box cutter and a pair of rusty scissors. The hood lifted, revealing a white pillowcase stretched tight over what could only be a skull. The mouth was a slit. The eye holes were filled with blue fire.

My STI cleared the holster and I opened fire.

The ragged man jerked and flinched as the bullets struck. There was a flash of metal and the chain erupted from the skull like the tongue of a frog. It snagged my forearm, wrapped around my wrist, and pulled taut. The muzzle of my gun was yanked to the side as the razor edge of the chain cut my armor. The chain tugged and it began to reel me back toward its demonic visage. The pair of scissors began to open and close rhythmically.

The chain sparked as a bullet struck it. The creature flinched and my wrist was freed. The chain snapped back into the monster's mouth hole like a retractable tape measure. The monster stumbled back, seemingly in pain. Seeing my chance, I jumped off the stairs, moved right between the four deadly arms, drove the muzzle of my .45 deep into one of the fiery eye holes, jerked the trigger and blew the back of its head off.

Flecks of stuffing floated in the air. The body fell silently, almost gently. The fog parted around it and the pile of rag-wrapped bones and metal implements landed in a disorganized heap. The blue fire winked out of existence. The back of its hood was split open and rather than brains, ragged chunks of bloody fabric fluff rolled across the floor. A fluid that glowed under the black lights came spilling out from every seam, soaked into the rags, and formed a puddle.

I stood over it, waiting, bleeding but breathing, keeping it covered, but it didn't so much as twitch. But just to be sure I pulled out my lighter and set the rags on fire. The flames spread greedily. The glowing goo was extremely flammable. I reloaded my guns as the fire consumed the body. "Whatever you were, you're dead now . . . Asshole."

The music stopped abruptly. "Up here!" Trip shouted. He was behind the DJ station on the second floor. He messed with something else and the normal lights came on with a blinding pop.

"Dude, that was an amazing shot. I can't believe you hit that chain all the way from over there!"

"I could barely see anything. I just hosed him and got lucky." Further proof that Trip must be living right. He was far too honest. I wouldn't have said anything and just let him think that I was that awesome.

The cuts on my forearm and calf burned, but they weren't bleeding too badly. Addressing them could wait a minute. Thank goodness for Kevlar. I limped up the stairs and made my way down the walkway. Trip had dragged Green onto one of the lounge couches and put a tourniquet around his leg. All Hunters keep a few of those in our kits. When you run into as many different things that can remove limbs as we do, you'd be stupid not to.

The blood loss had slowed to the rate of a mildly drippy faucet. The half of Green's face that wasn't covered in blood was deathly pale. Trip opened his med pouch and pulled out a pressure bandage. He gently lifted the shredded remains of Green's armor and revealed the terrible injury beneath.

Green moaned when the bandages touched him. "He sawed my foot off." His voice was barely a whisper.

"We know." Trip knelt next to him. "It's okay, man. We got it. You're going to be fine."

"Where's your partner?" I didn't even know who Green had been patrolling with.

"Gone . . . Dead . . . Ragman got him."

"Ragman?"

"Listen . . ." Green reached out and touched Trip's arm. "He was my first monster. In San Diego. Serial killer. Sold his soul . . . Turned into *that*. I killed him years ago . . ." Green coughed hard. "Guess he wasn't done with me yet." He coughed again, wheezed, then passed out. I checked his pulse. It wasn't good.

Another horror dredged from the back of someone's mind and set free. Hugo's last word had been *Nachtmar*. It was looking like *nightmare* was a good name for what we were up against.

When we got back to the conference center, we learned that the *Nachtmar* had struck in two places simultaneously this time. In addition to crippling Green and killing a Hunter from the Mexican company, by the name of Salazar, it had struck nearly simultaneously in another area. Pressfield, from Sticks of Fire out of Tampa, and Verne, one of the British liaisons from BSS, had responded to cries for help from one of the rooms. When they'd kicked in the door, Pressfield had been ripped to pieces by the demonic things that the anti-Hunting activists inside that room had mutated into.

The surviving Hunter fragged the room, then head-shot everything. He'd been so shell shocked that when he'd walked back into the main lobby where most of the trapped tourists had congregated, his wide-eyed and blood-soaked appearance had nearly caused a panic. That had only been three minutes before I'd run in, carrying Green and shouting for a medic.

Now the trapped tourists were ready to listen to us. Too bad we didn't really know what to do yet.

Afterwards, Pressfield's boss, Allen, was able to identify the creatures from the description as something similar to an oddity that Sticks of Fire had encountered and wiped out a year earlier.

"Pull the patrols back in. I want everybody in one area." Earl was pacing at the front of the conference room. He was chain-smoking again, but it wasn't like anyone present was going to give him grief about it. Representatives from every team were here, Hunters foreign and domestic, whether we got along or not, as well as some of the casino's night managers. I was sitting on a table with my pants leg rolled up while Trip sewed stitches in my ankle. "This thing is screwing with us."

"You think it's intelligent?" VanZant asked.

"Yeah . . . It strikes one way, creating a beachhead. So we spread out to keep an eye out for that kind of attack, so it changes tactics and starts picking us off one by one." Earl angrily lit his next cigarette. "Tell me that don't sound smart? We need to fortify here, where we can keep an eye on each other."

"What if it picks an isolated spot and pulls a stunt like it did in Hugo's room?" I asked. "By the time we knew, there could be an army of monsters coming at us. Then we're back to where we were this morning."

"Pitt is correct," Pierre Darne agreed. "Turtles have shells, but make for tasty soup."

"Is that like some old French proverb?"

"I made it up." Darne shrugged. "I thought it was a fine analogy."

"Okay, Pierre, put together a full team and send them down to the security room. I want that place locked down tight. Protect it at all costs. What's your new buddy's name there, Z?"

I didn't know if I would go as far as *buddy*. "Mitch."

"Tell Mitch that we're counting on him to be our eyes. *Nachtmar* makes a big move, he calls us and we vector in on it."

"Consider it done." Darne signaled two of his employees that were present and they left.

Earl was talking quickly now. The gears were turning. "VanZant, you're good with people. Take Tyler Nelson, he's a shrink, and whoever else you need. I want every single person that's locked themselves in their rooms brought down to this floor, and I want them here now."

"Some aren't going to like that," the diminutive man told him.

"*Persuade* them, but don't waste time on anybody who wants to do their own thing. If they want to hole up alone, leave them."

He didn't care for that. "We've seen how this thing works. It's just going to pick something nasty out of their heads, make it real, then kill them with it. If I leave them—"

"Their deaths aren't on our hands. I respect stubbornness and I respect folks who take personal responsibility, but we can't be everywhere. They don't want to come, write them off."

From what I knew of our California team leader, he was the last person who wanted to leave anyone behind, but our hands were tied. "You want persuasive? I'll give you persuasive." He gave Earl a sharp nod and then left the room. I heard him shout from the hall. "Jason Lacoco! You, large Polish man! Follow me."

The big fellow laughed with his hearty pirate laugh. "My name is Byreika, my small friend. Tadeusz Byreika! Let us go and scare all the people."

No way. If we lived long enough I was going to have to sit down with that guy and ask him about his genealogy.

Earl turned next to the night supervisor of the casino. She was a sharp-featured woman in her fifties, and was the senior employee stuck under quarantine. The name tag on her tidy black pants suit said BETH. "Are all your employees accounted for?"

"They are. In one way it's fortunate this happened when it did. This is our smallest shift. Just my shitty luck that it happens to be *my* shift . . . All of them are in this area except for the people in the security room and our guards at the vault."

"I'd suggest leaving the vault and getting their asses up here. It's only money."

"There are millions of dollars in cash in that vault. I'm not even authorized to know how much."

"Can't spend it if you're dead."

Beth shook her head. "I'm not authorized to do that. The last message I received from Management specified to turn all operating decisions over to you, Mr. Harbinger, but we were to keep staff in control of the vault, regardless of what you said. Management's orders."

If no one could call in or out ... "How did you hear—"

Earl held up one hand to silence me. "Leave it, Z ... Okay, Beth. This is what you do, pull those men out of there, because otherwise, when they die, it goes on your conscience. If we live long enough for Management to get mad at you, tell him that I forced you to do it. He knows that I'm pushy like that. If this is all a very elaborate scam to rob your vault, he knows where I live."

Beth looked really nervous. "They say he's—"

"He's not *here*," Earl specified. "I am. Get those men up here now. Then you're going to go with the red-bearded gentleman," Earl pointed at Milo. "And you're going to send some of your people to raid your stores and bring things here. Food, water, medical supplies, and anything else Milo can think of that might be useful, and trust me, he will surprise you with what he thinks is useful. Move."

"Yes, sir," Beth said, having been completely bull-dozed.

"You get used to him," Milo told her on the way out.

Earl continued handing out assignments. I knew I'd get my turn soon enough, and soon enough we were the only ones left in this part of the lobby. There was a sudden twinge in my ankle. "Dude, watch it."

"Sorry," Trip said. "All done. Five stitches. No biggie."

I inspected his work. The cut from the chain had almost been shallow enough for super glue. All things considered, I was really lucky. "They're way prettier when Holly does them."

"So sue me."

"Maybe I should, lousy stitching like that. You've ruined my chances of becoming a swimsuit model."

"You can still live your dream. That's what Photo-shop is for."

"Are you two done screwing around?" Earl asked. Trip gave him a thumbs-up as I rolled my ripped pant leg back down, pulled the armor guard back into place, and cinched it up tight. That stung. Everybody else had been dismissed. "Cody and the smart kids are inspecting the attack scenes, looking for clues about how to beat this damned thing. Get over to the nightclub and brief him on everything you saw. Take the elf with you, see if she can't . . . *wizard* something up. Hell if I know, whatever it is elves do."

I hadn't seen my wife in the meeting. "Is Julie with them?"

"I gave her a few more men and sent her back up to the roof," Earl answered.

"Why?"

"To keep an eye out . . ." Earl said, strangely defensive. "My call. Got a problem with that?"

Normally I wouldn't argue with Earl, but this was my wife we were talking about. "Yeah, I do. What's the deal, Earl? You've been weird about her since this started."

Earl frowned at me and moved his cigarette from one side of his mouth to the other, thinking. I wasn't about to back down, and he knew me well enough to know it. "Trip, give us a minute alone."

Trip, looking concerned that I'd just crossed some line with our scary werewolf boss, complied. "I'll be right out here when you need me."

Earl glanced around to confirm that nobody was close enough to listen. "I put Julie on the roof because the roof is safer. She's with solid Hunters in a wide-open space.

No civilians with nightmares to raid. And if anything happens she can keep an eye on things for us."

"As much as I appreciate the sentiment of keeping her out of harm's way, she's got to have hated that order."

"She did. She called me a few choice names and raised holy hell, but as much of a pain in my ass as that stubborn girl has been over the years, she trusts me enough to do what I ask."

Now I was just confused. Earl had never been overprotective of Julie before. She had started participating in MHI missions when she was still a teenager. Julie had actually cut her prom date short in order to tag along with Earl to take out an ogre. "She's one of the most talented Hunters we've got. Why waste her up there?"

Earl's manner made it obvious that he didn't want to be having this conversation. "Because if everything goes to complete shit, or that bastard Stricken makes his move early, she can make a break for it in the chopper with Skippy. No matter what, she needs to survive."

"Yeah, no kidding. We don't do this kind of thing and try not to survive. You yelled at her for going into 1613 too. I'm not leaving until I have an answer. What's the deal?"

"Listen to me, Owen..." Earl tossed the butt of his cigarette into a potted plant. "Here's the deal. I don't want her in harm's way because Julie's pregnant."

"Wait..." My stomach lurched. "What? How?"

Earl folded his arms and smirked at me. "How? Really, kid?"

"No, I mean..." My brain was having a really

difficult time sending messages to my mouth. Suddenly flushed and dizzy, I was really glad I was already sitting down. "Pregnant? How do you know?"

"You forget how sensitive my nose is. Humans are walking hormonal cocktails. Werewolves can spot a pregnant woman a mile away, you know, pick the slow ones out of the herd. Don't you dare tell her I said that. I could tell as soon as y'all flew in. So yeah, that's my first great-great-grandkid in there. You're gonna be a father. Congratulations. Now, no matter what, we make sure Julie lives through this. Not counting the Boss back in Alabama, who ain't no spring chicken, the last of the Shacklefords are all here, and I will not tolerate my family dying out. Period."

I wasn't mentally ready for this. We'd talked about it, but because of the Guardian's curse we'd been too scared of the repercussions to risk it. What if the baby inherited the marks? We'd taken precautions. Julie was on the pill. *Ninety-nine percent effective, my ass.* Thoughts and emotions were colliding in my head. I was too confused to know how I felt. "I... Wow...Oh, man. Does she know? Did you tell her?"

"Thought about it. I couldn't decide if that would make the situation better or worse. Quarantined with a nightmare creature? I figured she had enough to worry about without complicating matters. What was I supposed to do? Maybe I haven't been thinking too clearly myself."

"I'm sorry about Heather."

Earl shook his head. "I've not given up on her yet. Heather's a survivor. You'd like her. And now that I know more about what's going on, when I get out of here I will find her...So yeah, that's about it, Z.

I've been protective because your wife is gonna have a baby. Regular cause for rejoicing. Normally I'd say 'let's celebrate,' and you could fetch me a beer and a cigar, but right now I'll settle for 'let's not all die.' So now that I've ruined your calm . . ." He reached out and patted me on the shoulder. The gesture was about the most tender familial thing I'd ever seen from Earl Harbinger. "Get back to work."

CHAPTER 16

"Hey, Z. Are you okay?"

"Huh? Yeah, fine." Truthfully I was in a daze. I wanted to be talking to my wife, not wandering through this ridiculous flashy casino, looking for a nightmare monster. "Sorry, just tired is all."

Trip just shook his head and continued between the slot machines. He knew me better than almost anyone, so didn't bother bugging me further. Cutting through this gambling area was the quickest way to get back to the nightclub. Tanya and Edward were right behind us, Edward happily pointing and grumbling at the pretty lights and video poker. Finally Tanya said, "Jeez, chill, Ed. Don't get all tourist and make us look like hicks." I'd seen the trailer she'd grown up in. The girl wasn't fooling anybody.

I couldn't wrap my brain around it. Julie and I were going to have a kid. You wouldn't think that would be so mind-blowing—I'd fought alien gods, after all—but it really was. We had a lot to talk about, a lot to plan, a lot to get ready for. It was terrifying and exciting

at the same time, but right then, mostly terrifying.
Sort of like my job in that respect. Not that I wasn't
motivated to survive before, but now I really had a
reason to beat this thing.

A phone began to ring.

"Oh, heck..." Trip muttered. Tanya's pointy ears
weren't just for show, and she picked out the source
first. The sound was coming from the entrance to
a nearby sports bar. I found the phone under the
hostess podium.

"This is Pitt."

"This is Mitch. Are you guys okay?"

I glanced around. Everything was as normal as a
deserted, haunted casino could be. "We're fine."

"Good. We were watching you, but then you weren't
on camera anymore. Where are you?"

I read the sign over my head. "Johnny Football
Hero's Sports Bar and Grill."

"I'm looking right at it. That can't be right..."
Mitch's voice faded as he gave instructions to one
of his employees. "Where? Jump up and down or
something."

I sighed. "Everybody smile for the cameras. Move
around so they can see us." The rest of my team did
so, everyone picking out one of the silver balls in
the ceiling and waving at it. Edward waved at a slot
machine that had a clown on it.

"We can't see you. There's nobody on camera. You
guys aren't there."

Oh, that can't be good.

"What's going on?" Trip asked.

"Technical glitch with the cameras?" I asked hopefully.

"Impossible," Mitch said. "I'm going to call your boss and warn him something's up."

"Do that—" The air temperature was dropping rapidly. My breath came out as steam. "Mitch, we've got company. I'll have to call you back."

"There's something wrong..." Trip said as he lifted the KRISS to his shoulder. "Feel that?" Edward drew his short swords. Tanya pulled an arrow from the protective foam quiver and tried to nock it with suddenly cold fingers. Every shadow in the dimly lit gambling area was suddenly threatening. "Where's the fastest way out?"

"Back the way we came." I flicked Abomination's safety off with my trigger finger. "Walk fast." There was an awful moan. It was impossible to tell where it came from. "Real fast."

"You smell that?" Tanya asked nervously.

"Dead things," Ed answered.

"Movement on the left," Trip said. I turned, ready to shoot. "It's gone now."

"Aw, hell." I caught something in the corner of my vision and turned. Something had moved between two slot machines. "Contact right." Shadows were dancing along the wall, but there were so many different oddly placed light sources that I couldn't tell where they originated from.

"They're behind us too!" Tanya exclaimed. She was gesturing wildly at the sports bar we had just left. I turned just as several dark shapes were shuffling out the front door of the restaurant. Covering them with Abomination, I lit them up with the mounted flashlight. The shapes were illuminated in a brilliant white beam. At first I thought they were people, a crowd of at least eight, but then I noticed the blood and the torn clothing, then the exposed bones and missing chunks of flesh, and then their dead, blank eyes turned toward the light and they stumbled forward.

"Zombies!" Trip and I shouted at the same time, but no one could hear us because we started shooting at almost the exact same moment. Heads ruptured as I worked Abomination across their line, one, two, three, four, five, dispatched in just over a second. Trip had started with the other side, and the zombie in the middle got a neat .45-caliber hole in the forehead a fraction of a second before a 12-gauge slug removed three quarters of its skull.

I stared at the pile of corpses. There was no hesitation when it came to zombies. In any other situation our training would've demanded that we wait long enough to be a hundred percent sure that they were actual undead monstrosities and not people dressed up in costume, but here in Hotel Hell, I was ready to shoot first and ask questions later.

"Anybody we know?" I asked, but they didn't look like they'd been animated from any of the people I'd seen trapped here so far. *That meant* . . . I glanced at the others. Tanya was quaking, face pale, limbs quivering. Trip, having come to the same realization, was staring back at me. "These from my past or yours?"

"Either way it's bad." A chorus of undead moans filled the entire casino, dozens, maybe hundreds of them. "Keep going!"

The purple carpet near my feet ripped open and a rotting hand poked through, grasping wildly. Beneath the carpet was soft, crumbling black dirt. I flinched and jumped back. "Impossible," I muttered as I smashed the hand beneath my size-fifteen boot and took off after my friends.

Tanya screamed as a hand broke through a nearby wall and reached for her. She backed into a slot machine, and another hand shattered the glass and grabbed a tangle of her hair. Suddenly, Edward was by her side, his sword humming through the air, and the hand went flying. It landed on a nearby blackjack table, still twitching as spasmodically as the maggots poking out of it.

"How the hell does that work?" I took a step around the broken slot machine. There wasn't even room for a zombie to fit inside, but laws of physics be damned, there was still a zombie crawling out of it. The broken glass cut through its rubbery, bloodless skin. "I hate monsters that cheat." I blew its head off.

"This way." Trip was in the lead. Zombies were popping up all around us, clawing their way out of the floor as if it was made of soft cemetery dirt, crashing through the walls around us like they were old mausoleums instead of sheetrock and new wallpaper. Trip came running back, a mob of zombies blocking the direction we'd come from. "Not that way."

We were completely surrounded. There were hundreds of them. Was there any limit to what the *Nachtmar* could create? I killed a zombie with each shot left in Abomination's magazine, then dropped the shotgun to dangle from its sling and pulled my pistol. I lined up the sights and brain-shot the next zombie in line. Four more took its place. Even keeping our cool and dropping a zombie with each round, we'd be out of ammo and overwhelmed in no time. We needed an exit or at least a choke point.

"Over here," Tanya said. There was a set of double doors nearby that I hadn't seen earlier. Tanya ran to the doors and yanked them open. "They're unlocked." She looked in. "And zombie-free!"

Anything was a better option than getting eaten. "Get in there then." An arrow hit a nearby zombie in the chest. The thing rocked, but then kept walking, oblivious to the shaft sticking out from between its ribs. "Quit dinking around and move!"

Trip walked backward toward the doors, firing methodical, single, aimed shots the whole time. Edward was on the other side, and in a flash of movement, *zip zip zip*, three zombies fell to the floor, their heads rolling away. I emptied my pistol magazine on the way over to them. There was quite the pile of corpses all around us by the time I got there.

The four of us got through the doors, and they swung shut behind us. Edward found something on the ground, picked it up, and shoved it through the twin handles to form a makeshift crossbar.

We were in a long, straight, industrial-gray hallway. There were rows of green lockers on each side and multiple wooden doors with small glass windows inset in them. The fluorescent lights above us were flickering and humming.

I braced my shoulder against the door, reloaded Abomination, and got ready for the inevitable zombie onslaught. "We'll hold them until help comes. If they break through the door, the hall's narrow enough to funnel them down. Let's stack these sons a bitches, Trip." He didn't answer. Trip was busy staring down the hallway. I looked past him, but couldn't see anything worth fixating on. The hall terminated at a bulletin board. That wasn't nearly as interesting as an onslaught of flesh-eating zombies. "Trip?" I snapped my fingers. "Trip!"

My friend spoke very slowly. "This is bad . . . Really, really bad."

Shit. It was unlike Trip to lose it. "Ed, help me." The orc put one boot against the base of the door, sheathed one sword, then took the other one up in both hands, ready to thrust it through the intersection of the two doors to surprise-kill a zombie. With Captain Slice 'n' Dice by my side, any zombie hands that broke through were going to get lopped off real quick. We just had to hold until Harbinger hit them from the other side.

But there was no crash, no press of undead corpses stacking up against the door. It was quiet . . . Had the zombies been too stupid to follow us? That was possible depending on the type and strain, and those had been slow shamblers, the stupidest type I knew of. Or had the *Nachtmar's* magical effect worn off? If I opened the door, would they be gone and the casino turned back to normal, or would they be there waiting? I got up, realizing as I did so, it was no longer cold. In fact, it was hot. A deep, thick, muggy heat that made me feel like I was back in Alabama. The sudden temperature change made my skin tingle painfully.

"Heh . . ." Trip laughed absently. "This is *really* bad."

I looked back to the door. Still no zombies. But then I realized what Edward had used to jam the door handles closed. It was a pickax, and the metal tips were coated with congealing blood and tufts of hair. "Trip, *where* are we?"

"This is where I found out monsters are real . . .

We're in Florida." Trip said. "Lord help us, this is my high school."

John Jermaine Jones, or Mr. J, as he was commonly called back then, had been a teacher at a small-town high school in rural Florida when the zombie outbreak had occurred. Some local teens had antagonized a witch doctor, with gruesome results. The outbreak had been a small one by historical standards, but still bad enough to warrant a Level Three containment by the Monster Control Bureau. Luckily for them, the events had occurred only a few days before a hurricane, which provided a handy scapegoat to explain the number of dead and missing in the media. There had only been a handful of firsthand eyewitness survivors, and all except one had been rather easily intimidated into silence, but that one had been recruited by a private Hunting company and had signed all of the applicable NDAs, so by Monster Control Bureau standards, the Leonard, Florida, outbreak had been handled flawlessly.

Those facts were all irrelevant to Mr. J, who had spent the evening hitting his students in the head with a pickax.

Trip stumbled and crashed into one of the puke-green lockers. He was beginning to hyperventilate. I ran over and caught him before he could slide to the floor. "This isn't real! Trip, he's messing with your head. We're not really here." *Probably.*

"I can't do this again." Trip grabbed onto my arm so hard that it hurt. "Not this. I had to kill them, Z. I had to kill them all. I tried to save them, but there were too many. I had to leave some of the kids behind."

"That was a long time ago. You did the best you could. We're going to walk out of here. This is all an illusion."

Tanya rapped her knuckles on the wall. "Nope. It's real. We're just not in our world. We're *in between*."

"In between what?" I demanded.

"People are used to only being in one world. Hunters get used to seeing into others sometimes. Elves can see into some of the others a little. There's lots of other worlds bunching up against ours. That's where lots of monsters come from, you know, but this... This is part of some other world squished into ours. It's all twisted up so I don't recognize which one it is. I wish I could call Momma. She'd know."

"Nightmare-land," Edward rumbled, still watching the door. "Bad place."

Choosing between a casino full of zombies on Earth or wandering further into nightmare-land was an easy call. "Whatever it is, we're getting the hell out of here." I dragged Trip back to his feet. "Listen to me, man. I need you to focus. Now is not the time to lose your shit."

"I'm okay," he said wiping his eyes with the back of his glove. "Wasn't expecting this is all. Let's get out of here." There was steel in his voice as Trip lifted his gun. "Put your game face on."

"That's more like it. Ed, get ready." I pointed Abomination at the doorway.

Our orc yanked out the pickax and let it clatter to the floor. He kicked the door open and...

"Oh, come on..." Slowly lowering Abomination, I gawked at the scene. There was a sidewalk, some bushes, then the clearly marked handicapped parking area, and behind that were some tall street lamps being circled by clouds of reflective nighttime bugs, and beyond that was an empty street, then the bleachers for a football field, and on the other side of that was a dense, dark, swampy forest, clicking and buzzing with insect life. The door slowly swung back inside, then out, then in, then stopped, blocking the scene entirely. "Trip?"

It took him a moment to get his voice back. "That's what it looked like. I ran into the first zombies where they had been digging up a busted water pipe outside. That's how I got the pickax in real life."

I sighed. "We're not in Kansas anymore."

Edward muttered something, and Tanya gave him a friendly cuff. "Of *course*, Las Vegas is in Nevada," Tanya said. "That's from *The Wizard of Oz*. Didn't your momma let you watch any TV while you were growin' up? *Orcs*..."

"What do we do?" I asked her.

"Why are you asking me?" Tanya was terrified.

"You're the wizard!" I gestured at the doors that most certainly did not lead back into the casino. "That's a magic issue. Fix it!"

A low growling sound came from inside one of the nearby lockers. All of us jumped. Something thumped against the sheet metal. Then it thumped again, harder. Something was trying to get out. I put the EOTech on the center of the locker. Trip was saying something under his breath, repeating the same thing over and over, and I realized he was praying. "What is it?"

"Her name was Amy. She was on the softball team, sophomore, good kid. Bright future." Trip's whole body was shaking. "She was the only survivor outside. I

came in here to call for help, but I could hear more
of them ahead. This locker was open, so I told her
to get inside. I closed the door and told her to stay
real quiet . . . I didn't know what else to do. I thought
they wouldn't be able to get to her."

The locker rocked. The metal frame was bend-
ing around the latch. The zombie inside couldn't get
enough range of motion to break itself free.

"Don't cry. Don't cry. I'll get help. Just stay quiet
and they won't know you're here . . ." Trip whispered.

"She had already been bitten, hadn't she?"

"I didn't know what to do back then, Z. I did the
best I could."

Edward stepped forward, lifted his sword about head
high, and drove it cleanly through the sheet metal.
He wrenched it around then pulled out the blade,
now coated in fresh blood. The moaning stopped.
The locker was still.

There was a sudden bang as a door further inside
the school was opened. Someone screamed.

"This is how it happened . . . Exactly how it happened," Trip said. "This is exactly how it happened.
They all died last time." The screaming continued. It
sounded like a young woman, high-pitched and terrified.

"Focus, Trip. Listen to me, man." I grabbed him
by the shoulder. "Don't let him mess with your head.
It's not *real*."

"What if it is? We don't know who else is in here."
Desperate, he knocked my hand away. There was more
crashing as furniture was knocked over, followed by
the groans of the hungry dead. Then there was a
chorus of screams. "I can save them this time." Trip
took off in a sprint.

I should've seen that coming. "Damn it, Trip!" I shouted after my friend. "Stop!" I couldn't have tackled him if I wanted to. Trip was way faster than I was. "Hell. Come on," I told the other two.

Trip was running full tilt, and he'd been a college football running back. The dude could move. He got to the next intersection, hung a left, and disappeared. I got there a few seconds after him. There were bloody handprints on the walls. Trip had already rounded the next corner when I stepped in a puddle of blood, slipped, and landed on my hands and knees. Ed moved to help me, but I waved him on. "Catch Trip." Tanya and Edward did as I ordered and kept running. I got up and started after them, but as I reached the next corner, the fluorescents died. I was completely engulfed in darkness. I reached out to touch the wall that had just been there, but my hand fell through nothing. I took another step to where I was positive the wall would be, but it was only open air.

The world around me had vanished. "Oh, crap."

Everything was just gone. It was empty and dark and vast, and my muscles threatened to lock up in fear. I had to fight down the sudden urge to panic. I blundered forward, sightless. *No. Don't leave me here.*

Then there was a tiny flicker of light ahead, the fluorescent lights of the high school. I struggled toward it.

The figure of a man stepped into my path. "Wait, please." I squinted to see who it was, and with a shock, recognized the young man that I'd seen briefly at the wrecked gas station. He was in the same olive-drab utility clothing, free of any identifier. My initial reaction was to shoot him, but the look on his face was one of concern rather than menace. "Don't leave yet.

I pulsed you here so we can talk without him hearing us. It's getting worse out there, isn't it?"

"Yes. Who are you?"

The young man rubbed his face with his hands, the motion of a man who was desperately trying to wake up. "I don't remember."

"You'd better start remembering, sport. Are you the one behind this? Are you the Nightmare?"

"No. I'm trying to hold him back. I used to remember how to control him, but I've been asleep. They put me to sleep. I'm still trying to wake up. Everything's so confusing. I don't know anymore."

What the hell is going on here? "What do you remember?"

"Needles . . . They stuck so many needles in me. Hundreds and hundreds of needles. They gave me drugs. They shut down my brain. They thought it would stay inside me that way. The doctors thought it would sleep forever, but it dreamed the whole time. Such terrible dreams . . ." The young man shuddered, and that seemed to rouse him from his haze. "I've got to find her. Help me find her, mister. I have to know she's safe. In the dreams, he showed me over and over what he would do to her. That's how he woke me up. I've got to get to her before he does. Help me find her, then I can put him back to sleep. I can't rest until I know she's safe."

He'd mentioned finding someone last time. "Who?"

It was as if he didn't hear me. "He wants you to die here. You've crossed into his world. I'll try to make a door for you and your pals to go back through. I won't be able to do that for too many more times now that he's awake. He gets stronger, then he rests and comes back again. The stronger he gets, the more the worlds will blur together. I'll make you a door home, but promise you'll help me first."

What choice did I have? "Okay. I promise." The darkness parted just a bit more. The place I'd just been standing was ahead, shimmering as if it were under water. I took a step toward it, fearful that what felt like solid ground beneath my feet would disappear at any moment, then another step, and another. The light grew closer. "This woman I'm supposed to find, what's her name?" Then I realized that the light was fading, and soon I would be left in the darkness, trapped. There was no time. "Shit." I ran for it. As I moved past the young man, it was like being struck by an arctic wind, the cold was so piercing.

One freezing hand reached for me but it passed through my arm as if there was nothing there. The cold threatened to overpower me. "I remember something important. Topaz! Look at topaz!" he begged.

And then I was back in the light.

Turning around, there was nothing but the blood-smeared high school. The empty black was gone.

Another bloodcurdling scream brought me back to reality.

It was as if no time had passed at all, and I caught up to Tanya and Edward in a few seconds. Just ahead, Trip rounded one last corner and skidded to a stop.

I caught up. There was a mob of zombies waiting for us. Their clothing was ripped, red with fresh blood, there was a janitor, teachers and parents, but most of them were just normal kids. They were all focused on trying to get into a classroom, smashing themselves over and over against the splintering door. There were interior windows; those were cracked, held together only by the wire mesh inside, but the zombies were slowly pushing their way in. The screams were coming from inside the classroom. The zombies had heard the squeak of Trip's boots and their heads snapped around automatically, dead, glassy eyes fixated on him.

"This time I've got a gun," Trip said. The zombies started toward us. "And I know how to use it." Then he went to town. The first zombie caught a .45 right in the eye. The next two were going down before the brains of the first one had even splattered against the floor. The impact of the bullets made more noise than the firing of the suppressed KRISS. Brass tinkled across the floor.

A zombie lurched at us from a nearby closet. I blasted it square in the face. A dead cheerleader came from the other side, but Edward hurled a knife and stuck her head to a bulletin board. By MHI standards, slow zombies were easy money. Trip just kept on shooting real bullets into the imaginary zombies as they lurched and jerked their way toward us.

Trip's gun was empty. There was still one left tottering toward him. I pointed Abomination. "I've got this," he spat with uncharacteristic rage. Trip dropped his subgun and pulled the tomahawk from his belt. The zombie was wearing a white shirt and a tie. "Hey, Jim." The zombie kept walking obliviously toward his destruction. Trip took two steps forward and swung, planting the little ax into Jim's forehead. "You don't get them this time." Trip wrenched the tomahawk out, taking a huge chunk of scalp with it, then chopped Jim again, then one last time as the nearly headless corpse went down. Trip was panting. "Never again."

In less than twenty seconds there were more than twenty dead zombies littering the hall. Edward went over and jerked his knife out of the wall and the zombie's head. It dropped like a rock. Ed wiped his knife off on the cheerleader's skirt before resheathing it. Tanya went to the side and barfed in a trash can.

Trip was standing over the dead man in the tie, his tomahawk dangling at his side, dripping dark blood. "That was Jim," he said softly. "Friend of mine. Taught shop. Last time he was the one that broke in. He was the one that got the kids that I couldn't save. I put those kids in there. I told them to barricade the doors and stay put. I went to get help. I told them to pray. I told them to have faith and everything would be okay. I told them to *trust* me, but I failed them. I was too slow, too weak...I wasn't ready then. I didn't know what I was doing then. I wasn't prepared. Not this time...Never again."

I looked to the classroom. The screaming had stopped. It was quiet except for the buzz of the old lights. "What happens now?"

"I don't know. Last time I got this far they were already dead." Trip put his tomahawk away and stuck a fresh mag into his subgun. "Let's find out."

Stepping over corpses, we reached the classroom. The door was nearly destroyed. One sharp kick sent it flying inward.

As promised, he'd given us our exit. The four of us stepped out onto the empty gambling floor of the Last Dragon casino. The door we'd just come through led to nothing but an empty janitorial closet.

CHAPTER 17

Earl Harbinger wasn't even there for me to brief when we got back to the conference center. He was off taking care of another crisis called in by Mitch. Apparently, there was a kraken in the pool.

Cody, Paxton, and the other smart Hunters had come back from the nightclub without incident. They'd walked right through the area where we'd been initially attacked by zombies, and there hadn't even been a sign that anything had happened there at all. I gave them the rundown of what we'd seen, then had to repeat myself to Klaus Lindemann, who had been made the second-in-command of our operation. I hadn't been around for that part. It struck me as a cagey move by Earl, though, since Grimm Berlin was respected by many of the companies that didn't particularly care for us, and even the companies that didn't like either of us would have a difficult time not listening to the combined experience of those two men.

Nobody I briefed had a clue what the significance of topaz could be, but it immediately sent Lee on a research kick. We had monsters that had violent adverse reactions to silver, and more rarely from other substances like holy water, white oak jade, or salt, so why not topaz? Milo took a raiding party down to the gift shops to find some. There was bound to be some jewelry we could use. It would be nice to have another weapon to use against this thing.

Of course, that was all assuming that the kid I'd talked to was even real and not some sort of trick of the *Nachtmar*'s. For all I knew the damn thing thought topaz was delicious and was using us to forage for snacks. I didn't know what to believe, and since I'd just strolled through a hallway that had been filled with Florida, believing *anything* here was one hell of a risky assumption.

Lindemann told me that he'd put together one group of Hunters, hotel employees, and a few surprisingly useful volunteers from among the tourists to explore possible avenues of escape should time run out. There are always sewer systems and steam tunnels under a building of this size, and if we were lucky not all of them would be blocked by the MCB. None of us were real hot on the idea of dying in this quarantine. So far there hadn't been any luck.

All of the spare equipment available had been gathered in the conference center. One of the Russian Hunters had been trapped outside the quarantine, and his gear had several loaded eight-round Saiga magazines in it, so I borrowed those to resupply Abomination. It was lunch time, and Milo's raiders had brought back a literal ton of food. The conference center had facilities for everything, and the employees had gone to work preparing food. It kept their minds occupied and everyone else's bellies full. After picking up a couple of plates, I found Trip sitting on the carpet outside the main conference room with a thousand-yard stare, so I gave him a turkey sandwich and a Coke and sat down next to him.

"I've got no appetite," he said after a minute of staring at his food. "Go figure."

"Reliving the worst moments of your life will do that to you. Eat. Come on. You'll feel better . . . I know you want to." Trip finally relented, unwrapped the sandwich, and took a bite. He chewed listlessly, still staring off into space. I let him drink some Coke before bothering him more. He needed the sugar. "How're you doing?"

"Better than expected." Trip watched his hands for a bit. They were still trembling, but much less than before.

"Want to talk about it?"

"No." But when I didn't go away, Trip sighed and gave in. "Really, I'm fine. That was just a shock to the system. After Florida, once I found out that there was such a thing as Hunters, for the very first time I knew what God wanted me to do with my life. I'd found my purpose. There was real evil in the world, but it was okay, because there were good guys that could fight it. Knowing that's what got me by the first time. God had a plan for me."

Trip was a lot more religious than I was. I could only nod and agree. "Sounds reasonable."

"This *Nachtmar* wanted to scare me, wanted to break me, maybe? I don't know. Assuming it even thinks like we do at all. But if that was what it was going for . . . Big mistake on his part." Trip took a long

drink of the Coke. "What just happened only reaf-
firmed my faith that I'm doing the right thing. When
I was a normal guy, a whole bunch of innocents died
because I didn't have the skills that I do now. We
plowed through more zombies in five minutes than I
had in two hours back then. How many times have
we saved the day, Z? How many innocent people are
alive because we did our job?"

Trip was a true believer. It was going to take a lot
more than revisiting his past to shake him. "We've
saved bunches."

"We're the good guys. We're the heroes."

"Damn good-looking ones, too. I knew you'd be okay."

"Eternal optimists." Trip chuckled. "But I've been
thinking. If this *Nachtmar* could do that with what I
had in my head...My experiences are nothing compared
to what some of these Hunters have been exposed to.
What's going to happen when it gets to someone like
you? I mean, come on, you've been to hell."

"It wasn't really hell. It was more of an infinite
dimension of eternal suffering populated by awful
beings beyond comprehension. Totally different."

"Uh-huh . . ."

I tried to laugh it off. "Motherfucker can't handle
what's in my brain."

Trip often chided me for swearing too much, but
at least I could make him laugh. "I'm just glad Holly
isn't here. I mean, sure, she'd be valuable, kick butt,
take names, and all that, but you know...I'm glad
that no matter what she'll be okay."

I understood exactly what he meant. Holly was one
of us. We'd stood back-to-back surrounded by the forces
of really pissed-off evil many times, kicked the crap

out of it, and managed to walk away, but it was nice to know that no matter how bad things turned out in here, at least one of us would live on. I held out my soda and we clinked Coke cans. "Amen to that. Reminds me of something, though..." I got up with a grunt. "I need to talk with my wife."

"Want company?"

This was going to be weird enough by myself. "Naw, it's cool. Finish your lunch."

I probably should have taken some backup. Going anywhere alone was stupid. Everyone else was occupied working on something, and I was distracted by the idea of finally being able to talk to Julie about what Earl had told me earlier. It was a sloppy call, but I justified it to myself that it would only take a minute. I got to the elevators, tagged the button, and only had to wait a second for the last one on the left to *ding* and slide open.

I swiped the card Mitch had given me that allowed access to restricted areas, then pushed the button for the roof. Deep in thought, I leaned against the back of the elevator car and thought about what I was going to say to Julie. There were surely better ways to find out you were pregnant than during a siege from an incorporeal nightmare creature. *How would she react? Happy at first, then terrified, then what?* The doors slid closed.

The elevator began going *down*.

I reached out and pushed the roof button again. It wouldn't stay lit.

It was dropping so quickly that my stomach floated up into my lungs. This elevator wasn't fucking around. There was a digital display above the door, and it counted down L3, L2, L1, B3, B2, B1 in under four seconds, then it was blank and I was still going down. There was an emergency stop button. It didn't do anything. I hit the fire alarm. Nothing happened. "Crap." There was an emergency phone. I yanked the panel open and pulled the phone out, hoping to contact Mitch, but it was dead. The elevator was still descending.

There was a stab of fear. Had I just reentered the nightmare world?

There had to be a way to stop this thing. There had to be a trap door in the elevator car's roof, but as soon as I unslung Abomination, a voice came through a speaker in the wall. "Please remain calm, Mr. Pitt. Your excitable nature has already caused you to accrue significant charges since you began your stay here. Damaging one of my elevator cars would be exceedingly expensive." The voice was deep and commanding. "Please put your firearm away."

"Who are you?"

"I am the owner of this establishment as well as several other hotel-casino facilities in the Las Vegas metropolitan area. I am the primary sponsor and organizer of the First Annual International Conference of Monster Hunting Professionals. Most importantly, I am your host."

I lowered my shotgun. "You're the one they call Management?"

"That is I. You see, I normally operate through a group of intermediaries. Only a handful of my employees have ever met me in person. I do not take a hands-on approach very often. The duty of a good executive is to pick good managers, as they are my public face. Because of this, my existence has taken on something of an air of mystery, a situation which I do not find uncomfortable. I believe that a little fear improves employee productivity. Thus, you may call me Management for your convenience. That name will do as well as any."

The elevator was still cranking along. I had no idea how deep below the surface I had to be by now. Then the elevator stopped so suddenly that my knees clicked and I had to grab onto the handrails. The door slid smoothly open to reveal a... *mine shaft?* The walls were bare stone, roughly chipped into a rectangular passage, and reinforced every ten feet by a crisscrossing steel beams. Naked lightbulbs were affixed to the ceiling, following a single electrical cable. The tunnel descended into the unknown.

I pushed the roof button repeatedly. The doors didn't close.

"Please, Mr. Pitt. Time is money. We both have pressing matters to deal with. My office is at the end of the tunnel." I put my hand back on Abomination's grip. "Please do not do that. Violence upsets me."

"Really? Because getting kidnapped upsets me."

There was no answer. The intercom was quiet. I punched the button one last frustrated time. Since my only other option was to try to climb up the elevator cable for probably twenty stories, that left the tunnel.

The tunnel was clean of dust. The rocks were cool. It was a straight shot with no side branches. It sloped downward for a hundred yards before I noticed a much brighter source of light up ahead. The tunnel gradually widened until it opened up into a huge space.

The cave appeared to have been formed naturally,

and was at least as large as DeSoya Caverns, only this place was far brighter. You could play a football game in this cave and leave room for bleachers. The light was coming from intricate golden chandeliers hanging from the roof. Crystal formations were naturally growing out of the walls or sprouting from the floor, and they reflected the light in shades of purple, green, and blue. There were more lamps set all along the interior, some crafted metal, some made of exotic fabric, each of them different, but all of them gaudy.

The entirety of the space was filled with *stuff*. There were great gleaming heaps of coins, goblets, jewelry, crowns, and other expensive trinkets. There were sacks casually stacked off to the side that were spilling over with diamonds. There were rolls of silk so shiny that at first I thought it was an optical illusion. Paintings were casually stacked and leaning everywhere, and though I myself knew very little about artwork, I recognized many of these as the originals that graced the pages of Julie's many art books. There were pristine old classic cars parked down here, with even more stuff stacked on their roofs.

I'd seen a TV show once about people with a mental problem that caused them to hoard things. This cave had that vibe, only instead of junk, stacks of old newspapers, and cats, this place was absolutely packed with valuables and items that reeked of money. I carefully stepped over what I was fairly certain was a Fabergé egg that had just been left on the floor.

The cave smelled dry, sort of old, like an antique store, or an old lady's house where all the furniture was covered in plastic and there would be an inevitable dish of hard candies that had gradually melted into a solid, colorful block, and then the grandmother would complain that nobody ever came to visit... But beneath that antique smell there was something else, something that took me a moment to place. Back in college I'd had a roommate with a pet iguana. So the cave smelled like an old lady's house with a pet iguana.

And judging by the thick, musky lizard smell, we're talking a really *big* iguana.

"Hello?" I called.

"This way, Mr. Pitt," came the thunderous response. The noise caused me to instinctively crouch for cover behind a taxidermied white rhino. "No need to be alarmed." Management's voice was terribly loud inside the cave. "Please, excuse the mess. I have been meaning to organize but I have been so very busy."

Peeking over the rhino's butt, I couldn't see the source of the epic voice. Cursing myself for being an idiot, I made my way around a suit of armor that had a placard saying that it had belonged to Henry the Eighth and a figure that could only be one of the terracotta warriors. Now I could see that in the center of the cave was a gigantic stone pillar, big as a city bus flipped onto its nose. Something vast moved around the stone. Scales whispered against rock.

It was so big that it took me a second to sort out the images and categorize the horrific giant marvel with a word.

It was a dragon.

We'd covered dragons in Newbie training, but only briefly, since nobody ever thought we'd actually *see* one. There were two known types, eastern and western, and both were very powerful, dangerous, with intelligence ranging from smart to brilliant. They were so absurdly, extremely rare, and since no one had encountered one in generations, they were commonly assumed to be extinct.

They were definitely *not* extinct. There was at least one slithering along right in front of me, and if he wanted to eat me there probably wasn't a damn thing I could do about it. The gigantic creature took my breath away. He was so big that my brain was having a hard time calculating the dimensions. His head was the size of a small car. His shoulders were like two elephants squeezed together. I could only see the front legs, but they were shaped more like hands, only he could palm a cow like I could palm a basketball. One of the claws hit the floor, but with surprising gentleness. The enormous head dipped, fence-post horns tilting to the side, eyeballs the size of my head blinked. The eyelids actually made an audible *slap* as they closed. "Have a seat, Mr. Pitt."

The only chair I saw nearby was a gray stone throne. I pointed at that questioningly, but no sounds would come out of my mouth. "Yes, yes. A nice piece. It belonged to Nebuchadnezzar, a fine specimen of human leadership. I picked that up at auction for a very reasonable price. Please, we have much to discuss and there is little time." The massive head swung away as Management continued his path along the pillar.

I very carefully lowered myself onto the priceless historical artifact. The seat was a little small. The dragon continued speaking, obviously trying to put me at ease. "Forgive my rudeness. I will attempt to keep my voice down. I do not receive many visitors. Would you care for anything to drink? I have some very nice 1907 Heidsieck, purchased for the Russian royal family but then lost at sea, and only recently discovered by divers." I shook my head *no.* "Are you certain? It was a bargain at two hundred thousand a bottle. Ah yes, I forgot, my sources said you are a teetotaler. Very well, down to business then."

"You're a dragon?" Considering my current circumstances, it was a remarkably stupid question, but to be fair, I was still suffering from the awe.

"An astute observation. A dragon, the dark lords of the sky, the fire drakes, the savage lords of a time long since turned to dust. I am one of the last of my fading kind. A man of lesser fiber would have fled at the sight of me, but not you, Mr. Pitt. It appears that I picked the right human for the job." I had the distinct impression that the giant lizard was trying very hard not to sound patronizing. "Welcome to my humble abode."

The dragon turned, somehow not crashing any of its enormous body into any of the piled treasures. Now I could see that he had wings, but they were folded tight against his scaled back. The end of his tail whipped around the opposite end of the pillar, almost but not quite hitting a red supercar. It looked Italian. Too bad Mosh wasn't here. He would've known what it was and probably had the courage to ask the dragon if he could take it for a spin. My mind was reeling, trying to recall everything I'd read in training. Management was obviously a western dragon. The four limbs, long neck, separate wings, and general dinosaurlike build made that obvious. That also meant he could probably breathe fire and fly, all of which were completely irrelevant factoids at this juncture. I wished fantasy-geek Trip was here. He would've flipped out.

As Management moved, I realized for the first time that the stone pillar was absolutely covered in flat-screen TVs. There were hundreds of them, all on different channels. The dragon stopped. Once again, he was staring right at me. "Sell. Sell. Yes. Sell that too."

I looked around, then back at him, confused. "Sell *what?*"

The dragon held up one swordlike fingernail and pointed at his ear, revealing a Bluetooth headset, miniscule against his huge ear hole. "Not you. Yes, you. Sell when it gets to forty dollars a share." The dragon rolled his eyes. It was a very human expression for a giant lizard. "Do not question my wisdom, Stanley... Very well. Roll it over and purchase more Apple. Give my love to Mary. Goodbye... Now where were we?"

It turned out that talking to a dragon multitasking with a hands-free phone was even more confusing than when it was a person. "Me?"

"Yes, you. Keep up, Mr. Pitt." The dragon snapped his huge fingers repeatedly at a volume close to gunfire. "Chop chop."

Then it struck me. Unless his broker was locked upstairs, he was communicating with the outside world. "Your phone works?"

"Obviously. The MCB's petty jammers mean nothing to me. I own forty-two percent of the company that manufactures their jamming equipment, not to mention redundant shielded cables. Information is power. And if they had thought that far ahead, I have copious backup systems. I must stay connected at all costs. Of all the many things I collect, information is the most important. Display security cameras." The TVs were on a voice-activated system, and every screen changed to show the same views as Mitch's office. "Information is the reason why I organized ICMHP to begin with."

"I don't understand. Why—"

"By your current human legal definitions, I am classified as a monster. The conference guests, by career choice, are primarily hunters of monsters. The remainder are the administrators of the hunting of monsters or the scholarly that debate the minutia of any poor creature that falls into the category that you so flippantly refer to as PUFF-applicable. It behooves me to keep abreast of trends in the industry that very well might someday attempt to murder me in my sleep, would you not agree?"

"Sounds reasonable."

"Is there place for such reasonable creatures as I in such an unreasonable world as this?" Management's laugh shook the entire cavern. The sudden exhalation of hot air caused a stack of bearer's bonds to fly across the cave. I caught one, and for a split second owned a thousand shares of Ford. I put it back gently on the arm of the throne. "Of course, I have dealt with MHI before. I am fully aware of the character of your organization. Earl Harbinger has developed a reputation for integrity and honor in the monster community. Even foul and otherwise unlikable creatures have been ignored by MHI unless they are believed to be dangerous. You even spare *gnomes*." The dragon got a wistful look in his eye. "Ahh, gnomes, you can't eat just one . . . I believe you humans would say that they are like popcorn. But as I was saying, as long as I mind my own business, then I know I have nothing to fear from MHI. From the lowliest of humanoids to the spectral wendigo, MHI has demonstrated a willingness to put logic over profit... A concept that few of either of our species seem to grasp."

MHI took pride in being picky. There were far too many examples of creatures that had ended up on the PUFF table somehow, but weren't really any sort of danger to mankind. Those, we left alone. However, if we believed their type or species to be a threat, then it was game on, and we'd cash that PUFF check with a smile and sleep like a baby. It was an understandable ethic from a company run by a werewolf. "Thanks."

"However, I do not know so much about your competitors, nor your federal overseers. They worry me. They strike me as a sort of modern knight, ready to destroy that which they have predetermined to be evil, without ever granting the barest thoughts to determining if that classification is just. Do you know many annoying chivalrous knights I have had to eat over the years? I do not enjoy eating knights. Steel does not digest so well."

I nodded slowly at the creature that could swallow me and the throne of Nebuchadnezzar in one bite.

"Nor does chain mail. It sticks in the teeth. It has been centuries since I last ate a virgin, and that was purely by accident, I assure you. Human maidens taste about the same as anyone else, but old stereotypes die hard. I have changed with the times. I promise you that I am not coming to steal your maidens, and my shiny trinkets have been collected through honest labor and sound investment. MHI, being reasonable, would understand that I am no menace, and can be counted on to leave me in peace. The others, I am not so sure about. So you can see why it behooves me to pay attention to what Hunters are about. Thus was born the seed of the idea that would become the International Conference of Monster Hunting Professionals. A win-win, mutually beneficial situation for both of us. You are able to network and make valuable business connections, and for me, every conversation you Hunters have held has been recorded for my study, and dare I add, in some cases, amusement. How scandalous."

We had been used by a big lizard, but I wasn't going to argue with him about it. "Why did you bring me here?"

Management made a noise that had to be the dragon equivalent of a chuckle. It was about as loud as two dump trucks in a head-on collision. "I have been around for a very long time. Over the centuries I have seen humans come and go. I recognize your type. The various factions that constantly vie for control of this universe enjoy picking their champions. You are one such individual. Of course there are others like you here as well; however, you were the first one *courageous* enough to get into an elevator by himself since I decided it was time to make contact."

I had a sneaky feeling that *courageous* was a code word for *foolish*.

"I am as concerned about today's events as you are. This is, after all, my humble home that has been so crassly invaded by this dread *Nachtmar*. I would like to help repel this invader, and I trust that you are up to this challenge. I will attempt to assist you in defeating our common foe. All I ask in return is that you do not speak of my existence."

It wasn't like I could disagree with the monster

that could squish me like a bug in his own living room. "I can do that."

"There is no doubt that you can keep a secret, but as you can see, I have eyes everywhere. If you tell the world about me, I will find out. So I warn you first, Mr. Pitt..." *Here comes the part where he threatens to eat me.* "I will ask you to sign a non-disclosure agreement. If you reveal me, I can assure you that you will be hearing from my attorneys."

Okay, not what I expected. "Fair enough. How can I help?"

"This invader is disrupting the cash flow of one of my most profitable endeavors, not to mention the MCB slandering the reputation of my establishment. Our grand opening is soon, and I do not want the word on every critic's lips concerning the Last Dragon to be *Ebola*. I want this being destroyed."

"We've been working on it. If we don't succeed, it'll kill everyone here. That's already a pretty darn good motivator."

"I would agree with this assessment. These are dark days indeed, my friend. The quarantine alone has already caused my stock to plummet. A thousand deaths would be a marketing disaster. Today's activities have caused me grave concern. Display marked events." Every TV changed simultaneously, all of them showing different angles of the *Nachtmar's* various attacks. "I myself am nearly indestructible. However, I did not leverage my considerable wealth into building this marvelous palace only to see it burned down by do-gooder knights."

"Especially with us still inside. It sounds like we have compatible goals here. I'm okay with combining forces, Mr. Management." And to think Earl had accused me of lacking diplomacy. "So do you have any idea of what this monster is?"

"That I do not, young Mr. Pitt. The descriptor you have chosen for it seems apt enough, for it is a thing of nightmares. From listening to your conversations, I have come to a few conclusions that may differ from those of your learned fellows. From the evidence, I tend to agree that it is a relic of the madness that led to Decision Week, but I believe the proper question you should be asking yourself is, where did it come from before that?"

"What do you mean?"

The dragon snorted. It sucked the bearer-bond shower back across the cave. "I paid special attention to the events of that particular human war. A war so terrible that it intruded into the interests of my kind. These were not all new technologies the human scientist invented. Some were of the old ways, twisted. Your scientists were fools. The old ways do not enslave easily, nor do they bow willingly, and then only before the strongest of masters. Even among those, it is only a matter of time before the darkness corrupts them to its own nefarious desires. You have known a few men of this caliber, Martin Hood, for example, or Lord Machado."

Two very good examples of men poking around in things way over their heads. "You know about them?"

"As I said, I have eyes everywhere. I knew of Lord Machado when he was still *alive*. Yet, even men of will sufficient to overcome physical death still end up as mere pawns to the warring factions eventually."

"You know a lot about these things. Mind if I ask you a few questions?"

"Understandable, since the factions and their endless war are now hopelessly intertwined with your destiny, I would expect no less. I will be glad to address your concerns over tea and cookies once we are no longer under the pressing threat of imminent destruction... As I was saying, the learned men of Decision Week delved into mysteries far beyond their means. When the knights outside realized the tremendous nature of this threat they changed their plans, and like knights always do, decided to resort to violence." The dragon studied me quizzically. "I can see that I lost you. Display exterior intercepts." The screens changed to show the quarantine. "I have been monitoring the communications of the one you call Stricken. A soul of such indescribable foulness so very seldom pollutes this world."

"So you've met?"

A scaly ridge over Management's eye rose. "Oh, yes. Long ago. Do not trifle with that one, Mr. Pitt. He is no knight, deluded by chivalry or noble concepts. He is the devil made flesh. I intercepted this message fifteen minutes ago. The following transmission was encrypted; however, it was encrypted using software created under contract by a company that's mostly owned by one of my shell corporations. Play audio recording number thirty-four. Increase volume to normal human auditory levels."

The multitude of TVs all switched to the same view, a blue armored personnel carrier that had SWAT on the side in big white letters. There were a lot of antennas on the back of the APC. The next voice that came over the speakers was clearly that of Stricken.

"Things are getting worse inside. I want to bump up the timeline."

I didn't recognize the other voice. "How soon?"

"As soon as you get me approval I'll turn this place to ash."

"How's Director Stark feel about that?"

·"Forget Stark. He'll do what I tell him or we'll find a new guy. We own MCB now."

"POTUS won't give approval until we can at least finish questioning the scientists. We've got no assurance that Mark Thirteen won't just go incorporeal again and infect the rest of the city. There's a lot we don't know about it."

"I'm not worried about that. We found one of the Decision Week survivors in a retirement community not too far away and brought him in. Doctor by the name of Blish. I questioned him already. The old bastard confirmed what we suspected all along, but I think he's exaggerating the destructive capacity. They didn't have the ability to deal with this back then, but it's nothing we can't handle now. I've got enough information to take it down when necessary."

"Are you going to brief the Hunters inside?"

"Negative." Stricken's laugh was as cold as ever. "We wanted an excuse to restart the Nemesis Project. We're never going to have anything better than this. We'll let it play out, then provide the solution at the last minute. Let the Hunters do the bleeding until then. We're not out any resources ourselves. Then I can go up the chain and tell them if I'd had Nemesis assets ready to rock, this all could have been prevented."

"You'll get your budget. Don't worry. But there will be significant backlash against restarting Nemesis."

"You mean Frankenstein's monster? That lumbering freak has outlived his usefulness."

The other man quavered. "But Franks is hard as

fuck. He's untouchable. He's a national treasure. You know what'll happen—"

"None of you have to worry about Franks. I'll handle him. Same with Myers or any of the old guard that gets in the way, I'll burn them too. I've got a mission to complete."

The line was quiet for a long time. "That's cold, even for you."

"And that's why you keep me around. Just get me my approvals, Mr. Secretary, and I'll handle the messy details."

I'd heard Nemesis mentioned between Franks and the Unicorn man yesterday. The dragon turned back to me as the TVs returned to their wide variety of channels. "No, I do not know what this Nemesis is that they speak of. However, it seems to be something that Stricken wants, and is prepared to sacrifice my lovely establishment, my employees, and my guests in order to justify."

"Screw him. I'm not planning to die just so some asshole can justify a line item on a spending bill. They've got one of the Decision Week scientists right outside. If I could get to him, I can find out what this thing is and how to kill it." I looked around the opulent cave. The chaos of shelves, piles of furniture, and boxes made it difficult to see very far. "Do you have another way out of here?"

"I am afraid not. You see, this is my final home. This is where I plan to live out my days in peace amid my treasures. I had this site carefully selected and prepared for my comfort, then I flew in under cover of darkness and had the casino built on top of it. I plan on dying here, Mr. Pitt."

"Why?"

"Why? An interesting question." The dragon flexed his enormous body in a drastic imitation of a shrug. "Some of the hateful things that are said about my kind are, sadly, true. We do love our shiny things. A dragon has a pathological desire to amass a horde. It is an addiction, but one that I have learned to control." The dragon nodded at his display of moon rocks. "I tried a twelve-step program once, but it did not work out . . . So I make the best of it. Can you think of a more appropriate place than Las Vegas to accumulate such pretty things?" The dragon's head moved over me, engulfing me in shadow, but he was merely inspecting his treasures. He clucked disapprovingly, and one wing stretched outward, the tip of it gently dusting a display of delicate glass figurines.

"There is nowhere for me to leave to. My kind are dying. This world no longer belongs to us. The few of us that remain are a pale shadow of our once ferocious ancestors. The dragon gods began to die when the age of man began. You should have seen them in all their glory, Mr. Pitt. They were terrible and beautiful beyond all possible descriptors, but they were too magnificent for this petty age. The rest of us, their once-noble children, were feared and hunted nearly to extinction. The outside world has nothing left to offer me. If I come across something that strikes my fancy, I have it brought here to keep me company. I do love eBay." The massive chuckle shook me again.

"That's not what I—"

"Ah, of course. I realize now that you are asking in a tactical rather than a philosophical manner. Though I do not intend to leave, I am not stupid. There's a freight elevator back there. That is where I take my meals, usually a cow, sometimes a buffalo, or perhaps something exotic, like a giraffe, should the mood take me. I can fit up that shaft should I really wish to, but it is useless for your needs. It only goes up into the casino as well."

"Aren't you worried about the *Nachtmar* coming down here for you?"

"This is my home, Mr. Pitt. A dragon does not simply *leave* his home. I am far more concerned about the safety of my guests, and thus my bottom line, than I am about my own well-being. If you haven't noticed, I am rather fearsome." He lifted himself up onto his rear legs and puffed out his chest. Management was, indeed, pretty scary, but for the first time I realized that he seemed rather . . . *flabby*. "This creature of nightmares does not frighten me. As I believe you so eloquently told Mr. Jones earlier, and I quote, *Motherfucker can't handle what is in my brain*."

"Right on." Even a flabby old dragon with hoarding issues was still not something to tangle with. "Mind if I use your phone?"

"Who would you like to call?"

"Holly Newcastle. I've got her number—"

The dragon held up one epic claw. "No need. Dial Newcastle, H. Put on speakerphone. Increase volume to normal human auditory levels." There was a series of beeps as her number was dialed. "She was registered as a conference guest," Management explained. "I have her email as well. I was going to add all of you to the newsletter to keep you appraised of special vacation offers. I have a property in Bermuda that I have been told is simply to die for."

"Thank you. If we live I'll take you up on that." The phone rang several times before going to voice mail. "Damn it." I'd really been hoping to talk to an actual person, but she was probably up to something right this minute. Holly was just that crafty. I hurried and left her a long message detailing our status. I really didn't know if she would be able to accomplish this, but it was worth a shot. "Even though he knows how to beat the monster, Stricken is planning on letting us all die. What I need you to do is find a man named Dr. Blish. He's got to be old. Old enough to have worked on this project in the forties. Stricken is holding him somewhere close. Blish knows all about this creature. Find out what you can from him..." I paused. How would she get that info back to us?

Management cut in. "Have her call back on this number. I will pass it along to you."

I repeated that. "Wait a second, can you send her that recording of Stricken talking about maybe murdering Franks?" Management seemed to perk up at that idea and nodded his horns vigorously. "Okay, Holly. I'm sending you a recording you might be able to use as leverage. Stricken's ruthless. He'll kill you if he catches you. Do what you can, but be careful." I had just asked the one member of my team that was in a position of relative safety to go do something incredibly dangerous, but if we could learn what Dr. Blish knew, it might give the rest of us a fighting chance. Sometimes this job just wasn't easy.

"End." The dragon watched me with his huge black eyes. "You can gain the measure of a man by the nature of the friends he keeps. I have studied all of the ICMHP attendees. The courage of this fair maiden friend of yours speaks volumes about your character, Mr. Pitt. I'm certain she will succeed in this endeavor."

"Calling her a maiden might be a stretch, but yeah, Holly will get the job done, no matter what."

"If it is not presumptuous of me, I know that you have some other members of your stalwart company out there, and I would be willing to send this same message to them as well."

I'd heard that some of the Las Vegas team had stayed up north just in case anything else popped up in the aftermath of the spider problem. "That would be great."

"Very well. I will do so. There is one last order of business, Mr. Pitt. A subject that I am most loath to broach. We have already established that the nature of our current adversary is a mystery, but another question remains. What, or rather, who, woke it up? Display original images."

The screens changed, and now all of them were showing different still pictures, and though they were all different images, from diverse times and places, they were all of the same subject. Some were carved in stone, others were scratched in the dirt, a few were spray painted like graffiti, and one was scrawled in blood on the other side of crime scene tape. My throat was suddenly dry. It was the mysterious symbol first shown to me by my father, since seen by Hunters around the world, and most recently on the ceiling of the containment unit at Dugway.

"You know about this?"

The dragon nodded his head, and it was like having a car jangled above you by a crane. "Of course I do. Word had reached me from many sources about his sign appearing again. I'm afraid the time of his return is upon us."

The dragon collected information along with antiques. If Management could teach me about this new threat, then there would be no reason to involve my dad... "Give me a name and an address and we can start arranging his funeral."

"He has many names, none of which you would have heard. He comes from an age before this one, when dragonkind were still young on the face of the Earth. His faction in the eternal war has been silent for a very long time. They are enemies to the Old Ones, but that does not make him a friend to you, quite the contrary, in fact. He will remake this world and it will spell your end. The presence of these signs was another motivating factor for the organization of ICMHP, for though there is much I do not care for about the human world, its continued existence provides me a measure of comfort and amusement, and thus I would prefer not to see it destroyed. I would very much like to see him stopped."

I got off the ancient chair and made it a few halting steps toward the screens. "It's real, isn't it? The pattern that we discovered. There's an invasion going on."

"These are but the opening moves of the game. He has come forth briefly before, to test the waters, if you will, but each time before he found the world not yet ready, and returned to his slumber. However, this time feels different to me. If this is the case, then the invasion will come soon enough, and believe me, you will know. What we are seeing now is a testing of man's defenses. There are many things that are buried deep in the world or far beneath the sea, dead but

dreaming. He is waking them one by one, setting them
free, all in order to watch how man reacts. I believe it
was no accident that this latest creature has beset us
here today." The dragon regarded me for a long time.
"You Hunters are being tested. Pray to your God of
light and ask that you do not fall short. I would do
the same, if my gods were still alive." Management
gave a melancholy sigh.

"I want to know everything you know about—" There
was a sudden wailing noise and all of the monitors
flashed red. "What's happening?"

"Hmmm..." Management swiveled his head back to
the monitors. "Every alarm in the facility has gone off."
He growled low in his mighty chest and made a series
of clicks with his forked tongue. The computer system
understood the dragon language, and all the monitors
began to flick rapidly between different scenes, far faster
than my eyes could track. About half of them turned
to rapidly scrolling text. Management seemed to have
no trouble devouring all of the input simultaneously.
"Interesting. The exterior views are showing extreme
weather conditions. There is monitoring equipment
atop my hotel. It indicates that we are experiencing a
hurricane. From the humans' reactions, there seems to
be a disturbance upon the roof."

"Julie's up there!"

"Your mate, yes. Congratulations on your new egg.
The elevator has been unlocked." I ran for it, leaping
over priceless trash. Management called after me. "We
will continue this talk later. Make haste, Mr. Pitt.
Destiny awaits you."

CHAPTER 18

The elevator that had seemed so fast earlier now felt like riding a lethargic turtle. "Come on. Come on. Come on." With my wife possibly in danger, the elevator could have been going fifty and I'd still be ticked. The unmarked super-basement floors zipped by and the digital counter began showing numbers again. I readied Abomination and pulled the charging handle back a bit to confirm that I had a round chambered.

Management spoke over the intercom. "Mr. Pitt. Something peculiar is happening. My secondary lines into the building are failing. They are being severed. It is as if—"

The lights went out.

"Management?" *Nothing.*

The elevator stopped moving. "Shit." The background hum of machinery died. The elevator creaked and whined as it settled. It was pitch black in the car. Turning on the eyeball-melting flashlight mounted on Abomination in this tiny space would've blinded me, which was why I kept a little crook-neck LED flashlight jammed through some of the MOLLE straps on my armor. I flicked it on. There was nothing to see, but the light helped me stay calm.

It was stupid, but I tried the buttons anyway and got nothing. I was trapped in a stupid elevator while my wife was at the top, probably in danger. I kicked a furious dent into the wall and shouted something incoherent.

Other than the creaking of the elevator and my breathing, the car was quiet. My flashlight gave me a little bit of light. I realized that the temperature was dropping. *Not again.*

"Have you found her?"

The sound made me jump. The Asian kid that I'd originally taken for a rival Hunter had appeared out of nowhere and was standing in the opposite corner of the elevator car. "Don't do that!"

He just looked at me funny. "For some reason, you're the only one I can talk to easily."

"Just another perk of being me," I muttered.

"Everybody else, I have to shout and then bad things happen."

"What's going on?"

"I'm not sure. He's getting stronger. He's touching us to the other place, where the demons dream . . . It's not a very good place at all. He was born here, you know . . ." *That sounded just lovely.* He changed the subject. "You promised to help. Have you found her yet?"

With the kid, science experiment, entity, whatever the hell he was right there, it kept getting colder. As if fueling his presence required sucking all of the energy out of the space. Within seconds the temperature was similar to being shoved into a walk-in freezer. I began to shiver uncontrollably. "I need to know who *she* is."

"The names are gone. They took them from me. All I can see is her face." He was desperate, but growing angry. "They took them, they erased what they could, and smashed everything else. My head...It's filled with *splinters*."

The more agitated he got, the more the temperature seemed to drop. My face was going numb. "I want to help you, but I need more information. I need something to work with."

"You're out of time!" he shouted. Face red, veins standing out in his neck, he lashed out with one fist, only to have it pass cleanly through the elevator wall as if it wasn't even there. He jerked his hand back in surprise. Seemingly stunned, he stared at his hand in disbelief. "How—What is this place?"

"Las Vegas, Nevada. Planet Earth."

"Are you real?" he asked me. "Are you alive?"

My teeth were chattering. "I am." *You, I'm not so sure about.*

He shook his head as if to clear it. "No more tricks. You're probably with them. You bastards clouded my mind with your drugs and machines. I'm sick of walking around in a fog. You stole my life. You tricked me, and I'm not putting up with it anymore."

"I'm not with them." I wasn't even sure who *them* was, probably the scientists that had started this mess. "Calm down. I want to help."

"That's what they said last time. I took their tests. I did everything they asked me to, and all I got was tortured for it, and they just sit there in their lab coats writing notes on a clipboard while I begged for mercy. You listen and you listen good, buddy. You're going to give her back to me, and we're getting out of here. You do it, or I'll stop holding *him* back. I swear. Find her or you'll all pay."

Supernatural entity or not, I didn't put up with anybody's drama. "Listen to me. I don't know the people that hurt you. I want to help. Give me something to work with. I need a name, a place, something. And I can't do jack until we beat the *Nachtmar* and get out of here. You need to help me so that I can help you. That was your body buried in that containment unit, wasn't it?"

"Body? I'm right here. I don't get what you're saying."

This was infuriating. I was arguing with a delusional dead guy, while Julie was in danger. "You said they stuck you with hundreds of needles and filled you with drugs to keep the nightmare asleep. I found the room with all the needles. You've been—" I caught myself before I said dead. That probably wouldn't go over well. "—asleep for a long time. This woman I'm supposed to find, I don't even know if she's still around."

"Why wouldn't she be? How long have I been sleeping?"

"You've been buried for over sixty years." The kid just stared at me as I rattled off today's date. "I'm sorry."

Conflicting expressions clouded his features, shock, disbelief, grief, all in short order, but then he settled on angry denial. "I'm done being lied to. Find her or else I'll let him have his way." He took a step back through the wall and disappeared from view.

I swear, the dead never listen to reason.

The elevator and the air were still. The temperature slowly crept back above freezing. There was some creaking of cables above. I hit the emergency call button, but it was still dead. I waited a few seconds, hoping the emergency power would kick on, but it didn't. I really didn't have time for this. The last thing I'd seen on the digital display had been L2, only one floor off of where we'd set up shop. If I was lucky I'd stopped near the door and somebody might hear me. So I slammed Abomination's butt stock against the door and shouted for help.

Several tries of that nonsense and I was getting really pissed off, so I slung my shotgun around my back and drew my kukri. The curved, nineteen-inch Himalayan Chitilangi was thick enough to make a decent crowbar. I jammed the tip into the junction of the doors and started prying. It took me a few seconds to get it leveraged apart. No matter how hard I shoved, I could only get it open a few inches before it got stuck. There had to be some sort of safety latch I couldn't get to.

Through the crack, I could see there was nothing but a blank shaft in front of me. I'd stopped between floors. Now I was really angry. "Oh, come on!" I angled my little light up through the crack and could see what I thought was the doors of the next floor just over the roof. "Nothing can ever be simple."

I smashed the plastic roof sheeting out of the way. There was an access panel in the top of the car. It might have been locked, but I swung the kukri so hard that when the hatch broke open I didn't notice. We heavyset guys aren't known for our vertical leap, but I used the handrail as a step, and after a couple of tries caught the lip of the roof, and, grunting and swearing, pulled myself through.

"Stupid dead guys. Never easy ... Bitch bitch bitch. *Find her.* Whatever. Get me a friggin' address, asshole."

The elevator shaft stretched impenetrable black above. My little light only made a dent in it. The cables were greasy and rang with a strange pitch as I bumped them and they bumped each other. The doors for the lobby began at about the height of my waist. I wedged in my kukri and started pushing them apart.

The metal was icy to the touch. *Clang.* Jerking my head up, I stared into the darkness. Something had moved up there. The hairs on the back of my neck stood up. The rhythmic pings of the elevator cables changed and they began to jiggle violently. *Clang. Clang.* Drops of cold water fell out of the black to splatter me and my surroundings like a sluggish rain.

I could either bring Abomination around and turn on the big light to see what was descending, or I could get these doors open and get out of here right the hell now. There wasn't a lot of room to maneuver or defend myself, so prying took top priority. I poked my knife through the crack and threw my weight against the kukri's hilt. The doors began to slide. The shaft doors didn't seem nearly as hard to move.

Clang. Clang. Clang. Screeeeech.

It was getting closer. There were new sounds, small tings of impact, and the raspy scrape as something pushed against the walls of the shaft. A fat blob of cold water struck my head and rolled down my cheek. Instinct made me look up. Something blacker than the darkness of the shaft moved, glistening, above.

Its shape was so alien, so baffling, so unfathomable, that for a split second I could do nothing but gawk and try to comprehend. It reminded me of pulling weeds and looking at the hairy roots beneath, partially obscured in wet dirt, only these millions of roots and tufts were *wiggling*. It filled the entire shaft and was gradually descending, now only two floors above. In the middle of the mass was a single, awful, circular *mouth*, filled with row after row of blunt white teeth, stretching up inside like a tunnel until it disappeared into the thing's interior.

I slammed my body against the kukri. The door opened a few inches. I tossed my knife through, got my hands on both sides and shoved as hard as I possibly could. The doors slid open and I clambered through. It was dark here too. Rolling across the floor, I crashed into a set of legs. Thankfully, they were attached to a living human being. "It's coming!" I shouted.

A flashlight beam stabbed me in the eyes. "Z?" Milo Anderson asked. "What's coming?"

"Damn if I know," I gasped. Milo set his AR-10 against the wall and used his free hand to help me up. As my light came around, it illuminated a plastic bottle in Milo's hand. It was filled with gray powder. I pointed. "Explosive?"

"Yeah. Cooper made Tannerite. Why—"

I snatched it from him. Tannerite is the common name for a simple explosive made from a mixture of ammonium nitrate and aluminum powder. For the ammonium nitrate he'd probably stolen fertilizer from the grounds crew. The aluminum powder, I had no idea. But it would go boom, and a one-liter soda bottle was a decent sized boom, and best of all, it could be set off with the energy of a high-velocity rifle round. Abomination's buckshot was too slow, but a .308 would do nicely. I picked up Milo's rifle and thumbed on the flashlight. "Gonna borrow this."

I stuck the muzzle of his rifle into the shaft, risked

a peek, and saw the dangling wet root monster still gradually oozing its way down. Milo stuck his head around the corner and exclaimed, "Grinder!"

"Friend of yours?"

"No." Milo reached out, took the bottle back, and hurled it at the monster. The explosive struck the roots, but before gravity could bounce it back, half a dozen of the tendrils lashed out with blinding speed and encircled the bottle. It automatically slithered the bottle toward its mouth hole. The rows of teeth inside began to rotate hungrily against each other. The sound was like nails on chalkboard on triple speed. Milo pulled back and stuck his fingers in his ears. "Blast it!"

The AR-10 had an Aimpoint sight on it. The shot was easy. The angle was not. I fired once and the bullet slammed into the earthy mass right next to the bottle with a splash of black mud. The second round hit the Tannerite square.

The explosive wasn't very big, but in the enclosed space it was brutal. There was a terrible blast that struck me as I fell. It was like getting smacked in the face with a bat.

There was no shrapnel, and the shockwave alone usually wasn't too bad unless you were close enough for it to damage your internal organs. That was all good to know academically, but like I said, *bat to the face.* So I lay there for a moment, blinking stupidly. Milo's rifle was at my side, the brilliant beam of the flashlight still shining into the shaft as gray smoke came rolling out. Black gobbets of meat and heavy white teeth fell through the smoke to collect on the elevator's roof.

"Z! Z! Are you okay?" Milo had taken hold of the drag straps on my armor was attempting to lift me, which was tough since I was twice his size.

"Fine." My head was swimming. I was going to be hating life later. One of my electronic earpieces had shorted out. I smacked it a few times, but it was toast.

Milo took up his rifle, went through the smoke, and shined it up the shaft. There was an awful squeal and the cables shook as the creature climbed back up. Milo fired several rounds after it but then it was out of sight. "Hate those things!" Dizzy, I struggled to my feet. Milo caught my arm. "Grinders are gross."

"A what?"

He mistook my ignorance for deafness. *"Grinder!"* he shouted in my ear. "They burrow under houses, creep up through the floor, and suck folks out of their beds. That's why I refuse to sleep in basements. The name comes from that rotary mouth-hole thingy. It's like death by a thousand Dremel tools. Grinds bones right into pulp."

I didn't even want to know which poor bastard was unlucky enough to have that nasty thing sucked out of their memory. I shook my aching head. That was twice today that I'd been too close to an improvised explosive device.

"Secure these elevators in case something else comes out," Milo ordered a couple of Hunters that had coming toward the sound of the explosion.

"I've got to get to Julie."

"That might be hard." Milo picked up a backpack. It was filled with more bottles. "Elevators don't work. You can take the stairs, but you should see something first. Things have gotten *weird.* Even by our standards."

Our situation was so FUBAR that random rotary death monsters in the elevators were unremarkable, but Milo thought something else was weirder than that? This couldn't possibly be good. "Status?"

"Our bus took a detour to crazy town. Come on. I'll show you."

My first clue that something was drastically different was that our radios were working again. Luckily the MCB was no longer jamming us. Excited chatter in several different languages picked up in my one working earpiece. There were monster sightings everywhere. Competent team leaders were getting everyone sorted onto different channels and vectoring Hunters against threats. At least the uninterrupted radio waves were a welcome change.

It wasn't until Milo and I got to the windows of the conference center that I realized that having our radios back was actually a really bad sign. The reason the jamming wasn't working anymore was because the jammers weren't *here* anymore. Neither was the rest of the quarantine. Or the street. Or Las Vegas.

"What the hell is going on?" I stared out the windows and tried to wrap my brain around the scene. The manicured grounds of the complex stretched out for a few hundred yards and beyond that the ground just dropped off into nothing. There were crashing gray clouds that stretched above us and seemed to curve inward over the top of the connected hotel. The storm outside was brutal and unlike anything I'd ever seen, walls of seemingly solid fog were being driven about by fierce winds, but in different, conflicting directions. Every now and then the mist would swirl, revealing tunnels and cuts where we could see just a tiny bit further, but there was no city beyond.

The storm wasn't dark at all. It had its own strange internal illumination. The odd light coming through the windows made everything look washed out, nearly black and white. The hotel creaked and shook as it was buffeted by the wind. The sound coming from the storm was dampened by our shelter, but it didn't sound like any normal weather I'd heard before. It sounded *displeased.*

I didn't know if the sudden wave of nausea I experienced right then was from the concussive force of Milo's explosive or because of the sudden realization that we probably weren't on Earth anymore. "*Where* are we?"

"I was kinda hoping you would know," Milo answered. "You've at least been to other dimensions before."

"Not this one." The mysterious ghost had warned me about the blurring of the lines between worlds. *Things had just got real blurry.*

The conference center was shaped like a horseshoe. On the rounded bottom end of the horseshoe was the street, or where the street would've been if it still existed. I ran across the lobby area to get to the opposite bank of windows. The interior of the horseshoe was where the gardens and pools were. One leg of the shoe touched the casino and shops and the other ended at the hotel, the elevators of which Milo and I had just left.

From the windows on this side I could see into the manicured gardens one story below. The trees and bushes were shaking under the force of powerful gusts of wind. Hard rain was splattering the glass.

Lightning flashed, and it turned the fog around it green. The color lingered far too long before it faded back to gray.

I could see the edge of the roof of the hotel where Julie was positioned, but couldn't see anything moving up there. I tried the radio on my team's regular channel. "Julie, come in. This is Owen. Can you hear me? Over." I let go of the transmit button and waited. It was hard to tell from this angle, but the clouds couldn't be too high above the hotel's roof. It was like we'd been packed into a fluffy box of evil death clouds.

So not cool.

There was a sudden flash of purple lightning. It made the fog look like an angry bruise before the color gradually seeped away. "Come on. Pick up. Please pick up."

All around us was chaos. A crowd of about forty guests and employees had come in here to be able to see out the windows. There was screaming, crying, arguing, shouting, fervent prayer, and general pandemonium. The room was lit by bobbing flashlights and the unearthly pale light from the windows. Tyler Nelson had gotten up on a table and was doing his best to be a calming influence on the mob. I didn't think that psychology degree was much prep for something like this, but he was doing his best. A soothing voice might be helpful, but I'd seen some freaky shit in my life, and even I wasn't feeling particularly soothable right now.

My radio beeped. "This is Julie. Go ahead."

Oh, thank you. "Are you okay?"

"As much as I can be. You seeing this?" This time the lightning flashed Valentine's-Day red.

"I am. I'm at the interior window. Main level of the conference center." Waving one arm so she could pick me up through the sniper scope, I walked away from the others so I could hear. "I'm heading into the walkway over the garden."

There was a few seconds of static. She had to wait for the weird fog streaks between us to move. "Got you . . . From up here I've got a good view out into the . . . whatever. Space? Beats me. I've never seen anything like this." There was a lot of bad wind distortion from her end of the conversation.

"Me either. People down here are coming apart."

"I'm trying real hard not to do that myself, dear."

You and me both. "Does it look like we can walk out? Maybe make a run for it?"

"Don't do that. There are *things* out there. I've just gotten glimpses. They're gigantic, Owen. I don't think there's anywhere to walk to. It looks like we're floating."

"Say again, what?"

"Floating. Like an island. All I can see in every direction is this storm. We're definitely not in Las Vegas anymore."

Damn it . . . This was where demons dream. "I think the *Nachtmär* has dragged us into his world."

Julie was quiet for a moment, surely thinking over the consequences of that awful idea. The radio was filled with wind. "Find Earl. We need to figure out how to kill this damned thing *now.*"

Was that even possible? This was far worse than I'd imagined. The *Nachtmar* was unspeakably powerful. He hadn't just blurred the lines, he'd ripped a chunk of our reality right out of the ground and sucked it to a whole different dimension, along with all of the poor bastards inside. What else was he capable of? Even if we could defeat him, was there any way home?

There were only a few others on the walkway, all Hunters, all of us staring stupidly out the floor-to-ceiling windows. One of them was muttering the same thing over and over, *"No debemos estar aqui." We're not supposed to be here.*

I put my hand out, and even through the glass and the glove, I could feel the energy humming on the other side. "Come inside. It's not safe." I let go of the transmit button and waited for her response. There was a crash back in the conference center behind me as one of the guests' arguments turned violent. The big lady with the mobility scooter was beating a bellhop with her purse. Milo moved over to separate them. "Julie? Julie, are you there?"

"Incoming!" Julie ordered. "Get dow—"

A fiery comet fell into the gardens and hit like a bomb. The shockwave sent a circle of semi-solid mist hurtling outward. The windows of the walkway shattered. I barely got my arms up in front of my face as I was pelted with shards of glass. The alien fog crashed around me with the force of a tidal wave and I was knocked from my feet.

The mist was sickly cold. It clung to my face like wet spiderwebs. I couldn't see through it.

The hotel shook under repeated explosive impacts. I couldn't see what crashed against the building, but something vast struck a few feet away. The roar of cracking concrete drowned out the panicked screams. The floor bounced beneath me as if we were in a terrible earthquake. The shaking continued for several seconds, bouncing me along the walkway's carpet. I groped blindly, trying to grab onto something solid, but then I realized I was sliding as the floor broke and tilted beneath me. There was a constant rattle and crash of falling debris. Bits and pieces of the building struck me as the floor tilted more violently. Then I was rolling crazily as the walkway tore from the conference center and collapsed around me.

I couldn't see. I didn't know which way was up. Then I was falling, part of a cascade of shattered glass.

My shoulder hit first. Then my face. There was another tearing roar that blotted out everything else, then another hit, spinning through the dust and fog, and then I slid and crashed my way to the ground. I was engulfed in choking dust, something else struck me in the head, and everything went black.

The first sound I heard over the ringing in my ears was the wind. It was screaming like a million people being tortured to death. It was alien, haunted, and it made my soul ache. It was the wind of a desolate place where no man should ever go. Beneath the scream of the wind were the screams of the people trapped here. Those were what brought me back to consciousness.

Then the pain in my skull hit and I added my scream to the rest. That woke me right up. Everything hurt. My ribs ached. My head felt like it had been split open.

It was wet. Water was running over me. I was lying in the mud. I forced my eyes open. Immediately the hurricane winds tried to rip them out of my head. The water was pouring from a broken fountain. I was in a flowerbed. Grunting in pain, I rolled over.

Above me, half the walkway of the conference center was *gone*, blown apart, flung down and spread around me. The other half was still attached, and I saw a Hunter dangling from the far edge being pulled back inside by another. There was a jagged hole in the conference center above and it looked like the building had puked its guts out. I could see that the people closest to the blast had been scattered. People inside were just beginning to get to their feet, and those that had been further away were dragging limp bodies away from the hole.

I had ridden a ten-foot section of the overhang into the gardens. Chunks of concrete with broken bits of rebar sticking out of them were all around me. There was broken glass everywhere. It was a miracle that I hadn't been impaled or crushed to death. I wiped my stinging eyes. My glove came away red with blood. It was streaming from a deep cut on my forehead.

Everything hurt, but I couldn't tell how badly I'd been injured. I got to my hands and knees, crawled a couple of feet, but was too dizzy, and face-planted into the mud. There was another person just ahead. I hadn't been the only one caught in the collapse, but they hadn't been as lucky. Half of their torso had been caught beneath the sliding debris and crushed. I was too disoriented to even tell who it was.

There was another roar, and this one wasn't the wind. Gunfire erupted above as Hunters began firing into the alien hurricane. They were shooting out into the garden at something just ahead of me. Someone up there was shouting orders, struggling to be heard, trying to direct the innocent toward safety. Another flaming comet, smaller than the first, streaked across the gray

sky and hit the building. The entire world shook under
the explosive impact, and flaming bits rained down
around me. The Hunters above me were driven back.

Raising my head, I could make out brightly colored
shapes moving in the garden, some orange, some red,
just quick flashes as the things maneuvered through
the thrashing bushes. There was the briefest glimpse
of an oddly shaped head and weird multiple eyes
before the creature took cover. There was a terrifyingly
familiar whistling noise as a cloud of projectiles was
launched from the garden against the breach in the
wall. Inside, humans cried out in agony as they struck.

I tried to stand, but a lightning bolt shot up the
nerves of my leg and I went back down. Something
was screwed up with my foot. There was movement
to my side. Another survivor of the crash had staggered upright. It was a female Hunter that I'd seen,
but never spoken to. She was shell-shocked, staring
out into the mist, only her wide eyes visible through
a mask of blood and dust. She turned to look up at
where we'd just been standing. I shouted for her to
take cover, but either she couldn't hear me or no
sound actually came out of my throat. I wasn't sure.
There was another whistling noise, a *thud*, and she
lurched forward and fell.

Head swimming, face bleeding, I crawled through
the wreckage. My hands landed on her warm body.
There was a short spear sticking out of the dead
woman's back right between her shoulder blades.
Without thinking, I wrenched it out with one gloved
hand. I recognized the alien spine clenched in my
fist right away, because I'd been killed with one just
like it once.

It made sense, trapped here in the realm of night-mares, that this is what would be sent to end us. There were several survivors amongst the senior MHI staff here. If the *Nachtmar* had been looking for one consistent horror that many of us shared, this would be it.

It was the demons from Natchy Bottom. It was the creatures from the Christmas party.

We were all going to die.

My legs didn't want to respond. The explosion and resulting fall had shaken me badly. I needed a minute to collect my bearings, but I didn't have a minute. These things were too fast, too lethal. Once they got inside they'd rip us all to pieces, only since I was stuck outside with them, I'd be dead long before that.

I'd fought these things once before. They were horrific foot soldiers of the Old Ones. They came from an alien dimension, with many different shapes, sizes, and capabilities, some were small and fast, others were lumbering armored insect tanks, others could fling parts of their bodies as poisonous projectile weapons, and every one of them were tenacious and deadly. It was only the intervention of me using Lord Machado's artifact that had saved our lives last time.

There was no way I could climb up the jagged face of the building and get back inside without being speared. Abomination was still slung to me, but I was too dizzy to walk, let alone fight effectively. I could see dozens of flashes of bright color through the mist. They were almost here.

"—hear me? Owen! Hide! Hide now!" It was Julie. My radio was still working. "They're coming!"

She could see me. Julie was on the opposite roof, watching helplessly through a scope as her husband flailed around stupid and injured in the mud with a horde of interdimensional insect demons heading right at me.

Screw that. I didn't want her to see me die.

My first inclination for most problems was to shoot them, but that would only get me killed here. Julie was right, I needed to hide. Crawling back to the big chunk of concrete, I found the partially crushed body. He had been squished into the soft dirt and was a real mess. We had no idea how smart these things were, and in any case, these probably weren't the real thing anyway, rather figments of our imagination made real. I had no idea if this would work. Grimacing, I lifted the unmangled arm, and then lay down beneath, trying to squish myself as far into the soil as possible. *Sorry, man.* I tried to stay perfectly still. I was immediately coated in hot, sticky blood.

It was disgusting. It was infuriating. It was better than dying.

"They're right on top of you," Julie whispered in my earpiece, and then she too was silent, unsure if they would be able to hear even that much noise. I shut the radio off before anybody else made noise on this channel. Then I held my breath.

There was a narrow gap between the concrete and the dirt. Dozens of demonic limbs charged past, claws ripping up grass or elephantine feet smashing great circular tracks into the dirt. Bullets landed throughout the garden as the Hunters tried to hold them off.

Fall back. Get to a choke point. Come on, guys. Stay alive.

There were hundreds of demons. The first wave of black and orange bodies hit the breach only to be washed away by machine-gun fire. More arrived within seconds, clustered all around the hole, twitching and moving like bees on the surface of a hive. They were too occupied with the living to search the dead. *Yet.*

There had only been a handful of Hunters inside that area when the hotel had been hit. Not nearly enough to stop the tide of demons.

Milo must have left more of his explosives behind to slow them, because a few seconds later a final explosion rocked the breach, clearing the swarm off the wall and flinging demon bits in every direction.

By the time the gray smoke cleared, the fastest of the creatures had already swarmed in after the fleeing humans. The spine-flinging warriors continued inside after them.

But I wasn't alone... Now the claws around my hiding place were moving more slowly, methodically. These feet were smaller. The workers had arrived. Like four-foot-tall, yellow, bipedal grasshoppers, their joints clicked and popped as they moved, and as I watched, horrified, they began pulling a body from the wreckage to systematically rip apart. Every direction I could peer through the gap, there were more twisted legs, dozens of them.

A grasshopper demon took hold of the limp arm resting on my back and began to tug. I was alone in the middle of them, but not helpless. I slowly moved one hand to Abomination's grip. I'd take as many of them with me as possible.

Please let Julie escape. That's all I ask.

There were demons everywhere.

So this is how I die...

"Not yet, Z. You don't get off that easy."

My radio was off, but I'd heard the familiar voice as clear as day.

It can't be. He's dead. Ray Shackleford killed him. I was fading in and out of reality. I was injured worse than I thought. Now I was hearing voices from my past.

But . . . Was that Copenhagen chewing tobacco that I was smelling?

"You're not in the real world anymore, Z. You've all been shanghaied into a place between worlds. He's killing you with things from your own pasts, things that are already dead and gone. Well, me and the other guys are sick of that shit, and *here* we can do something about it. This evil son of a bitch isn't the only one that can cheat."

A demonic claw wrapped around my boot and I was pulled from underneath the body parts and concrete. The worker demon grabbed the back of my armor and flipped me over. The creature loomed over me. Its pack of eyes flickered back and forth and then it clicked hungrily as it realized I was alive. It leaned over to slice my face off with one of its jagged mouths.

The demon's face exploded, splattering me with hot bits. A figure stepped over me and kicked the headless corpse aside. The man knocked a second monster down with the stock of his rifle. Another monster ruptured in a shower of yellow bile. He worked a Marlin lever-action rifle and fired from the hip, disemboweling a third creature. He kept shooting and shooting and shooting, driving the demons back. Somehow the rifle never seemed to run out of ammo.

He was wearing MHI-issued body armor, bandoleers of individual rounds of .45-70, and on his arm was a patch featuring a walrus with a banjo.

It can't be.

I'd never seen these demons show fear before, but *this* Hunter scared them. Screeching and chattering in their incomprehensible language, the horde retreated. "That's right, you bugs!" he bellowed after them. "Run back to your master and tell him he's not the only one with friends at this party."

"But you're dead," I croaked.

"Duh." Sam Haven turned around and grinned at me from beneath his gigantic mustache. "But screw death. I've got shit to get done. Come on."

"Are you from my imagination?"

"No. That's stupid." Sam snorted, reached down, grabbed my armored collar, and hoisted me as if I weighed nothing. "Can you walk?"

It hurt like a son of a bitch. I'd wrenched one leg on the way down. My ankle felt like it had been sprained, same one the stupid rag monster had torn up earlier. I wasn't going to win any races, but there wasn't time to whine about it. "Yeah."

He pulled me along, through the ruined gardens, through the evil swirling fog, and away from the breached wall. "You've got no idea how much it sucks being in the spirit world watching my people get their asses kicked in the world of the living and not being able to do anything about it. We can't see everything, but we can watch those that we're close to a little. We're still in this fight, we just haven't been allowed to participate yet."

The red haze in my head had cleared a bit, enough to know that I wasn't imagining this. I'd been rescued by a dead Monster Hunter. And judging from the gunfire in the gardens, he'd brought friends. "We?"

"See for yourself."

I was still blinking away someone else's blood so it was hard to see clearly, but there were several men waiting ahead of us. Some were dressed in modern MHI armor, but a few were wearing armor that seemed more old-fashioned, and a few were even in the archaic high-necked leather suits that I'd seen Bubba Shackleford in. They seemed somehow blurry. The strong winds didn't so much as muss their hair. I could have swore that it was Chuck Mead that gave me a small nod as we passed, but Chuck had died at DeSoya Caverns.

"Terminate these insect assholes with extreme prejudice," Sam ordered. "Be ready for him to throw anything at us. He will not let up. Keep the living safe as long as possible. They're counting on us. Move out." The ghostly figures faded away and were gone.

Sam carried me around the corner, where there was a bit of shelter from the screaming wind, and set me down with my back against a low wall. He squatted next to me, looking remarkably good for a dead man. I rubbed the blood off of my face and realized with a shock that the blurriness of his features wasn't due to crap in my eyes at all. Everything else in the world was sharp and focused, but the lines that made up Sam seemed to flicker. "How're you feeling?"

"Confused."

"I was asking about physically, but that's under-standable. Listen carefully, Z. You need to know that you aren't in this alone. There's a war coming, and it's bigger than just the living, and it's bigger than just the Earth. A lot of those that came before you still have skin in this game. There are legions of us. *Legions.* But until the war starts, there's rules set that we have to follow, including not meddling with the living. Ah, but you know I've never been too good with authority." He chuckled.

I raised one shaking hand and pointed upwards questioningly.

Sam nodded. "Pretty much. It's mostly hands-off the living world for reasons I don't get myself. Way over my pay grade. But this place isn't in the living world right now. Nobody important has laid claim to this place except for scum that live here. So the rules are in sort of a gray area, which is how come some of us came here to help. We're buying you some time, but this needs to be finished by the living. I've got a message from Mordechai that'll help. Since the Old Ones messed with your head, you can read other people's memories. Think of this as a download."

Sam reached out, put his palm on my forehead, and *SNAP*.

It was like getting a stun gun to the brain. But when the white-hot electrical vise grip unlocked from my synapses, there was a gigantic pile of new memories in my head. I'd watched other people's memories unfold before as a result of my connection to the Old Ones' artifact, but never anything like this. It was quite literally an infodump, and I was surprised to see who it was from . . .

CHAPTER 19

He had been called many things since he'd died. He did not like being referred to as a ghost and preferred *protector spirit,* which seemed to him to have more dignity, though *restless dead* also had gravitas, but often had negative connotations. Usually the living that he had dealt with simply referred to him as the old man, since that was how he still tended to perceive himself, and thus how the living perceived him as a result. Regardless of what he was known as, the most common adjective applied to any of his titles by his superiors was usually *stubborn.*

Come on, girl. Pick up your telephone . . . There is not much time. Pick up the telephone, girl!

The girl in question was Holly Newcastle. The old man knew that she was the most suitable person available and time was of the essence. It was not often that he was allowed to interfere in the affairs of the living, but this was a prelude to the big war, one of his own flesh-and-blood descendants was in danger, and the Hunters could not afford to lose their champion.

The old man knew Holly well. He had seen her grow and mature, fighting alongside the champion, always with conviction, never showing fear. But she wore a mask, crafted so well that even she thought it was real. On the inside there was still some of the old girl left. She had her own destiny yet to fulfill, but sadly, most of her choices would lead her to a dark end. Her road was a difficult one.

She was dressed in a manner that would have been scandalous and completely unacceptable during the old man's mortal time on earth, but was normal now. She had left the other Hunters with excuses of "partying" or such mortal nonsense, but that had only been at first. It had been an excuse, to the others, but mostly to herself. Squandering her money and poisoning her body were distractions from what was really on her mind. She had done that for a time, but there was something far more important that she had to tend to that she'd been avoiding, and this was the first time she had returned home since she had discovered the real world.

So she had paid a cab driver to take her far to the outskirts of the city, to a rusting industrial area. It was the sort of place where only the most unsavory ruffians would be found, but Holly was not afraid of the human kind of monster. She was here to confront her memories of the other kind.

It had not been difficult to find, because a place where such evil and horror occurred was always visible to a spirit's eyes. Even long after the evil had taken place, it would still glow like a hot coal. The ruin had once been a factory of some kind. The police had put a chain and a padlock on the door. So Holly had smashed out a window with an old board and crawled inside, ripping her dress in the process, but not caring.

The old man had found her deep inside, sitting at the edge of a hole in the ground. The hole was not so big, but big enough to hold many captives, and deep enough to keep them from crawling out. It was a horrible thing, this pit. Vampires were vile beasts, and the things they did to survive were terrifying to comprehend. The old man had survived much in his mortal life, but even he had a hard time understanding what it would be like to be kept as a prisoner and used as food. She had become strong to protect the others, and eventually herself. All of the other captives had broken and then died.

Yet, Holly had survived the pit. And that had made her strong.

While the others had wilted and died and come back and died again, Holly's determination had grown, until she'd used her cunning to kill a vampire and then go for help. Hunters had come and eradicated the rest of the nest, and Holly had found her destiny. The girl had two sides, one made of anger, and one made of love. Anything that provoked the anger or endangered that which she loved was doomed. The old man approved.

She had come back to the site of her horror. The old man wondered if the hole seemed smaller to her now. Did it seem insignificant? Compared to the other things that she had faced without flinching, it must seem insignificant, this dark place. But then again, it must not, because she had sat next to the edge of the pit for hours, always remembering, hating the vampires that had taken her, sometimes crying, occasionally talking to herself, or perhaps to the ones that had died around her. The old man could have saved her the time. Those spirits had moved on. They were not restless, like him.

Holly was strong, stronger even than she or any of her friends realized. Coming back and facing again the test that had made her a Hunter would hone that commitment. She was an ideal choice for this task.

The only problem was that she wouldn't heed his words. *Your friends need you!* He was practically shouting. Even with all of the excess magical energy leaking into the city from the rift, she wouldn't hear his voice. *Why will you not listen to me?*

Because there aren't very many living that can hear us good, his companion told him. *The champion's in tune with the dead. Most folks ain't.*

Then we need another alive person to serve as messenger. And that gave the old man an idea. The champion came from a special bloodline, prepared and honed over generations to fulfill a prophecy. That particular challenge had been won, but then he'd been drafted for another. There were no more prophecies, and fate would be determined by mortal choices. But the champion was not the sole inheritor of that prepared bloodline. *Come, my friend. New strategy I have. Not a Hunter, but I know a man who will hear us.*

I hope this works, Mordechai.

The spirits left in search of another. Holly, exhausted and emotionally spent, had finally had enough and decided to leave the warehouse. She contemplated setting the place on fire and burning it to the ground, but her conscience wouldn't let her, on the off chance there were some bums sleeping in the neighboring buildings. As Holly made her way back into the light, she checked her messages and found one from Owen Zastava Pitt.

David "Mosh" Pitt woke up on his hotel room floor with an agonizing headache. He was no stranger to hangovers, but this one was particularly epic.

After Owen had sucker-punched him and stormed out, Mosh had finished off the contents of one of the bottles he'd found on his table. He wasn't even particularly sure what brand the nasty concoction was. It could have been jet fuel for all he cared at that point, and since he hadn't made it to his bed, it might actually have been. He couldn't tell what time it was. His watch was missing and the alarm clock was blinking 12:00 over and over again. "Where's my watch? Oh yeah, that one groupie stole it from me last week... Stupid chick. That Rolex was totally fake..." He'd had to sell the real one. Besides, he didn't need a watch. The light coming around the curtain hurt his eyes enough to tell him that it was in the afternoon, so close enough. He just needed to be coherent enough to play some half-hearted crap before eight P.M.

Staggering to the bathroom, Mosh discovered that he was still wearing one boot. He splashed some water on his face and took stock of the damage. His bottom lip was split and his front teeth hurt. His brother always could throw a mean punch. Mosh poked at the sore spot. "Damn it, Owen, you self-righteous asshole. I can't believe you did that. Ah, that stings." Talking to himself wasn't a recent development. He had always done it, but usually only when he was lonely, not that he would admit it.

Owen was such a jerk...It wasn't enough to drag his business into everyone else's business, but now he was into something that was going to endanger Dad? Not that Dad would care. He was psycho too. Hell, the whole family had problems. Mosh found himself staring back at his own bloodshot eyes. "Look at you. You used to be something. What happened to you?"

"I do not know this answer. You should turn on the television set. Watch news."

Startled, Mosh spun around to see who had said that. He could've sworn that the voice had come from right behind him, but the bathroom was empty. Had the maid come in? Walking lopsided because his remaining boot had very thick soles, Mosh went into the suite to find that it too was empty. The security latch was still locked.

"I'm losing it." Mosh rubbed his face in his hands. He could've sworn he'd heard a man's voice, like an old dude, with a thick accent, sort of Eastern Europe, kind of like Mom when she got excited, but way worse. He found a bottle of Tylenol in the kitchenette and popped four of them. "Can alcohol give you hallucinations? Is it a hallucination if you *hear* it?" Unlike many of his peers in the music business, Mosh didn't mess around with drugs. He'd seen too many other musicians fry their brains, and he liked being the smart one too much.

The drinking was just to help him sleep...Until things picked back up.

"What is it with this family? None of them can listen to instructions!"

Mosh leapt back and crashed into the refrigerator.

"Who's there?" There was no response. He had heard that clear as day. "If you're messing with me, it isn't funny."

Who would play a trick on him? His so-called friends had bought the government's line. Nobody wanted to have anything to do with him. His name was mud. The only people that would have anything to do with him anymore weren't the kind he wanted around. A bunch of sycophant groupies weren't the best company, and he couldn't even remember the names of the ones he'd found here in the mornings.

"None of the Pitts can listen. Is simple request. Watch news program, dummy."

Mosh jumped. That had come from right behind him. Now he was really freaked out. "Okay, assholes. It's on now." He hobbled back to the bedroom and picked up the Glock 19 he kept on the bedside table. He wasn't the family gun nut—that honor went to his brother—but he'd been raised by a fanatical survivalist, which meant that Mosh knew damn good and well how to take care of himself. After a death cult had kidnapped him, and a psychotic bitch had sawed his fingers off, Mosh was more than happy to shoot first and ask questions later. "You want trouble, you got trouble." He came back around the corner with the 9mm in both hands. "You better get out of here. I've got a piece and I will shoot your ass dead. I mean it."

"This wreck is the best we can do?"

"G'ah!" Mosh turned around and stabbed out the gun. That voice had come from a different man, deeper, with a slow southern drawl. His hands were shaking. His finger was on the trigger. But there was nobody there. "Stop that!"

"Can make contact. Is same blood as champion. You have better idea?" the disembodied old man's voice said. "Idiot boy. Turn on television."

"This place is haunted!" Mosh shouted.

"Yes. Boo," said the southerner. "I'm a haint. Now do what Mordechai said already. We're burning daylight."

"Mordechai?" *Owen's imaginary friend?* His brother had told him some crazy stories, only half of which he believed, and only then because he'd seen giant monsters and been teleported himself. When Owen had talked about ghosts and time travel, he'd wondered if his older brother had started licking toads. What was it Earl Harbinger had told him when he'd tried to cheer Mosh up, *flexible minds?* Like that helps when your whole life has just been ruined. "What do you want from me?"

"I am messenger, appointed by one side in big war to help Hunters. You are only person I can reach in time to warn."

"You've got to be kidding me. So you're really Mordechai Byreika?" He was supposedly the dead guy that had guided Owen through his first brush with cosmic weirdness. "I've got to be tripping."

"You are not going anywhere right now. Yes. Is I. Now hurry."

Mosh found the remote control and turned the TV on. It was still on one of the adult movie channels. "Damn, boy. Times have changed. In my day you had to work to see nekkid ladies," said the southerner.

"Easy, Bubba," the old man's voice took on a cautionary tone. "Is strange world now, but still worth saving. Sometimes."

Embarrassed, Mosh quickly flipped through the

channels until he found a cable news show. There was a special bulletin with the Las Vegas Strip in the background. The announcer was rattling off information about fires, the CDC, Ebola, a chemical spill, and an evacuation, but he'd jumped in midstream and Mosh's aching brain was having a real hard time catching up. The live video showed a line of fire trucks, police cars, and military vehicles, and behind them was a wall of whirling gray smoke.

"You are only one we can reach. Much magical energy spilling out of vortex. I use it to talk to you. You are close. You are blood of champion, so we can talk. Surprised I am, how good your mind works for this. Is more easy than your brother's even. He has to be close to death for me to even say hi anymore. Remarkable how good you are at listening to the dead."

That was a whole lot to take in on short notice while suffering from a hangover. As far as Mosh was aware, he'd never talked to any dead people before. So either more of his brother's nonsense was intruding into his life again, or somebody had slipped him something last night. Either one was equally possible.

"We need your help."

"Wait a second. I recognize that place." Mosh pointed at the TV. "That's the new hotel where Owen's staying. Is this more of his monster bullshit? Look, dead guys, I don't want to get involved in my brother's crazy-ass business ever again. Last time I lost my fingers and wrecked my career. This isn't my thing."

"Is everyone's *thing*. Not time to be selfish, boy. Hunters, how you say, kidnapped. Taken to another world. Whoosh. Whole place, taken away. If you do not help, one by one they all will die. When they all used up, the monster come back here to feed on more. Your brother needs you, Mosh."

"Mosh? What kind of name is Mosh?" the southern ghost asked. "Thought you said he was a musician."

"What kind of hillbilly-ass name is Bubba?" Mosh answered. "You a NASCAR driver?"

"What's a nascar?"

The live feed changed to an aerial shot from a helicopter. Mosh couldn't believe his eyes. "Shut up for a minute . . ." Mosh walked over to the window and pulled open the curtains. The sunlight drove a shaft of pain through his eyeballs and deep into his cerebral cortex. "Man, I think I need to cut back on the drinking."

The street below was packed with cars and people, all fleeing. After a few seconds of throbbing agony he could see the pillar of gray smoke rising from the opposite end of the Strip. This sure didn't look like smoke from a big fire, though. It was as big around as a city block, twisting like a leisurely tornado, rising up over the city until it blotted out a giant chunk of the sky. It was really weird looking, and didn't seem to be dispersing like a normal smoke cloud. Instead, it seemed to be hanging together, coherent. And worst of all, it was *huge*.

"Damn it, Owen. What have you got into this time?"

Making it to Owen's hotel was a lot harder than expected. The city was being evacuated so it was like trying to swim upstream. Mosh was still unclear on whether that was a mandatory evacuation declared by the governor, or if everyone was just getting the hell out of town because there was a several-mile-tall, eerie-as-hell smoke pillar shooting out of the ground.

A Ford Focus was quite a step down from his repossessed V12 Vanquish, but it still had a radio. The news was a mess, repeating all sorts of garbled nonsense. It was like they weren't sure what story they were supposed to be spreading. This had to be someone else's doing. That jackass Myers had at least been smooth when he'd come up with a cover story blaming Mosh for Montgomery. Myers had taken all the crazy pieces of the truth and hammered them until they'd fit a basic, believable, monster-free narrative, and he'd done it fast. This current media clusterfuck didn't have that vibe at all. Mosh found himself hoping that they wouldn't find a way to blame this one on him too.

Finally he had to give up on trying to drive there. The cops kept flagging him out of the way for more emergency vehicles and turning him around with dire warnings. The evacuation was general, and they weren't dicking around. So he parked on a side street and decided to walk in.

At least the dead guys had stopped hounding him. The old Jewish dude had said it took too much energy, but he'd be back periodically.

"I'd better not be going insane. Washed-up rock star goes crazy. That's so cliché. Bet it'll look awful on the magazine covers ... Shit. I probably don't even rate the cover anymore." They said there was no such thing as bad publicity, but Mosh knew that was a bunch of crap.

Sure, some no-talent hacks loved being the bad boys in the media and collecting a bunch of disaffected loser fans. Those assholes would bounce right back from being blamed for causing the deaths of

innocent people through their careless actions, then
go on to being self-proclaimed bad boys of rock or
some nonsense like that. But Mosh had been successful
because he'd been the best, not through trashy PR
manipulation. So now that his fingers were senseless,
clumsy blobs of lunchmeat and his playing sounded
awful, the only options he could see were either to
struggle along as a terrible musician, capitalize on
his bad name, and live Myers' lie as a D-list celebrity, or blow his own brains out and get it over with.
Auhangamea Pitt hadn't raised any liars or quitters, so
that left playing guitar in second-rate establishments
with the wrong hand, every minute of which he hated,
and each performance sucked just a little bit more of
the joy out of his miserable life.

And it was all Owen's fault, and now Owen's not-
so-imaginary friends wanted him to go rescue him or
something. "Man, this is bullshit."

"Is no bulls here. Turn right," the ghost told him
in his head.

So much for leaving him alone. "Stop that!"

Mosh had absolutely no idea what he was supposed
to be doing. He'd thrown on a long-sleeved shirt and
left it untucked to hide his Glock under it. He was
kicking himself for not doing like Dad had always said
and having a bug-out bag ready to go. Dad had always
kept a backpack of useful stuff next to the door. But
oh no, Mosh was too proud to listen to Dad. Whatever you needed, for any possible problem, Dad had
something in the bag. It was like magic. Need to start
a fire? In the bag. Purify water? In the bag. Hell, he
had *rope*. Mosh had a pistol because he'd once been
abducted by a death cult, and a Leatherman that he

only carried because the screwdriver and pliers came in handy for setting up the stage show, and here he was heading toward a supernatural cataclysm. Maybe Dad wasn't as crazy as he'd always thought.

The walk gave him a chance to clear his head. Not everybody was running for it. There were still plenty of people on the sidewalks, most of them taking pictures or video of the pillar. The cops were trying in vain to shoo them away. A few times a squad car came by using the loudspeaker, telling everyone to get off the street for their own safety. On the second pass the cop had called them idiots and said something about the *chemical fire*. Even the cops hadn't been given the same story. The Monster Control Bureau was really botching it this time.

"Well, I am surprised. Go in that shop. A friend is inside."

The sudden voice in his ear startled him. "Stop sneaking up on me," Mosh hissed. A few of the tourists that were filming the pillar turned to study him. "Not you. You guys are fine. Carry on."

"Cool. A Mosh Pitt impersonator," said one of the tourists. "Nice goatee. Oh no, he's going to go on a rampage and hit us with his bus!" She laughed and took his picture.

"Yeah. Okay. Whatever."

"Hold the pig steady, man," said the other tourist as he threw the horns.

Mosh sighed and walked toward the shop that the ghost had indicated. It was a costume shop, and like most establishments of its type in this part of town, it was mostly naughty costumes. He had no idea what sort of *friend* he was supposed to find in here. As he pulled open the door, a thin Hispanic man caught the handle on the other side and stopped him. "Sorry. We're closed. I'm on my way out."

"Uh . . ." Mosh glanced around. If it wasn't for his stupid brother he'd be hitting the road too. "You sure?"

"If you ain't noticed, buddy, something weird's going on down the street."

"I'm looking for a friend."

The man frowned. "Crazy blonde chick?"

Mosh pursed his lips. *Stupid ghosts.* He figured he might as well run with it. "That's her."

"I told her to get lost. She gave me a thousand bucks *in cash* and said she only needed ten minutes to pick out an outfit. A thousand bucks! Your friend is nuts. Hot, though. Come on in." Mosh followed the proprietor into the costume shop as he shouted ahead. "Hey, lady. Your friend is here. You got five minutes left and then I gotta go."

"Friend?" a woman called from the back of the store.

Mosh walked between the racks of costumes, sexy nurse, sexy kitty, sexy librarian, sexy construction worker, and then got to the more mundane area. A woman in a slinky party dress was flipping through a spinner of jackets. Since he'd come up from behind, Mosh took a moment to enjoy her curves. At least his new friend was stacked. *Hey, thanks, dead guys.*

She looked up in surprise. "Wait. You're Z's brother . . . *Mosh?*"

He recognized her right away. She certainly had a face that was hard to forget. They'd met at the MHI compound right after he'd escaped from Force and Violence and blown up an overpass in Montgomery. "Holly? Holly Newcastle?"

"What're *you* doing here?" She was obviously confused.

Her presence made him so very happy. First off, it meant that he wasn't insane. The odds of him randomly running into one of his brother's people in a situation like this in a place like this were absurd, which meant the voices in his head were real. Plus, Holly was supposed to be a badass, so she'd know what to do, and it helped that she was also by far the best looking Hunter he'd ever met.

Because regardless of how bad things got, or how much life was kicking him when he was down, Mosh Pitt would always love the company of a beautiful woman.

Holly snapped her fingers a couple of times. "Mosh. Focus. Why are you here?"

There was no use beating around the bush. Holly was a Monster Hunter. The girl hung out with orcs. She was supposed to be used to weird shit like this. "When I woke up there were a couple of ghosts talking to me. They said I need to go help rescue my brother. They led me to you."

"This day just keeps getting weirder..." Holly reached around and unzipped her dress and began shrugging out of it. She stopped. "Turn around, dumbass."

"Sorry." Mosh turned to face the front of the store, only to realize that there was a mirror nearby. Holly tossed the party dress. He had dated swimsuit models that weren't as built as she was. However, Holly made her living killing horrific things with bullets and fire and pointy things, so Mosh swallowed hard, decided not to get his ass kicked, and studiously watched the floor.

She put on a pair of jeans and a T-shirt. "I bought these clothes from the cabbie that dropped me off

here. I smell like boiled cabbage. The things I do for
this job...You can turn around now." Mosh did so.
"This ghost, was it Mordechai?"

"Yeah, and a guy named Bubba."

"The only Bubba I know is a Shackleford...The
founder of MHI. Z met him when he got all zombi-
fied." Holly nodded slowly, like that actually made
sense. "Okay then...This supernatural nonsense ticks
me off, but I'm not going to turn down help, no matter how clueless it is."

"Hey—"

"No offense, but I'd trade you for any Newbie
with a month of training. This is way over your head.
You're untrained, uneducated, inexperienced, but I
need another pair of eyes and all of my coworkers
are inside that cloud or won't be here in time. So
you'll have to do."

The last time they'd spoken, she had been a lot
nicer to him, but Mosh figured she was just estab-
lishing dominance. Not that it mattered. He wasn't
about to give her any lip. He didn't know anything
about this sort of thing. It was actually a relief to
have someone to turn the decision-making over to.
"I just want to help."

"Okay...What size are you? You look like a 2X."

"Sure...What—" Holly tossed a blue windbreaker
at him and Mosh barely caught it before it hit him
in the face.

"We're lucky in one way. They wouldn't have anything here that would fit your brother. Put that on,
Agent Pitt. Come on. We've got to hurry."

Mosh flipped the jacket around and saw that the
back had DEA in big gold letters. "Seriously?"

But Holly had already gone to the front counter and slapped down another hundred-dollar bill. "Yo, Jorge. You got any business shoes? Some plain flats maybe? Anything conservative?"

"No. Sorry. Just high heels and clown shoes. We don't carry normal shoes."

"Damn it." Holly looked down at her feet. She already had on a pair of high heels, expensive ones, from the look of them. "These do not look like cop shoes. Keep the change, and if I were you I'd get the hell out of town. Let's go, Mosh."

He caught Holly on the sidewalk, where she was pulling on her own blue windbreaker. Holly's read FBI. "Here's the deal. These aren't very convincing disguises, but they don't need to be. It'll be chaotic in there, and MCB usually pretends to be some other agency anyway."

"In where?"

"We're sneaking into the quarantine. Try not to talk to anybody. If you act like you belong, then nobody will bug us . . . Maybe. Stand in front of me for a second." Mosh did as he was told. Holly reached into her purse, pulled out a pistol, quickly stuck it in her waistband, then covered it with her jacket. A few extra magazines went into the jeans pockets. "I'm glad you showed up. I might need a lookout or a distraction or something. You ever picked a fistfight with federal agents before? How good's your attorney?"

"He's not talking to me because I still owe him money from when the city of Montgomery sued me." You knew things were really bad when your own attorney put you in collections. "Why are we sneaking into . . . a *quarantine*?"

"No big deal. It's just a stroll through the MCB's

secure area without proper ID to talk to a mad scientist. If we're seen by a certain scary albino, I'm going to shoot him in the face. We get caught or we don't. Either way, we've got to figure out how to stop *that*." She nodded her head toward the frightening pillar. From this distance it seemed even more unnatural. "Any questions? No? Good." Holly raised her voice and spoke directly at Mosh's forehead. "Listen up, ghosts, if you're really in there, and you can do anything to help, I'd appreciate it."

Apparently Mosh was the only one that could hear the voices, because Holly showed no reaction when Bubba chimed in. "I really wish we could've contacted her instead of this bum."

"She is not blood of champion. Must work with what we have."

Great. I'm being insulted by the voices in my own head. Just do like she asked and send the cavalry.

Bubba laughed. "Kid, you are the cavalry."

Holly, who apparently couldn't hear any of that, put on a pair of dark shades and a matching fake FBI ballcap. "How do I look?"

"Like a gorgeous FBI agent?"

"Why, Mosh. Even when you're in way over your head and scared shitless you can be *so* sweet. Come on." Holly had only made it a few feet when she spotted one of the tourists that had talked to Mosh on his way into the costume shop. "Excuse me, ma'am. Nice shoes. Are those size seven?"

The surprised woman looked down at her plain black tennis shoes. "They're eights."

"Close enough." Holly's grin was sort of frightening.

❖   ❖   ❖

Holly's plan worked. Briefly.

Piercing the outer layer of defense had been easy enough. Because of the sudden chaos the authorities were still disorganized. Adding to that was the evacuation order, which was taxing everyone's resources. There were police and sheriff's deputies from different departments, representatives from multiple agencies, and they'd called in the National Guard. The weirdness of the unnatural smoke funnel made a great distraction. Holly had simply picked a spot on the perimeter and walked right between the barricades, talking on her cell phone like she was getting directions from a superior, and waving at the distracted soldiers.

Mosh figured that it helped that all of the law enforcement and military types were distracted by the screaming death cloud. And it was, quite literally, screaming. Having spent years of his life on a stage listening to vast crowds making all sorts of noise, the sound coming from the whipping smoke was uncomfortably similar. It might have only been the wind, but the frequency of this particular wind sounded like thousands of people crying out as one, and they didn't sound like they were having a good time.

All eyes were on the smoke so Mosh couldn't blame them for the lax security. Screw watching for trespassers breaching the perimeter. Who'd be crazy enough to want to come close to this thing anyway? The smoke seemed alive. It was moving, but not billowing outward like smoke should, just going straight up, not deviating from its path until it was a quarter mile up. It was moving, like the whole thing was rotating around some unseen axis, but it didn't seem to be moving fast enough to be making that screaming noise.

After a few minutes of walking through chaos, the two of them stopped behind a fire truck to take a look around. It wasn't marked in any way, but it was obvious that this was the line where regular law enforcement stopped, then a no-man's land of pavement, and then there was the *special* government on the other side. That was where their scientist would be.

Holly was watching the smoke and shaking her head. "That is some major weirdness. It's so...*contained*..." Normally you'd be able to see a fire or something, but this was just gray. Not only that, but the pavement ran right up to it then seemed to drop off, as if the smoke was coming out of a hole. "It's like it's held inside some sort of force field."

"What happens if the force field comes down?" Mosh shuddered at the thought of all that smoke getting loose. It looked...*sticky*.

"How should I know?"

"You're the professional Monster Hunter."

"Newsflash. I've never seen anything like that before, and I've seen a ten-story walking insect tree, so chill the hell out." Holly reached out and popped the collar on Mosh's jacket. "Cover your neck tattoos. The next line is going to be MCB. Try to look professional. Think paramilitary business casual, but with a bureaucratic stick up your ass."

He had six inches of dyed pointy goatee hanging off his chin. Mosh wasn't sure how he was supposed to look *business casual*, but then again the jacket said DEA. He'd just say that he worked undercover...And then they'd probably ask to see his ID or badge, or whatever DEA agents had, and when he couldn't produce one, they'd probably shoot him. "So what is the plan, exactly?"

"Look for someplace where you'd put the expert on this sort of thing, so some sort of command center probably. I saw the Feds use a giant rubber tent for that once, but they've commandeered all the local buildings, so they're probably in one of those. If we can't find him, then find Franks."

"The big scary one? Are you out of your mind?"

"Maybe. If he doesn't just arrest us, then I trade information for a chance to interview this Dr. Blish."

"Information?"

"I can't really call it blackmail, because I'm not stupid enough to try to blackmail Stricken. Think more along the lines of me giving Franks an excuse to murder somebody."

"Subtle."

"As a train wreck. I give Franks a license to kill, he lets me interview the scientist, and then we get that to our friends."

"Assuming they're still alive," Mosh said as he watched the cloud of the damned. Holly glared at him. "I'm not trying to be a downer, but look at that thing."

"When it comes to survival, Hunters make cockroaches look like quitters. So man up, Mosh." She quieted down as several SWAT cops jogged by. "They're still alive. I know it."

He waited until they were alone again. "I'm kind of scared of Franks."

"Oh, he's cuddly. Don't worry. Him and your brother are *tight*."

"That's not exactly how Owen tells it—"

"You know how Z likes to exaggerate. Enough talking. Put your big-girl panties on and follow my lead."

Holly kept them on the normal cop side of the line,

paralleling no-man's-land, trying to spot anyone that looked like an old scientist. Unfortunately, there were several big vehicles, a few tents, and even a couple of small buildings that had been taken over inside the inner perimeter. Whenever someone would come near, Holly would either walk past like she was on a mission, or if they looked like the sort of people who might try to talk to her, she'd get out her cell phone and have an imaginary conversation with her superiors as they gave her imaginary directions to their imaginary position.

It took half an hour to walk all the way around the site, and they were just as clueless as when they'd started. "We're wasting time. I'm going to have to go in," Holly told him finally. "You stick out like a sore thumb. Stay here."

"That's not going to happen," Mosh answered with more bravado than he felt. "I can't let you go in there alone."

"You going to protect me, stud? Ninja your way in there all badass and choke out the guards?"

It sounds stupid when she puts it that way. "Sorry, I left my wall-climbing boots at the hotel. Maybe the dead guys have an idea? Gimme a sec. Hey, ghosts, you got any ideas?"

Holly was suspicious. "Does that work?"

"I don't know. A couple of hours ago I thought I was having an aneurism when they started talking to me. I'm not Owen."

"No kidding. He'd actually be useful." Holly put her hands on her hips. "Hurry up and do . . . whatever." She turned back to the smoke pillar. "Being psychic must run in the Pitt family."

"Psychosis runs in the Pitt family," he muttered. Mosh closed his eyes and concentrated as hard as he could. It made him feel completely ridiculous. *Mordechai, Bubba, come in. Help me out here.* He put his head down and folded his arms. *Do I like need to meditate or something?*

Now that he was more familiar with the effect, he could tell that the voice only seemed to be coming from around him, when in actuality it was completely inside his head. No wonder his brother had gotten so weird, living with this kind of thing. "Go with the men," Mordechai told him.

What men?

"The secret policemen who will shoot you in the back if you try to run away."

Mosh opened his eyes to find himself staring down the muzzle of an assault rifle. Behind the rifle was a dude in black body armor, helmet, and face-covering balaclava. Three other men moved up behind him, coming silently from around the corner of a military truck. "Uh, Holly?"

She was still watching the MCB line. "What now, Mosh?" She turned around to see the SWAT team pointing four guns at them. "Oh . . . Hey there."

"Put your hands in the air," said the first gunman.

She slowly raised her hands. "I'm looking for the Las Vegas FBI SAC, I was told—"

"Save it." Two kept covering them while the other two moved up. Mosh's face was shoved hard against the truck, and in a flash he was relieved of his Glock and handcuffed. He finally managed to look over to see Holly getting the same treatment. "Holly Newcastle, you're under arrest."

Holly snarled at Mosh. "I swear you are the worst lookout ever."

"I was meditating!"

"Worst. *Ever!*"

The four masked men didn't say another word as they dragged the cursing Holly and the frightened Mosh across the pavement of no-man's-land and into a Pancake Hut. It still smelled like breakfast and that just made the still-hungover Mosh feel nauseous.

The restaurant had been cleared out. They were seated in a booth, hands cuffed behind them. Through the window, only a few hundred yards away, was the swirling smoke that concealed the site of the Last Dragon. That was too depressing to look at, so Mosh read and reread the labels on the syrup bottles. Three of the men kept watch on them while the fourth disappeared for a bit. There were no logos or markings on any of their clothing, just empty spots of Velcro. Between that and the masks, Mosh had no idea who these men were, if they were regular cops, or MCB, or worse, whatever shadowy bunch that Holly was so nervous about. They seemed to be the only people inside the Pancake Hut. The lack of witnesses struck him as a bad thing.

"What's going to happen?" Mosh whispered to Holly after five minutes of awkward silence.

She whispered back. "If we're lucky, they let us go. If we're unlucky, they send us to prison. If we're really unlucky, they drag us into the freezer and put a bullet in the back of our necks."

"I'm liking that first option best." On the bright side, at least if he got sent to prison he'd probably already have a lot of fans there.

"Keep your fingers crossed." Holly raised her voice. "So, what does a girl have to do to get some service around here? I'm not leaving a very good tip at this rate." None of the men said a word. "Really? Nothing? I hear the blueberry waffles here are great. Well, up yours then. I want to talk to Agent Franks of the MCB. Come on, I know you assholes know who he is. Big guy, lots of muscles, always looks sort of angry, usually hitting someone. Ring any bells?"

But the men didn't say a word. Another minute passed before the fourth man returned, leaned his rifle against the wall, and slid into the booth across from them. He was still wearing a mask and kept his voice artificially low and raspy. "What've you got to say to the big man?"

"Are you trying to sound like Batman? Because if you're not, I've got some throat lozenges in my purse. How'd you spot us anyway?"

"You kept pretending to talk on your phone in the area where all cell signals are being jammed. Dumb move." The man put his hands on the table, then noticed that he'd put his Nomex gloves in some sticky syrup. "Aw . . ." He reached over, took some napkins from the dispenser and cleaned his gloves off. He turned back to them, started to ask another question, but then decided to wipe the rest of the syrup up first.

Holly began to laugh. "Seriously, Agent Archer? Are your OCD meds not working?"

The man across from them got defensive. "I don't know who—"

"Really, Agent, the growly fake voice thing doesn't work, and besides, I've always thought you had the most beautiful eyes. Which, by the way, I can see. You're not exactly a master of disguise."

He seemed to deflate as he reached up and pulled his balaclava off, revealing a thin-faced young man, with a blond flattop haircut. "All right, Holly. You got me."

Mosh looked between them. Apparently they knew each other. "I'm confused now."

"Mosh, this is Agent Archer of the MCB," Holly explained.

"MCB?" *Oh shit. Oh shit. Oh shit.*

"Who was also one of your brother's ineffectual bodyguards against the Condition. And I lied about the eyes, Archer. Torres was the hot one, too bad he was a nut bar. Where's Franks? I really do have a message for him. It's important."

"Not so fast. You're in a restricted area impersonating a federal agent. You're in big trouble." Though sounding far less ridiculous without the cheesy threatening voice, he was still trying to play it tough. "First off, you need to tell me what you're doing sneaking around in here."

"I was sneaking because if I'd run into Stricken and he found out what I wanted to tell Franks, he'd more than likely kill me. This is one of *those* things. Come on. I'm not stupid. If I can't talk to Franks, let me talk to Myers. This is legitimate big time. Stricken knows how to beat this monster, but he's planning on letting all those people in there die first."

Archer's tough-guy facade slipped. *Surprise.* "How did you hear that?"

"So you know, but you're cool with it? You planning on letting that thing murder all my friends and a bunch of innocents while you MCB tough guys sit around on your asses?"

"Oh, hell no! What do you think we are? Some of

us—Well . . . There's official orders, but you'd have to be an idiot to believe them. We're trying to stop this thing before anyone else gets hurt."

Mosh had no idea what was going on, but it seemed like not all of the government people were on the same side here, and he didn't know if that was a good thing or not. Especially since Holly was talking to the side that had mercilessly ruined his life, and they were supposed to be the nice ones.

"So let me talk to Franks or Myers!" Holly demanded. "I know you're not stupid, so you know I didn't come in here for kicks. Get your boss."

"There might be a problem with that . . . See, there are some communication issues . . ."

"Oh, come on. Communications was like your thing, wasn't it? So communicate with your damn superiors and fix this mess. I know you can't like that psycho Stricken bossing you guys around. What I've got will totally burn him."

Archer looked to one of the other masked men and shrugged. That one spread his hands as if to say *beats me*. Archer sighed. Holly looked at the other one suspiciously. "Wait a second . . . You guys are up to no good, aren't you? Where's the rest of the MCB? Does Stark know about this? Oh my gosh, Archer, you're a *vigilante*? Haw! MCB agents have gone off the reservation. You've gone rogue! This is golden. I knew the new guy sucked, but I didn't know he sucked that much."

"No. That's crazy . . ." Archer stammered. "That's . . ." He looked back at the other agent for help again.

"So much for plausible deniability. Way to go, Archer." The other agent gave up and pulled his mask off as well. "Good to see you again, Holly."

Holly laughed, harder this time. "No freaking way! You?"

Mosh was totally confused now. "Who? What?"

The other agent was a handsome, square-jawed, chiseled-feature type. One of those guys with that sort of natural confidence of somebody born to be one of the beautiful people. Despite having just been wearing a ski mask, even his hair seemed neat. He nodded in greeting. "Nice to see you again, Mosh. I'm Special Agent Grant Jefferson, Monster Control Bureau."

"Wait . . . I know you."

"We met briefly at the MHI compound."

He'd been at Sam Haven's funeral. "You're the dude my brother beat up and stole Julie from!"

"That's not how it . . . Hell. Never mind." Jefferson sighed. "Listen, Holly, we need to tread carefully here. I need you to know that not all of the MCB are happy with the official plan."

"So what are you going to do about it?" Holly snapped.

Someone else answered from behind them. "We intend to save the day."

Mosh craned his neck around to look over the back of the booth. A middle-aged man in a charcoal-colored suit had come up silently behind them, and it wasn't the manager of the Pancake Hut. Mosh immediately recognized the smug, obnoxious, lying face of the man who had orchestrated the ruination of his life. "You . . ."

"Yes." Agent Myers stopped next to the booth and gave Holly a nod of recognition. "You, I'm not surprised to see here meddling." He looked next at Mosh. "You, I didn't expect. Your psychological profile suggested you were a narcissist that didn't suffer from heroic delusions like your brother. When did you get suckered into joining MHI?"

"Never. I'm a *freelance* ass-kicker. So uncuff me now, asshole."

"Or what?" Myers asked slowly.

Mosh hadn't thought that far ahead. "Or you'll be hearing from my lawyer."

"I already bribed your leech of an attorney into failing miserably during your civil-liability cases last year, Mr. Pitt, and he did a rather spectacular job of it too. I was surprised he came so cheaply as well. Apparently, he didn't much care for you to begin with. So spare me the sanctimony."

"What? Max sold me out? That son of—"

Holly made a shushing noise. "Quiet. Grownups talking...Okay, Myers. So I know what you know, and you know that I know, but you don't know *all* I know, and there's something else that I simply must know...So we need to make a deal."

"I'm listening."

She leaned forward conspiratorially. "I know that Stricken is planning on letting everyone inside the Last Dragon die before he makes a move."

"Unfortunately, it would appear you are correct. Mr. Stricken feels that an event of this magnitude will result in him receiving the permissions necessary to go ahead with a very controversial plan. My guess is that he considers these deaths an acceptable loss in order to reach his goals."

"That's the difference between us. I don't consider any losses *acceptable*. Are you mounting a coup against Stricken, or what?"

"Coup is such a nasty word."

Despite being in handcuffs, Holly seemed completely at ease. Mosh found her confidence almost annoying. "You know what else I hear is a nasty word in some circles? *Nemesis.* I've heard that Stricken is willing to murder you and Franks over it."

That got his attention. Myers waved his hand dismissively at Archer, and the junior agent slid out of the booth to go stand next to Jefferson. Myers sat down across from them. He steepled his fingers and studied them with cold eyes. "Ahh, Ms. Newcastle, how you never cease to amaze me. Now on you, the Las Vegas MCB truly dropped the ball. Your resume was rather underwhelming, and the routine psychological profile pegged you as a rather mundane specimen of an attack survivor. Your background suggested that you wouldn't be the type to talk about trauma, since you obviously know how to keep a secret. So you were simply warned, filed, and forgotten. If we had realized what a spitfire you'd turn out to be, then the MCB would have made you a job offer. I hate to see this much talent wasted on the private sector."

"Why, thank you, Agent Myers. That's the sweetest thing an MCB representative has ever said to me. But my parents weren't first cousins, so I'm afraid I'd be ineligible."

"Such a loss." Myers nearly smiled. "And the information that you need?"

"How to defeat this monster and save my friends. Preferably today. I want to talk to Dr. Blish."

"You are remarkably well informed." Myers glanced around theatrically. "Are there gnomes here that I don't know about?"

"I hope not. Little bastards give me the creeps.

You help me and in exchange I give you an audio recording of Stricken being all plotty and nefarious."

"What good does that evidence do me? I'm more than aware of Stricken's nature, and he's not the sort of man that you can touch with things like the truth."

"Like you'd know the truth if it bit you in the ass," Mosh muttered.

"Compliments will get you nowhere, Mr. Pitt."

Holly shook her head. "I don't care if you use it to hold a congressional hearing or stick it on YouTube. Personally, I planned on just playing it for Franks and letting that murder machine *sort things out*. I'm straightforward like that."

"Agent Franks is currently indisposed," Myers said. Holly began to ask another question, but Myers held up one hand to silence her. "I'll level with you, Ms. Newcastle. When I arrived, I attempted to speak with the scientist, Blish, but was ordered out of the area. I'm supposed to be on a plane to Washington right now. Direct command of my strike force was taken over by Director Stark. He is in total operational control."

"Sounds like you're not a fan of the guy." As Holly said that, Jefferson had to suppress a laugh.

"Cutting to the chase? He's a puppet. Doug Stark has been a quisling searching for a boot to lick for a very long time. With him in control of the Bureau, I fear for America's safety. Luckily for us, the men that I've trained are intelligent and loyal to the MCB's primary mission. Despite your organization's feelings about mine, we are first and foremost professionals, and will do what we must to keep this nation safe. Once I found out what was going on, I sent Franks to procure some items that I feel will be necessary to defeat this being. There's an MCB storage facility here in Nevada—"

"Area 51?" Holly asked excitedly.

"Don't be absurd."

"Seriously. It's Area 51, isn't it?" But Myers' deadpan expression didn't change. "Okay, okay, never mind. Franks's picking up a secret weapon; go on."

"I've gleaned a small amount of information, but some of what I've learned has been conflicting. I want this situation resolved just as quickly as you do. If, in the process, embarrassing facts surface that are damaging to my replacement and his pink-eyed handler, I would be a very happy man."

"And in the process maybe get your old job back... Yeah, I know, you don't care about that, but we both know the MCB needs strong leadership in these troubling times." Holly grinned. "You've been remarkably forthcoming, Agent Myers. I'm impressed. Now, as for our deal—"

"I've already heard your recording. It was downloaded on your phone. I listened to it after my men confiscated it from you. I have no need of a *deal*."

"You prick!" Mosh exclaimed. "I should—"

"Chill out, Mosh," Holly ordered.

"Yes, *chill out*, Mosh," Myers said. "Really, I never thought I would say this, but you're making your brother seem rational and level-headed in comparison."

Holly seemed completely unperturbed at losing her ace in the hole. "If Myers was just going to screw us over, he wouldn't bother to brief us with a bunch of sensitive intel first. He's a busy guy. Am I right, *Director*?"

"Correct, Ms. Newcastle. There are a few policy

disagreements. I am one side of the battle and Stricken is on the other. In this battle, information is power. Stricken has one of the original scientists, and thus, he is keeping that information from me. What I do need is more information, and to achieve that now I need resources with plausible deniability. My loyal men are known. If we are caught attempting to speak to the scientist, then there will be repercussions. Stricken can't know that we are aware of his plans. However, nobody would be surprised if a member of MHI was caught trying to speak to the good doctor. You have a reputation for being meddlesome."

"We do work at it."

"Go with Agent Jefferson. He'll provide a way in, you get what you need, and in return you report back to my men."

"You're on," Holly answered without hesitation.

But Mosh was still suspicious of the slimy bureaucrat. "Aren't you worried about us talking if we get caught?"

"Absolutely not. Because if it comes to that, they will more than likely shoot you on sight. Though very capable in their own right, STFU's greatest weakness is its relatively small number of staff, which is the only way something so shrouded in secrecy can exist. In operations like this, they depend on us or other government agencies to provide security and firepower. In our current situation, Stricken, knowing he's in a power struggle, won't endanger his secrets by leaving their protection in the hands of men that may be loyal to me. So he hired some outside contractors on short notice and put them under the supervision of one of his pets seeking a PUFF exemption. They strike me as the shoot first and ask questions later type. If by some miracle you are taken alive, by the time they confirm the information that they torture out of you, I personally will be on the way to Costa Rica to live out my days under a new identity. Thus, I would strongly recommend not being caught."

Torture? It wouldn't come to that. Mosh knew that he would gladly blab Myers' name the second they got caught.

"You know, Myers, I like you a lot better as a subversive terrorist. Super villainy really works for you," Holly said with forced cheer. "We're in. Let's go for it."

Mosh glanced nervously at the MCB agents. The ones with visible faces looked as nervous as he felt. This whole sinister inter-governmental rivalry thing was way over his head. He despised the MCB for everything they stood for, but Holly seemed to think that they were a whole lot better than the alternative. That was really saying something about the alternative.

The ghost of Mordechai chuckled inside his head. "Boy, these policemen are not your friends. They are liars who hide monsters and threaten poor survivors. They do terrible, misguided things, but they are so much better than the pale one. Him, you avoid. I have seen with my own eyes what happens when his kind becomes in control. Now go. Next part may become...difficult. Hurry. Time is short."

If I live through this, I want you the hell out of my head, old man. No wonder Owen had gotten to be so nuts. This talking to dead people business was a bad trip. "So what's next?"

Agent Myers slid out from the booth, carefully adjusted his tie, and said, "Try not to get shot."

CHAPTER 20

Mosh Pitt, former rock superstar, had woken up with a nasty hangover and a bad taste in his mouth, which was a fairly normal state of affairs lately, but after that his day had just gotten progressively worse. His stupid older brother was in danger, the whole city of Las Vegas was being evacuated, he was hearing dead people, and somehow he'd ended up working with the government agency that had used him as a scapegoat. Now he was in a sewer.

"Is not so bad," Mordechai told him. "This is not actual sewer. Only tunnel. Sewer much worse."

Sure, there was no river of poop like in the movies, just close concrete walls and a lot of pipes, several of which he'd already managed to hit his head on, but there were still rats. Mosh could hear the rodents, just crawling with fleas and rabies, scurrying to stay ahead of their flashlights.

"You cannot *hear* rabies, boy."

"Shut up," Mosh said, sick and tired of the helpful voices in his head.

Grant Jefferson was in the lead. "What was that?" The MCB agent looked back over his shoulder.

"Nothing. Just talking to myself."

Jefferson shook his head, muttered something about Newbies, and continued down the narrow passage. As the flashlight moved away, a cold dread began to worm its way back into Mosh's guts. There was something bad ahead, he could just feel it. He jumped when Holly came up from behind and tapped him on the shoulder. "Relax, Mosh."

"You relax."

"Jeez, dude, calm down. I don't like being in the dark or in enclosed spaces either. Believe me. Nothing to be ashamed of. Hell, me and Grant have both been captives in some pretty nasty underground holes and you don't see us being jumpy little babies."

"It's not that. I've got a real bad feeling about this..." It was hard to explain. It was more than just the possibility of being shot by the guards. He knew that something bad was waiting for them. "I can just tell. Okay?"

"Like a premonition?"

"What? No. Cut that out already. I'm not my brother. He's the magic one. It's only a feeling, but I feel like something is going to try and stop us."

"That's like the definition of a premonition. You freaking Pitts. I should have taken Z out gambling with me last night. He could've used his psychic powers to predict where that stupid little ball was going to land on the roulette wheel." Holly put her hands on his back and shoved Mosh along. "I blew through two zombies' worth of PUFF in less than an hour."

"It makes me sad that she feels she has to wear a

mask," Mordechai said. Mosh had absolutely no idea what that was supposed to mean.

Mosh followed Jefferson's flashlight beam. As far as he could tell, the plan made sense. Myers' MCB agents couldn't risk tipping their hand by being spotted trying to talk to the scientist, so they were going to cause a distraction and sound the alarm while Holly and Mosh snuck into Stricken's base of operations.

They reached an intersection. "All right, Holly." Agent Jefferson aimed his flashlight down the service tunnel. "Here's where we part ways. You go to the right. We're now under the Taj, that's the casino that was next to the Last Dragon. You'll find the access door to the basement in about two hundred yards. Archer cut the camera wires, picked the lock, and disabled the alarm earlier when we thought we were going to have to do this on our own. Last we knew before the MCB got tossed out, Dr. Blish was one floor up in the main office area." Jefferson looked at his watch. The hands glowed in the dark. "In approximately ten minutes there will be a massive security breach. That should get the guards' attention. I wouldn't expect them to stick around if they think the monster has come through the smoke. They'll run. They're only contractors."

"Watch it, Grant," Holly warned. "Contractors are bailing your ass out right now."

"Only kidding." Jefferson lied smoothly. "Everyone here will think the monster has broken out. From what Myers knows about him, Stricken will go there in person to oversee its takedown. He wants just enough carnage so the president will green-light his pet project, so having everyone in the Last Dragon die is perfect, but he won't want it to escape into

the city because that will make him look bad, since
he's in control."

"Or if it does escape, then Stricken will just blame
it on Stark. Your boss will be the fall guy, and the
MCB loses even more authority," Holly said. "There's
no way that slippery bastard is taking the blame for
anything that goes wrong, which is why Myers wants
to steal his thunder and stop this monster before
Stricken's little task force can get all the credit."

"Not bad." Grant smiled. "You sure you don't want
a federal job? The benefits are great... Okay, relax.
Stricken knows how to stop this creature, and we'll
be watching to see how he reacts to our false alarm.
He'll more than likely take his actual Unicorn personnel with him, so at least you won't have to worry
about any of those *things*."

"Things?" Mosh asked.

"Long story." Holly's brief answer didn't make him
feel any better. "How do you plan to rig this break-
out, Grant?"

"A car bomb, weird lights, smoke, bangs, a whole
bunch of tear gas, throw in some garbled communications. Help me, help me, we're all going to die
sort of thing. Then someone," Jefferson made quote
marks with his fingers, "will direct fire on the parking
garage of this casino. By the time the entire Nevada
National Guard has emptied a magazine or two into
it, Stricken will think the monster is inside."

"You really think that's going to work?"

"Trust me. MCB are masters of hoaxes. If too
many people are getting curious about a real monster
phenomenon, then we make up some evidence to
add to the real pile. Then when everyone is looking

at that, we arrange for it to be revealed as a clever fake. That makes the real evidence look bad too, and pretty soon everyone forgets about it and moves on with their lives. There's a certain psychology to this sort of thing...It really is rather impressive."

"This is my not impressed face, Grant."

"Fine, it only has to work for a minute. Anything else?"

Holly shook her head. "We've got it."

"I've got to hurry." Jefferson got a really awkward look on his face. "Be careful, Holly. I know we've got some history with me and MHI, but—"

She held up one hand. "It's cool. Water under the bridge. You did what you thought you had to do. I can respect that. We'll see you back at the Pancake Hut. Good luck." And with that, she turned on her own flashlight and turned down the appropriate tunnel. Jefferson watched her for a moment, as if trying to decide to say anything else, then hurried in the opposite direction.

Mosh only banged his head on pipes twice more while trying to catch up to her. Holly was waiting for him next to a big green door. She kicked at a passing rat with her stolen shoes. "You think this is going to work?" Mosh asked.

Holly was inspecting the door, confirming that Agent Archer had already tampered with it. "I think we're another part of the distraction. I think Myers' real plan all along was to see what kind of weapons or tactics Stricken uses to respond to this fake attack so he can copy them. That's his real goal. Our showing up was just gravy. Myers probably thinks that we'll get caught, and when we do, by then Stricken knows the other attack was a ruse, MHI will get the blame."

"But that means..." Mosh was flabbergasted. "What about the whole running to Costa Rica thing?"

She snorted. "Puh-leese. Don't tell me you bought that noble for God and country duty-and-honor shtick. If anybody should know how good that professional liar is, it's you. We get caught and tattle on Myers, he denies that he ever talked to us, and anything we say is just a lame attempt to get out of trouble. We end up in a shallow ditch in the desert, Stricken maybe has a few nagging doubts about some of his coworkers, but then he and Myers go back to their chess game of which bureaucrat has more clout again tomorrow. If we actually pull this off, then it's just a happy bonus for Myers."

"But you were like all friendly... You even said that you and Jefferson were cool—"

"That backstabbing son of a bitch? Of course not. The thing about Grant is that he really does think he's doing the right thing. In his mind, he's the hero. He's got his own set of morals. Problem is, whatever he decides to do is automatically right. Anybody who gets in the way gets tossed under the bus." Holly tried the door handle. As promised, it was unlocked. "Grant's a real piece of work. Why do the really good-looking ones always have so much baggage?"

"I'm considered good-looking. I was in the top twenty of *People Magazine*'s Sexiest Man Alive once." It had been a couple of years ago, right after *Hold the Pig Steady* had hit number one, but it still counted.

"That's because girls will always love musicians, but like I said, baggage." She shut her flashlight off, then slowly opened the door a crack to peek inside. The lights were on, revealing a metal stairwell. "Coast is clear. Now we wait for Grant and Archer to do their thing."

The tunnel was humid and hummed with the noise of distant equipment. Occasional suspicious hissing noises didn't do much to alleviate Mosh's nervousness. "What do you mean 'baggage'?" he whispered.

"Never mind."

"No, really."

Holly sighed. "I swear I always have to be the one that tells the truth, even when it sucks." She kept looking through the crack. "Well, from what I hear, and your general state, the way I see it, you're still wallowing in self-pity about what happened to you. You're bitter, pissed-off, and won't accomplish shit until you move on. You'll either accept what happened, or let it eat at you until you die."

Mosh wasn't used to people being so blunt. Which was one of the main reasons he avoided his family. "You don't know me, Holly."

"Shhh. Keep it down," she snapped. Mosh hadn't realized he'd raised the volume. "Voices carry down here. I may not know *you* well, but I know a lot of people like you. I volunteer at an insane asylum full of them. Specifically, I know what happened to you with the Condition. Yes, it sucked. Yes, it ruined all your plans. You got screwed over. So what? At least you're still alive. You're a survivor. Every single minute you have after that is a gift, but you've forgotten that."

That stung. "You don't understand how bad—"

Holly turned around. They were cloaked in shadow, but he could still tell that she was giving him an angry glare. Her voice was hard. "You want to compare notes about how hard life has been? I'll win. I'll win handily, and that was before I had to kill my best friend with a *bone* I sharpened on a *rock*. So shut the fuck up and listen. I'm telling you things that your brother should have said to you a long time ago. Evil can kill you, break your body, and sometimes it can even break your mind, but only you can break your spirit. You know what I see at Appleton? That's the insane asylum for monster attack survivors. I see people where their sanity just *shattered*, and I see quitters. I feel sorry for the first bunch, and the second group just pisses me off. So quit pissing me off."

"I'm not a quitter," Mosh protested. "I lost my fingers. I was the best and they took that from me. I lost all my money—"

"Did you lose your life?"

Mosh paused. "No . . ."

"Then quit your crying and shut up." Holly checked her watch. "It's time to go. We'll continue this therapy session later."

"So you're my therapist now?"

"Apparently, I'm a life coach for idiots." Holly opened the door. She shined her flashlight up the stairs. When she didn't see anything, she climbed the stairs quickly and quietly to the next door. When she tested the handle, it was also unlocked. "Archer, you are the man . . ." Her voice was barely a whisper. "Follow my lead." She reached under her jacket and pulled out her pistol. It was a 1911 of some kind, like the sort of old-fashioned pistol that his father preferred.

"But the guards are just people. They're Hunters like you, just from a different company. You can't just shoot them!"

"Sure I can. Point and click." Holly glanced down

at the pistol. "Okay, fine. I don't want to and I'll try not to, but if I have to choose between saving my friends' lives or their lives?" She shrugged. "Easy call."

Mosh had done a lot of stupid things in his life, but murder wasn't one of them. "Promise me you won't kill anybody."

"Seriously? Okay, fine. I promise I won't kill anybody *unless I really need to.* You think I like this fly by the seat of the pants stuff? I'd love to have time to come up with a plan that doesn't end with shooting them, but we don't have time."

As if to punctuate that statement, there was a distant rumble. Mosh couldn't be sure, but he suspected that it was an explosion. *Right on time.* Holly crouched down and opened the door a bit, revealing a dimly lit storage area. A single red light began to flash high on the wall above. An annoying repetitive wail emanated from the ceiling along with a calm, prerecorded voice: *"Proceed to the nearest exit. Proceed to the nearest exit."* It was extremely loud. The MCB's distraction had begun.

The storage area was filled with props and costumes, most of them with a Bollywood vibe. "This way." Holly ran between the rows of shelves, looking for a way out. They didn't have a map or any idea how this floor was laid out, just general directions from the MCB, but there was supposed to be an office area around here somewhere. Holly found another door that led into a carpeted hallway. There were filing cabinets and corkboards with memos tacked to them, so it felt like they were on the right track. Mosh got ready to charge out, but Holly stopped him. "Stay hidden. Give them a minute to react. We want the Unicorn troops to leave first."

The wait was killing him. He couldn't shake that feeling that something terrible was about to happen. Holly waited for what seemed to him like far too long, but that was probably just the adrenalin rush making it seem that way, then she opened the door the rest of the way and slipped into the hall. At least the Proceed to the Nearest Exit lady was so loud that there was no way anybody would hear them coming. Of course, as soon as Mosh thought that, the prerecorded message stopped.

"Hurry," Holly said.

Hurry? They didn't even know where the scientist was, so for all they knew they were hurrying in the wrong direction. The entered a room full of cubicles.

"Go left here," Mordechai told him.

"Turn left," Mosh said immediately. Holly looked at him incredulously, but Mosh just pointed at his temple. "Dead guy said so."

"Freaking Pitts." But Holly didn't argue. She turned down the next hall. They entered another desk- and cubicle-filled room. There were doors on each side and half of each wall was a frosted glass window.

"Stop. Get down." Mordechai ordered. Mosh repeated the warning without even thinking about it. Holly took a knee behind a water cooler. Mosh crouched behind her. Holly held up one hand. *Voices.*

The sound was coming from the room ahead of them. "It's for your own safety, Doctor." The man sounded confident, in control. "Our security's been breached. There's activity in the parking garage. Follow me."

"Coming here was a mistake. If he knows I'm here he'll come for his revenge, mark my words." The second man sounded old and raspy. "There's nothing you can do against him. Save yourselves."

"You heard Mr. Stricken. Everything will be fine, sir. In the meantime we'll be moving you to a more secure location outside of the city. We have a car waiting."

"You're not listening, idiot. There's no such thing as a secure location when Mark Thirteen is involved."

The first speaker was losing his patience. "Grab him. Let's go."

The doctor protested, swore, and called them names, but then the sound was moving away. Mosh lifted his head enough to see shadows moving through the frosted glass. There were four upright figures. One of those was pushing a fifth in what could only be a wheelchair.

Holly was already crawling forward. Mosh realized what she was doing. They were going to have to move through this area, and she intended to surprise them. She looked back at him, mouthed the words *get ready*, then rolled into a cubicle across the aisle. Mosh fell back into the cubicle behind the water cooler and squished himself next to the desk, which, judging from the nameplate, belonged to someone in marketing named Arlene. There were lots of framed pictures of a plump woman with her cats and another one where she was posing with Elton John at this very casino. *Focus, Mosh!* The men would pass Holly. She'd make a move and then he'd back her up. Mordechai had steered them to the perfect spot.

"Thank you."

Not now, Mordechai! Having gotten his Glock back from the MCB, he took it out and held it in his clumsy, nerve-damaged hand. Owen and the other Hunters were counting on him. He couldn't let them down.

Holly had called him a quitter, but Mosh Pitt was no quitter. A quitter wouldn't pull a gun on armed Monster Hunters in order to kidnap an old man in a wheelchair... *Shit. That doesn't sound any better.* Footsteps and a repetitive wheeled creak were coming their way. Mosh was so nervous he could barely breathe, but at the same time he was excited. It was like how he used to feel back in the days when he'd first started playing in front of an actual audience. *I'm ready to rock.*

"That's the spirit, boy."

Mosh gritted his teeth together and blinked his eyes rapidly. The Hunters moved past Holly's hiding place. The continuous stream of complaining from the scientist was like a tracking beacon. They were almost on him and he knew that they'd see him as they went past and he'd get shot to death.

"Don't move!" Holly shouted.

Mosh leapt up and aimed his Glock over the top of the cube. The men were in the process of turning back toward Holly. Dressed in matching camouflage uniforms and wearing bulky tactical vests, all of them were carrying rifles that would be a lot more devastating than his little 9mm. He hadn't really thought about what to say, and on TV cop shows they usually said *drop the gun* or *freeze*, but unfortunately what came out of his mouth was, "Drop the freeze!"

The tiny man in the wheelchair was ancient and he stared at Mosh with rheumy eyes. "Drop the *what?* Are you an imbecile?"

The Hunters had been caught completely flat-footed. Eyes flashed between Holly and Mosh. They were holding rifles, but their muzzles were down. The man in front regarded Mosh with calculated belligerence and ice-blue eyes so cold that they suggested he'd killed a *lot* of people. The Glock was shaking all over the place. The Hunter was doing the math, deciding if he could raise his rifle to shoot Mosh in time. Even if Mosh got a shot off, he'd have to hit the man in something unarmored, which wasn't that big an area...

"Don't you move, Armstrong. Don't even think about it." Holly had a good command voice. "I'll drop you like a sack of shit."

The man in front turned slowly to study Holly. Her pistol was moving slowly back and forth between the four heads. Now she didn't look like she would miss. One of the men must have made some movement that Holly didn't approve of. She turned the pistol on him. "Is that vest bulletproof? It looks bulletproof. Let's find out." *BLAM.* The sudden noise made Mosh jump. The bullet hit the Hunter square in the chest. He gasped and stumbled back a few feet, but stayed on his feet. Holly quickly shifted her gun back toward the leader. Her eyes flicked over to the man she'd shot. "Yep. Bulletproof. Bet that still hurt, though. Don't waste my time, Armstrong. I'm in a hurry."

The Hunter named Armstrong smiled disarmingly, but his eyes still betrayed murderous intent. Mosh had never seen teeth so white and perfectly even. This guy had paid his dentist's mortgage off. "Well, seems we've been bushwhacked right in our own base of operations. Put them down, boys."

"Nice and slow. One at a time," Holly suggested. All of the black rifles were clipped to their armor on slings, and it took the men a moment to undo them and place them on the floor. "Pistols too. In a pile. That's good...

I know some of you are packing backups, but I only like surprises on Christmas and birthdays. Sudden moves make me twitchy. Put your hands on top of your heads and keep them there. Next round goes into something softer than Kevlar." They did as they were told.

"FBI?" the old man had read Holly's jacket. "Are you kidding me? Don't you know who I am?"

"She's no cop," grunted the man Holly had shot. He was red-faced and wheezing. "She's Monster Hunter International."

"That's right, so I guess you can say I'm violating the shit out of your restraining order. Hey, are those zip ties?" She gestured her pistol at one of the vests. "Awesome. You get to zip-tie your buddy's wrists together. You heard me. Nice and tight." She waited until he'd done the other three. "Mosh, bind him. Watch out, that's Ultimate Lawyer. He's a kung-fu expert *and* an attorney."

"Kung-fu? Please. I do Krav Maga, Muay Thai, and Brazilian jujitsu." That particular Hunter was rather intimidating and Mosh really didn't relish the idea of going near him. He saw Mosh looking at him. "Mosh, huh? Thought you looked familiar. Relax, buddy. I know the drill." He stuck his own hands through the zip-tie loop, then bit the end and pulled it tight with his teeth, securing himself. "By the way, love your work. 'Hold the Pig Steady' is my favorite workout song."

"Thanks," Mosh answered, not really sure what else to say.

Once they were bound, Mosh made sure the zip ties were tight, and then used the rest of the zip ties to attach their hands to the straps on the next Hunter's armor. He figured that would make pursuing them sort of like playing Twister. It only took a minute, and none of the Paranormal Tactical men tried anything, but he was sure that was all due to Holly's readiness to shoot any troublemakers in the face. He tied Armstrong's wrists to one of his men's pistol belt; that way, Armstrong's hands were pressed against the other guy's crotch.

"Is that necessary?" Armstrong asked.

"Necessarily hilarious," Mosh answered.

"Pick up their guns," Holly ordered. Since there were four rifles and four handguns, that was a lot more difficult than it sounded. But he got the pistols partially tucked into various pockets, and managed to sling a rifle over each shoulder and one in each hand, all without shooting himself on accident. So he called that a win. "Listen, guys. We didn't have a choice." Holly got behind the wheelchair. "We've got to run, but this was nothing personal."

"You shot me!"

"Yeah, yeah. Sue me."

Ultimate Lawyer chuckled. "Oh, don't worry. We will."

Holly looked to the leader. "Look, Armstrong. Stricken is using you. He already knows how to stop the monster, but he's willing to let all of those Hunters in there die first just to score some political point. I'm not going to let that happen, and the doctor here is going to tell me how. After that, you can have him back. Don't come after us. You don't want that much blood on your hands, and I don't want your blood on mine."

But Armstrong wasn't in a listening mood. "You'll pay for this. Kidnapping—"

"It isn't kidnapping." Holly began pushing the wheelchair away. "It's borrowing."

"Assault—"

"Attempted murder," corrected Ultimate Lawyer.

"You'll pay for this, Newcastle!"

"Buh-bye," Holly said. Armstrong was still shouting after them. The old doctor was cursing. Holly took the next corner and pointed them back the way they'd come in. The wheelchair was capable of a surprisingly high rate of speed. Mosh followed along carrying almost forty pounds of extra guns. At one point a Hunter's pistol worked its way free from his waistband and landed on the carpet with a *thump*. He turned back to retrieve it. "Leave it," Holly ordered. "We've got to keep moving. I think Armstrong's got help on the way."

"How?"

"I didn't think of it at the time, but the way he said he was being bushwhacked and where was too convenient. It was probably because he had his radio on."

"Oh, man!" Mosh looked back down the hall. He couldn't hear anything now, but that was probably because the Hunters were trying to figure out how to free themselves from the zip ties. "They're going to be *really* mad."

"Well, duh. I did shoot that one guy."

"You promised not to shoot anybody!"

"I promised not to *kill* anybody. Huge difference." They reached the storage room and went inside. "This will do. Help me barricade the door. It'll buy us some time. This is the only way into this room other than the service tunnel."

"How do you know that?" Mosh asked incredulously as he dumped the black rifles on the floor. They had practically sprinted through here the first time.

"Situational awareness. Try to keep up." Holly turned the doctor's chair to face her. "Okay, Doc. We've got to make this interview fast and then you can go back to your friends."

"They're no friends of mine. Times may change, and men come and go, but there will always be opportunistic wastrels like Stricken, attached like leeches to a project like Mark Thirteen. The more secretive and expensive the project, the more leeches."

"Great." Mosh was surprised to discover how out of breath he was from the short run. He had used to work out religiously but had let that slide along with everything else. He picked a nearby heavy metal shelf stacked with plastic elephant heads, and struggled to drag it in front of the door. "We're on the same page. We only want to stop this monster."

"Nonetheless, I refuse to share any classified data with you."

Mosh stopped to study the scientist for the first time. He was a tiny, shriveled man. His skin was thin and blotchy, with purple veins right below the surface. He had a blanket over his shrunken legs, but was wearing a white shirt, neat red tie, Mr. Rogers sweater, and a gray tweed sport coat. "Please?"

"What're you supposed to be anyway?" The doctor squinted to glare back at Mosh. "Some sort of gypsy?"

By Mosh's standards he was dressed rather conservatively. "I'm a guitarist."

"Devil music, I bet." The doctor snorted. "In my day the only men that had tattoos on their necks were queers and convicts. I'm not telling you anything. Disrespectful youth have no understanding of what it means to keep an oath."

Not having a good answer for that and expecting a bunch of angry Hunters to kick down the door any minute, Mosh went back to stacking heavy boxes of paper onto his freshly moved shelf. "Don't expend too much energy," Holly warned. "When they find us, if they can't get through the door easily, they'll blow a hole in the wall. Okay, Dr. Blish—"

"Don't say my name!" the old man shrieked. "Are you trying to get us all killed? If he realizes I'm here, he'll destroy us all. He hates me, and for good reason. I warned Stricken not to bring me this close, but he said that he wanted my visual confirmation. The manipulative swine. He had me dragged from the rest home and brought here despite my protests. I think Stricken merely wanted to see if my presence would provoke him into revealing himself. I am the worm on the end of the hook."

Truthfully, the idea that they might draw the monster's attention freaked Mosh out. A bunch of scary, six-armed, snaggle-toothed monster costumes stared back at him. Holly looked around cautiously, but didn't seem convinced. "Fine. No names then. But I really need to know how to kill this thing."

The old scientist's cranium seemed way too big as he shook his head in the negative. It reminded Mosh of a pinkish-purple lollipop sticking out of a sweater. "Foolish girl, it is *incapable* of dying. We killed his body once, but he simply willed himself back into existence. If we could simply kill it then we wouldn't have needed to bury the host. By every calculation it should still be lying dormant. If you could totally destroy its host, it will simply find a new one and the nightmare will continue."

"Whatever. I only want to get my friends back. They're trapped inside the Last Dragon."

"Then you have my condolences, because they're already dead. I will not help you. I am sworn to secrecy, and I am a man of principles."

Holly swore under her breath as she paced back and forth. It was obvious she was thinking hard. Her expression changed subtly before she gave Mosh a malicious look. "Is that how it's going to be, then?"

"I am afraid so, my dear."

"Well, that's too bad . . . *Dr. Blish*, scientist from Decision Week, who worked on the Mark Thirteen project at Los Alamos and who knows our monster personally. You would've been a young man back then. I should probably point that out in case he doesn't recognize you, Dr. Blish."

"Stop! Are you mad? If he hears, he'll kill you as well!"

"That's a risk I'm willing to take." Holly raised her voice. "Did you get that? Blish. It's spelled B-l-i-s-h." Suddenly she reached down, grasped the arms of his chair, and jerked him around. She bent over and stared him square in the eye. "Man of principles, my ass. Quit wasting my time. Tell me what you know or I swear that I will get on the intercom and call this son of a bitch down on top of us. Talk!"

"Please, stop." The doctor quavered. "I'll tell you everything."

The ancient scientist seemed like he might begin crying. Mosh had never helped abuse a senior citizen before. "Damn, Holly. You don't screw around."

"Sure I do, just not when my people are in danger. Spill it, Doc."

Blish's lower lip was quivering so badly that for a second Mosh thought the old man was having a seizure. "We never intended for the project to end this way. We were the best and brightest, the superior scientific minds of our day. I was the youngest member of the team, but my theories on disembodied entities were considered revolutionary. Our goals were noble. We were trying to end the war with the smallest loss of life possible. The host subjects were all volunteers. They knew the risks going in. We simply never could have imagined this outcome. We would never have sacrificed those men. Only he doesn't know that. He thought that I lied to him. I swear that I didn't."

Mosh was confused. "Host subjects?"

Blish wiped his nose with his sleeve. "You don't even know about them?"

"Enlighten us. Back up a little."

"The being that is terrorizing your friends is only half the issue. The destruction is merely the manifestation of one man's anger over his betrayal. However hopelessly they are entwined, we are facing two separate foes, a human test subject and the disembodied creature which was bonded to him. The creature that is farming nightmares is merely an alp."

"Bull," Holly said. "There's no way. Alps are pathetic."

The only thing Mosh knew with that name was a mountain range. The skiing was awesome, and the nights were cold, but the women were beautiful . . . But he was fairly certain that wasn't what they were talking about. "What's an alp?" Mosh asked.

"They're parasites. Little floaty ghost bastards. We only spend like thirty minutes on them in Newbie training. They're the monster under the bed that gives little kids nightmares and then feeds on their terror. A really strong one can give an adult bad dreams, maybe. That's it. Ignore them long enough and they get hungry and go away. They're not even PUFF applicable because they don't have a corpse to turn in. You're telling me this thing that's killing professional Hunters and sucking giant buildings into other dimensions is an *alp?*"

"Yes, in part. It is the driver, but it is not the engine. The goal of my original experiment was to capture one of these nightmare feeders and find a way to magnify its strength."

"Your goal was to make the boogieman *stronger?*" Mosh was incredulous. "Are you nuts?"

"Shhh." Holly put her hand on his arm. "The boogieman is different."

The doctor sighed. "I will try to keep it simple for our sideshow freak."

"Now that's just unnecessary—"

"The alp, or nightmare feeder as it is colloquially known, hails from another . . . plane. It is a sort of nightmare world that only rarely connects with our own, and when it does, it barely registers in the human subconscious. My doctoral research documented the creatures, and we even succeeded in capturing one for study. Though fascinating, it was relatively weak, hardly dangerous at all. Our worst side effects were discomforting dreams and headaches. After the war began, we were invited to continue our work at Los Alamos, where we succeed in capturing several more alps. One of the other projects came up with a way to magnify the alp's strength through exposure to . . . Never mind. I could talk for days about the details.

What matters is we made the alps far more capable. Now the test targets were overwhelmed with nightmare stimuli, even while awake. It was astounding. Imagine, ending a war simply because the enemy populace was too terrified and distressed to continue fighting…"

"You tried to enslave otherworldy creatures to use as a weapon." Holly spat. "Gee whiz, I'm *shocked* that didn't work out."

That offended him. "I was trying to save lives, young lady. My project was considered a psychological weapon rather than a destructive one. You have no idea how desperate we were. Nothing was off the table. My compatriots were a diverse group, ranging from the keenest scientific minds to the strangest masters of the occult. Compared to the other projects that were being contemplated at the time, mine was one of the least lethal. We were trying to use imaginary horrors to prevent real horrors. We had no choice. The things that the other side were dabbling in were just as terrible or worse. The alp itself, even after being augmented, is an unfocused, erratic—"

"Evil," Holly supplied.

"*Misunderstood* being. Alps are not intelligent enough to be capable of esoteric concepts like good or evil. They are little more than cunning animals that feed on psychic distress. Ours were more capable, but still a far more pleasant alternative than dropping an Elder Thing on Berlin. We had a weapon, but no way to control it, no way to *aim* it. We needed a delivery system. But what if we could give the alp a controller? My research suggested that we could *bond* the creature to a human controller, sort of like how they bonded to a dreamer naturally while they fed, but a more complete, synergistic bonding. We found volunteers, young soldiers who fit certain psychological and intellectual criteria, and who were also physically and culturally capable of blending into the target populations. The first bonding procedures worked fine. Early testing demonstrated we would be able to break the connections and release the alps from their human hosts when the war was over. It seemed to be a smashing success, only we didn't realize what would happen when Project Thirteen went off the rails."

"No kidding."

Mosh heard a noise. Someone was trying the door. "They've found us."

"They won't do anything too fast. They're worried about hurting their charge. I'm assuming PT's pay will get docked if they kill him on accident. Keep going, Doc. How do we stop this super alp of yours?"

"The creature isn't the problem. It is merely following its instincts, creating nightmares and feeding upon the resultant terror. The danger comes from its human host. One of our volunteers turned out to be something . . . special. He was our most promising subject, so we picked him to receive what seemed to be our most capable alp. When a creature was bonded to him, it unleashed some surprising side effects. What had previously been figments of the mind were given actual form. Nightmares became real. Physically *real*. They were small at first, but this sort of phenomenon was unprecedented. My team was delighted. The energy necessary to accomplish this feat was simply inconceivable. Our experiments had unleashed the unexpected."

The rattling of the doorknob stopped. Mosh picked

up one of the rifles. It was an unfamiliar, bulky, plastic thing, heavier than it looked, but the controls made sense. It had a safety, a trigger, charging handle, and mag release where expected. Auhangamea Pitt had taught him well, so Mosh knew he could fire it if he needed to, but it wasn't the *technical* part of shooting someone that was troubling him. Somebody kicked the door hard, but it barely moved the shelf.

Holly raised her voice and shouted through the door. "If you use an explosive to breach . . . the shock's liable to kill the old guy!" Then she went back to normal. "Let them chew on that for a minute. Please continue, Doc."

Dr. Blish didn't seem to notice the noise. It was as if telling the story he'd kept bottled up for so long was consuming all of his attention. "The sudden increase in the alp's abilities was all due to the volunteer. He seemed like a normal enough young man, rather brave considering what he was willing to do for his country. However, as time went on, things became worse. The nightmare creations became far stronger and unexpectedly aggressive. Members of my team died. We tried to break the bond, but it wouldn't work. This particular alp had either gained sentience, or some dark aspect of the human host's personality had become imprinted on it. The immaterial being didn't want to give up its new source of power, so it began to manipulate him, first physically, then mentally. He tried to keep it in check, but it eventually turned him against us. It was a hard decision, but we had no choice but to terminate the project."

That's a nice way to say they decided to murder the dude. "I thought you said you couldn't kill him?"

"That was the problem. Anything capable of destroying the host would merely free the now intelligent, hyper-evolved alp. Though certainly no longer as powerful, freed from a physical anchor, it would be able to roam the world doing harm. The range of the nightmare effect was limited to within a few hundred meters of the host's body. The unexpected physical changes caused by the bonding had rendered the host unaging, theoretically immortal, with many of the mutations that we see in advanced types of undead. Unmolested, there was no reason to believe that he wouldn't live forever. So we did the next best thing we could. We rendered the host catatonic."

"You couldn't risk killing him, so you made him a vegetable, and buried him in a chemical weapons dump..." Holly whistled. "But now he's back, and he's pissed."

"The idea was to leave him in stasis until we could find a cure," Dr. Blish said, but then he looked away evasively. "You must understand, after Decision Week, almost all of the supernatural projects were scrapped, and the evidence was placed in storage. We were not allowed to look for a cure. The survivors of the research team had no choice but to move on with our lives. The decision was out of our hands."

"I'm sure it was..." Holly muttered.

"I petitioned to reopen the study, but was denied. I am not the guilty party here."

Mosh didn't think they had time to debate the moral implications of mad science. "If we're not supposed to kill him, what can we do?"

"Our safest solution is to convince him to go back to sleep, but good luck with that," the doctor answered.

"The behaviors being exhibited this time are different than before. It would seem that its physical form is capable of moving between planes now, Earth and the nightmare realm. Which is why the host body has seemingly been able to move so rapidly about in this world. I would assume that is where your casino has gone as well. It seems that the evolution of the symbiote has continued during their long stasis. There is no telling what their capabilities are now."

"You keep talking about this host." Holly picked up another one of the rifles and chamber-checked it. The door-kicking was making her nervous. "What's his deal?"

"One of the other research teams had hypothesized the existence of this kind of rare individual . . . The mystics and occultists referred to them as children of special destiny, individuals who had been chosen by some higher power and given special gifts. At the time I thought that was nonsense, only now I must admit there really is something to it. We know there are other worlds, other realities, that infringe upon our own. These are the source of some of the creatures that end up here. Sometimes there is a rare individual inexorably connected to one of these other realms. It is as if they are chosen to accomplish something, sometimes good, sometimes evil, or even completely incomprehensible. They exhibit strange abilities, even connections to tap into these other unknown realms. Intrusions by other worlds seem to create these specimens. Sometimes the abilities are passed down genetically, though they rarely manifest, but when they do, remarkable things happen."

Mosh and Holly exchanged a glance. "We know somebody that fits that description."

"I strongly doubt it. The odds are astronomically against it."

"Odds go out the window when my brother's involved," Mosh said. "Owen has collected some absolutely bizarre karmic baggage. He's why I'm here. He's one of the people trapped inside the Last Dragon."

Dr. Blish's mouth fell open but no sound came out. For a second Mosh thought that he'd simply died of shock. Then his mouth began to move again, like a fish out of water gasping. Finally he was able to get the words out. "No, no, no. Another one of them? And he's on the other side? This is terrible. Absolutely terrible. Do you have any idea what this means?"

"No." The door was kicked again. There was still no give. Mosh was just glad they had a hostage so they couldn't just start shooting through the walls. "Not really."

"In the intervening years we have learned from other incidents involving the bonding of humans to spirit entities from other planes. Stricken has procured some ancient weapons that he believes will not only destroy the host, but at the same time permanently banish the alp back to its home . . . But if the host is destroyed, and there is another one of these chosen vessels present in its home realm . . ."

"We'd be banishing it to someplace where it could just take over another body . . ."

"And doubtlessly continue to travel between our worlds, wrecking havoc on us all," Blish finished for her.

"Oh, hell no. This nightmare thing is not going to possess my brother." Mosh looked to Holly. "Is that possible?" She shrugged. Holly had no idea either. "No way, man."

Mordechai's voice came into his head for the last time. "Thank you, boy. We know enough now. The Champion will be warned. Now you must prepare yourself. You must face your fear."

The lights flickered. The banging against the door ceased. Mosh realized that Holly's breath was visible as steam. A tingle of dread rolled down his spine. He began to shiver uncontrollably.

"It's too late." Dr. Blish sounded utterly defeated. "He's found me."

"Crap. He's here!" Holly sprang into action. She grabbed onto the shelf that was keeping out Paranormal Tactical and began pulling it aside. "Help me, Mosh!" Potentially getting shot by angry Hunters, but maybe having help, sounded a lot nicer than being stuck inside with the nightmare monster. The metal of the shelf was cold to the touch.

The lights died.

There was a new presence in the storage room with them. Mosh could feel it, only a few feet away, standing dark and cold over the wheelchair that held the cowering scientist.

I remember you . . . The words pounded their way into Mosh's thoughts.

"I'm sorry." The doctor's voice cracked. "I'm so sorry for what we did to you, Marcus."

It's too late for apologies.

Mosh screamed as the world was swept away.

CHAPTER 21

Mosh!

I was Owen Zastava Pitt again.

It all hit me in fast succession, leaving me with what felt like the worst ice-cream headache ever. "Oh, man."

Sam Haven took his ghostly hand away from my head. "Yeah, that looks like it really hurts. But soak that shit up quick. I need you motivated. This is a job for the living. And since you're the guy with all the connections between worlds, you got the job. Congratulations. That's getting to be a habit with you. All us dead Hunters have nicknamed you Short Straw. Believe it or not, we mean it in the nicest way possible."

I was still being overwhelmed with information, and as it came grinding to an end, I realized with a shock that my brother was in danger. "The *Nachtmar's* got Mosh!"

"Among others. It's spreading out into Vegas, looking for minds to raid. So you need to hurry up and waste it before it's too late."

"How—"

Sam pointed up like I had seconds before.

"God will smite him?"

Sam laughed at me. "I was pointing at the *roof*. Get to the chopper. Power's out. You up to twenty flights of stairs?"

My wife was up there. Damn right I could take the stairs. "Ankle's buggered, but I can do it."

"Ace-wrap that fucker and walk it off," Sam ordered like any good SEAL would. "This casino is drifting in dreamland, but you can still fly out. You'll need to piss the monster off good so it'll chase after you, but knowing you, that shouldn't be a problem. Mordechai pulled some strings and will have what you need waiting. He's sort of your guardian angel. Turns out there's a lot invested in you, Z, so when it comes to meddling in your particular business, we get a little more leeway. You'll find backup on the way. Me and the boys need to go waste some demons. We'll hold them off as long as we can. Tell Milo I said hi, and I'm really honored he named his kid after me. That was mighty cool of him."

I could see *through* Sam. "Wait—"

But then Sam Haven simply vanished as if he'd never even been there at all.

My radio had only been turned back on for a few seconds when I received, "Was that *Sam*?" from Julie. "I mean, visibility is garbage and the wind keeps moving the fog around, and it took me a while to find you in all the debris, but . . . Sam?"

"Yeah." I was limping along as fast as possible, Abomination in hand, just waiting for something to pop out of the fog. "It was Sam."

"But Sam's gone."

"We got reinforcements."

There was a pause as Julie took a deep breath. "I thought I'd lost you for a minute there. I . . ."

"Me too."

The rest went without saying. Julie didn't have time to get emotional. This was business. "Hang on. This stuff is pissing me off. I'm switching rifles . . . Milo and Nelson got most of the innocents away from the breech. Earl's got nearly everyone boarded up on the main floor. They're holding the demons in the lobby. There were a few other teams out, but there's nobody close to you."

"Tell Skippy to warm up the chopper. I'm on my way to meet you. I've got a plan."

I'd sliced my forehead open, but my armor had kept me from getting cut in too many places. However, I'd whacked myself really hard in several spots during the ride down. I'd pulled muscles and wouldn't have been surprised if there were a few bones cracked. There wasn't any part of me that wasn't hurting, but there weren't any bones sticking out and nothing was squirting blood, so I could do this. It was weird, though, I felt stronger than I probably should have. Either I was in shock and working through the pain or there had been something else to Sam's help than just the memories from my brother.

Hang in there, Mosh. I'm coming.

"Hold still," Julie ordered. I froze in place. All I could see around me was the wretched churning fog. There was a solid *THWACK* ten feet in front of me. Something hit the ground. "Got it. You can keep going now."

I found the body of one of the warrior demons just ahead. Julie had shot it through the vulnerable juncture of neck to body. Steaming goo had sprayed

everywhere. It was still twitching as I went around
it. "You on thermal?"

"Sure am. Told you I was switching rifles. When the
fog rolls around it's the only way I can see." Anything
that emitted body heat would positively glow in this
cold mess, and these demons always seemed feverishly
hot. "The wind keeps changing, so this might get tricky.
There's an external stairwell to your left." I couldn't
see a damn thing. "Keep turning. Turning . . . Okay.
Head that way. I'll cover you. The garden's crawling
with monsters."

I set out with a sort of hopping, hobbling jog. The
demons were shrieking and clicking at each other.
There was a trumpetlike bellow from one of the big
acid throwers. "They know you're there. There's more
coming." It took a moment for her bullet to arrive.
THWACK. There was a gurgling noise as another
creature choked to death on its own blood. *THWACK.*
"Two down, but they're surrounding you. Hurry."

Hurry was a relative term when all you could feel
from one foot was lightning bolts whenever it touched
ground, but I ran like everyone's lives depended on it.

"Monsters on your right. Two. Don't have a shot."

I turned and lifted Abomination. The rapidly moving fog was so wet that rather than raining, water just
accumulated out of the air and soaked you. Gusts were
like being smacked with a damp towel. The water
picked up the blood and ran off me in pink rivulets.
The mist swirled. I was ready. The instant a bit of
orange broke the fog I shot it to death. Its companion
pushed by, only to have a pile of silver rip through
its thorax, spilling it in a wet heap.

"Clear. There was a tree in the way. Didn't have

an angle." *THWACK*. "That time I did." Julie was an absolutely lethal shot. "Hit the deck!" I did exactly as she said, diving forward and landing on the soft grass. Several spines passed through the air where I'd been standing. There was a series of loud impacts as Julie opened up on them. "They're down. Move."

I got up and ran. Blood kept running into my eyes. It turned the fog red, then pink as I blinked it away, then clear. Repeat every few seconds. I vaulted a low iron fence. Hitting the ground hurt so bad it nearly made my legs buckle. The wall of the hotel came into view. I was right under Julie. She must not have realized she was still transmitting. "Edward, hold onto my belt. I've got to lean over to see. Don't let me fall." I had a sudden vision of Julie toppling over the edge of a twenty-story building while trying to keep the demons off my back. There was a sudden impact off to the side and my heart jumped into my throat, but it was only another monster catching a .308 round right through the top of its bulbous skull. "Door should be straight ahead of you. Two dozen monsters coming your way."

There was the door. I tried the handle but it was locked. It was a fire exit. Of course it was locked. It opened outward so I couldn't kick it. I didn't have any breaching rounds, so being really hopeful that I wouldn't kill myself with a ricochet, I stuck Abomination's muzzle next to the frame and blasted the lock into shrapnel. There was enough metal still engaged that it still wouldn't open. So I overreacted and jerked the trigger twice more. That did the trick, but a chunk of metal ripped a tear in my armored sleeve and drew more blood. The movies always made it look so easy.

"Going in," I said as Julie killed a few more of the demons chasing me. The interior of the fire-escape stairwell was nothing but plain concrete walls and metal stairs. I looked up. They seemed to go up forever.

"Climb fast. Ed, get ready to toss that black backpack over the side... Yes. That one. Careful. It'll go off on impact... Yes, boom... Yes, it is heavy... Owen, climb *really* fast."

"Crap." Each step felt like taking a hammer to my foot as I put my weight down, but it sounded like Julie was throwing down something nasty, so I gritted my teeth and hauled ass up the stairs. Behind me, bullets fell like rain as Julie kept the monsters off the door. "Second floor." *Pain. Pain. Son of a bitch. Pain.* Two steps at a time. Not fast enough. Three steps at a time. "Third floor!"

"Reloading," Julie said. "Keep going, Owen."

My leg hurt so bad I could taste it. "What is it?"

"I don't know. One of the bomb nuts made it out of chemicals from the nail salon."

There was a crash below me as one of the demons thrashed its way through the broken door. "Fourth floor," I gasped.

"Let it go, Ed. *Ahhhh!*" Julie screamed. "Not *me!* The bag! The bag! Drop the bag. Hold onto me!"

"You okay?"

"Fine. Orcs can be so literal sometimes."

I was still climbing when the improvised explosive device hit amid the demons crowding their way against the entrance. The boom wasn't as big as I'd expected, either that or I was so frazzled that my system just wasn't registering concussions anymore, but a look over the railing showed me that the bottom floor had been sprayed with colorful blood and entrails. A foul smoke was drifting up the stairwell. The chemical stink of acetone burned my eyes as it hit, but nothing else was trying to get through the door. "Clear?"

"For a minute. They're milling around."

"Who made that one?" I asked as I resumed climbing. Talking kept my mind focused on something other than my foot, which felt like it was so swollen that I was expecting my boot to pop open.

"Cooper, Lee, or Milo. I'm not sure. I think those three are having a competition to see who can build the most dangerous thing out of household chemicals."

There was a fierce rumble. The hotel shook. Dust fell down the stairwell. "What was that?"

"Damn! Half the conference center just blew up. It was the overlook area where the demons broke in. That was *huge*. I think Milo just took the lead."

"Right on." Getting those particular pyromaniacs together was like a Discovery Channel show gone horribly wrong. The Mythbusters had nothing on our guys.

"I'm sending a couple of the men down to meet you. Skippy's prepping the chopper. I hope you know what you're doing, Owen."

Not really. "Sure do. Don't worry." I thought about telling her about the baby, but quickly dismissed that thought. We needed to concentrate on not getting killed first, then talk about the future. Now I could understand why Earl hadn't said anything. Normally it was the woman that knew about this sort of thing first. This was supposed to be happy news, not *hey, we're trapped in a nightmare dimension surrounded by demons and a nightmare creature that's going to swallow our souls, but you're pregnant! Yay!* This sucked. *Keep climbing.*

Keep your head in the game, Owen. I had to focus on the task at hand. Not my stupid foot, not fatherhood, but focus on beating the *Nachtmar*.

Beating him required getting his attention first. "I've got to talk to Earl." I toggled through the channels and found the main band. It was chaos.

"Holding on two, but Kantrowitz is down."

"Demons are stalled at the escalators. I don't know who, but somebody's flanked them."

"There's fifty of them at the conference side entrance. We can't hold them. Falling back."

"No, damn it. Belay that. This is Nate Shackleford. I'll hold that side. We fail here and Russians will be stuck in the open. Don't you dare move!" I'd never heard Nate so fired up before. He was a Shackleford after all. *"Haights on me. Hold this fucking line until everyone is in!"*

Every second counted. I had to get the *Nachtmar's* attention away from the others, but if he knew what I was planning, he'd take me out before I was in position. I had to wait. My chest hurt. I could barely breathe, but I kept taking the steps three at a time. Abomination banged back on its sling against my back as I used my hands to pull myself up the railing. I listened to the radio chatter for several awful minutes. The world's Hunters were taking a beating.

"We've got some of those acid-tank bastards coming through the hole." Nate was shouting into his microphone. *"Gregorius, I need more ammo for that fifty-cal."*

"Hang on, Shackleford. Omaha Stakes on the way to back you up. Shit! They're coming through th—" Static.

The Hunters were losing.

CHAPTER 22

There was movement above me on the stairwell.
Footsteps. It was quicker to draw my pistol than reach
for my shotgun. I put the STI in my left hand so I
could keep using my right to hurl-drag myself up the
rail. A flashlight bounced above. It was the Hunters
Julie had sent. Someone bellowed a challenge. "Pitt,
is that you?"

"Yeah. It's me." It was time to get the monster's
attention. I switched to Earl's command channel, but
somebody else was talking.

*Earl. This is Lindemann. I believe I just saw my
father killing demons. This is troubling, since he died
fighting vampires when I was young. Am I losing my
mind? Over.*

"This is Pitt. Negative. The Hunters' ghosts are on
our side. They'll stall the monsters as long as possible.
It's a long story. Over."

Earl came on next. *"Z, I thought you were dead.
Milo said you got blown up by that meteor."*

"Nearly." My ankle made an audible popping noise

as I reached the fourteenth floor. "I've got a plan." It was hard to talk and run stairs at the same time. "Mordechai showed me how to kill the *Nachtmar*."

"We're in a world of his creation. He can certainly hear you," warned Lindemann.

"Good. He should listen. I know his secret. If he can read minds, then he knows what I'm going to do next. Come and get me, asshole." *Only four more floors.* The flashlight from above shined in my eyes. It was Jason Lacoco. The squat shadow behind him could only be Edward. "Get ready," I warned them. Once I got the *Nachtmar*'s attention, things would probably get really hairy. Lacoco only grunted. He might have hated my guts, but this was business. Edward took the lead. Lacoco grabbed onto my left arm and helped me along. The son of a bitch was so strong that he actually began dragging me. Not that I was complaining. My leg muscles had turned to jelly.

The information that Sam had given to me was all there, crammed painfully in between my own orderly memories. Of course I was the one picked for this. My brain was like a filing cabinet stuffed with folders from multiple people. Hell, I spoke sixteenth-century Portuguese because of this sort of thing. I was prepped for this sort of craziness. Thanks, stupid Old Ones and your stupid artifact. I flipped through the files, examined what my brother had overheard, until I found what I needed.

I kept broadcasting. "We've been calling him *Nachtmar*, Nightmare, things like that. We guessed right all along. That's all he is. He's nothing without us. He needs humans to give him form. He can't do anything without us. He feeds on our fear. The Nachtmar is just an alp. He's a parasite. He's a worm. Humans made him strong and he's only this powerful because of his human host. If he's connected to somebody weak, he's nothing. He's a pathetic little alp. The *Nachtmar* ain't shit."

It was working. I could tell the monster was listening. The hotel rumbled. Edward turned to look at me as if to ask *are you sure this is a good idea?*

"This particular little nightmare spirit was lucky enough to find a powerful human to stick himself to a long time ago. One of the Chosen." *Like me,* I didn't add. There was only so much fate I wanted to tempt at one time, and I didn't know what to make of that possession business that Dr. Blish had spoken about near the end of the memories. "The *Nachtmar* was too pathetic to take a man like this over on his own. It was the scientists that broke him and let the *Nachtmar* in. All of this? The dream monsters, the destruction, it's all from the power of a special human mind. The *Nachtmar* likes being thought of as a wrathful god, but he's just a manipulative little prick piggybacking off a great man."

"This is Julie. Owen, you've got incoming."

"What now?" There was a violent crunch. The cement wall on the landing above us was suddenly riddled with cracks. Lacoco and I stopped.

"Gargoyles. You've got three gargoyles on the exterior of the stairwell."

Edward ran back past us, hit the nineteenth floor landing, yanked the door open and looked inside. He nodded quickly. *Clear.* The concrete on the twentieth floor was raining down in dust and chunks. An enclosed space was a stupid place to take on an animated stone monster. We went after Ed.

His response had been much faster than expected, but I wasn't done provoking our monster. "Gargoyles? Probably the same ones from Appleton. See, what did I tell you? Now he's cherry-picking Julie's memories. He can't do anything on his own. He's a chump. He's got no imagination." The three of us entered the nineteenth floor. It was pitch-black, but Lacoco and I turned on our flashlights. Ed could see in the dark. This floor was still under construction, and was a mess of half-finished metal frames, dangling wires, scaffolding, and stacked sheetrock. There had to be another interior stairwell in the middle, and we could take that to the roof. "He's limited to the weapons we provide him, and even the poor deluded human he's keeping alive isn't powerful enough to handle the things I've got in my head." I could only hope that the great Old Ones were so sanity-bending and incomprehensible that they couldn't be copied, otherwise we'd all just get squished.

There was a horrendous crash as the gargoyles broke into the fire stairwell. We kept moving as fast as we could, but I'd seen how quick these things were. It was a straight shot down the middle. Ed found the door for the next set of stairs and jerked it open. Ed looked inside, up, down, then back at us and nodded. *Clear.*

I got back on the radio. "Screw you, *Nachtmar.* Your world is nothing. You cobbled together all of this from your host's subconscious. Your days are numbered. They know your secret back on Earth. They know how to kill him and banish you now. They're going to find your poor human, waste him, and you'll go back to being nothing. You might find someone else to bond with, but it'll never be the same. Your glory days are almost over. You'll be so weak that you won't even show up on the PUFF table. You're a nuisance. The best you'll be able to do after this is make a five-year-old wet the bed."

The hotel was experiencing a continuous low-level earthquake. "You're really pissing him off," Lacoco said as we went up the last flight of stairs. I had one arm draped over his broad shoulder. It was faster than trying to walk on my own swelling foot. Lacoco was half ox, and though huffing and grunting, was dragging me along fairly quickly. "You better know what you're doing."

"I'm winging it."

"The only reason I haven't dumped your ass is because I trust Earl Harbinger. You're making that really difficult." The crashing told me that the gargoyles had entered the hotel. The stairs ended earlier than expected. There wasn't an opening to the roof. We had to go back out onto the twentieth floor and go back to the first set of stairs. "Hell." Lacoco murmured when he came to the same realization. Ed led the way through the door.

The gargoyles were below us. Their movements were so destructive and heavy we could feel them vibrating the floor. We'd have to pass back over them. *We're almost there.*

The twentieth floor was an even more chaotic construction mess than the nineteenth. Some walls were in, others were just metal skeletons waiting to be dressed. There was a low animal growl from the opposite end of the hall. A primal fear instinct caused all the hair on my arms to stand up. Something was waiting in the dark between us and the stairs to the roof. With no hesitation, Edward drew his swords. "Ed! Wait!" But the orc was already charging the unknown threat. Ed leapt over a wheelbarrow and disappeared into the dark.

"After him." There was a sudden movement to the side. Something incredibly cold collided with me and Lacoco. Our flashlight beams whipped about, adding to the confusion. I was knocked head first into the opposite wall.

What now? Dazed, I managed to get to my hands and knees. I reached for my pistol, but caught a kick in the ribs so hard that it lifted me off the floor. "Ooof!" The air in my lungs came shooting out. I caught the framing, struggling to rise, but a big fist caught me right behind the ear. The framing collapsed on top of me.

In the conflicting light, I'd seen that it was a man. A big dude, at least my size, shirtless, and thickset with muscle.

Lacoco came up with his shotgun, but our attacker blocked the muzzle with one hand and slugged Lacoco in the face with the other. The Remington landed a few feet away. The Hunter roared and drove himself forward. They collided. Lacoco caught an elbow drop to his back, but rammed his opponent through one frame and into another solid one. They came right off, whirled around, and Lacoco was the one that hit the opposite wall, tearing a huge gash through the new sheetrock.

His enemy was me.

Lacoco froze, shocked, and the nightmare version of me hit him again, and again, and again. Harder and faster than I'd ever been capable of in real life.

Blood splattered the sawdust as Lacoco's nose shattered. The fists kept pumping, falling over and over like pistons. The look on my evil mirror twin's face was completely dispassionate, emotionless. It was my face, but it was younger, free of scars, and the eyes were dead, blank, all humanity shoved aside and focused on only one thing, utterly destroying his opponent.

It was exactly how I'd looked when I'd ruined Jason Lacoco's life.

Lacoco tried to shove him off, but it was an overwhelming assault. Lacoco hit the floor, and the copy followed him down, knowing exactly how to manipulate an opponent on the ground. He got a knee over one of Lacoco's arms, and hit him, and hit him, and hit him. Lacoco's face was being pulverized. An elbow fell and his glass eye had popped out and rolled across the carpet.

It was exactly like last time. I'd lost it. I'd broken his skull open. I'd put out his eye. If I hadn't been pulled off I would've beaten him to death. I'd put him in a coma.

Of course this creature was here. It was made of nightmares. This younger, blank-faced version of me had been Lacoco's nightmare. I was his monster.

But like the rest of us, Lacoco had gotten a lot better at fighting monsters.

WHUP. The fake me lurched. The bloody hands left Lacoco's face and grabbed for his leg. The knee that had been used to block one of Lacoco's arms. Lacoco's hand came off the floor, holding something boxy and orange, and he drove it against his opponent. WHUP. A black circle appeared in the copy's chest. *WHUP. WHUP.* Two more.

Lacoco had landed on a powder-actuated nail gun.

As the copy rolled off, Lacoco got one big boot up and kicked him in the face.

The copy crashed into the far wall, reached up emotionlessly, and ripped one of the nails out of his sternum. He immediately started to rise. There was a sharp crack. The nightmare copy looked down in surprise at the new, much larger hole that had appeared in the center of one pectoral. Screw the nail gun, Lacoco had gone for his pistol. His XD .45 extended in one shaking hand, Lacoco lumbered back up, blood streaming from his battered face.

Hands pressed against the holes in his chest as blood trickled between his fingers, the copy turned his head and studied me, speaking with my voice. "You mocked me, Chosen, but I'm not the only one here that causes bad dreams." He began to laugh.

Lacoco shot him again.

The *Nachtmar* grimaced and slid down the wall, leaving a smear of blood, until he came to a rest, seated, chest full of weeping holes. "It is all for nothing. The human I am bonded with is beyond your reach. You cannot kill him."

"I know," I said as I slowly got to my feet. "That's why I'm going to talk him into doing it himself."

And then the ancient nightmare creature realized what I intended to do. "No! You—"

This time Lacoco walked over, put his pistol against the copy's temple, and blew a reasonable facsimile of my brains across the twentieth floor. Lacoco spit on the corpse. "Shut up." His lips were so mangled and the words were so slurred that they were barely understandable. The big man turned toward me, quivering with fury. One side of his face seemed shrunken without the eye. The other side was battered into split-open pulp. I was amazed he was still standing.

I looked at the pistol dangling in his hand. "That wasn't me."

"It was once . . ." He looked back at the body.

"Neither one of us is the man we were once, and I'm sorry for the man that I was, for what I did to you."

Lacoco put his pistol back in the holster. "Apology accepted. You can buy me a beer when we get back to Earth."

"Deal." I moved my arm around from behind my back, revealing that I'd pulled my own .45, originally to shoot the copy, but had kept it hidden until Lacoco had put his own gun away. "What?" Lacoco shook his head ruefully when he saw that, but he still came up to help me limp along. "I've got things to do. I didn't have time to get shot by you."

He grunted in acknowledgement as he put my arm over his shoulders and took some of my weight. Then he said, "I gotta say, it felt awfully good to shoot you . . . the old you."

I chuckled, then paused to listen for the gargoyles, but I couldn't hear them. Maybe even here the *Nachtmar* could only pay attention to so many things at once, and there was an army of demons below. But now that the *Nachtmar* realized what I was up to, it would be coming for me with everything it had, which was exactly what I wanted. That would distract it from the others. There was a sudden crash and a cry from the other end of the hall. "Ed!"

We ran toward the commotion. Lacoco's flashlight illuminated Ed with his back to us. He had a sword in each hand, one raised over his head to slash downward, one extended in front of him to ward off danger. He moved slowly, legs bent, gradually setting his weight on his toes. On the other side of him, something growled and slinked along the ground. I lifted Abomination and flicked on the big light.

Something furry was crouched on the other side of our orc. It was low and ready to pounce, but not wanting to impale itself on Ed's sword. Bright yellow eyes were unblinking as it prepared to strike.

It was a werewolf.

I was no stranger to werewolves. I'd killed a few of them and I was absolutely terrified of the savage things. It was a werewolf that had nearly killed me and introduced me to the existence of monsters. Werewolves scared the hell out of me. The *Nachtmar* was getting personal now. "Out of the way, Ed!" I shouted as I searched for a clear shot. Ed leapt smoothly to the side. I pulled the trigger.

My buckshot tore a dozen holes in the ceiling. Lacoco had knocked my muzzle aside at the last second. "Hold on. I recognize her. Hey, Red! Is that you?"

It was red. I'd never seen a red one before. The werewolf tilted its head to the side, nostrils flaring as it smelled us. Ed kept his swords up. I put the monster in my sights again, but kept my finger off the trigger. Lacoco had better know what he was doing.

"It's me, Jason. Can you hear me, Deputy?"

The werewolf stood upright and dipped its—no, her—head, seeming almost *calm*. I'd only been around a few fully transformed werewolves in my life, but I'd never seen anything like that before. Normally they were all fury and snapping. Edward, totally confused, even lowered his swords a bit.

The change back into a human was incredibly rapid. I'd seen fast werewolf transformations before, but never anything like this. It made Earl look sluggish. Bones popped out of now ill-fitting sockets. Fur receded. "What the hell?" Within thirty seconds there was a naked redheaded woman standing in front of us. When she lifted her head, her eyes were still glowing gold. "Damn."

"Jason Lacoco?" She still sounded too deep.

"This is the second time I've seen you naked. I'm starting to think you like me or something."

"Are you real?" she asked suspiciously, her voice already returning to a normal tone.

"Are you?" I asked her back. I wasn't ready to believe anything here in crazy world.

The golden eyes had dimmed. "I've been fighting every crazy thing you can think of since we got stuck here. When I saw your little friend I thought it had started throwing ninjas at me." She bent over and picked up some camouflage clothing from the ground and used that to cover herself. "Quit staring."

"If it helps, I'm focusing on my sight. Not you. No offense."

Ed, seeming satisfied that the scary werewolf lady wasn't going to eat him, sheathed his swords and bowed. The werewolf woman gave Ed a look that suggested she didn't trust him at all. There was a huge bloody gash in her side, but it was already knitting itself closed. It didn't seem to be bothering her much now, but Ed had tagged her good.

"Gonna introduce us or what, Lacoco?"

"Z, this is Heather Kerkonen."

Heather? Earl's girlfriend? Blame it on the head

injury, but I'd been too frazzled to realize who I was talking to. I'd met the red werewolf at last. "Your team went missing."

"I'm the only one left. It's been a *long* day. You're MHI then. Yeah, you've got the happy-face patch." She was suddenly hopeful. "Is Earl here?"

"He's down in the casino. But how'd you get here?" I was still suspicious that this was another trick. I was no longer pointing Abomination *at* her, but I was pointing it *near* her.

"We tracked the Mark Thirteen after it escaped Dugway. We caught him, fought him, and next thing I knew we were wandering through a fog filled with monsters. At least until this hotel appeared out of thin air. I was checking it out when your little buddy stabbed me."

"That's how he says hello." There wasn't time to chit-chat. Every second I was here the Hunters in the casino would be under siege. "We've got to keep going. I need to get to the roof now. I know how to beat this thing."

"Not until I get to talk to Earl Harbinger," she insisted, but she did pick up her backpack and follow.

The need for haste was suddenly punctuated by a loud crashing noise from behind us. The floor popped, cracked, and lifted. The *Nachtmar*'s gargoyles were active again.

Heather sighed. "More? Hell . . . not again." She looked over at Lacoco. "Leave me your radio. I'll contact Earl myself."

I was surprised when the big man didn't argue. Lacoco really trusted her. He unclipped his radio and passed it over. "It's on the right channel."

"I've got this. Go do what you've got to do." Heather began quickly shoving the clothing back into the backpack at her feet. There were even shoes in there. I'd never heard of a werewolf with the presence of mind to keep its human things with it before. "This is such a pain."

Werewolves were tough, but . . . "That's a gargoyle."

"So? Fifth one I've seen today. One of the guys on my team hated gargoyles. Why couldn't Benny be terrified of My Little Ponies? No. Has to be gargoyles."

"You're unarmed!"

She smirked at me. "The only thing that bothers me about these things is that I can't *eat* them. Even the soft monsters turn to sand after you kill them. I'm starving. I'd murder a nun for a cupcake right now . . . From Earl's description, you must be Z, the mystical accountant. Here." She reached into the backpack, pulled something out, and tossed it to me. I caught it with one hand. It was a set of military dog tags. "I snagged them off our target in Dugway before he blinked us all into la-la land."

The gargoyle would be through the floor in a matter of seconds. "Good seeing you again, Deputy," Lacoco said as he dragged me down the hall.

"You too. I'll be in touch." Behind us, Heather took a moment to use the radio. "This is Heather Kerkonen. Come in, Earl Harbinger."

"Is this some sort of trick?"

I keyed my radio. "Negative, Earl. This is Z. I think she's legit."

"Heather? You're . . . alive? Is it really you?"

"Yeah, Earl. It's me." Her voice was choked with emotion. I'd never seen a werewolf start to tear up before. "I didn't think I'd ever hear you again."

"Where are you? I'll come get you."

I almost felt sorry for any demons that would get in Earl's way.

"In a minute. I need to break some gargoyles first." She placed the radio on top of the backpack, took one last look at us with her now-gleaming golden eyes, and wiped her cheek. "You'd better not screw this up."

"I won't." And then Lacoco was helping me away as a massive stone gargoyle clambered into the hall to face off against the rapidly transforming werewolf. We moved away as fast as we could, which wasn't saying much. I was wobbly and Lacoco was blowing bloody snot bubbles through his broken nose with each labored breath. Ed got the door. Back in the fire stairwell, the wall was shattered from where the gargoyles had burst in. Behind us Heather howled and there was a terrible noise as the gargoyle attacked.

Clinging mist was billowing through the hole. The alien damp tried to suck our will to live, but anger drove me on. Under the sound of the wind was the hopeful noise of our helicopter, our ticket home. We were almost there. The door to the roof was open. Julie was waiting for us, standing like a dark blot in front of the angry static of the storm, hair whipping loose behind her. "Owen! How bad are you hurt?"

"It's not my blood. Mostly."

A foreign Hunter I didn't recognize grabbed onto my arm and took me from Lacoco. From the way he appraised me, I probably looked worse than I felt. "You both need medical attention."

"No time. Get to the chopper."

"Do it," Julie ordered him.

"How many men do you have up here?"

"Counting you guys, eight."

That would be a very tight fit. "Load them up." Julie shouted for the others and waved them toward the Hind. Ed helped me up the stairs to the landing pad, and a few seconds later I was climbing inside the Hind. It appeared that Skippy was ready to go. Julie got in behind me. "What's your plan?" she shouted, trying to be heard over the rotors. I mostly read her lips.

I pulled down a headset from the overhead rack and pulled it on. "Skippy, as soon as everyone is loaded, get us in the air."

"Go where?" Skippy asked.

"Pick a direction and run, fast as you can." Gargoyles were capable of surprising speed, but they would be no match for Skippy. Though driving in a helicopter through a magical hurricane was probably stupid, Sam said we could fly right out of here. Being dead didn't make you infallible, so I sure hoped he was right or we were totally screwed.

Edward climbed in next, and then extended his hand to help in a slight figure. I realized it was Tanya the elf, but before Julie or I could say anything, Ed looked at us and put his finger over his face mask to indicate silence. If his brother realized that there was an elf on his chopper there would be absolute hell to pay. We couldn't leave any of our people up here to die, but I wasn't sure if Skippy would agree that elves counted as people, and there was no time to argue about it.

Julie's snipers were moving back from the edges. John VanZant came running up, carrying a Barrett M-82 that was nearly as big as he was. Lacoco was being helped along by the stranger. They were almost to the chopper when there was a flash of red lightning. The running Hunters were swept off their feet. The

Hind rocked and swayed on its tires, our spinning rotors dipping wildly toward the ground.

"Look!" Julie pointed out the door.

Gargoyles were swarming over the side of the roof, their blank stone eyes focusing on the Hind. There was a flash of purple lightning, the sky broke open, and shadows flashed above as dozens of beating wings filled the sky. The gargoyles had seemingly appeared out of nowhere. They were circling, preparing to dive-bomb their stone bodies against our only escape.

The hotel rocked under another tremendous assault, which bounced our chopper, sending it turning sideways. It felt like the hotel was going to collapse. Skippy shouted something that had to be orcish profanity. The other Hunters were knocked off their feet and sent jittering wildly across the shaking roof. Lacoco realized that he was coming dangerously close to our dipping rotor and scrambled away on his hands and knees.

A gargoyle fell out of the sky. It didn't even spread its wings before hitting the roof hard enough to make a crater. The unfamiliar Hunter disappeared, smashed beneath the creature. It had only missed our rotor because of the wild bouncing of the building.

The gargoyle was between us and Lacoco. More were crashing into the roof all around us. One hit and we were done.

The other Hunters weren't going to make it.

Julie began unstrapping herself. She was going after them.

If we fail here, everyone dies.

"Stone birds! Stone birds!" Skippy bellowed. "Must go!" A gargoyle hit on the other side and the shrapnel cracked the window.

It would be a lie to say that my decision was hard or easy. Those concepts imply having the luxury of time enough to think it through. It just was what it was. We couldn't risk hundreds of lives for two. I reached out and grabbed Julie's hand before she could finish unbuckling herself. She tugged against my bloody hand until she realized what I was doing. I made the call. "Skippy! Get us in the air!" I shouted.

"No! Those Hunters—" Julie was stunned.

"Fly, Skippy, now!"

Skippy complied. The Hind rolled forward on the landing pad.

VanZant had managed to maneuver his gigantic sniper rifle around in the prone position and began firing the .50 at the gargoyle embedded in the roof, splattering molten rock with each massive impact. Lacoco staggered to his feet. Understanding registered on his battered face that he wasn't going to reach us in time, and then we were moving up and forward and I lost sight of him through the door.

Julie was staring at me, eyes filled with disbelief. *The* Nachtmar *is after me,* I told myself, trying to not make it any more painful than it already was. *He'll concentrate on me. They can fall back. It'll concentrate on me. If we fail here, everyone dies.* I repeated it like a mantra.

"Hold on to something!" Skippy roared. The Hind nearly turned on its side as we left the hotel. Loose items rolled free. Tanya hadn't gotten strapped in yet, but one of Edward's hands flew out with lightning speed and snagged her by the shirt. Ed pulled her in and wrapped one arm around her to keep her in place.

A black shape streaked past our open door. Wings

tucked in and falling like a bomb, the gargoyle had missed our rotor by mere inches. It slammed into the edge of the hotel, obliterating twenty feet of it, and hurtling over the edge. It would've gotten us if we'd stayed any longer. The entire world shifted as Skippy turned us the other way. Another gargoyle screamed past. Sparks flew as something nicked our chopper's side. Then I didn't know which way was up, as the view through the door was gray nightmare fog, then ground, then fog again. The chopper shook as something clipped us toward the rear. A warning buzzer sounded and a red light began to flash in the interior.

But then we were upright again, the hotel was behind us, and we were hurtling into the unknown. We'd made it through the hail of gargoyles. *"Frolugsh!"* Skippy exclaimed. "Stone bird hit! Not tail row-tor again. Not good. Not good." I tugged the door closed. The angry red warning light was still flashing. I couldn't read Cyrillic but I was pretty sure that one said something about Kiss Your Ass Goodbye. Smoke was pouring into the cabin.

"Keep going straight, Skippy," I said. We could crash, just please let us get out of this world first. Looking around, Edward seemed calm as usual, Tanya was utterly terrified, especially since the only thing that had kept her from flying out the door had been Ed's reflexes, but Ed hadn't let go of her yet.

When I glanced at my wife, she was giving me the angriest, most hurt expression that I'd ever seen from her. Who could blame her? I hated myself too. "I had no choice."

"You always have a choice!" Julie got on her radio. "John? Jason? Come in John? VanZant, Lacoco, can you hear me? Damn it...Get inside, fall back, find cover. John?"

"I'm sorry." It was too much for her. Julie hit me. We were sitting too close for her to get much energy into it, but she tried. She hit me again. I let her. "I didn't have a choice."

"I've heard that before! They're going to die. You abandoned them!"

Yes, I had. *Hanging onto a metal ladder in a hot engine room with a vampire below me and a hatch slammed shut in my face.* I knew exactly how it felt. "If we don't make it out, then every single mortal trapped in this realm is as good as dead. I have to get back to the real world." It was a new feeling, seeing such anger directed at me from my wife. It hurt a lot worse than my physical injuries. "You've got to trust—"

"Shut up." Julie held up a hand. "I've got something on the radio. John? Are you okay?"

I picked it up in my headset. The voice of the *Nachtmar* was deep, thick, hoarse, and every bit as chilling as his physical presence. *"You will not escape me that easily, Chosen...For I know what you are now. I can see the chains of destiny you wear. I will take your chains. I will taste your fear and I will grow strong. My essence lingers upon you. There is no escape for you."*

If he concentrated his energies on me, then he wouldn't be able to expend them against the other Hunters. "Come and get me, alp."

"A word. There are many words. That is the wrong word." The *Nachtmar* hissed. *"Your learned humans were fools. They believed I am less than I am. They*

did not capture me as they captured my children. They did not take me from this place. I allowed them to take me from this place. They did not use me. I used them. I am king here. I have been and always will be. They did not give me thought. I have tasted the fear of Chosen before. I took their words and made them mine. I took their words and told new stories. When dogs feasted upon the bodies in the streets of Bactria, I was there. The harvesters of flesh allowed me to harvest their dreams. I am and always will be. This is my finest vessel yet, and I will not allow you to take him from me until the superior vessel is ripe."

I was developing a rapidly sinking feeling that this thing wasn't an ordinary alp.

"*I have travelled the dark paths of your mind world. Many of your paths are closed to me by the Others. Your mind is a cage. It contains stories that only wish to be told, but humans fear the freedom of the words. I will break through your mind cage. I will taste your fear. I will take your words and tell your story. I will take your chains. You will become a harvester of the flesh on my behalf. In my name. For I am and always will be.*"

The chopper shook as we were buffeted with winds that were stupidly dangerous to be flying in. "Skippy, are you seeing anything up there that looks like Earth yet?"

"Pretty lights," Skippy answered over the rattling and squealing warning sirens.

Great. That was either Las Vegas or Hell. It really could go either way right then and I wouldn't have been surprised in the least. "Just get us there."

The voice on the radio changed. "*I'm sorry, Mr.*

Pitt. It would appear that I have underestimated our foe..."

"Management? Is that you?"

"*Yes.*" The dragon sounded weak, pained, his breathing labored. "*I did my best, but I could not stop him. He ripped it from my mind. He combed through my treasures ...*" There was a long wheezing noise. Management was in pain. "*He went back to the beginning, when I was a hatchling. and the great dragonfathers ruled the sky. Beware... He means to devour you.*"

The *Nachtmar* returned. "*I have taken the great beast's words and I will tell his story.*"

And the radio turned to static.

Edward's head swiveled from side to side, suddenly suspicious. The orc was sensing something. Without a word he disentangled from Tanya, unbuckled himself, moved to the door, unlatched it and slid it open. Disregarding the wind and the potential fall into eternal nothingness, Ed looked back the way we'd come from and twitched in surprise, which was a remarkable display of emotion for the orc warrior. Then he signaled that Julie and I needed to come take a look.

The Last Dragon complex was in the distance, partially visible only as the sheets of mist moved and the unnatural lightning provided illumination, but the gaping hole in the middle of it was obvious. Something had torn its way out of the ground. The central gardens had been replaced with a fresh new hole.

Julie looked at me and mouthed the word, "*Management?*"

The lightning cracked the gray open above us, and for the briefest instant we could see shape of something vast and winged coming after us.

CHAPTER 23

I had never been so happy to see Las Vegas before.

One second the Hind was plowing through the storm, and the next we were streaking over the blinding lights of the Strip. The churning mist stopped behind us like it had crashed into an invisible wall. The chopper was vibrating madly. There was a distressing noise coming from our gargoyle-struck tail, but at least if we were going to crash, it was going to be on the solid ground of my home planet.

We had done it. We'd escaped. There had been enough of a head start that the *Nachtmar*'s newest creation had never been more than a shadow in the fog behind us.

"We made it!" Tanya bit off her yell, probably because she wasn't sure if Skippy would toss her out if he found out there was an elf aboard.

But Skippy was preoccupied and hadn't heard. "Row-tor spirits . . . they fight me. Must hurry. Land . . . in road," he warned. "No problem. No problem." The chopper rotated in a series of jerks and fits. Out the window was a shockingly well-contained pillar of whirling nightmare. Our passage hadn't made so much as a ripple. "Probably no explode."

"Can the *Nachtmar* come across?" Julie asked.

"I've got absolutely no idea." The streets a few hundred yards below seemed surprisingly clear of traffic. There were hundreds of police cars, fire trucks, and military vehicles around the phenomenon, but beyond that, the vehicles I saw seemed to be heading away from the disturbance. In the distance was a continuous chain of barely moving headlights that could only be I-15. Mosh's memories had been spot-on. The city was being evacuated.

Mosh . . . I had to reach him. The host's physical body had been there with him and Holly. I spotted the Taj, the casino that had been holding Dr. Blish. I was unsure how much time had passed since Mosh had been cut off, but it was after sundown here. It felt like we'd only been in the nightmare world for maybe an hour, but time must pass slower there than in the real world.

Skippy picked a clear area, then, grumbling and fighting the stick, he brought us down. There were soldiers and rescue workers running toward where we were about to set down. Hopefully there would be someone with a clue nearby that could get me to the host. Stricken was a conniving dirtbag, but theoretically we could be on the same team at least enough to defeat this monster. Stricken didn't want too much collateral damage either. But after that, I was going to snap his neck. If I was really lucky Agent Franks would be back from his secret weapon-supply run.

The ground was a hundred feet away and coming

up fast, but despite the chopper's damage, it didn't look like it would be too much harder than a normal landing. Skip was just that good. Julie had moved on to focusing on what we needed to do next. There would be time to dwell on my mistakes later. "What do we need to do now?"

"The monster is in two halves. My brother was in that casino right there with the half I need to get to. I think I know how to stop—"

ROOOOOOOOOOAAAAAAR!

The sound was louder than our helicopter.

We had been followed.

Far above us, the nightmare dragon erupted through the barrier like a bullet through glass. The pillar of smoke split open around it. The walls of reality unfurled and the nightmare world came pouring into ours. The shadow of the dragon streaked across the sky. Despite its incredible speed, it was so long that it blocked the moon for several seconds, and then cut it in half for another second just with the length of its tail. I hadn't gotten the best look, but it was *huge*. It was like standing under one of the MCB C-130s coming in for a landing. Briefly visible out the opposite window now, wings spread wide, the dragon banked, turning over the city, coming back around toward us.

"Punch it, Skip!" Julie shouted.

Our pilot did. Angry rotor spirits be damned, we were not putting down with that thing heading our way. There was a sudden surge of power and we were moving forward just as the now-released mists of the nightmare world came spilling through the street below, engulfing the quarantine and swallowing the soldiers. I couldn't tell if they were consumed or simply hidden from view, but then we were barreling down the Strip in front of a tsunami of nightmare fog.

The dragon was now above and behind us. It was the color of the night sky, and only random reflectivity from the city lights marked its presence as it tore through the air. Then it was behind us and I could no longer see it, but I could sense the *flapping*. Something that big and unaerodynamic didn't fly. It beat the air into submission, and every concussive strike of those membranous wings shook the world. "Can we outrun it?"

"Skip get away." Suddenly, the world around us turned to scarlet. Fire licked the glass. The chopper screamed as Skippy pointed us straight up. "Fire!" The color turned back to black, and we were free. However, the strain on the chopper had made something worse, and now the vibration was trying to remove the fillings from my teeth. That had changed Skippy's opinion too. "Never mind."

"The son of a bitch breathes fire too!"

"It's a dragon. Did you expect flowers? Skippy, try to shake him between the taller buildings." Julie got out of her seat, then clipped one of the bungee cords attached to the ceiling to a carabineer on her armor to keep her from falling out. She checked her rifle. She was thinking the same thing I was.

"This asshole wants to dogfight, he's got himself a dogfight." I grabbed another one of the cords. Abomination was a short-range weapon, but the case for Milo's machine gun was still secured under Ed's seat. I signaled him to get it out. I took the case and opened it up. Ed pulled a belt out of the ammo can. There was only one left. Which was enough to solve most problems, but I didn't know if a .308 would even put a dent in a monster that big.

Julie was way ahead of me. "Skippy, try to maneuver around him. When you can, head back toward the Feds' quarantine. They're bound to have something big enough to shoot a dragon down."

But the pillar of smoke had collapsed and was flooding outward into the city, seemingly heavier than air. "Assuming they can see through the fog."

"Or that they didn't all get sucked into the nightmare world already," Julie answered. "You got a better idea?"

"Trying..." It was taking all of Skippy's mad skills to keep our damaged bird in the air, and now we were asking him to play high-speed tag between a bunch of casinos.

"If we don't die, then I'm making you employee of the month," Julie said.

"Great honor. Skippy not let die!" There was a moment of nauseous weightlessness as Skippy dove at a ten-story building. "Great honor for tribe."

"What can I do to help?" Tanya asked me.

I loaded the belt into the 240, slammed down the feed-tray cover, and worked the bolt. "Got any fancy elf magic tricks up your sleeve?"

Tanya didn't even have sleeves. "Not for nothing like this."

"Then start praying."

"I'll ask Elvis Presley for his divine help," she promised, and I think she was dead serious.

"You do that." I yanked the door open and was blasted with wind. Edward came over and helped me get the machine gun onto the door mount. "Ed, your girlfriend is one weird chick." The orc just gave me a *she's not my girlfriend* snort of denial. "Whatever, dude."

My wife opened the other side door. As Skippy turned, at least one of us would have an angle. "Five bucks says I'm the first one to hit him in the eye," Julie stated.

"You're on." I leaned out. The dragon was behind us. We were flying south down the Las Vegas Strip. The monster's wingspan was wider than the street, the body long and lean. This was the best look I'd gotten of it so far, and it was frankly terrifying. Its skin was obsidian, so black that it seemed to absorb the brilliant lights of the casinos below. Its head alone was as wide as our chopper. It dwarfed Management. It was a nightmare from a being that caused nightmares. Each rise and fall of the wings was enough to create turbulence to batter the snot out of our damaged vehicle.

It opened its mouth, and inside was an unfurling stream of liquid flame. It lit up the night. "Evade, Skip! Evade!"

The bolt of superheated gas spanned the distance between us in a heartbeat. Skippy turned us hard as the dragon's flames filled the space we'd just been in. Hanging on for dear life, I gasped as we narrowly avoided a high-rise tower. I hadn't even seen it coming.

The dragon was right behind. One of its wings clipped the edge of the Illusions building and obliterated two floors' worth of windows. It didn't seem to notice. The beast was coated in licking flames from flying through its own fiery breath. The fires died, beat out by the wind. So it was impervious to that too. *So let's see how he likes bullets.* Having a clean

shot, I mashed the trigger and walked a stream of
tracers across the dragon's body. It was so damn big
that missing was virtually impossible.

The bullets simply disappeared with no visible effect
whatsoever. The nightmare dragon screeched at our
defiance. The sound pierced my headset. If at first you
don't succeed, shoot it another hundred times. That's
what's nice about belt-feds. "Come on, motherfucker!"
I kept on shooting, hammering the dragon as the FN
churned out spent brass and muzzle flashes. I hit it in
the wings, in its dinosaur snout, and all across its body,
but didn't so much as get a flinch. Skippy cranked us
hard the other way, I lost sight of the dragon, and
then there was another building and Diamond Steve's
roller-coaster track between me and the dragon. We
swayed, and it was Julie's turn. I had volume, she had
accuracy, and there was a series of shots, about two
a second, as Julie probed for something vital.

"We're going to need bigger guns," she stated with
forced calm. The dragon crashed *through* the roller-
coaster track. Mockups of famous landmarks were
pulverized into dust and splinters. "*Way* bigger."

Skippy was swearing. We were slowing down. It was
as if our chopper was starting to rotate along with the
main rotors. The tail wasn't keeping up. We were going
to corkscrew it into the ground at a hundred miles an
hour. With a few mighty beats of its wings, the dragon
halved the distance between us. "Skippy, he's gaining!"

"I try. Not know why...Spirits are displeased!"

"Because we got hit by a gargoyle missile." The
dragon's jaws snapped shut a few feet behind us.
"Tell your spirits to quit their crying and lose this
son of a bitch!"

Another fire bolt streaked past. Somehow Skippy rolled us out of the way at the last instant. The hotel just ahead of us took the hit. The concussion shook us hard, then we were *ping*ing and *bang*ing our way through a cloud of expanding shrapnel. Tanya screeched as a chunk of hot metal punched a hole through the wall next to her head. The girl had a set of lungs like you wouldn't believe.

"What? Is that...Elf! There is filthy *elf* here! No wonder spirits displeased!" Skippy sounded relieved, like that explained everything. "Stow way... Edward, throw out window elf, please. Fix good."

Edward grumbled, "No...Elf girl. Nice."

"*What? Exszrsd,* no!" Skippy was shocked and dismayed at his brother's betrayal. "Noooo!" The Hind turned on its side to fit between two towers. The dragon was forced to swing around. Skippy launched into a giant tirade in his native, guttural, nearly incomprehensible language. Despite my having a great natural talent for learning languages, so far Orcish had eluded me. It was like trying to understand someone shaking a bucket of rocks. Edward snapped something back. Apparently he was just as terse in Orcish as in English. They went back and forth as the dragon's tail swept the twenty-foot neon sign off the top of the Paradisio.

Tanya, who I think understood even less of their angry exchange than I did, didn't help by adding "Yeah!" every time Ed said anything.

"Now is not the time to debate your feelings on interspecies dating," Julie shouted as she cranked off several more ineffectual shots. Luckily my wife understood a lot more Orcosh than I did. "Tanya, promise Skippy that you won't use your elf magic to steal their souls."

"Uh... Okay. I promise?" Apparently soul-stealing hadn't been on her To Do list. "You better not try to put my ears on your elf-ear necklace."

"Fine." Skippy grunted in frustration. "Curse you, row-tor spirits! Stubborn... *Exsrzd!*" and then Skippy rattled off some complicated instructions in Orcish. The only word I'd picked out of that was *sacrifice*. "Fast now go!"

Edward slid to the back of the cabin and rummaged around behind the rear seat. He came out a moment later with a cardboard box that had been wedged in. Ed reached inside and pulled out... *a chicken?* I'm pretty sure it was the same chicken he had stolen up north. The bird was alive and seemed very nervous. For good reason, too. "Seriously, Ed? Seriously?" Julie groaned. "Okay, fine. Whatever. Do it!"

"Go toward the light, brave little bird," Tanya said.

"More sacrifice!" Skippy bellowed.

The orc grumbled something to the tail rotor spirits, squeezed next to me, and hurled the chicken like a football right out the door. It zipped straight into the smoking tail rotor and disappeared in a flash of feathers.

"Holy crap! Did you see that?" But then I had to concentrate, since the dragon had swung back around on my side. I lit the beast up with the 240.

The shocking part was that our improvised chicken repair seemed to actually do *something*. Skippy at least sounded happier. "Much better... Hang on."

The Hind tilted up, then rolled over, and over, and over, and then we were *upside down*. Every one of us screamed. The lucky ones were pressed against their seat by the g-forces. A gigantic aluminum case that had been wedged beneath the chicken box came free and smacked Ed in the arm. I floated in the air, holding onto the grip of a machine gun, hit my head on the roof, and then landed back on the floor. I was so temporarily disoriented that I'm not even sure what kind of maneuver we performed, but then we were heading back the way we'd come from and the dragon was below us, furious and trying to turn around.

"Go, Skippy, go," Julie gasped.

The Hind was still making a terrible rattling noise and there was dark smoke trailing behind us. The dragon was banking hard, wings spread wide, and for a moment it was illuminated in a brilliant spotlight for the entire world to see. I didn't know how complete the evacuation was, but somebody was going to have to some explaining to do. "Get us back to the quarantine line. Let me off and then the rest of you, run like hell."

Julie looked at me like I was stupid. "That's not going to happen."

"You can't come with me."

"Really? And why the hell not?"

I really wish there was a better way to handle this . . . I screwed up my courage and dropped the bomb. "You're pregnant."

"Wha—wait . . . What?" She really hadn't seen that coming. "I can't be. How?"

I couldn't resist. Near-death experiences bring out my inner smartass. "When a mommy and a daddy love each other very much—"

"Aargh! No. But I'm not . . . How do you know? Wait . . . Earl . . . That *ass*."

"Yay! Babies," said Skippy as way of congratulations.

Tanya agreed. "Aw, cute."

Julie went white as a sheet, and not just at the prospect of impending motherhood. She was the smart one in our relationship. "It might be hereditary..." She'd realized what I had been thinking. "The *Nachtmar* called you *chosen*. He talked about breaking into your mind and enslaving you."

"Right. That whole bloodline thing. I don't know, but the poor bastard that's stuck as its current host is sort of like me. Will this kid be like me too?" I was some sort of cosmic intersection of weirdness, and Julie was all sorts of cursed. I wouldn't take odds on this one. "Maybe. I hope not, but we're not going to find out. This thing is not going to possess *my* kid. No way. Screw that."

"I can't leave you—" but even as she said it, she knew she was wrong. Julie bit her lip and nodded. It was a lot of information to process.

"I'll hit the ground running." That was wishful thinking. I'd hit the ground limping. "I'll find Mosh and Holly. They were with the host last. I want the *Nachtmar* to intercept me. I want both halves of it, him, whatever, in the same place."

"And then what?"

"I talk them into surrendering."

"Talk?"

"Yeah. Pretty much."

"You? Talk? Oh, we're screwed."

"Thanks, hon." I checked out the door. The dragon had got turned around and was heading back up the Strip. I wouldn't have much time at all. My leg was throbbing, and since I hadn't walked on it for a bit, it was probably going to be extra stiff. "I'll go as fast as I can."

Edward was more perceptive than he looked, and he'd seen how buggered up my leg had been earlier. He handed me a flask. "Drink." It smelled like rancid pond water. "Gretchen make. Help feets." She was their healer, after all, and I'd benefited from some of her crazy remedies before. She insisted that her magical remedies needed to be fresh and made for a specific person, but this was worth a shot. It tasted worse than it smelled, and burned going down. I passed Gretchen's magic energy drink back to Edward and tried not to puke. My injured foot began to tingle, which was either a good sign or a bad sign.

I could only hope that the Feds would have some weaponry down there that would buy me some time. Edward was rubbing his arm. The big case that had struck him was leaning on the seat next to him. "What's that?"

The case had a pink invoice on the outside, *Anzio Ironworks. To: Milo Anderson/MHI. For Test and Evaluation Purposes.* It was one of Milo's *free samples* that he had bragged about picking up at the tradeshow. I popped the latches. *Please be good. Please be good.* "What the *hell* is that?" Since I was the biggest gun nut in the company, me not recognizing a firearm was especially notable.

Julie adjusted her bungee cord so she could come over to see. She whistled. "I don't know, but it's *huge.*"

It was ridiculous. It was shaped like a rifle, but it made my Barrett look like a .22. It was also disassembled to fit in the foam cutouts of the case, but it looked like it went back together fairly rapidly.

"Where's the rest of it?" Ed pointed at another case that had been under this one. Julie began dragging it out. Put together, this gun had to be longer than I was tall. The case felt like it weighed a hundred pounds. "Is there ammo?"

Julie cracked open the other one. "Here's the barrel, muzzle brake is the size of a phone book, owner's manual . . . Okay, there's a few rounds." Julie hefted one. "But they're the size of bowling pins."

"What is that? Freaking twenty millimeter? Isn't that what fighter jets shoot? Never mind. I need to move fast. I'll never be able to lug this thing around with me." *I guess there is such a thing as too much of a good thing.* "I was hoping for a weapon, not a piece of farm equipment."

"Almost there," Skippy warned. "Much fog. Hard to see."

I closed the case. The ground below us was soupy, but lights glowed through the thick mist. It seemed heavy enough that it had congealed close to the ground. The actual pillar of smoke was entirely gone, spilled loose into the city. And there, battered and looking like it had been the victim of an air raid, was the Last Dragon hotel and casino, the top floors blasted and scorched, dark without power, but most importantly, it was *here*. Hopefully our friends had returned with it.

"Put me on top of the Taj parking garage. You see it? Straight ahead. Next to the white one with the big dome in the middle." The Hind turned and we were heading for the top. Most of the cars were gone, so there was plenty of room to land. I checked behind us, but couldn't pick the dragon out of the dark. I couldn't feel the buffeting effect of its mighty wings, so that was a good sign. Maybe I'd be able to get inside before I got stepped on. Unhooking my safety cord, I got ready to hop out.

Julie grabbed my arm. "You can't—"

"I have to." I took her hand. She was worried about me, but I was mostly worried that I was wrong, and it wasn't after me at all. If the *Nachtmar* was after a different potential host... "Promise me you'll keep moving."

She pulled me in and gave me quick kiss on the lips. There wasn't any time to enjoy it. "Be careful."

And then our tires struck the top of the parking garage and it was time to go. "I will. I love you." No time for hesitation, I took Abomination in hand and leapt out the door. Pain shot up my legs, but I managed to not spill over. Extending one hand, I waved at the Hind as it rolled away, blasting me with rotor wash. Julie waved back, hiding the fact that she was terrified, but for me. She was never scared for herself.

It wasn't until they lifted off that I realized that she hadn't promised to flee like I'd asked. "Oh, please don't go stubborn on me this time. Run, Julie, run." The chopper turned away and I lost sight of her. I jumped when Ed tapped me on the shoulder. He was so damn quick that I hadn't even seen him go out the opposite door. "What are you doing here?"

Edward shrugged like *I'm a sword master, what was I supposed to do in the sky?*

There was a breeze. Then it was calm. Then another breeze. The dragon was flapping its way here, pissed off, on fire, and filled with a thousand years of nightmares that it really wanted to share. "Let's go." We had to get out of the open. The fastest way to do that was down the nearby car ramp. Every step was agonizing, but I limped and cringed along. Gretchen's energy drink wasn't helping much, but I could stop and whine about it when I wasn't in imminent danger of getting squished. "Mosh is inside, downstairs."

Ed just grunted. He didn't care about the particulars. He just wanted the opportunity to stab a dragon. Tanya had no idea what a catch she'd made.

I got on the radio. "Come in, MCB. This is Owen Pitt with MHI. There is a dragon inbound toward the Taj parking garage. Repeat. Dragon. Anybody listening?" The ramp led down to the next level. It was darker here. The escaped nightmare fog clung to the floor, so thick that we couldn't see our feet. The fog had no smell; it was simply moist and dense. However, the air smelled like oil smoke. Grant and Archer's distraction had been nearby. Even if somebody was listening to the radio right now, I was probably the boy that cried wolf. "I say again, there's a dragon about to land on the Taj parking garage. I'd recommend shooting it down. Stricken, if you can hear me, you'll know I'm telling the truth *real* quick."

There was nothing. Back in the real world, they might still be jamming, or they might have all been killed by the spilling of the nightmare world. *Thinking of that . . .* I looked toward the unseen floor. It reminded me of the glycerin fog of the nightclub where Green had got his foot sawed off. Would the *Nachtmar* stay in dragon form, or would it turn into something else and come at us sideways? Would it pick a new vision, or would it be too proud to give up the epic nightmare skin it was wearing?

There was a sudden roar and a crash as the dragon

slammed into the concrete above us. That answered that question. The *Nachtmar* screamed its fury and filled the sky with an arc of fire. It illuminated the entire garage through the open sides. He probably didn't realize he'd done me a favor, because the reflection made it easy for me to spot the enclosure that led to the casino. "Over there!"

Limping along, I tried to ignore the rumbling as the dragon shifted above. The jackhammer strikes that were making concrete flecks fall from above were its claws as it moved toward the ramp. Car alarms began going off, only to be silenced as the *Nachtmar* flicked the cars over the edge in annoyance.

Ed was half my size, so it wasn't like he could help me as I hopped along nearly as effectively as Lacoco had, but he was also really fast, and I was just holding him back. He ran over to the door and opened it for me. Ed began fiddling with the door mechanism with a knife. I had no idea what he was doing. "Mosh is down a few floors."

"Great war chief," Ed agreed. "Go save."

"Save everybody," I agreed. Edward pressed something into my hand. It was a small leather bag. "What's this?"

"Give Tanya for Ed," he answered cryptically.

The dragon was coming down the ramp. Even with its wings tucked in tight and scraping along the walls, it was a tight squeeze down the path that could hold two buses side by side. Its head came around the corner first, undulating on its long neck. The beast was craggy, armored in plates, and covered in spikes the size of rhino horns. It was lightless black, but at the edges where the plates met was just the hint of red light, as if a great internal furnace was leaking heat through the cracks.

It was so imposing that for a moment I was frozen with fear. I was no stranger to terrifying beasts. This was something different, something that gnawed at the very edges of your psyche. I shook my head and broke the spell. In those few seconds it had drawn itself fully into the garage. Cars were crushed beneath its feet, or struck by a horn or tooth, lifted effortlessly, and rolled out of the way.

There was no way we could escape that thing. It was just too big, too powerful, and there was nothing standing in its way it couldn't just plow through. But I still had to try.

I entered the casino. Edward shut the door behind me . . .

With him still on the other side.

"Ed?" I turned back. There was a small glass window in the center. He was watching me through it with sad yellow eyes. *Time to go.* "What're you doing?" I grabbed the door, but the handle wouldn't engage. He'd disabled it with his knife. "Ed!" I pounded on the door. "Come on! Ed!"

The orc tilted his head to the side, studying me. The dragon was growing behind him, plowing its way through the fog and the parked cars. He took off his ski mask, revealing his real face. Ed gave me a little bow.

This was his fight. His greatest challenge. His sacrifice.

"Ed, you obstinate asshole!" I kicked the door. I kicked it again. It was too solid. I pulled Abomination around to blast the lock open.

Edward just shook his head disapprovingly. I was wasting time.

His time. He was buying me time.

I lowered Abomination. Edward nodded. *Thank you.*

All orcs are born with one gift, one area where they could achieve absolute perfection. Ed was the most lethal mortal thing I'd ever seen at hand-to-hand combat. Each orc was the best at one particular thing, but how could they know for sure if they never tested it? Orcs needed challenges, and Edward had finally found one worthy.

Edward turned around, drew his swords, and faced the onrushing nightmare dragon.

Surprisingly enough, it came to a grinding halt, tilting its massive head quizzically. Having a single tiny creature stand up to it with nothing more than a few sharpened pieces of metal was unexpected.

The *Nachtmar* had no idea what it was getting into . . .

The brave orc gave me one last look through the window. *Go.*

I wouldn't fail him.

CHAPTER 24

I ran through the darkened hall. My brother's memories had been clear. I had a good general idea of what part of the building he had last been in. My biggest hindrances to finding him were the typical, stupidly confusing layout of most casinos, the fact that the power was out so I had to navigate by flashlight, my leg was fragged, and the fact that I didn't know if they'd still be in the same place. Mosh and Holly might already dead.

They're alive. Edward's alive too. He's too fast to die. Not like that.

I had heard the dragon's roar and felt the vibrations of their battle for quite some time. He'd slowed it. Maybe even stopped it, because nothing had come after me. Yet.

I'd found the right part of the building, the offices of the evacuated casino. I recognized the frosted glass of the cubicle area where Mosh and Holly had kidnapped Dr. Blish. Nightmare fog covered six inches of the floor. It was freezing cold. My leg hurt so bad that it had moved into a whole new territory of pain. So I had put the pain in a drawer in my brain and shut it. Something was torn in there, I knew it, but I could still move relatively quickly and I could still put weight on it, so screw it. Lee would be in a leg brace for the rest of his life because of me, and I'd never once heard him complain about it.

That was just one of the many people whose lives were screwed up because of me. The list was a long one. Lee's leg had been ruined, but how many Hunters had died that day at DeSoya Caverns because I hadn't been strong enough to take out Lord Machado faster? I was here searching for my brother, his talent had been extinguished, his soul had been cut up along with his fingers, and that had been my fault too. I was never good enough. I never had been, and never would be. Edward was probably dead now too, just bones stuck in the dragon's teeth.

The fog was crawling up the walls.

The Hunters that had been holding out at the Last Dragon were surely dead. There was no way the *Nachtmar* let that hotel back into this world if they were still alive. They were either dead, or worse, locked up in the dream world to be endlessly tortured, while the *Nachtmar* wrung every last bit of terror he could out of their minds.

They're fine.

No. They're not. They're all dead. Lacoco and VanZant were dead too. A couple of minutes after I learned that I'd been just as awful a force in Jason's life as everyone else I'd ever known, I'd abandoned him to die, ripped to bits by a flock of gargoyles.

I didn't have a choice. If I didn't reach the

Nachtmar, *everyone would have died. If the Hind had been crippled—*

No. I could have gone back. I could have reached him. I could have gotten those other Hunters onto the helicopter. I was a hypocrite. I had tried to drown Grant Jefferson for abandoning me to monsters once, but I had done the exact same thing, only worse, because I'd done it to several Hunters. I hadn't left to fight the *Nachtmar.* I had fled out of cowardice.

That's not right. I'm forgetting something.

As I looked back over my life, all I could see was a long parade of failures. Even my successes were only postponing the inevitable. I'd defeated the Old Ones' invasion. So what? They'd be back. Their victory was inevitable. All I'd done was use my finger to plug one hole of a leaking dam, only the whole thing was cracking and falling apart, and when it collapsed it would wash away the whole world. What was the point?

I found myself on the carpet, but I couldn't remember falling down. The nightmare fog covered me completely, drifting over my face in a comforting cocoon. The cold was relaxing. I should just stay here for a while. Pushing on would only make things worse, cause more trouble, ruin more lives. It could be somebody else's problem for once, somebody else's responsibility. What was the point? It was like my father had always said, I wasn't tough enough, I wasn't smart enough, I didn't try hard enough. Hell, I was supposed to end his life too, and the last thing I'd ever see in his dying eyes as the cancer consumed his brain was disappointment. The cycle never ended. They'd be better off without me.

Get up. Get up and fight. That's the Nachtmar *talking.*

But I didn't know which thoughts were my own. They were conflicting, colliding. Everything had gone dark. My flashlight had died, batteries leeched by the unnatural cold.

That helped me focus. It was trying to do the same thing to me.

Pushing myself up, the fog tried to drag me back down with chains made of self-pity. Images of sadness and failure filled my mind. "I'm stronger than you!" I roared. It was horrible, this terrible weight, but I managed to get back up. The fog wasn't just around me, it was in me. Was this a glimpse into the sort of manipulations the human host had been enduring all this time? Lies, distortions, and half-truths... regardless of who you were, you would break eventually. The fog had taken on the consistency of foam and was clinging to my face. I had to physically grab bits of the stuff and hurl it away. "You'll have to do better than that."

I could have sworn that something moved in darkness of the corner of my eye. There was the rustle of dry leaves and a whisper. "You are good."

"You're not, you wretched piece of shit. Where's my brother?"

The *Nachtmar* didn't respond. Batteries dead, I blundered forward in the dark. The cold was making me stupid. It took a second for me to remember that Hunters always had a backup for everything. *Two is one, one is none.* There were glow sticks in a pouch on my armor, so I drew them out, cracked them, and shook them until I had a small comforting green glow to light my way. I tripped over a body on the floor.

It might have been one of the Paranormal Tactical men or maybe somebody from STFU, but I couldn't tell because his face had been dissolved.

"Mosh! Holly! Can you hear me?" They were here. Somewhere . . . But I had a sinking feeling that here and *here* were two different things. The *Nachtmar* was distorting reality. They were so close that I could feel them, but I felt like we were slipping in and out of the real world. The fog's power was growing. The *Nachtmar* was feeding on everyone who was trapped in the mist. The nightmare realm was spreading. Good thing they'd evacuated. I couldn't even imagine what this thing would be like if it could entrap an entire city. "Mosh!"

I got no answer.

But maybe that was because I was calling the wrong name . . .

The host had once been a normal man, corrupted. Heather Kerkonen had given me a pair of dog tags torn off the body buried in Dugway. My hands were shaking so badly from the cold it was hard to draw them free from my pocket. I held them up to the glow stick and squinted to see.

Kitashima, Marcus

I knew what all the info was for because of my dad's tags. There was a service number, blood type A. The religion was an *X*, which if I recalled for that time period, meant something other than Protestant, Catholic, or Jewish. The name of the next of kin was *Mary Kitashima*. A wife? A mother? Was that who he had been demanding I find? The address section for the next of kin contact seemed to be only partially complete, *Topaz WRC*.

Look at Topaz.

That had been the host's words. It had been a place. In his confusion, with his will being sapped and his mind being manipulated, the host had been searching for his home. *WRC?* It sounded vaguely familiar... Dr. Blish had told Mosh that all of the subjects had been volunteers that could blend in with the target populations. WRC... War Relocation Center.

I'd learned about this. My dad had *made* me learn about this. He'd wanted me to understand the fine line between men's reason and fear, and just how quickly that line could be crossed. During World War II the Japanese on the west coast had been rounded up, rights stripped, homes and property confiscated, and then they'd been imprisoned in several different godforsaken camps in the middle of nowhere. Over a hundred thousand people, just like that... Dad's goal had been to instill a healthy mistrust for authority in his kids. That was one lesson that had stuck.

Topaz had been the name of one of those concentration camps.

"Marcus Kitashima! Come out and face me." The fog recoiled away from me. It had been a long time since the *Nachtmar* had allowed that name spoken out loud in the presence of its host. "I kept my word. I know how to find *her*. I know how to find Mary. I know you can hear me. You need to push your way through the fog. Don't let the *Nachtmar* stand in your way. Don't let him stop you."

The fog pulsed with an unnatural light. Something rose to my left, forming out of the floor in a vortex. It took on the shape of man, and for a brief moment, my hope surged... Only a hideous, shrieking ghoul surged forth, snapping ragged jaws and clawing bone fingers for my throat.

I calmly raised Abomination and blew its head off. The entire figure exploded into congealed mist globules. "Don't let the nightmare cloud your mind, Marcus. Come toward the sound of my voice. I'm here to help you." Other monsters formed in the fog, and I killed them, one after the other, not even thinking. Not even taking the time to assess them further than it took to see that they weren't who I was looking for. I kept talking the whole time. Calm. Rational. Killing. "The *Nachtmar* is controlling you. He's using you. He doesn't want you to have the truth."

Werewolf on the right. Two rounds of buckshot dissipated it back into nothing. The darkness was lying, spewing blasphemy and horror. Demons came out of the ceiling. I killed them. Whipping tentacles came out of the walls and exploded one after the other. I reloaded without thought and dropped a charging wight. It was an endless parade of beasts. It was so dark that I could only react at the last instant. It was pure instinct. Movement on both sides. I switched Abomination to my off hand and drew my pistol in the other. I drove my arms out and killed both of them before they could even fully form. "Come on!"

Moving forward, I found another real body, this time one in a wheelchair. It was Dr. Blish. Dead. Only there wasn't a mark on him. His face was frozen in a final, rigid scream, killed by his own fear.

The fog crawled into his open mouth. The corpse turned his dead face toward me. The lips didn't move, but he spoke with the *Nachtmar*'s voice. "I will not let him go. I will not go back to the silent lands."

"You won't have a choice. He's stronger than you are."

There was a scream to my side. I raised Abomination, but that had been a human scream, and despite the *Nachtmar*'s trickery, I knew this one was real. "Holly?"

"She dwells in my world now. She fights me, as you do. She will not give in to her fear like most, but she will break. I will—"

I slammed Abomination's butt stock against the corpse's skull hard enough to crack it wide open. "Zip it." The doctor's body spilled into the fog and the *Nachtmar* was silent. "Holly! Hang on. I'm coming." It was difficult to tell with only the light of a few glow sticks, but this seemed like the storage room they'd hid in before. The door had been badly damaged and there was a big shelf lying on its side. I recognized the leering costumes. I took another step forward and my feet sunk into the floor. I didn't need to see it to know that it had turned to soft dirt. The lines of reality were blurring hard in here. "Holly!"

There was a depression in the floor. The fog was toppling into it, telling me that it was a rather big hole. "Z?" Holly called from inside. Her voice reeked of desperation. "I need help. Get a rope."

It could have been a trap, but I didn't have time to think through the consequences. "Is that really you?"

"No. I'm the Easter Bunny. Rope, now, asshole!" That certainly sounded like the real Holly, but then something else snarled at the bottom of the hole. I tossed the glow stick down. It fell about a dozen feet, cutting through the gray, until it hit the ground between two figures. One was Holly, covered in mud and holding something gray and pointy in her hands, using it to ward off the second figure. The other person was in far worse shape, ragged, tattered, so absolutely filthy that I could barely even recognize it as a human being, and couldn't even tell what sex it was. "A little help would be nice, Z!"

The batteries on my holographic sight had died along with everything else, but it was an easy enough shot. The silver buckshot hit in a loose wad, blowing a hole through its jaw, neck, and shoulder. The body hit the far wall of the pit, but kept on snarling.

"Hold on," Holly snapped. I took my finger off the trigger. She used the distraction to lunge forward and plunged her weapon into the creature's chest just above the sternum. Holly levered it up, then drove it down with a sick, wet crack, right through its heart. She put her foot on its stomach and shoved it away, where it rolled to a stop.

"Good shot," I said.

"Rope, Z," Holly demanded, and then I realized why she was in such a hurry. The one with a now perforated heart hadn't been her only problem. The glow stick hadn't landed on *ground*. The floor was an uneven layer of dead bodies. The entire floor was *squirming*. It was a vampire feeding pit, and the newly minted undead were waking up. Holly had to brace herself against the wall as the man she was standing on tried to rise, knocking her off balance. She stomped ineffectually on his head. "Hurry."

I didn't have actual rope, but I always kept a small roll of paracord. It was nearly as useful as duct tape. I wrapped one end around my hand a few times, then tossed the remainder at her. "Catch." She found the roll and held on for dear life. I pulled hard and dragged her up. Her weight made the narrow cord slice into my flesh and cut off the circulation to my fingers, but there hadn't been time to secure it any better. Holly got her shoes on the side and tried to kick her way up the mud wall. Hands came out of the fog, grasping listlessly for her.

Holly latched on for dear life as she cleared the edge. I let go of the cord, grabbed her by the wrists and dragged her to safety, cutting a path through the fog. Her fake FBI windbreaker had been shredded. Holly lay there gasping for breath. "I thought I was toast."

Holly had survived one of these in real life; of course the monster would use that against her. "The *Nachtmar* is getting into your head—"

"Yeah, yeah. I figured that out. He probably thought he could ruin me with this." She took a deep breath. "He'll need to try harder. The real one was worse. The problem there wasn't when our dead occasionally woke up before the vampires could drag them out and chop them up. It was the starvation and the monotony." Holly snorted. "He went for flash and missed the whole point."

I couldn't even imagine. "Good thing you had a stake."

Holly shook her head. "I wish. I ran out of ammo and had to improvise. That was a jagged broken femur... Just like old times..."

"Can you move?"

She must have seen how I was standing, favoring one leg. "Probably faster than you."

"Where's Mosh?"

"I don't know. Once things got weird, we were separated...Wait, you guys are back?" A smile split her filthy face. Despite everything else, Holly was actually an optimist. "We did it. Awesome."

"Maybe. I don't know. Long story. Come on." Dragging Holly out of the hole must have messed with the *Nachtmar*'s plans. The fog seemed more erratic, more desperate. I helped her up. "We've got to find somebody named Marcus Kitashima."

"Marcus... I think we met. Dr. Blish said that name. Undead, dark, and creepy, plunged the world into a psychotic nightmare? Yeah, he took that doctor you told me to find. I heard him die screaming. At least I hoped he died, because it sure did sound awful otherwise."

"That'd be our guy."

"Marcus... Project Thirteen... *Mark* Thirteen's a nickname? Son of a bitch." Holly was excited. "So we kill this Mark dude, we fix everything?"

"Actually, I'm here to save him."

Holly sighed. "Oh, for fuck's sake. Really, Z? Did you at least bring help?"

"Ed, but he's upstairs fighting a dragon." There was a sudden *bang* from the opposite end of the storage room. That had been a gunshot. "Mosh?" I asked.

"Maybe."

"I haven't seen any of the nightmare creations use a gun yet."

"Quiet, Z. You trying to give him ideas? It might be Mosh, or there were a few of the PT boys here too when everything went to hell." Then there were several more shots, followed by a crash. "One way to find out."

I cracked more glow sticks, gave Holly some, and since her gun had long since been emptied on newly minted vampires, handed over my compact .45. We found my brother at the opposite end of the storage area, only he wasn't the one in need of rescuing.

The area was actually well lit, having taken on the guise of the mortuary in New Zealand where my brother had been tortured. The fog had curled inside the lightbulbs and was fueling them with a sick pale light. The nightmare creations had been cultists from the Church of the Temporary Mortal Condition. There were four of them, but their red robes had been riddled with bullet holes.

Mosh was standing in the middle of the area, over a fifth body. He swung around and pointed a pistol at us when he heard our footsteps. He was shaking so badly I was amazed that he didn't just shoot. "Owen?"

"Yeah, man. It's me." I was flooded with relief. "It's okay now."

He'd been cut, beaten. His face was a mess of spreading bruises. His clothing was hanging in strips, and his flesh had been abraded beneath that. Blood was dripping down his arms and splattering into the fog. He held up the hand without the pistol and wiggled his fingers. "Kept them this time. They tried to take them again, but I wouldn't let them."

"What happened?"

"I . . . I don't know. It was like before, only this time I knew what was going to happen." He held up the nickel-plated Browning Hi-Power. "I stole this earlier off one of those PT guys. I don't know how I got a hold of it now . . . But I got them. I got them all. Even her." Mosh stepped aside, revealing the last corpse. "Remember her?" Intellectually, I knew it wasn't the real Lucinda Hood, but it sure was a convincing facsimile. She was a rather attractive young woman with a hacksaw in one hand, but it had been twisted, wedged up under her chin and stuck clear through her throat, surely driven by desperate strength. Mosh giggled. "Bitch didn't see that coming."

My brother was seriously out of it. "I'm impressed. I didn't know you had it in you. Now let's get you out of here."

"I should've did that the first time." Mosh was going into shock. "But I'm not like you."

I put my arm around his shoulder and steered him toward the exit. "Only in the good ways."

I'd get these guys out, then I had to go back. I had to find Marcus and break the *Nachtmar*'s spell. There were hundreds of Feds and rescue workers trapped in the foggy area, and if the *Nachtmar* was feeding on all of them, then there was no telling how strong it was going to become.

Lucinda Hood spoke. Mosh had nearly removed her head with the saw blade, but the *Nachtmar* didn't need vocal cords or air to speak. "Wait, Chosen."

"I already told you, no autographs!" Mosh turned around and shot Lucinda half a dozen times. The slide locked back empty, but he kept jerking on the trigger uselessly. "Fucking die already."

I pushed the empty pistol aside. "Get him out of here, Holly." She took my incoherently shouting brother by the arm and pulled him away gently. "What do you want, alp?"

The *Nachtmar* hissed. "I see now you are stronger than my last. Parlay with us, Chosen."

"Sure. You go back to where you came from, leave us alone, and I don't destroy you forever."

"No. I am and always have been. The old realm can no longer satisfy my hunger. The mind worlds have all been explored. Their stories have been told.

It is silent now. I would starve there. To go back is to end that which has always been. Ally with us."

"That's not going to happen."

"Together we will shape this world in whatever fashion you see fit. You wish to halt the coming war? We can help you. We ask little in return. We will heed your stories. We will serve you. We will turn aside the invasion, for you will be the teller of this world, not a mere harvester of the flesh. You are stronger than the last. With our help, only that which you wish shall be."

I scowled. The evidence all pointed to something big on the horizon, and the mysterious mark had been inscribed into this thing's tomb in Dugway. "You know about the invasion that's coming?"

"Yes . . . I am and always have been. We have seen his stories told before. His stories are beautiful. Even his silence is art. It was he who awoke us from our slumber. It was he who sent us forth to travel your mind worlds and tell your stories in flesh."

"Why?"

"To test his foes."

"Who is *he?*"

"He is that which ends all things. He will end you as well, if you do not accept our alliance. We will show you."

The fog changed color, becoming a deep red the color of fresh blood. Lucinda and the fake cultists disappeared, to be replaced with brief flashing images, stacked on top of each other, going on forever and ever. I saw the world I knew in flames, cities collapsing into great tears in the earth. I saw everyone I'd ever known, and I saw each of them die horribly. Last of

all, I saw Julie, only she'd been changed, every inch
of her was covered in the marks of the Guardian. She
had become nothing more than a desperate weapon,
and had lost all of her humanity in the process. She
alone survived, but at that point, it no longer mattered,
because she was no longer *her* anymore.

The images stopped flashing. Above the chaos there
was a single mastermind, plotting. He was watching
me right now. The red faded and the false Lucinda
reappeared before me.

"I'm sick of nightmares."

"Those are not your nightmares, those are your
future. We know this is not the story you wish told...
Ally with us, Chosen."

If I'd learned anything in this business, it was that
you never made deals with the devil. "You know what
I think of your offer?" I went over, slammed my boot
down on Lucinda's chest, grabbed the saw, and finished
what Mosh had started. A few seconds later, the head
went rolling away. "That's what I think of your offer."

When I finished sawing the teenage girl's head off,
I realized a mummy was politely waiting to speak
with me.

It was as if he'd grown out of the fog. His flesh
was desiccated, skin pulled tight and parchment thin
over the bones. The eye sockets were empty black
pits. The hair had long since fallen out, and the skin
had split in places over the top of the skull, revealing white bone beneath. I recognized the cut of the
uniform from when I'd met him before, only now it
was ancient, frayed, and falling apart, bleached nearly
colorless by decades of rotting away beneath the sands
of a chemical weapons dump.

"Marcus?"

The mummy nodded. The lips had long since peeled back, revealing yellow teeth. The jaw moved, as if he were trying to speak, but no sound came out. The parts that could make sound had long since turned into jerky.

I'm remembering. That was my name once.

The fog was swirling around us, furious. The *Nachtmar* was gathering its energy, preparing to try another tactic, but it couldn't stop what I was about to do. It had been a long time since I'd embraced the power granted to me by the Old Ones' foul magic. Mordechai had understood what I could do. There was a reason he'd risked Mosh's life to get me here. "I told you I'd help. I kept my promise. I know how to find the woman you're looking for. Come with me. I need to show you something." I held out my hand.

The handshake was like grasping iron bars wrapped in a thin leather glove, and a wave of unbearable cold rushed up my arm and threatened to seize my heart.

CHAPTER 25

"Where are we?"

The mummy had been replaced by the same young man that I had met earlier. His uniform had gone from dusty rags to a neat olive drab. His skin was normal instead of a dried-out husk, where before there had been splits in his scalp there was thick dark hair. This was how he saw himself, or, more likely, how the *Nachtmar* ensured he saw himself. The mummified corpse was all that really remained.

I knew that our bodies were still in Las Vegas. This place was real enough, but we weren't. This was incredibly dangerous. As Mordechai had warned me long ago, when you leave a perfectly good body empty for long enough, something would come along and live in it.

"Where are we?" the ghost of Marcus Kitashima repeated.

"Look around. You tell me where we are."

Much like how the mummy had been replaced by what looked like a normal human being, the fog-filled casino had been replaced by a wide-open desert of scrub brush. In the near distance were the shadows of mountains. It didn't seem that different from the terrain I'd been in earlier in Dugway. After all, in terms of actual miles, we weren't really that far away. Marcus had been buried not very far from his last earthly home.

"It seems . . . familiar. Why are we here?"

"Because I need you to understand that truth."

It was freezing cold, but not from the strange energy-siphoning effect of the *Nachtmar*. This place really was that miserably cold in real life. The wind was howling. There was a dusting of snow on the sand. It was a barren, ugly place.

"Where have you taken me?" he asked, suspicious.

"You brought us here. This is what you've been looking for all along. I don't know how to get here, but you've known all along, and he's been leading you astray. The only thing I've done is help you get out from under the demon's thumb. I'm like you." I didn't understand a fraction of what the Old Ones' artifact had done to me, and I hated letting someone else tap into that strength. As I'd been told, everything from the other side came with a price, and I was going to have to pay for this somehow. "The *Nachtmar* isn't strong enough to stop us both."

He studied the horizon. It didn't matter that it was dark. It wasn't like his eyes were real anyway. He could see our surroundings just fine. "It does look familiar." Marcus walked forward a few feet, squatted down, and poked at something in the sand. It was a chunk of an old bottle. Nearby were a few scraps of lumber rotting back into the ground. "But this . . . This can't be... I know this place. There was a town here. Well, not really a town... They were only shacks, but..."

"They're gone. They've been gone for a really long time. I tried to tell you before."

Marcus went to his knees and laid his hands flat on the sand. "This *feels* like the place. I lived here. This isn't another of his lies, is it?"

"I'm sorry. This is now. This is real."

"This is where I left her. My wife... I promised her I'd come back."

"But that was over sixty years ago. You've been asleep a long time."

"It can't be. That means..." he trailed off.

"Yeah." It meant that everyone he'd ever know was probably dead, or so old that he wouldn't be able to recognize them anyway. The world had passed him by. He was quiet for a long time as the terrible ramifications set in. "This isn't your time anymore."

"We'd only been married a year. She was going to have a baby." The dead man's voice cracked. "I promised her I'd come back when the war was over."

"You have. Not making it in time isn't your fault."

The clock was ticking, but I needed the host to come to terms with reality.

Marcus stared at the ground, deflated. "They came here and asked for volunteers. Really? After throwing us out of the house I built with my own hands, after taking my father's orchard away, and putting us out here in a shack that wasn't even fit for pigs, where the wind blew right through the walls, and I was supposed to leave my wife in that damned shack, and they wanted me to go fight their war?" The ghost stood up and stared off into the distance. "But I did, because

I was born in this country. It's all I'd ever known. I felt like it was my responsibility... Did we win?"

"Yes, we did, because of guys like you. Now listen to me. I need you to do something—"

"No, you listen to me, stranger." I could hear the anger creeping in. "When those doctors interviewed me, said they had a special assignment, said I could help end the war faster, and then we could all go home... I believed them. Then they drilled a hole in my head and filled it in with evil. Every time it tried to take over more of me, I fought it off, but then they'd just drill another hole." He curled his hands into fists. "They've got to pay for this."

"*They* are all gone. They're either long dead or about to be. The only people paying now are a bunch of innocents that had nothing to do with any of this. Your wife was pregnant? Well, so is mine. And she's in danger *right now*. Some of those people dying out there might even be your grandkids for all you know."

That thought took him by surprise, but this was a lot for a ghost to digest. "But how—"

"I need you to call off your monster. I need you to take him and go back to the dream world."

"But I can't. He's become too strong. I was trying to keep him in check back when I first met you, but while we were asleep, it's like he got stronger while I got weaker."

"Then we've got no choice," I said slowly. "I need you to die."

Marcus stared at me, incredulous. "What?"

"You're already dead. I just need you to accept it and move on. If you don't, he'll just keep on using you. You need to move somewhere beyond his grasp. You need to move on to the place where he can't follow. Without your power, the *Nachtmar* will become weak, vulnerable. It'll try to take someone else over... Probably me. But if it does, they can put me to sleep before it gets too strong, just like they did to you before."

"That's nuts. You don't know what you're asking for. The dreams. They never stop. They get worse and worse until you can't tell what's real. Don't volunteer for that."

"You volunteered for a tough job knowing damn well you might die, but you got stuck with something even worse. At least I know what I'm getting myself into. I need you to die. We all need you to die, Marcus."

"I can't..." he stammered.

I slowly drew my kukri from its sheath. "Yes, you can. Problem is, if you want to live, you'll just come back. I don't understand how this works exactly, but for men like us, our will makes a big difference, and if you give us an inch we'll take a mile. You need to move on willingly. If you don't, the *Nachtmar* will just keep using you, and more innocent people will die. They killed you before, but between your desire and the *Nachtmar's* magic, you came back. That's why they put you to sleep, but the *Nachtmar's* done sleeping. You need to die and stay dead."

Marcus watched my knife, but he didn't move away or try to defend himself. He was pondering what I had said. There was steel in his response. "What do I need to do?"

"Just don't come back."

He slowly nodded, finally understanding what was at stake, and he stood there bravely, awaiting his fate.

I raised the kukri. "She'll still be waiting for you," I assured him.

Marcus kept his eyes open. "Do it."

I struck.

The mummy stood before me in the foggy storage room. My arm was extended. The heavy blade of the kukri had sliced cleanly through Marcus' neck.

And then he collapsed. Skin ruptured into dust and the bones fell with a clatter.

The *Nachtmar's* scream shook the world. The fog boiled, furious, away from Marcus' body, fleeing.

Killing its host would seriously wound it, but it wasn't done yet. It would be stunned momentarily, disoriented, probably expecting its Chosen to return to life like he'd done before. Marcus had been its main source of power, its anchor to Earth. When he didn't come back to life, the *Nachtmar* would become desperate. The alp by itself had grown strong, but it would need to find someone else to bond to if it wanted to remain here. And why wouldn't it? Earth was an all-you-can-eat buffet of fear.

Our mental journey to Topaz must have only taken a few seconds of real time, because I caught Mosh and Holly in the hall. They were pushing their way through the thick fog, heading for the tunnels. "Not that way," I shouted. "Out the front. We need to find Task Force Unicorn."

"Oh, come on, Z!" Holly got the still-stunned Mosh turned around. "First help the dead guy and now find the bad guy? Any other horrific assholes you want to hang out with?"

"The dead guy's gone. Now we just have to worry about the ancient nightmare monster. Piece of cake." We made our way in the direction of what I thought was the front. At first I thought the fog was dissipating, because it was certainly taking up less space, but when I looked closer it appeared to be coagulating, becoming thicker, slimy. It was soaking my boots and freezing my toes. It was alive, and seemed to be leaking through the floor, or gathering on the vents, searching for a downward path.

"It's collecting," Holly said. "There's tunnels under here."

"I cut off the main battery. I think it's gathering its remaining strength in one place."

"Why? Shit. Never mind. It can't possibly be good."

I hobbled along behind Mosh and Holly. Luckily Mosh was beginning to snap out of it. We came to a heavy, locked door, and in Pitt family fashion, Mosh simply roared and kicked it open. We were on the casino floor.

"Turn right," Holly pointed.

These places were so damn confusing. "How—"

"I lost a thousand bucks here last night . . . Look out!"

A man crashed through a glass wall to our right. I flinched away from the stinging glass as he landed flat on his back with a splash in the flowing nightmare goo.

I didn't get a good look at what had tossed him, partially because of the bad light, partially because it was made out of nightmare fuel and was rapidly disintegrating, and partially because it had started out looking like an eight-foot-tall bipedal porcupine with six arms. It was so close that I just angled Abomination and fired from the hip. Two quick shots and the creature ruptured like a water balloon. I was splattered with slime, but most of it just oozed away with the rest.

Mosh moved to help the fallen man. "Are you okay?"

"No . . . but I'll live," the man gasped, obviously in pain. He was wearing armor, but was so covered in nightmare slime that I couldn't recognize him, but he recognized Mosh. "You!"

"Oh crap, it's Ultimate Lawyer," Holly said. "Sorry about earlier."

"Save it. Let's get the hell out of here first. I can sue the hell out of you later." Mosh pulled him up. He pointed with one dripping hand. "My team's over here. We could use some help—"

"No problem," Holly answered.

"We could use some help because *someone* stole all our guns." Embarrassed, Mosh handed over the Browning that still had slide-locked open. "You've got Mindy!" he exclaimed. "Come to daddy. Did the bad man hurt you?" Ultimate Lawyer promptly pulled a mag from his vest and reloaded. "If you so much as scratched her I swear that I will beat you to death," he told Mosh nonchalantly. "Name's Durant. This way."

We followed the terrifying attorney to where the remaining members of the Paranormal Tactical team were holding off more melting super-porcupines with bar stools. They'd been split into a few groups, using rows of slot machines as choke points. Ultimate Lawyer broke off and began shooting one of them. I headed toward another of the creatures that had someone trapped behind a blackjack table.

Armstrong had managed to survive, and I had to hand it to the guy, even if he was a complete prick, he could fight. He was beating the monster over the head with a pipe, but the slimy beast didn't seem to notice as it pursued him around the table. The two circled around each other, Armstrong was desperately trying to keep the table between them. He saw my approaching glow sticks. "Over here! Help!"

Because I really am a jerk, I simply couldn't resist. "I'd love to, but this is way closer than a hundred yards."

"Pitt..." Armstrong snarled, then had to duck as the monster came over the top of the table. I shot the monster in the back and it burst and sloshed the walls with nightmare slime.

"Clear!" Ultimate Lawyer shouted from the other side.

That seemed to be all of them. We were safe for a minute. "Clear," I responded. Armstrong was on the floor, wiping goo out of his eyes. I extended a hand to help him up. "You can thank me later." He was pissed, but he grudgingly took my hand. Mostly because it is really difficult to stand up when you're wearing heavy armor and the floor is slippery. "Right now I need to find Stricken. I know he hired you, so I'm hoping you know where he was going when everything went crazy."

"And why should I help you?"

I pointed at the ground. The slime had congealed more and was now glowing with a faint gray light. It was inching along, leaving moisture in its wake, but the actual substance was escaping. "We've got a very limited amount of time before all that stuff gets together and does something really nasty. Your new boss has a secret weapon to kill this thing and I'd like to use it. We can save the animosity toward each other for later when the big nightmare demon isn't about to eat Las Vegas."

Armstrong shook his head. "We have a principal to protect. I have to find him first—"

"I'll save you the time." I held up Abomination and pointed at the butt stock. "I had to cave Dr. Blish's head in with this. Don't worry. He was already dead. It's a long story. But as I was saying, secret weapon?"

"Uh . . ." Armstrong was looking at Abomination. I realized there was still some blood and hair stuck to it. "One of his men had it. Hang on. Comms have been sporadic since the fog showed up." Armstrong tried his radio. "This is Swift Fury Six. Anyone read me?"

"Swift Fury? You guys really do take yourselves way too seriously."

But Armstrong had gotten someone. "Where is Command?" he looked over at me. "Because we've got something big coming." I pointed at the floor. "I think from underground . . . Roger that. We're on the way."

"Where?"

"Right out front. There's a plaza on the street by a bunch of fountains. Know it?"

The others had gathered around us. The Paranormal Tactical team looked exhausted. Every one of them was injured somehow. My people appeared even worse. "Ready? Let's go," Holly said.

"One thing first," I said. This part sucked, and I knew that Holly wasn't going to like it and Mosh would probably flip out. I turned to Armstrong. "I want to hire Paranormal Tactical for a job."

"Wait. What?" The poor guy had been having a very confusing day. "Hire us?"

"What the hell are you doing?" Holly asked.

"Whatever your standard rate is, don't worry. I'm good for it. I got one of the biggest PUFF bounties in history, remember? Two-part deal. First off, send a couple of your men to the top of this place's parking garage. I've got a friend there who might be dead or injured. Get him." And with these money-grubbing bastards, I felt the need to clarify. "Just to be clear: He's an *orc*. But he's *not* PUFF applicable, so if you mess with him, I'm not paying you."

"You got some strange friends," Armstrong said.

"Second part is more complicated, so listen close. Here's the deal. The *Nachtmar* is going to come after me and try to beat me into submission."

"You? Specifically? Why?" Ultimate Lawyer asked.

"Because I'm the Chosen One." Paranormal Tactical shared incredulous glances. "There's no time to explain. It's a long story..."

"You say that a lot," Armstrong said suspiciously. "I'm all about taking your money, but I can't do anything that would be a conflict of interest with our current contract."

"Oh, don't worry. Stricken will love this." I looked Armstrong right in the eyes. He needed to know how sincere I was. "This next part is important. If it looks like the *Nachtmar* has won, and it looks like I've been possessed, you need to knock me out. Don't kill me, because then it'll just go looking for someone else. You need to knock me cold, drug me if you can, secure my body, and then turn me over to Stricken."

"Z!" Holly protested. "Are you insane? He'll kill you!"

"He won't." *He'll just turn me into a vegetable and bury me in a chemical weapons dump.* Mosh began to say something but I cut them both off. "It's our only chance. Hopefully we can just kill it or banish it, but if we can't then we can imprison it again. Otherwise it'll keep floating around until it finds someone else like me or Marcus and then we're screwed all over again." I looked back to Armstrong. "Can you do it?"

He shrugged. "I don't see why not. I'm down with tranqing you and turning you over to a megalomaniacal nut job so he can throw you in prison. I'm not really seeing the downside here."

"And it sounds like we'd get paid twice," Ultimate Lawyer said. "Wait ... If you die, how do we collect?"

Armstrong stopped him. "Naw, Shane. It's all good. I'd do this one for free ... But Pitt here is going to owe us a *huge* favor when this is over."

There really wasn't time to debate it. "*Only* if I'm possessed," I warned.

Armstrong's big fake smile looked even more malicious when he was covered in slime. "Of course, Mr. Pitt. Paranormal Tactical is the best in the business. You're in good hands."

This had damn well better work.

CHAPTER 26

The Strip was entirely clear of the choking fog. The power was out. It was strange to see Las Vegas so dark. The casinos around us were big, silent ghosts. There were some lights in the street, headlights mostly, but from only a fraction of the vehicles, and many of those seemed too dim. There were lots of people out here, military and law enforcement mostly, but only a small percentage of them appeared to be okay. Many were just wandering around shell-shocked. Understandable, since they'd all just gotten glimpses of their worst nightmares. Not everybody had the flexible mind that was a prerequisite for being a good Hunter.

At least I didn't see any bodies, so the quarantine line had been spared for the most part. I sure hoped that wouldn't be changing soon.

Armstrong pointed out a big, rubberized command tent, similar to the one that I'd seen the MCB use in Natchy Bottom. "That was where Stricken's strike team was working out of. I'm going to find the rest of my men, I'll send a few after your friend, and then I'm getting my tranquilizer gun."

"Awesome . . ." I muttered as I set out for the command tent. I was so tired I could barely think.

The silhouette of the Last Dragon towered above us. It had seen better days. Most of the windows were broken. Gigantic chunks of the conference center were missing. The gardens were one big muddy hole. The spot where I'd fallen down and hurt my leg was now just a smoking ruin from Milo's last improvised explosive device. I couldn't see any movement and had no idea if any of the others had made it back.

"Do you think they're okay?" Holly whispered.

"Most of them," Mosh answered. I looked at him and he blinked slowly. "What? You can't hear him? Mordechai just said that most of them made it back."

"Well . . . Huh . . ." At least now I wasn't the only psychic in the family.

"You can have your dead guy back now," Mosh insisted. "What? No . . . Why? Because I don't want to be a crazy person, okay . . . Back off, old man. Shit. He says I'm easier to talk to than you . . . Go screw yourself. I'm evicting you as soon as this is over."

I winced as I made it down the stairs. This had better be over soon, because my ankle and foot had swollen so much that I was now bleeding between my boot laces. At least Gretchen's healing swill had really kicked in because I wasn't in as much pain, either that or the nerves had just given up and died. *Great. Whatever worked.*

There was a Blackhawk parked in front of the tent, and it must have been here when the fog hit, because the pilots were sitting inside. One was crying and rocking back and forth while the other one was just staring blankly out the window. "I think that's Franks' ride."

Normally there would be guards posted on the entrance, but they had probably fled. One MCB agent was curled up in the fetal position behind the tent flap, wearing his gas mask, and muttering something about crocodiles over and over again.

"Looks like it was a real party out here when that pillar came down," Mosh said.

The interior of the command tent was in disarray. Most of the equipment had lost power. Half the screens were dead, and the other half were static. Most of the stations were unmanned, and there were a couple of people hiding under their desks, but there was a group of men in the center of the tent, and these were coherent enough to be arguing.

I recognized the new MCB Director Doug Stark from his address at ICMHP. He was on one end of the group, red-faced and shouting. There were half a dozen other MCB agents around him. Across from Stark, with his back to me, was the broad, imposing shape that could only be Agent Franks. It took quite a bit of guts, or perhaps insanity, to yell at Franks, but Stark was going for the gold.

"You will stand down, mister. You violated direct orders. Direct orders from the highest authority! You broke into a secure facility and stole top-secret government property. You've gone too far this time, Franks. They're going to burn you for this!"

Franks shrugged. "Eh..."

One of the other agents stepped forward. It was Grant Jefferson. "Director, we're being used by STFU.

I saw their attempt. They tried their weapon and when it didn't work, they bailed out to let us take the blame."

"Nonsense," Stark shouted. "You're another one of Myers' loyalists. You're all out to get me. You and those fish men!" Stark shook his fist in the air. I looked around. *Fish men?* Holly shrugged. "The monster has been defeated, and now you want to snatch defeat from the jaws of victory. We need to concentrate on damage control and what we're going to tell the press."

I spoke up. "The monster will be back soon."

Franks turned around. He didn't seem surprised to see me. "Did you kill the host?"

"Permanently this time. The alp is coalescing in the tunnels before it goes hunting for a new host. I figure we've got a couple of minutes, tops."

"Alp? That's classified!" Stark sputtered. "Who told you that?"

Franks looked me over. "You understand the risk?" I nodded. *I was host bait, and if we didn't manage to kill this thing fast and it got me, I was going to end up in a coma.* "We'll meet it in the open."

"The open! We've been ordered not to take any public action. The open is like ... extra public!" Stark bellowed. "You will all stand down. Mr. Stricken said—"

"The situation has changed, sir. Stricken has left the area. He got on the last chopper out ahead of the fog," Grant said gently. He turned to me. "If the host is gone, now's our chance. STFU tried to attack the creature with one of the ancient weapons we had in the vault. The thing was, with the host still being alive it didn't work. It might now."

"Ancient weapon?" I asked.

I hadn't seen Agent Archer standing off to the side. "We watched when Stricken's men responded to our dist—uhm..." Agent Stark was staring at him. "When that car blew up in the garage earlier. They had an old sword."

"A sword? That's it?" But then again, I'd already seen repeatedly that our forefathers had been very creative when it came to coming up with mystical ways to win this fight. Hell, I'd blown up an Old One with something originally conceived by Isaac Newton.

"A *magic* sword," Archer corrected. "I identified it from our inventory roster. MCB's been seizing mystical items since our founding. We've got a warehouse full of interesting things for study. STFU checked this one out and then locked down the rest of the collection. According to the write-up, this one was supposed to be able to banish otherworldly creatures. Too bad their plan didn't work, probably since the monster wasn't otherworldy enough when it was still attached to a human being." Archer held up the broken hilt of what looked like an old Viking sword. "We found this still attached to the STFU man's hand."

Franks pointed at a long nylon case on the ground at his feet. "I stole more. Want one?"

"That's it. Seize Agent Franks!" Stark ordered. All of the other MCB agents seemed really nervous, but none of them made a move. Having worked with Franks, I couldn't blame them. I'd rather seize a rabid honey badger. "What are you waiting for? Place Agent Franks under arrest!"

Apparently Franks had finally had enough. He covered the distance in two big steps and grabbed Agent Stark by the throat. Stark reached for his pistol but Franks simply took it away and dropped it on the floor. The other agents were too shocked to do anything. Stark struggled, but Franks dragged him in and, almost gently, placed him in a choke hold.

While Stark struggled and gasped for air, Franks calmly began to give orders. "Archer, get comms up. Call air support. Pasztory, evacuate the locals. Jefferson, Liu, on heavy weapons. The rest of you find anyone who can fight. Meet out front in two minutes." Stark was turning blue and flopping around from lack of air. Franks looked at his men, obviously displeased that they hadn't snapped to.

"Uh . . . The director . . . You're sorta . . ." Archer was trying to frame it as a question. "That's not good . . ." He looked to the other agents for support, but they were all too aware of what Franks was capable of. "This is bad, isn't it?"

Stark was finally unconscious. If Franks wanted to kill him he would've just snapped his neck. The big agent dumped his superior's limp body on the ground. Stark lay there drooling down his cheek. "Move out."

The MCB agents fled. I didn't need to be a government employee to know that this was going to cause some really serious repercussions for Franks, who wasn't human and only existed because the MCB allowed him to. "Will you be in trouble?" I asked.

"Yes," he answered simply. Franks went over to the bag and unzipped it. He rummaged around inside, pulled out a battle-ax and tossed it to me, heedless of whether I was ready to catch something heavy and razor-sharp or not. "Familiar?"

I managed to snag it by the handle and kept both my thumbs. Lighter than it looked, it still had a bright orange inventory sticker on it. The wooden handle was worn smooth and strangely comfortable in my grip. The metal seemed warm to the touch. I knew this blade. I didn't just know it from using it myself, but I knew it from another man's unholy memories. "Holy shit." It was thousands of years old, and if it was in fact magic, it was only because of the sheer number of lives it had taken had given it a sort of life of its own. "This is Lord Machado's ax."

"I'll need it back," Franks said. He removed a Roman gladius from the bag and tested the weight by tossing it back and forth between his hands. It looked way too small on him.

"You got any more magic swords in there?" Mosh asked hopefully. Franks pulled out a bone-handled dagger. It was about the size of a glorified steak knife. Mosh took it reluctantly. "Seriously?"

Holly had relieved the stunned guard in the entrance of his G-36K carbine. She laughed at Mosh's little knife. "I'd be embarrassed to let anyone see me with that."

"Shut up," Mosh said as he read the inventory sticker. "This one's called the *Black Heart of Suffering*. That sounds evil. Is it evil?"

"Way evil," Franks said.

"Sweet."

The ground quaked beneath our feet.

"It's coming."

The brief glimpse into the nightmare world had rendered most of the quarantine line into what Franks would refer to as *combat ineffective*. The sane had run. That left a handful of MCB that were in the know, about a dozen members of Paranormal Tactical, and a tiny group of cops and soldiers who were getting a real fast tutorial on the fact that monsters existed and one was about to come eat us.

"How do you think this is gonna go down?" Mosh asked me nervously.

"My guess is that the slime will take some sort of form. Whether that will be one big thing or a bunch of little things, I don't know. What I do know is that it won't last long, and it'll probably get weaker as it falls apart or gets damaged. It normally wouldn't be able to manifest here at all, and what he's got going on now is a result of human beings. The *Nachtmar* is on its own now. The more we hurt it, the weaker it'll get, and then we can get it and stick him with one of these things and send it back to hell where it belongs."

"And you know this . . . how?"

"It was in the MHI employee handbook," I said. Mosh snorted. "Okay, I just know. Call it instinct . . . How're you doing?"

Mosh surprised me with a grin. "Remarkably well, actually. Believe it or not, this is kind of cool. Crazy, but cool."

I bet the *Nachtmar* hadn't realized that giving Mosh a chance to work his anger out against a bunch of death cultists would be so therapeutic. "Dad always did say you were the warped one. Stay back here, okay? I don't want you doing anything stupid."

"I came after you, didn't I?"

He had me there. "Damn right you did." I reached over and rubbed my brother's shaved head. "For luck."

I had stuck the ax handle through the straps on the back of my armor, so it was at least semi-secure.

The ax wouldn't do me any good until the *Nachtmar* got close, which meant that I would be using Abomination until then.

The rumbling in the earth had gotten steadily louder. Anything small that wasn't tied down was jittering about from the vibration. "Get ready!" one of the MCB agents shouted. A crack appeared in the street a hundred yards away and began to grow. A chunk of the road split away, lifted, and then fell into the Earth.

Everyone had taken cover, but there had been no time to really prepare. The defenses that had been in place during the quarantine had been disabled or abandoned. We had a haphazard bunch of small arms and whatever else they'd been able to lay their hands on fast. I wasn't feeling super confident.

The crack in the Strip spread further. Steam came shooting out from the hole. A police car disappeared into the crack. The hole was spreading rapidly, but we still hadn't seen the *Nachtmar*'s form yet. Something long and black undulated briefly through the steam then disappeared. Someone jumped the gun and opened fire. Unfortunately that led to several others following his example and wasting their ammo against broken asphalt.

ROOOOOOOAAAAAAR!

The sound was deafening. "Dragon! It's the dragon!" I shouted. Of course it was the dragon form. It was the greatest nightmare the *Nachtmar* had found so far, and once he'd gone through the work of ripping it out of Management's head, he wasn't going to waste it. A mountain rose in the middle of the Strip. The road lifted, breaking. Cars rolled down the side. Pipes broke and sprayed. It got bigger, and bigger, and bigger, the *Nachtmar* lifting itself on its hind legs, wings wrapped around its body, and when it suddenly flung them outward we were in a world of hurt.

Several of us shouted for everyone to get down, but the air was instantly filled with debris. Tons of rock and dirt were launched in every direction. Men screamed and died, impaled on bits of rebar or smashed beneath flipping cars. Mosh, Holly, and I were behind a fire truck that took most of the hit.

The air was filled with choking dust. Holly leaned around the back of the truck and began popping off shots. There was a horrendous noise to the side as one of the MCB fired some sort of antitank rocket. Fire streaked across the sky and terminated against the dragon's wing. The explosion was terrible, sending the gigantic beast reeling to the side. All of us were peppered with a fine mist of nightmare slime. A few optimists cheered.

The dragon responded by opening its jaws and engulfing that entire area in fire. The section where the rocket had come from was consumed. Gas tanks cooked off in the surrounding cars, causing a chain reaction of explosions.

I had to get close. Slugging it out at range would only cost lives. "Stay here," I ordered Mosh, then I took off into the dust.

Running, heedless of the pain shooting up my leg, I scrambled over obstacles. The dragon was still pulling itself out of the earth. The entire world turned red as a gout of fire erupted overhead. The heat scalded me. The dragon lowered its head and burned a path down the Strip. I slid across the hood of a police car and took cover behind the safety of some upturned asphalt.

So hot. The fire struck twenty feet away and immediately melted the asphalt into a circular puddle. Another nearby gas tank ignited and ruptured. As soon as the sweeping fire passed, I got up and ran again, trying to get closer. Moving Abomination's selector to full auto, I cranked off a magazine as I approached, not slowing, not even bothering to aim. The dragon was so big I couldn't miss, but it was like mosquito bites on a rhino. I dropped the mag and rocked in another one full of slugs.

Closer now. Its head was less than a hundred yards away. The world around me was on fire. I aimed at the long sinewy neck and held the trigger down. I could barely make out the ripple pattern of impacts, and that was only because the beast was coated in its own fiery breath and when the slugs hit, the nearby splash of slime put out the fire. It turned quickly, spinning as something got its attention from behind, and as it did, a spray of glowing ooze splattered across the Strip from its shattered wing.

It was bleeding. It was shrinking. We could do this.

Then I realized what had gotten its attention. The Nachtmar was taking fire from the area around the Last Dragon. *Hunters!* They had to be low on ammo and hurting, but they weren't giving up. There were dozens of figures moving around the front of the conference center, leapfrogging their way forward, pouring a continuous stream of gunfire into the monster.

It was a valiant effort, but they didn't have anything left big enough to really hurt it. Abomination empty, I dropped it onto its sling and reached over my back for Lord Machado's ax. This had to work. It was our only hope. Still running, I headed straight for the nearest piece of dragon. One of its forearms was touched down ahead of me, claws dug deep into the sidewalk, balanced as it turned its long neck over its shoulder to launch a stream of fire at the Hunters.

Ax freed, I lifted it overhead and charged. I swung downward with all of my might, aiming for the claw. One finger was as big around as a log. Lord Machado's ax struck and sliced right through the alien meat like it wasn't even there. The ax sparked when it hit the sidewalk beneath. The claw fell away and a flood of slime came pouring out. The *Nachtmar* screamed so loud that it almost knocked me out.

"Suck it!" Then the other couple of tons of worth of claw came off the sidewalk and hit me like a train.

Spinning through the air, I saw sky, then ground, then sky, and then I hit *so* hard.

It took me a moment to blink myself back to reality. The pain was unbelievable. I'd landed on my side. There was no air left in my lungs. I was twenty feet away from where I'd just been. I could tell because the severed claw was still there.

I'm okay. Get up. Get up and finish this. Lord Machado's ax had landed blade first just ahead of me and was embedded in the street. I put my hands down to push myself up, but nothing happened. *Come on. Nobody likes a fucking quitter. Move.* I got my right hand on the ground and struggled up. I realized what the problem was with the other, because it was hanging at a funny angle and there was a bone sticking out of my forearm, having poked right through my armor. Blood was leaking out around it. I stared at it with clinical detachment. *That can't be good.*

I took two faltering steps toward the ax. But then

the entire world was filled with the head of the great dragon *Nachtmar*. Its nostrils, each big enough to put my head inside, stopped mere inches above my head. Its mouth was open before me, like I could ride an escalator up his tongue, but only if I hopped over the picket fence of teeth. Blood slime was pouring out of the dragon's nostrils, leaking from one ruined eye, and splattering around me like rain. "Well...shit."

Bullets were still striking the beast, sounding almost like a hard rain on a metal roof, but for that split second it was just me and the *Nachtmar*, all alone in the world. Time dilated down until the instant was an eternity. He'd come to take me, to steal my destiny, to remake our world in his nightmare image, and as that mouth opened around me, I came to the terrible realization that he didn't mean to possess me; he meant to *consume* me. He wanted to be one all right, but now the *Nachtmar* would be the host. I would live forever in his *guts*.

But then someone blew a hole through the top of the dragon's head big enough to see the stars through.

I was washed away in a sudden burst of slime, sent spiraling out of control down the street. The *Nachtmar* rose, spraying glowing fluid in every direction as another colossal hit ripped through its back and out its chest. I saw the flash that time. It had come from out of the sky. There was a helicopter turned sideways, hovering over the conference center.

Looks like Franks got his air support. But then I recognized the familiar, odd, bulbous shape of MHI's MI-24 Hind. That wasn't MCB air support. That was my wife hanging out the side of a helicopter with a free sample 20mm cannon.

The dragon opened its mouth to engulf the helicopter in flames. "No!" I slipped and scrambled my way forward, trying to get to the embedded ax. Fire arched across the sky, but Skippy was too fast, and the Hind rose up and away just ahead of the attack and out of the dragon's range. However, that wasn't even close to being out of Julie's range, and as the chopper turned and with just enough time passed to work the bolt, a third round blasted through the *Nachtmar*'s jaw, through one of its arms, and through the engine block of an upside-down police car.

The street was aglow with spilled dragon blood. The bitter taste was in my mouth. The *Nachtmar* was visibly smaller, deflating as its essence was spilled from its wounds.

Someone passed me quick on the right. The *Nachtmar* had returned to all fours, but only for an instant as a two-foot line was slashed along one wrist. Franks appeared on the other side as the claw rose, easily dodging the same type of attack that had crippled me. Franks had learned from my mistake, and as the claw went past he hacked a chunk off of it the size of a Thanksgiving turkey with his ancient Roman sword.

Movement on the left. This was even faster, just a flash of red fur, and claws sunk into one of the rear legs. The werewolf was gone as quickly as it had struck, and by the time the dragon's tail pulverized that area into nothing, Heather Kerkonen was attacking the other leg.

The *Nachtmar* rose up on its tail and hind legs, one unscathed wing covering the entire street. It aimed its head downward, preparing to engulf the street directly beneath it in flame, taking us all to hell with it. But then Julie's next round creased the side of its skull, took one horn completely off, and the burst of flame went to the side to melt the front of another casino and to cook their world-famous fountains into steam.

I reached Lord Machado's ax and grabbed on with my working hand. Desperate, still being peppered with bullets from all around and now being hacked to bits from beneath, the *Nachtmar* slammed its remaining wing inward against its body. The concussion hit the street and a massive blast of wind swept everyone away. The others were closer. I saw Franks hurled through the air to disappear into the steam. Heather was knocked through the windshield of an army truck.

I held onto the ax as the wind washed over me. It tried to carry me away, but I was as embedded to the earth as the ax. *Fuck you,* Nachtmar. *I'm not done yet.*

When the wind passed, I wrenched the ax out of the ground and started forward. The *Nachtmar,* now half its original size and rapidly disintegrating, was trying to steady itself on four damaged limbs. The head came around, searching for me desperately, its final hope.

But instead I was its doom.

The mouth gaped wide before me. I swung from the shoulder. The ax tore the end of its snout off. I blinked away the slime and stepped to the side as the teeth slammed shut where I'd just been. I swung again, removing half of its bottom jaw.

The head struck the ground hard. I followed, striking, lifting, striking. Each hit took another chunk from its neck. The muscles of my arm burned. My blood was rushing out of my injuries. I stumbled, but kept going. The head rose, trying to get away, trying to escape the hungry ax.

Too weak, I couldn't follow it. I was about to pass out. The *Nachtmar* was coming apart all around me, great chunks of the creature disintegrating and falling to explode on impact. I couldn't reach its head, but its body was still here. I turned toward its torso and just in time to be hit by one of its falling limbs.

I found myself on my knees. The dragon had lost too much mass to remain cohesive and its body began to split and flow into dead nightmare slime. The dark body became translucent and I could see the opposite side of the street through it as it melted.

There . . .

Deep inside of the dragon's chest cavity was a small, misshapen figure, manlike, the size of a child, only twisted and distorted, its limbs too long and uneven, its head too big. It was the actual alp, the actual form of the creature here on this plane.

It stared at me with big red eyes. It knew I was the cause of its failure, the cause of its banishment and future starvation, and its last act of defiance in this world would be to kill me. The remainder of the dragon's body turned, angling itself to fall and crush me beneath. I lifted Lord Machado's ax, and with all of the strength I had left, hurled it through the air. It spun, end over end, as the alp's already gigantic eyes widened in fear. The ax split the dragon's belly, but my aim was off and I only struck the alp on one side.

The alp let out a silent scream, bubbles appearing in the fluid around its mouth. It began to disintegrate around the ax wound, but it was still alive for the moment, and the melting dragon corpse took another tottering step toward me. I was about to be crushed.

A second object came flipping through the air, only

this time the aim was true, and the bone handle of a knife suddenly appeared in the center of the alp's face.

It was the *Black Heart of Suffering*. The tiny creature seemed to swell the instant it was struck by the knife. It twitched and jerked spasmodically, wailing in agony that none of us could hear... It thrashed as its form broke into pieces.

And then it was perfectly still, floating in the bowels of its gigantic creation.

"Good shot, Mosh..." I croaked as I turned to look over my shoulder. Mosh was there, but he was staring at his open hand that had just had a magic knife snatched from it. Standing next to my surprised brother was Edward the orc. *Well, that makes more sense.* Ed's clothing was scorched and charred, but he was in one piece. Ed raised one arm defiantly and flipped the bird at the dead alp.

The nightmare dragon was dead, and what was left of it was splitting into multiple chunks, spreading apart, with long mucus strings dangling between the pieces. I got to my feet. Deliriously thinking that I really needed to get my arm looked at before I bled to death and that I was still really close if this damn thing decided to fall on me.

I was hit hard in the neck. I reached up, found something hard jammed in there and pulled it out. It was a dart. "Son of a..."

But then the remains of the Las Vegas Strip rushed up to hit me in the face.

CHAPTER 27

I woke up slowly in a hospital. Not the best place to wake up, but at least I was waking up, period... That meant that we had won. It took me a minute to remember what we'd won against, and how I'd wound up here. We'd defeated the *Nachtmar*.

Everything was fuzzy. Looking down. One of my feet was in a cast. My toes were ugly and purple sticking out the end of it. Looking to the side. My opposite arm was also cast. I could feel the dull ache of other injuries, and the itch of stitches in several places over my body. I'd gotten messed up. *Again*. Despite being hurt, I didn't care about myself. The only coherent thought I could latch on to was who else had made it? Who had we lost? I looked to the other side...

"Stricken..." I croaked.

The head of the nefarious Special Task Force Unicorn was leaning in the corner, watching me from behind his strangely colored sunglasses. "You're awake. About damned time."

He sounded funny, like I had water in my ears. I

was still too doped up to be angry, but I still tried to sit up. I tried a few times, but couldn't quite make it. I gave up and sunk back into the pillows. I'd kill him later. Right now I was just tired and thirsty.

Stricken walked over and stood over the bed. It was the first time I'd met him in person. He was too tall and too thin. It was like he tried to avoid the sun coming through the miniblinds. "Owen Zastava Pitt... I'm going to make this simple for you. I'm going to ask you some questions. Your answers will determine the rest of your life. Ready?"

"Up yours," I whispered.

"Let me set the stage for this next question, help you get in the right frame of mind." He gave me an eerie smile. "You met the dragon under the casino."

"Management?"

"No. The other dragon. Yes, Management, you idiot. While my people were investigating the scene, it came to my attention that our dragon friend had a problem with eavesdropping. That's a terrible habit. Shows a real lack of character. So here's my question. What do you know?"

I meant to say *fuck you*, but what came out instead was, "Nemesis."

Stricken chuckled over my surprise. "Don't be alarmed, Mr. Pitt. There's a potent chemical cocktail in your IV bag. You couldn't lie to me if you wanted to... I was afraid of this. What do you know about Project Nemesis?"

"Nothing about what it actually does. Something big, I think. You want it. Franks and Myers don't. It scares them. You'd let everyone die to make your point." It hurt to talk, but I couldn't stop. It was like there was no stop between my mouth and my brain. "Heard you..."

"I was afraid of that." Stricken picked up a pitcher of water. "You look thirsty. Want a drink?" I nodded. My mouth was very dry. "Who else knows about this?"

I bit my tongue until I could taste blood.

There was something sinister about the way Stricken leaned over me. Like he was an undertaker and I was in a coffin. It made me giggle. "Don't be like that, Mr. Pitt. What else do you know?"

"Your real plan..."

Stricken filled a plastic cup with water from the pitcher. "Oh, really? And what would that be?"

"The Last Dragon and all those folks dying wasn't the important part. They were just targets of opportunity when you figured out how tough the *Nachtmar* was. You wanted to expose Hunters to it. You knew it would think we were tasty. But even if you got your permission to do your project, you'd still have to deal with Franks, and he'd just kill you, because he just don't care. Even if you aren't scared of him, your collaborators are. This whole thing was to push Franks over the edge."

That caused him to pause. "Interesting. Go on."

"Sure, the deaths would help your agenda, especially since it was a bunch of professional Hunters. That ought to scare 'em. But you knew you'd get that permission anyway eventually. But then Franks would stop you. You need him gone, but he's too important to just pop. You set this up. You made it impossible for him to do his job without breaking the rules... You knew what he'd do. Franks can't *not* do his job. But now that he's in trouble, you've got an excuse to get rid of him."

Stricken was nodding along. "That dragon was way more tuned in than I expected."

"Naw." I waved my good hand dismissively. "I figured that out myself."

"Remarkable," Stricken agreed. He put the water cup on the table next to me. "You MHI types are just full of surprises. What else do you know?"

"You plan on killing me."

"Well, that goes without saying. Anything else?"

"You're not gonna kill me."

This was amusing him. "Want to bet?"

"You can't kill me because I'm the only one that can stop the *real* bad guy...He's coming." I sang that last part for some odd reason. It made sense at the time. "You know he's real. You've seen his signs all over the place...Wanna know a secret?" I lifted my head and tried to lean in conspiratorially. I couldn't even whisper right. "I'm the Chosen One."

Stricken stepped away from the hospital bed, stroking his pointy chin thoughtfully. "I see..." like that messed with his schemes.

"Yep. I'm the Champion of everything. You kill me, you're on your own. I don't know what your fancy secret Nemesis thingy is, but it won't work. You're gonna need us. You're gonna need *me*. Like, my family's been prepping for this for like *forever.* Prophecies and stuff, generations of this kind of thing, people coming back from the dead. The works." My words were really slurred. The stuff in the IV was potent. "He's *scared* of me."

Stricken didn't seem convinced. "You really believe that, don't you?"

"Yup. It's my destiny."

"Hunters never cease to amuse me. I'm not too worried about this new threat. I know all about him. With Nemesis assets in place we'll be able to handle anything the other side throws at us. No more being puppets on a string for a bunch of cosmic superpowers and their endless bickering. I'm changing the rules of this game once and for all."

Stricken turned and walked to the door, then paused, deep in thought. "But, tell you what, Pitt, just in case you're not completely delusional . . . I wouldn't drink that water if I was you."

I looked over at the cup, then back at Stricken, but he was already gone. I hadn't even seen the door move. I reached over, picked up the cup of water, poured it back in the pitcher, dumped the whole poisonous thing into a potted plant next to the bed, and went back to sleep.

"Oh, my head . . ." This time I woke up to a much more welcome sight next to my bed. "Hey, hon."

Julie startled awake. She'd been sleeping in the chair next to the bed. "You're up." I was glad to see the relief on her face. "Thank goodness. You've been out forever. How're you feeling?"

"Sore and drugged."

"You took a beating. Two broken bones in your foot, a compound fracture in your arm, and a whole bunch of other stuff. Sore is understandable."

"Is Stricken still here?" I asked suspiciously.

"No . . . He was never here. Nobody's seen him since he left the city during the dragon attack. There are several hundred Hunters in town who'd love to make him have an *accident*."

"He was just here," I looked over at the potted plant, suspicious that it would be turning brown already, but it was fine. "I think he was." The concept of linear time was still a little fuzzy.

Julie reached over and stroked my cheek. "I've been here almost the whole time, and when I wasn't, somebody else was. Trip and Holly have been practically camped in the hall. We didn't see anybody."

Weird. Had I imagined that conversation? I felt okay. The memories started coming back. "You . . . You came back on the chopper . . ."

Julie nodded. "What's a girl supposed to do? And by the way, that twenty millimeter is great. It's so big I had to use all the bungees to hold it up, stick the barrel out one door, then hang myself out the opposite side to aim it."

"But the *Nachtmar*—" It had wanted to possess a new host. "The baby!"

"Don't worry." Julie patted her abdomen. "Tanya promised she could ward it off with elf magic if it came around. Skippy almost had an aneurism when he found out she was drawing runes on his helicopter, but I talked him down because they were only in Sharpie. Tanya said she could handle anything disembodied."

"And you *trusted* her?" I raised my voice.

Julie raised an eyebrow. She won the argument. "And if I hadn't come back . . ."

"I'd be getting dissolved inside a dragon right now," I admitted. "Sorry. It's one thing to worry about one of you. I don't know if I can handle two."

"Better get used to it. I took a test an hour ago. Earl's nose was right. I guess this is official."

"What if—" There were a thousand questions.

"We'll deal with whatever happens, like we always do."

And that pretty much summed it up. We'd be okay. "You'll be a good mom."

"And you'll be a great dad."

We sat in silence for a long time. It was weird to have time to think again. I didn't want to ask, but had to. "Who'd we lose?"

"We're still trying to figure that out, but he hurt us."

"Lacoco and VanZant?"

Julie shook her head. "MIA."

I closed my eyes and tried to sink back into the bed. They were dead because of me. "I had to make the call," I whispered.

"You were right, though. The *Nachtmar* concentrated on us. The demons attacking the conference center lost focus, and when the *Nachtmar* followed us through the clouds, it broke the spell. If he hadn't followed us, who knows what would've happened. If we hadn't made it off that roof, the Last Dragon might still be on the other side."

Being right didn't make it any easier. Lacoco had a little girl. "I had to make the call."

She patted my hand as she began to cry. "I know."

EPILOGUE

Mosh stopped the rental car at the end of the driveway. He took way too long to shut the engine off. It was like he was debating putting it back in drive and making a run for it. I couldn't blame him.

"Ready?" I asked.

He glanced over at me. He'd gotten out of Vegas in better shape than I had physically, but his face was still bruised, swollen, and scratched from his fight with the nightmare cultists. Basically, the Pitt brothers looked like crap. "We could just pretend this whole thing never happened."

"Like that ever works out."

Mosh sighed and shut the car off. "Let's do this and get it over with."

It took me a minute to get my crutch out of the backseat. Even with Gretchen's additional attentions, she said the human doctors were right, and I was going to be on that crutch for a while longer. My brother met me on the other side of the car and the two of us stared up at the house with dread. There was still a discolored spot on the driveway from where a Condition cultist had bled all over it. This part was much harder than squaring off against a nightmare monster.

"You hear anything new?" Mosh asked, obviously stalling for time.

I shook my head in the negative. The news was still the same. The MCB had finally picked one of its conflicting stories and run with it. Las Vegas had been the site of an awful terrorist attack, first with weaponized Ebola, then with chemical weapons that may have caused crazy hallucinations, and finally with high explosives that had caused considerable damage down the Strip. "Last I'd heard they were still attempting to bring those horrible miscreants to justice."

"Good. I hear they're real jerks."

Like Julie had told me in the hospital, MHI had gotten hurt. Of our thirty-three members that had attended the first and final ICMHP, six had died, two were missing, and ten had been injured, with three of those being severe enough that they would probably end up retiring. We'd had another two Hunters that didn't get a scratch on them that had quit as a result of being exposed to their worst fears in the nightmare realm. None of the other companies had come out unscathed either. Everybody had lost someone. Earl had to say his goodbyes to Heather again. She still had one year of service left before she gained her PUFF exemption. It had been a bittersweet and too-short reunion for those two.

At least we had managed to protect the vast majority of the innocents who had been trapped inside the Last Dragon with us. As expected, they had all been threatened and silenced by the MCB. Some would make the transition to accepting the real world, others would end up in Appleton, a handful of them would end up like us.

ICMHP had left everyone with scars.

On the bright side, we had made some valuable new allies. The agreement that Earl had put together to share information and resources on the first day of the conference had managed to stick. We now had a strategic partnership with most of the other companies. Nate Shackleford and a small MHI crew had sealed the deal by risking their lives to hold the final wave of demons until every single other Hunter could fall back past them. That had gotten us a lot of respect. The kid had gained a reputation as a hero, maybe even enough of one to overcome the shame his father had brought on the family name years before.

It felt good to have allies. Sure, we'd compete against each other when it came to regular business, but when the time came that this new enemy showed his face, those differences would be set aside, and the world's Hunters would collect their pound of flesh.

I'd been surprised that so many of our new friends had stopped by to see me in the hospital. News travels fast among Hunters, and within a few hours of me catching a tranquilizer dart in the neck, pretty much everyone knew roughly what had gone down in order to defeat the *Nachtmar*. Just when I felt the worst, I had an army of strangers thanking me for saving their lives. As Earl Harbinger would say, they were *all right*. Sadly, White Eagle had gone home already, so I didn't ever get to ask that loud guy if he was related to Mordechai or not. Grimm Berlin had taken the PUFF money they'd received from Stricken and divided it out evenly to be given to the families of the Hunters that had died at the Last Dragon. Klaus Lindemann was a class act.

The only other bit of happy news that had come out of our Las Vegas trip was that our bomb expert, Cooper, had gotten hitched. One of the party girls that had crashed Grimm Berlin's celebration had wound up following him around learning how to build improvised explosives during the siege. I guess that had led to love at first blast. Once they'd gotten back to Earth, having decided that life was short, they had immediately gotten married at a twenty-four-hour wedding chapel by an Elvis impersonator. Tanya had approved.

As for that particular odd couple, I never found out what it was that Edward the orc had given me to give to Tanya in case he died. He had taken it back and hadn't said another word about it. I wasn't going to push the guy that had single-handedly sword-fought a dragon about it, either.

"Crap," Mosh said, drawing me back to the present. "I can't do this."

"What're you worried about? I'm the one that has to kill him."

"We'll see about that. Once he tells us who sent him back, I'll—"

"What?" I asked, genuinely curious.

"I don't know. Something. But they're not taking Dad if I can help it."

That's the spirit. I reached over and rubbed his bald head. "For luck."

Mosh swallowed hard and followed me up the steps. I screwed up my courage and rang the doorbell. We were about to face the hardest man in the world. A

minute later there was much rattling as many sets of
locks were undone.

The door opened and Dad was standing there. It
was hard to read his expression, but he knew right
away why I'd come. "I've been expecting you. I knew
you'd do the right thing." If he was a little surprised to
see me, he was really surprised to see Mosh. "David?
What're you doing here?"

"Being responsible, I guess."

Dad hadn't expected him at all and I think it might
have shook him a little. "Come in, come in. Your
mother's not home," He led us inside. "But I'm guessing this surprise visit shouldn't involve her anyway."

"How is she?"

"She's had years to get used to it. You're the ones
that have had to learn all this on such short notice.
And for that, I'm sorry." We all sat at the kitchen
table. "Judging by the shape you two are in, Las
Vegas. Was that your work?"

"Afraid so," I answered.

Dad looked at Mosh. "You too?"

Mosh nodded quickly. "A little."

"He saved a lot of lives," I said. "We wouldn't have
made it without him."

"I'm proud of you, son," Auhangamea Pitt said to
my brother for probably the first and only time in his
life. "I'm proud of you for that, and I'm proud of you
for having the guts to come here today." Mosh had
to look away, blinking rapidly.

My father turned back to study me for a long time.
"Something's changed since I saw you last, Owen."

"We lost people," I said simply.

"Naw . . . That's not it. You've lost people before." He

shook his head. "But this time was different. Either you sent them or something you did made it happen. I can see it in your eyes."

My voice cracked. "How can you know?"

"Because, son, I see that exact same thing I see on your face right now every single time I look in the mirror. It's a heavy burden, and it don't ever go away. You do what you have to do. Leadership is a hell of a thing."

I rubbed my face. "I can't—"

"They won't be the last," he promised. "That's war, and yours is just beginning."

"I know it is," I answered. "But we've got a lot bigger army than I thought. There's legions of us."

The men of the Pitt family sat at that table for a while, mulling that over. Dad waited patiently to begin. He'd already waited most of his life for this moment.

It was time to fulfill his destiny.

It was time for me to start mine.

"Dad, it's time we talk..."

The following is an excerpt from:

WARBOUND

Larry Correia

Available from Baen Books
August 2013
hardcover

☙ Chapter 1 ☙

It was not so many years after magic first manifested in this world that the first members of the society gathered. We were to be a shield against injustice. We were motivated by righteousness. We become Grimnoir in order to become heroes, to sacrifice our lives in the pursuit of a higher cause, to defend the defenseless . . . I've found that means attending a lot of funerals.

—Toyotomi Makoto,
knight of the Grimnoir,
testimony to the elders' council, 1908

Paris, France
1933

Faye thought that Whisper's funeral was very nice. Even though it was a rainy afternoon, there was a huge turnout, which was still to be expected since Whisper had been such a friendly girl. It made sense that she'd been popular. There had to be a hundred people down there all dressed in black. Faye hoped that when she died, she'd have a funeral this nice too, with all sorts of people coming from all over to say pleasant things about her before they stuck her in the ground. Dwelling on that thought gave Faye a touch of melancholy, since her friends probably already did think she was dead, blown to bits along with the God of Demons in Washington, D.C. Only Francis knew that Faye was still alive, and she was counting on him to keep her secret.

For all she knew, they'd already held her funeral and she'd missed it. Hopefully it had been well attended.

She couldn't make out the carving from this far away with the spyglass, but the tombstone would have the name Colleen Giraudoux carved on it. Nobody Faye knew had ever called her Colleen, it had always been Whisper. It had been months since Whisper had died, but she'd died far across the Atlantic Ocean, and Washington had been in a terrible state at the time, what with a big chunk of it being ruined or set on fire. Sadly, there had also been a lot of other bodies to sort out, so Whisper's corpse had been stacked in one of the overflowing morgues along with thousands of others for weeks before Ian Wright had identified her and had her remains shipped back to her home in France for a proper burial like Whisper would've wanted.

Faye had made a solemn promise to Whisper right before she'd died. So Faye had crossed the ocean, stowed away with the coffin in order to make sure that promise was fulfilled. The long journey across the sea had given Faye time to ponder on what Whisper's sacrifice had meant. Whisper had taken her own life in order to save the city from the big demon's rampage. Whisper had given up her magic in order to make Faye's stronger.

Faye was special, even by Active standards. She had known that for quite some time now. Her connection to the Power seemed positively endless when compared to anybody else. Blessed with what she figured was the best kind of magic ever, she was maybe the strongest Active around, especially after she'd managed to kill the Chairman and he wasn't competition anymore. Everybody had said that Okubo Tokugawa had been the strongest in the world, but she'd shown him. *Greatest wizard ever, I don't think so.* Faye snorted as she thought about it. The Chairman wasn't so tough after she'd Traveled his hands off.

Faye was unique. The problem was thats he had never realized just how come she was that way, and why her magical abilities had grown so quickly, but Whisper had told her the secret. A long time ago, a terrible spell had been created, one that stole people's connection to the Power as they died. The man the spell had been bound to gobbled up more and more magic until it had made him crazy. They called him the Spellbound, and he had done some horrible things to make his magic better. The Grimnoir had finally killed him, only the terrible spell hadn't died along with its creator. It had simply moved on and found a new home.

For some reason, it had picked her. She really wished that it hadn't.

Faye was the new Spellbound. There was no way she could have known it at the time, but it was the spell that had enabled her to defeat the Chairman and save the *Tempest,* just as it was the spell that had let her defeat the big super-demon Mr. Crow had turned into. It seemed like she'd inherited a gift, but

Whisper had made it sound like a curse. The fella that had created the spell had started out as a good man with noble intentions, but the more he used it, the more evil he'd turned.

The Grimnoir elders were so scared of what a new Spellbound might do that they'd been ready to murder her. It probably didn't help that they already thought she was kind of crazy anyway, so she figured she was already halfway there in their eyes. They'd even secretly sent Whisper to keep an eye on her and to kill her if she turned bad. Instead, Whisper had made Faye promise to stay good, and then shot herself in the heart to save a city.

Faye had held a bunch of very complicated one-sided conversations with Whisper's coffin on the trip over. Now they were lowering that coffin into the ground, and Faye had hidden herself several stories up on the rooftop of a fancy old church between some very ugly gargoyles. She was studying the mourners through a spyglass, trying to decide which one of them was supposed to become her teacher.

Jacques Montand was the expert on the Spellbound, and Whisper had asked her to seek him out. Jacques was one of the Grimnoir elders, one of the seven leaders of their secret society. Faye was proud to be a member, a knight as they called themselves, since they did a whole lot of good heroic stuff, but she did object to the part about preemptively murdering her just in case she decided to turn evil. That made it sorely tempting to teach them all a lesson...

Faye refocused on watching the funeral. Those kinds of murderous thoughts were probably the evil sort that she should be trying to avoid. It was hard not to think that way, though, because she was just so very talented when it came to killing folks. She'd *borrowed* the spyglass from the ship she'd stowed away on. She moved her focus from face to face around the coffin, studying each one, trying to figure out who was the secret magical warrior who had trained Whisper to be a Grimnoir knight, and which ones where just friends from Whisper's normal, not-secret life. It was hard to tell, especially with all of those darn umbrellas. Plus, on half of the people, she could only see the backs of their heads, but Faye didn't dare go down there. She had to stay hidden. The only way this was going to work was if the elders still thought she was dead.

Which did raise another question. What if, after she talked to Jacques, he decided to rat her out to the other elders? Then she'd either have to kill him to keep him from blabbing, or let the same folks who'd sent Whisper to kill her know that they needed to try again harder. She knew which one made more sense, but that sure seemed to go against her promise to Whisper to stay good, and she really didn't want to get into the habit of murdering other good guys, even if it was in self-defense.

This sure is complicated.

Being picked to be one of Grimnoir elders didn't mean you were old, just that you were supposed to be wise; but Jacques had to be older. Old enough to have beat the last Spellbound when Faye was still a baby, but there were several grey-haired men in that crowd. Faye knew from meeting a couple of the others that the elders were crafty and tended to keep a lot of protection around, which was understandable since the Imperium, the Soviets, and who knew who else was always gunning for them. So she tried looking for people who looked like bodyguards. There were a few tough-looking fellows, but for all she knew, they were just some of Whisper's multitude of boyfriends. And besides, in Grimnoir circles, you didn't have to be a side of beef like Jake Sullivan or Lance Talon to be dangerous. Faye, being skinny and unremarkably plain, was a perfect example of that.

One nice thing about her particular Power was that she was able to see the world around her so much better than everyone else. It was basically like a big map inside her head. It wasn't like Faye could see through walls with her eyeballs, but she instinctively knew perfectly well what was on the other side of those walls. For example, this big church, or cathedral, she supposed it should be called, had fifteen people moving around inside of it, and she could even get a feel of what was in the first level of tunnels beneath it. *Rats and bones mostly.* She could sense danger or any objects large enough to hurt her if she should Travel into them.

Faye hadn't known too many other Travelers in her life, as they were the rarest of the rare. Grandpa hadn't known how to do the trick with the head map like she could, none of the Grimnoir books knew anything about it either, and the few Imperium Travelers' she'd met, well, they'd been too busy trying to kill each other to talk about how their Powers worked.

Her head map could sense life, and she could pick out magic. If she tried really hard, she could even sort of trace the individual links back to the Power. Faye concentrated, drew in the width of her head map, and focused on the people at the grave site. Sure enough, there was magic in that crowd, several different kinds in fact. And a few the Actives had connections to the Power that were quite strong.

Was this how the last Spellbound turned evil? Since he was a Traveler too, did he have a head map of his own that could show him who had Power and who didn't? And was that what tempted him to kill folks and steal it? Though Faye could sort of understand the appeal of gaining even more magic, the thought sickened her.

She had to pause to wipe the raindrops off the lens. The spyglass blew up the faces of the magical folks, and she studied each one. It was easy to pick out the Grimnoir. Sure, they were sad, just like everybody else. The difference was that they all shared this same look of resignation, like they'd been to way too many funerals already. She supposed that was to be expected, since members of the society were getting themselves killed all the time. Those had to be Whisper's fellow knights.

The spring rain shower was annoying, and you can't exactly sneak around spying on folks while carrying an umbrella. Plus the rain had softened up the years of pigeon poop on the roof so everything was slick and her traveling dress was a mess. *Come on, Jacques . . . Which one are you?*

Faye had focused her head map so intently on the mourners that she hadn't even sensed the danger until it was almost on top of her. *There was somebody else on the roof!*

She hadn't heard him approach, which was saying something since the top of the cathedral was slick as a milk-barn floor and anything you could stand on was at an obnoxious angle. She'd simply Traveled up this vantage point, but the newcomer was climbing up the tiles behind her and slinking along around a gargoyle. He'd scaled the side of the cathedral and wasn't even breathing hard. If it hadn't been for her head map, he would easily have been able to creep right up next to her.

Well, this mysterious fellow had picked the wrong girl to try and sneak up on. She carefully collapsed the stolen—*borrowed*—spyglass and stuck it into a pocket so as not to accidentally scratch it. Faye picked out a narrow ledge just to the side of where the stranger had crawled onto the roof. Her head map confirmed that it was safe to Travel there. Rain drops were soft and easily pushed aside by her passage, so she focused on the spot and Traveled.

Faye appeared out of thin air and landed easily on the ledge. She didn't even need to put out one hand to correct her balance. Faye was rightfully proud of her Traveling skills. The science types had taken to calling her form of magic with the much fancier name of Teleportation, but she still preferred to think of it as Traveling. That name had been good enough for her adopted grandpa, Traveling Joe, God rest his soul, so it was good enough for her.

The climber was still focused on her last position. Faye studied him for a moment. It was hard to tell since he was all crouched over behind a gargoyle, but he seemed to be a tall, thick fella, gone soft around the middle. He must have lost his hat on the climb, because all men wear hats, and he didn't have one on. It was hard to tell his age, because though he looked old, he wasn't moving like an old fella. He was magic all right, she just couldn't tell what kind yet. His hair was stark white, thin, and plastered to his head by the rain. He was wearing what appeared to be a nice, dark-colored suit, but it was now smeared grey because of the stupid pigeons. *Well, serves him right for skulking around like an Imperium ninja.*

Still unaware of Faye's new position, he collected himself, reached inside his suit coat and came out with a small black pistol. Faye had a gun too, though hers was a much bigger .45 automatic, but she figured she wouldn't even need it. She watched, bemused, as the stranger rose from behind the gargoyle and pointed his pistol at nothing.

She Traveled, appearing only a few inches behind the man and shouted, "Boo!"

Startled, the man turned toward her with lightning speed. Faye had figured he'd be some sort of physical Active in order to have made his way up here so easily, so she was ready. The gun turned in her direction, but she was already gone, appearing effortlessly now in front of him. Even if he was a mighty Brute, he was in a rather bad position, what with being so close to the side of a really tall building, and so Faye simply reached out and gave him a shove.

Arms windmilling, his dress shoes squeaked on the rain- and pigeon-shit-slick roof as he tried not to fall over the edge. He almost would have made it too, but the tiles cracked and gave under his heels, and, top-heavy, he started going over the edge. *"Merde!"*

She knew a similar word in Portuguese, since Grandpa had used it a lot on all things relating to dairy cows, and apparently the exclamation translated over in French.

Before he could fall, Faye reached out and snagged his skinny tie with her right hand and a gargoyle's wing with her left, managing just enough of a grip to stop them both from tumbling to the street below. Of course, since she could Travel, only one of them would be going splat if she let go of that gargoyle.

"Whoa there, mister." She loosened up on the tie for a split second, just to demonstrate who was in charge. She snagged it again and kept him from falling. He grabbed her arm with both hands, nearly crushing it, though she could tell he was holding back—he was probably a Brute. Only his toes were still touching the edge of the roof and even Faye was mostly hanging over open space.She hoped he spoke English. "Don't do anything stupid. Let go of my arm."

He shook his head, then spoke with a light French accent. "If I fall, we both fall."

She'd been right to begin with. He was older, probably in his fifties, maybe sixties, but age was hard to tell with some folks. Eyes wide, the man looked first at the ground, then back at Faye, and then back at the ground. He was leaning back way too far to do much of anything except fall. A sufficiently skilled Brute might survive a fall like that, but it probably wouldn't be much fun. He'd dropped his pistol in a vain attempt to grab the gargoyle. He looked forlornly at the gun sitting in the rain gutter. "I did not see you coming."

"They never do."

Faye realized that the old man was studying her face, specifically her odd grey eyes. All Travelers had grey eyes, and there weren't very many Travelers. "You must be Sally Faye Vierra."

"That's me."

He looked around. *Faye. Ground. Gun.* Then, realizing that he was in a very bad way, he settled on looking at Faye. "Please pull me up?"

"Maybe." Faye answered, noting the black-and-gold Grimnoir ring on his gun hand. "Why'd you try to sneak up on me?"

After the initial shock of almost falling, the old fellow had regained his composure. "Why were you spying on us?"

That was a fair question, though she was rather disappointed that her spying skills weren't turning out to be very good. "I'm looking for somebody in particular. He was a friend of Whisper's."

He was a distinguished-looking man, well dressed, despite the pigeon poop and new tears that he'd put into his clothing trying to sneak up on her. He probably would have been rather handsome in his youth. It was hard to tell if he had the commanding presence of a Grimnoir elder, since nobody really had much of a commanding presence when the only thing keeping them from falling off a roof was a little girl holding onto their tie. He was old enough to have fought the last Spellbound. "Are you Jacques Montand?"

"I am . . . You've come to kill me, then?"

Not really, but he didn't need to know that yet. "I'm thinking it over."

"So you know what you really are?"

"The Spellbound. Whisper told me before she died."

"I see . . ." Jacques sighed. They both knew there wasn't a whole lot he could do right then if Faye decided to just let go of the gargoyle. She could easily Travel to safety before hitting the ground and Jacques knew it. He slowly released the death grip on her arm. "I do not know everything she told you, but I would ask you to leave the other members of the Grimnoir leadership out of this. They voted to leave you alone. Our last instructions to Whisper were to observe you but to take no action. The majority of the elders thought that though you had been cursed, you yourself were innocent of any wrongdoing."

"Uh huh...On this vote, how close was it?"

"Five against two."

Well, she was even more popular than she expected. "How'd you vote?"

He looked her square in the eye as his shoes slipped a little further. "I understand more about the threat of the Spellbound than the others. I voted to have you eliminated immediately."

"I didn't ask for this!" Faye exclaimed. It would have been so easy to just let go of him. That big of a fall might've even killed a Brute as tough as Delilah or Toru. Then Faye could simply take Jacques' link to the Power and make it her own. But then again, that was probably just the mean side talking. Faye had made a promise, and Faye always kept her promises. "I should drop you, jerk."

"It was nothing personal. I have seen what the spell will eventually cause, and I have evidence which makes me believe this will happen again. I do not regret my decision." He closed his eyes and waited for her to let go. "Do it. I am not afraid."

Faye was impressed. The Frenchman had guts. "I didn't come all this way to kill you, Jacques." Faye pulled hard. It was enough to shift both of their centers of gravity back over the edge, and he stumbled forward onto more solid tile. It was also hard enough for the tie to choke the heck out of him, and he had to stop and adjust it before he could breathe a sigh of relief. Jacques stood there on trembling legs. He may have been a Brute, but he didn't have near as much physical Power as some of the others Faye had met. By the time he opened his eyes, Faye was ten feet away, sitting on a gargoyle's head, just in case he tried to do something stupid and heroic. "I came here so you could teach me."

—end excerpt—

from *Warbound*
available in hardcover,
August 2013, from Baen Books

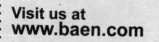